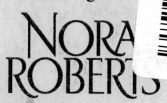

Dear Reader,

We all have a dream—that thing, that place, that person that's going to change our lives, if only we had the courage to reach for it.

In *Irish Rebel*, Brian Donnelly's dream was to be one of the preeminent horse trainers in the world, and he had the courage to leave his home in Ireland and travel halfway across the world to Royal Meadows to attain it. It would be his big break—as long as he did everything right. That certainly didn't inlcude falling for the boss's daughter, the coolly beautiful Keeley Grant. She was a temptation he couldn't afford…and a challenge he couldn't resist.

Cassidy St. John was Irish painter Colin Sullivan's dream—of a model, that is. As soon as he started painting her, he knew he was making the piece that would take his career to new heights. But after he'd made the last stroke of his brush, could he let her walk out of his life as easily as she'd come into it? Or would he have the courage to reach for the dream of his heart and make her *Sullivan's Woman?*

We're sure you'll fall for these passionate dreamers and root for them until they find their happy ending. Enjoy.

The Editors,
Silhouette Books

NORA ROBERTS

Irish Dreams

Published by Silhouette Books

America's Publisher of Contemporary Romance

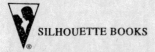

SILHOUETTE BOOKS

IRISH DREAMS

ISBN-13: 978-0-373-28151-0

Recycling programs
for this product may
not exist in your area.

Copyright © 2007 by Harlequin Books S.A.

The publisher acknowledges the copyright holder
of the individual works as follows:

IRISH REBEL
Copyright © 2000 by Nora Roberts

SULLIVAN'S WOMAN
Copyright © 1984 by Nora Roberts

This edition published by arrangement with Harlequin Books S.A.

For questions and comments about the quality of this book please contact us
at Customer_eCare@Harlequin.ca.

® and TM are trademarks of Harlequin Books S.A., used under license.
Trademarks indicated with ® are registered in the United States Patent
and Trademark Office, the Canadian Trade Marks Office and in other
countries.

Visit Silhouette Books at www.Harlequin.com

Printed in U.S.A.

CONTENTS

IRISH REBEL

To Nancy Jackson and Karen Solem,
who took a chance on a very green writer
and made her part of the Silhouette family.

And to readers who took the story
of a young Irish woman into their hearts.

Chapter 1

As far as Brian Donnelly was concerned, a vindictive woman had invented the tie to choke the life out of man so that he would then be so weak she could just grab the tail of it and lead him wherever she wanted him to go. Wearing one made him feel stifled and edgy, and just a little awkward.

But strangling ties, polished shoes and a dignified attitude were required in fancy country clubs with their slick floors and crystal chandeliers and vases crowded with flowers that looked as if they'd been planted on Venus.

He'd have preferred to be in the stables, or on the track or in a good smoky pub where you could light up a cigar and speak your mind. That's where a man met a man for business, to Brian's thinking.

But Travis Grant was paying his freight, and a hefty price it was to bring him all the way from Kildare to America.

Training racehorses meant understanding them, working with them, all but living with them. People were necessary, of course, in a kind of sideways fashion. But country clubs were for owners, and those who played at being racetrackers as a hobby—or for the prestige and profit.

A glance around the room told Brian that most here in their glittery gowns and black ties had never spent any quality time shoveling manure.

Still, if Grant wanted to see if he could handle himself in posh surroundings, blend in with the gentry, he'd damn well do it. The job wasn't his yet. And Brian wanted it.

Travis Grant's Royal Meadows was one of the top thoroughbred farms in the country. Over the last decade, it had moved steadily toward becoming one of the best in the world. Brian had seen the American's horses run in Kildare at Curragh. Each one had been a beauty. The latest he'd seen only weeks before, when the colt Brian had trained had edged out the Maryland bred by half a neck.

But half a neck was more than enough to win the purse, and his own share of it as trainer. More, it seemed, it had been enough to bring Brian Donnelly to the eye and the consideration of the great Mr. Grant.

So here he was, at himself's invitation, Brian thought, in America at some posh gala in a fancy club where the women all smelled rich and the men looked it.

The music he found dull. It didn't stir him. But at least he had a beer and a fine view of the goings-on. The food was plentiful and as polished and elegant as the people who nibbled on it. Those who danced did so with more dignity than enthusiasm, which he thought was a shame, but who could blame them when the band had as much life as a soggy sack of chips?

Still it was an experience watching the jewels glint and crystal wink. The head man in Kildare hadn't been the sort to invite his employees to parties.

Old Mahan had been fair enough, Brian mused. And God knew the man loved his horses—as long as they ended by prancing in the winner's circle. But Brian hadn't thought twice about flipping the job away at the chance for this one.

And, well, if he didn't get it, he'd get another. He had a mind to stay in America for a while. If Royal Meadows wasn't his ticket, he'd find another one.

Moving around pleased him, and by doing so, by knowing just when to pack his bag and take a new road, he'd hooked himself up with some of the best horse farms in Ireland.

There was no reason he could see why he couldn't do the same in America. More of the same, he thought. It was a big and wide country.

He sipped his beer, then lifted an eyebrow when Travis Grant came in. Brian recognized him easily, and his wife as well—the Irish woman, he imagined, was part of his edge in landing this position.

The man, Grant, was tall, powerfully built with hair a thick mixture of silver and black. He had a strong face, tanned and weathered by the outdoors. Beside him, his wife looked like a pixie with her small, slim build. Her hair was a sweep of chestnut, as glossy as the coat of a prize thoroughbred.

They were holding hands.

It was a surprising link. His parents had made four children between them, and worked together as a fine and comfortable team. But they'd never been much for public displays of affection, even as mild a one as handholding.

A young man came in behind them. He had the look of his father—and Brian recognized him from the track in Kildare. Brendon Grant, heir apparent. And he looked comfortable with it—as well as the sleek blonde on his arm.

There were five children, he knew—had made it his business to know. A daughter, another son and twins, one of each sort. He didn't expect those who had grown up with privilege to bother themselves overly about the day-to-day running of the farm. He didn't expect that they'd get in his way.

Then she rushed in, laughing.

Something jumped in his belly, in his chest. And for an instant he saw nothing and no one else. Her build was delicate, her face vibrant. Even from a distance he could see her eyes were as blue as the lakes of his homeland. Her hair was flame, a sizzling red that looked hot to the touch and fell, wave after wave, over her bare shoulders.

His heart hammered, three hard and violent strokes, then seemed simply to stop.

She wore something floaty and blue, paler, shades paler than her eyes. What must have been diamonds fired at her ears.

He'd never in his life seen anything so beautiful, so perfect. So unattainable.

Because his throat had gone burning dry, he lifted his beer and was disgusted to realize his hand wasn't quite steady.

Not for you, Donnelly, he reminded himself. Not for you to even dream of. That would be the master's oldest daughter. And the princess of the house.

Even as he thought it, a man with a well-cut suit and pampered tan went to her. The way she offered her hand to him was just cool enough, just aloof enough to have Brian sneering—which was a great deal more comfortable than goggling.

Ah yes, indeed, she was royalty. And knew it.

The other family came in—that would be the twins, Brian thought, Sarah and Patrick. And a pretty pair they were, both tall and slim with roasted chestnut hair. The girl, Sarah—Brian knew she was just eighteen—was laughing, gesturing widely.

The whole family turned toward her, effectively— perhaps purposely—cutting out the man who'd come to pay homage to the princess. But he was a persistent sort, and reaching her, laid his hand on her shoulder. She glanced over, smiled, nodded.

Off to do her bidding, Brian mused as the man slipped away. A woman like that would be accustomed to flicking a man off, Brian imagined, or reining him in. And making him as grateful as the family hound for the most casual of pats.

Because the conclusion steadied him, Brian took another sip of his beer, set his glass aside. Now, he decided, was as good a time as any to approach the grand and glorious Grants.

"Then she whacked him across the back of his knees with her cane," Sarah continued. "And he fell face first into the verbena."

"If she was my grandmother," Patrick put in, "I'd move to Australia."

"Sure Will Cunningham usually deserves a whack. More than once I've been tempted to give him one myself." Adelia Grant glanced over, her laughing eyes meeting Brian's. "Well then, you've made it, haven't you?"

To Brian's surprise, she held out both hands to him, clasped his warmly and drew him into the family center. "It appears I have. It's a pleasure to see you again, Mrs. Grant."

"I hope your trip over was pleasant."

"Uneventful, which is just as good." As small talk wasn't one of his strengths, he turned to Travis, nodded. "Mr. Grant."

"Brian. I hoped you'd make it tonight. You've met Brendon."

"I did, yes. Did you lay any down on the colt I told you of?"

"On the nose. And since it was at five-to-one, I owe you a drink, at least. What can I get you?"

"I'll have a beer, thanks."

"What part of Ireland are you from?" This was from Sarah. She had her mother's eyes, Brian thought. Warm green, and curious.

"I'm from Kerry. You'd be Sarah, wouldn't you?"

"That's right." She beamed at him. "This is my brother Patrick, and my sister Keeley. Our Brady's already on campus, so we're one short tonight."

"Nice meeting you, Patrick." Deliberately he inclined his head in what was nearly a bow as he turned to Keeley. "Miss Grant."

She lifted one slim eyebrow, the gesture as deliber-

ate as his own. "Mr. Donnelly. Oh, thank you, Chad."
She accepted the glass of champagne, touched a hand
briefly to the arm of the man who'd brought it to her.
"Chad Stuart, Brian Donnelly, from Kerry. That's in
Ireland," she added with an irony dry as dust.

"Oh. Are you one of Mrs. Grant's relatives?"

"I don't have that privilege, no. There are a few of
us scattered through the country who are not, in fact,
related."

Patrick snorted out a laugh and earned a warning
look from his mother. "Well now, we're cluttering up
the place as usual. We'll move this herd along to our
table. I hope you'll join us, Brian."

"How about a dance, Keeley?" Chad asked, standing at her elbow in a proprietary manner.

"I'd love to," she said absently and stepped forward.
"A little later."

"Have a care." Brian put a hand lightly on Keeley's
elbow as they walked away. "Or you'll slip on the
pieces of the heart you just broke."

She slid a glance over and up. "I'm very surefooted,"
she told him, then made a point of taking a seat between her two brothers.

Because he'd caught the scent of her—subtle sex,
with an overlay of class—*he* made a point of sitting
directly across from her. He sent her one quick grin,
then settled in to be entertained by Sarah, who was
already chattering to him about horses.

She didn't like the look of him, Keeley thought as she sipped her champagne. He was just a little too much of everything. His eyes were green, a sharper tone than her mother's. She imagined he could use them to slice his opponent in two with one glance. And she had a feeling he'd enjoy it. His hair was brown, but anything but a quiet shade, with all those gilded streaks rioting through it, and he wore it too long, so that it waved past his collar and around a face of planes and angles.

A sharp face, like his eyes, one with a faint shadow of a cleft in the chin and a well-defined mouth that struck her as being just a little too sensuous.

She thought he was built like a cowboy—long-legged and rangy, and looking entirely too rough-and-ready for his suit and tie.

She didn't care for the way he stared at her, either. Even when he wasn't looking at her it *felt* as if he were staring. And as if he'd read her thoughts, he shifted his eyes to hers again. His smile was slow, unmistakably insolent, and made her want to bare her teeth in a snarl.

Rather than give him the satisfaction, Keeley rose and walked unhurriedly to the ladies' lounge.

She hadn't gotten all the way through the door when Sarah bulleted in behind her. "God! Isn't he gorgeous?"

"Who?"

"Come on, Keel." Rolling her eyes, Sarah plopped down on one of the padded stools at the vanity counter and prepared to enjoy a chat. "Brian. I mean he is so *hot*. Did you see his eyes? Amazing. And that mouth—makes you just want to lap at it or something. Plus, he's got a terrific butt. I know because I made sure I walked behind him to check it out."

With a laugh, Keeley sat down beside her. "First, you're so predictable. Second, if Dad hears you talk that way, he'll shove the man on the first plane back to Ireland. And third, I didn't notice his butt, or anything else about him, particularly."

"Liar." Sarah propped her elbow on the counter as her sister took out a lipstick. "I saw you give him the Keeley Grant once-over."

Amused, Keeley passed the lipstick to Sarah. "Then let's say I didn't much like what I saw. The rough-edged and proud of it type just doesn't do it for me."

"It sure works for me. If I wasn't leaving for college next week, I'd—"

"But you are," Keeley interrupted, and part of her was torn at the upcoming separation. "Besides that, he's much too old for you."

"It never hurts to flirt."

"And you've made a career of it."

"That's just to balance your ice princess routine. 'Oh hello, Chad.'" Sarah put a distant look in her eye and gracefully lifted a hand.

Keeley's comment was short and rude and made Sarah giggle. "Dignity isn't a flaw," Keeley insisted, even as her own lips twitched. "You could use a little."

"You've got plenty for both of us." Sarah hopped up. "Now I'm going to go out and see if I can lure the Irish hunk onto the dance floor. I just bet he's got great moves."

"Oh, yeah," Keeley muttered when her sister swung out the door. "I bet he does."

Not, of course, that she was the least bit interested.

At the moment she wasn't particularly interested in men, period. She had her work, she had the farm, she had her family. The combination kept her busy, involved and happy. Socializing was fine, she mused. An interesting companion over dinner, great. An occasional date for the theater or a function, dandy.

Anything more, well, she was just too busy to bother. If that made her an ice princess, so what? She'd leave the heart melting to Sarah. But, she decided as she rose, if their father hired Donnelly, she was keeping an eye on him and her guileless sister over the next week.

She'd barely taken two steps out of the lounge when Chad appeared at her side again, asking for a dance. Because the ice princess crack was still on her mind, she offered him a smile warm enough to dazzle his eyes and let him draw her into his arms.

Brian didn't mind dancing with Sarah. It would be

a pitiful man who couldn't enjoy a few moments of holding a pretty young girl in his arms and listening to her bubble over about whatever came into her head.

She was a sweetheart as far as he was concerned, miraculously unspoiled and friendly as a puppy. After ten minutes, he knew she intended to study equine medicine, loved Irish music, broke her arm falling out of a tree when she was eight, and that she was an innate and charming flirt.

It was a pure pleasure to dance with Adelia Grant, to hear his own country in her voice and feel the easy welcome of it.

He'd heard the stories, of course, of how she'd come to America, and Royal Meadows, to stay with her uncle Patrick Cunnane, who was trainer in those days for Travis Grant. It was said she'd been hired on as a groom as she had her uncle's gift with horses.

But guiding the small, elegant woman around the dance floor, Brian dismissed the stories as so much pixie dust. He couldn't imagine this woman ever mucking out a stall—any more than he could picture her pretty daughters doing so.

The socializing hadn't been so bad, he acknowledged, and he couldn't say he minded the food, though a man would do better with a good beef sandwich. Still it was plentiful, even if you did have to pick your way through half of it to get to something recognizable.

But despite the evening not being quite the ordeal

he'd imagined it would be, he was glad when Travis suggested they get some air.

"You've a lovely family, Mr. Grant."

"Yes, I do. And a loud one. I hope you still have your hearing left after dancing with Sarah."

Brian grinned, but he was cautious. "She's charming—and ambitious. Veterinary medicine's a challenging field, and especially when you specialize in horses."

"She's never wanted anything else. She went through stages, of course," Travis continued as they walked down a wide white stone path. "Ballerina, astronaut, rock star. But under it all, she always wanted to be a vet. I'm going to miss her, and Patrick, when they leave for college next week. Your family will miss you, I imagine, if you stay in America."

"I've been coming and going for some time. If I settle in America, it won't be a problem."

"My wife misses Ireland," Travis murmured. "A part of her's still there, no matter how deep she's dug her roots here. I understand that. But…" He paused and in the backwash of light studied Brian's face. "When I take on a trainer, I expect his mind, and his heart, to be in Royal Meadows."

"That's understood, Mr. Grant."

"You've moved around quite a bit, Brian," Travis added. "Two years, occasionally three at one organization, then you switch."

"True enough." Eyes level, Brian nodded. "You could say I haven't found the place that wants to hold me longer than that. But while I'm where I am, that farm, those horses, have all my attention and loyalty."

"So I'm told. The boots I'm looking to fill are big. No one's managed to fill them to my satisfaction since Paddy Cunnane retired. He suggested I take a look at you."

"I'm flattered."

"You should be." Travis was pleased to see nothing more than mild interest on Brian's face. He appreciated a man who could hold his own thoughts. "I'd like you to come by the farm when you're settled."

"I'm settled enough. I prefer moving right along if it's all the same to you."

"It is."

"Fine. I'll come round tomorrow, for the morning workout, and have a look at how you do things, Mr. Grant. After I've seen what you have, and you've heard what I'd have in mind to do about it, we'll know if it works for both of us. Will that suit you?"

Cocky young son of a bitch, Travis thought, but didn't smile. He, too, knew how to hold his thoughts. "It suits me fine. Come on back inside. I'll buy you a beer."

"Thanks just the same, but I think I'll go on back to my hotel. Dawn comes early."

"I'll see you tomorrow." Travis held out a hand, shook Brian's briskly. "I'll look forward to it."

"So will I."

Alone, Brian took out a slim cigar, lighted it, then blew out a long stream of smoke.

Paddy Cunnane had recommended him? The idea of it had both nerves and pleasure stirring in his gut. He'd told Travis he'd been flattered, but in truth, he'd been staggered. In the racing world, that was a name spoken of with reverence.

Paddy Cunnane trained champions the way others ate breakfast—with habitual regularity.

He'd seen the man a few times over the course of years, and had spoken to him once. But even with a well-fed ego, Brian had never thought that Paddy Cunnane had taken notice of him.

Travis Grant wanted someone to fill Paddy's boots. Well, Brian Donnelly couldn't and wouldn't do that. But he'd damn well make his mark with his own, and he'd make sure that would be good enough for anyone.

Tomorrow morning they would see what they would see.

He started down the path again when the light and shadows in front of him shifted briefly. Glancing over, he saw Keeley come out of the glass doors and walk across a flagstone terrace.

Look at her, Brian thought, so cool and solitary and perfect. She was made for moonlight, he decided. Or perhaps it was made for her. What breeze there was fluttered the layers of the filmy blue dress she wore as she crossed over to sniff at the flowers that grew out of a big stone urn in colors of rust and butter.

On impulse, he snapped off one of the late-blooming roses from its bush, and strode onto the terrace. She turned at the sound of his footsteps. Irritation flickered first in her eyes, so quickly here and gone he might have missed it if he hadn't been so focused on her. Then it was smoothed away, coated over with a thin sheen of cool politeness.

"Mr. Donnelly."

"Miss Grant," he said in the same formal tone, then held out the rose. "Those there are a bit too humble for the likes of you. This suits better."

"Really?" She took the rose because it would have been rude not to, but neither looked at it nor lifted it to sniff. "I like simple flowers. But thank you for the thought. Are you enjoying your evening?"

"I enjoyed meeting your family."

Because he sounded sincere she unbent enough to smile. "You haven't met them all yet."

"Your brother in college."

"Brady, yes, but there's my aunt and uncle. Erin and Burke Logan, and their three children, from the neighboring Three Aces farm."

"I've heard of the Logans, yes. Seen them round

the tracks a time or two in Ireland. Don't they come to functions here?"

"Often, but they're away just now. If you stay in the area, you'll see quite a bit of them."

"And you? Do you still live at home?"

"Yes." She shifted, glanced back toward the light. "That's why it's home."

Which was where she wanted to be right now, she realized. Home. The thought of going back inside that overwarm and overcrowded room seemed unbearable.

"The music's better from a distance."

"Hmm?" She didn't bother to look at him, wished only that he would go away and give her back her moment of solitude.

"The music," Brian repeated. "It's better when you can barely hear it."

Because she agreed, wholeheartedly, she laughed. "Better yet when you can't hear it at all."

It was the laugh that did it. There'd been warmth then. The way smoke brought warmth even as it clogged your brain. He reached for her before he let himself think. "I don't know about that."

She went rigid. Not with a jerk as many women would, he noted, but by standing so absolutely still she stiffened every muscle.

"What are you doing?"

The words dripped ice, and left him no choice but to tighten his grip on her waist. Pride rammed against pride and the result was solid steel. "Dancing. You do dance, I saw you. And this is a better spot for it than in there, where you're jammed elbow to ass, don't you think?"

Perhaps she agreed. Perhaps she was even amused. Still, she was accustomed to being asked, not just grabbed. "I came out here to get away from the dancing."

"You didn't, no. You came out to get away from the crowd."

She moved with him because to do otherwise was too much like an embrace. And Sarah had been right, he had some lovely moves. Her heels brought her gaze level with his mouth. She'd been right, she decided. Entirely too sensuous. Deliberately she tilted her head back until their eyes met.

"How long have you been working with horses?" It was a safe topic, she thought, and an expected one.

"All my life, one way or another. And you? Are you one for riding, or just for looking from a distance?"

"I can ride." The question irritated her, and nearly had her tossing her collection of blue ribbons and medals in his face. "Relocating, if you do, would mean a big change for you. Job, country, culture."

"I like a challenge." Something about the way he said it, about the way his hand was spread over her back had her eyes narrowing.

"Those that do often wander off looking for the

next when the challenge is met. It's a game, lacking substance or commitment. I think more of people who build something worthwhile where they are."

Because it was no more than the truth, it shouldn't have stung. But it did. "As your parents have."

"Yes."

"It's easy isn't it, to have that sensibility when you've never had to build something from the ground up with nothing but your own hands and wits?"

"That may be, but I respect someone who digs in for the long haul more than the one who jumps from opportunity to opportunity—or challenge."

"And that's what you think I'm doing here?"

"I couldn't say." She moved her shoulder, a graceful little shrug. "I don't know you."

"No, you don't. But you think you do. The rover with his eye on the prize, and stable dirt under his nails no matter how he scrubs at them. And less than beneath your notice."

Surprised, not just by the words but the heat under them, she started to step back, would have stepped back, but he held her in place. As if, she thought, he had the right to.

"That's ridiculous. Unfair and untrue."

"Doesn't matter, to either of us." He wouldn't let it matter to him. Wouldn't let her matter, though holding her had made him ache with ideas that couldn't take root.

"If your father offers me the job, and I take it, I doubt we'll be running in the same circles, or dancing the same dance, once I'm an employee."

There was anger there, she noted, just behind the vivid green of his eyes. "Mr. Donnelly, you're mistaken about me, my family, and how my parents run their farm. Mistaken, and insulting."

He raised his eyebrows. "Are you cold or just angry?"

"What do you mean?"

"You're trembling."

"It's chilly." She bit off the words, annoyed that he'd upset her enough to have it show. "I'm going back in."

"As you like." He eased away, but kept her hand in his, then angled his head when she tugged at it. "Even the stable boy learns manners," he murmured and walked her to the door. "Thank you for the dance, Miss Grant. I hope you enjoy the rest of your evening."

He knew it could cost him the offer of the job, but he couldn't resist seeing if there was any fire behind that wall of ice. So he lifted her hand, and with his eyes still on hers, brushed his lips over her knuckles. Back, forth, then back again.

The fire, one violent flash of it, sparked. And there it simmered while she yanked her hand free, turned her back on him and walked back into the polished crowd and perfumed air.

Chapter 2

Dawn at the shedrow was one of the magic times, when fog was eating its way along the ground and the light was a paler, purer gray. Music was in the jingle of harness, the dull thud of boot and hoof as grooms, handlers and horses went about their business. The perfume was horses, hay and summer.

Trailers had already been loaded, Brian imagined, and the horses picked by the man Grant had left in charge already gone to track for their workout or preparation for today's race. But here on the farm there was other work to be done.

Sprains to be checked, medication to be given, stalls to be mucked. Exercise boys would take mounts to the oval for a workout, or to pony them around. He imagined Royal Meadows had someone to act as clocker and mark the time.

He saw nothing that indicated anything other than first-class here. There was a certain tidiness not all owners insisted upon—or would pay for. Stables, barns, sheds, all were neatly painted, rich, glossy white with dark green trim. Fences were white too, and in perfect repair. Paddocks and pastures were all as neat as a company parlor.

There was atmosphere as well. It was a clever man, or a rich one, who could afford it. Trees in full leaf dotted the hillside pastures. Brian spotted one, a big beauty of an oak, that rose from the center of a paddock and was fenced around in white wood. In the center grass of the brown oval was a colorful lake of flowers and shrubs. Back away, curving between stables and track, were trim green hedges.

He approved of such touches, for the horses. And for the men. Both worked with more enthusiasm in attractive surroundings in his experience. He imagined the Grants had glossy photos of their pretty farm published in fancy magazines.

Of the house as well, he mused, for that had been an impressive sight. Though it had still been more night than day when he'd driven past it, he'd seen the elegant shape of the stone house with its juts of balconies and ornamental iron. Fine big windows, he thought now, for standing and looking out at a kingdom.

There'd been a second structure, a kind of minia-
ture replica of the main house that had nestled atop a
large garage. He'd seen the shapes and silhouettes of
flowers and shrubberies there as well. And the big,
shady trees.

But it was the horses that interested him. How they
were housed, how they were handled. The shedrow—
should he be offered this job and take it—would be his
business. The owner was simply the owner.

"You'll want a look in the stables," Travis said, leading Brian toward the doors. "Paddy'll be along shortly.
Between us we should be able to answer any questions
you might have."

He got answers just from looking, from seeing,
Brian mused. Inside was as tidy as out, with the sloped
concrete floors scrubbed down, the doors of the box
stalls of strong and sturdy wood each boasting a dis-
creet brass plaque engraved with its tenant's name.
Already stableboys were pitching out soiled hay into
barrows or pitching in fresh. The scent of grain, lini-
ment and horse was strong and sweet.

Travis stopped by a stall where a young woman
carefully wrapped the foreleg of a bay. "How's she
doing, Linda?"

"Coming along. She'll be out causing trouble again
in a day or two."

"Sprain?" Brian stepped into the box to run his

hands over the yearling's legs and chest. Linda flicked a glance up at him, then over at Travis, who nodded.

"This is Bad Betty," Linda told Brian. "She likes to incite riots. She's got a mild sprain, but it won't hold her back for long."

"Troublemaker, are you?" Brian put his hands on either side of Betty's head, looked her in the eye. A quick, hot thrill raced through him at what he saw. What he sensed. Here, he thought, was magic, ready to spring if only you could find the right incantation.

"It happens I like troublemakers," he murmured.

"She'll nip," Linda warned. "Especially if you turn your back on her."

"You don't want a bite of me, do you, darling?"

As if in challenge, Betty laid her ears back, and Brian grinned at her. "We'll get along, as long as I re-member you're the boss." When he ran his fingertips down her neck, back again, she snorted at him. "You're too pretty for your own good."

He murmured to her, shifting without thought to Gaelic as Linda finished the bandage. Betty's ears pricked back up, and she watched him now with more interest than malice.

"She wants to run." Brian stepped back, scanning the filly's form. "Born for it. And more, born to win."

"One look tells you that?" Travis asked.

"It's in the eyes. You won't want to breed this one

when she comes into season, Mr. Grant. She needs to fly first."

Deliberately he turned his back, and as Betty lifted her head, he glanced back over his shoulder. "I don't think so," he said quietly. They eyed each other another moment, then Betty tossed her head in the equine equivalent of a shrug.

Amused, Travis moved aside to let Brian out of the box. "She terrorizes the stableboys."

"Because she can, and is likely smarter than half of them." He gestured to the opposite box. "And who's this handsome old man here?"

"That's Prince, out of Majesty."

"Royal Meadow's Majesty?" There was reverence in Brian's voice as he crossed over. "And his Prince. You had your day, didn't you, sir?" Gently Brian stroked a hand down the dignified nose of the aged chestnut. "Like your sire. I saw him race, Mr. Grant, at the Curragh, when I was a lad, a stableboy. I'd never seen his like before, nor since for that matter. I worked with one of the stallions this one sired. He didn't embarrass his breeding."

"Yes, I know."

Travis showed him through the tack room, the breeding shed and birthing stalls, past a paddock where a yearling was going through his paces on a longe line, and then to the oval where a handsome stallion was being ponied around in the company of a well-behaved gelding.

A wiry little man with a blue cap over a white fringe of hair turned as they approached. He had a stopwatch dangling from his pocket and a merry grin on his weathered leprechaun's face.

"So you've had your tour then, have you? And what do you think of our little place here?"

"It's a lovely farm." Brian extended a hand. "I'm pleased to meet you again, Mr. Cunnane."

"Likewise, young Brian from Kerry." Paddy gave Brian's hand a firm shake. "I told them to hold Zeus until you got here, Travis. I thought you and the lad would like a look at his morning run."

"King Zeus, out of Prince," Travis explained. "He's running well for us."

"He took your Belmont Stakes last year," Brian remembered.

"That's right. Zeus likes a long run. Burke's colt snatched the Derby from him, but Zeus came back for the Breeder's Cup. He's a strong competitor, and he'll sire champions."

At Paddy's signal, an exercise boy trotted over mounted on a magnificent chestnut. The horse gleamed dark red in the strengthening sun, with a blaze like a lightning bolt down the center of his forehead. He pranced, sidestepping, head tossing.

Brian knew, at one glance, he was looking at poetry.

"What do you think of him?" Paddy asked.

"Beautiful form" was all Brian said.

Twelve hundred pounds of muscle atop impossibly long and graceful legs. A wide chest, sleek body, proud head. And eyes, Brian saw, that glinted with ferocious pride.

"Take him around, Bobbie," Paddy ordered. "Don't rate him. We'll let him show off a bit this morning." Whistling between his teeth, Paddy leaned on the fence, pulled out the stopwatch.

With his thumbs hooked in his pockets, Brian watched Zeus trot back onto the track, prance in place until the boy controlled him. Then the rider rose up in the stirrups, leaned over that long, powerful neck. Zeus shot forward, a bright arrow from a plucked bow. Those long legs lifted, stretched, fell, flew, shooting out clumps of dirt like bullets as he rounded the first curve.

The air roared with the thunder.

Inside Brian's chest, his heart beat the same way, at a hard and joyful gallop. The boy's hat flew off as they turned into the backstretch. When they streaked by, Paddy gave a grunt and flicked his timer.

"Not bad," Paddy said dryly and held out the watch.

Brian didn't need to see it. He had a clock in his head, and he knew he'd just watched a champion.

"I think I've seen the like of your Prince at last, Mr. Grant."

"And he knows it."

"You want your hands on that one, boy?" Paddy asked him.

There was a time, Brian thought, to hold your cards close, and a time to lay them out. "I do, yes." Struggling not to dance with eagerness, he turned to Travis again. "If the job's being offered, Mr. Grant, I'll take it."

Travis inclined his head, extended a hand. "Welcome to Royal Meadows. Let's go get some coffee."

Brian simply stared as Travis walked off. "Just like that?" he murmured.

"He'd already made up his mind," Paddy said, "or you wouldn't be here in the first place. Travis doesn't waste time—his or anyone else's. After you're done with your coffee and such, come over to my place— above the garage. You'll want a look at the condition book, and have a little conversation."

"Yes, I will. Thanks." A bit dazed, Brian headed off after Travis.

He caught up, surprised, and a little embarrassed, to find his palms were sweaty. A job was only a job, he reminded himself. "I'm grateful for the opportunity, Mr. Grant."

"Travis. You'll work for it. We have high standards at Royal Meadows. I expect you to meet them. I'd like you to start as soon as possible."

"I'll start today."

Travis glanced over. "Good."

Scanning the area, Brian gestured toward another small building, with the paddock set up with jumps. "Do you train jumpers, show horses, as well?"

"That's a separate enterprise." Travis smiled slightly. "You'll work the racehorses. You can move your things into the trainer's quarters when you're ready." Travis flicked a glance toward the garage house.

Brian opened his mouth—then shut it again. He hadn't expected housing to be part of the package, but wasn't about to argue it away. If it didn't suit him, they'd deal with it later.

"You have a beautiful home. Someone likes their flowers."

"My wife." Travis turned onto a slate path. "She's particularly fond of flowers."

And Brian imagined they had a staff of gardeners, landscapers, whatever it was, to deal with them. "The horses appreciate a pretty setting."

Travis stepped onto a patio, turned. "Do they?"

"They do."

"Did Betty tell you that when you were speaking to her?"

Brian met Travis's amused eyes levelly. "She indicated she was a queen and expected to be treated as such."

"And will you?"

"I will, until she abuses the privilege. Even royalty needs a bit of a yank now and again."

So saying, he stepped through the door Travis held open.

Brian didn't know what he'd been expecting. Something sleek and sophisticated. Something grand, certainly.

He hadn't been expecting to walk into the Grants' kitchen, nor to find it big and cluttered and despite the gleam of snazzy appliances and fancy tiles, homey.

Certainly the last thing he'd expected was to see the lady of the manor herself in an old pair of jeans, bare feet and a faded T-shirt standing at the stove with a skillet while she rang a peal over the head of her youngest son.

"And I'll tell you another thing, Patrick Michael Thomas Cunnane, if you think you can come and go at all hours as you damn please just because you're going off to college, you'd best get that thick head of yours examined in a hurry. I'll be happy to do it myself, with the skillet I have in my hand, just as soon as I'm done with it."

"Yes, ma'am." At the table Patrick sat with his shoulders hunched, wincing at his mother's back. "But since you're using it, maybe I could have some more French toast. Nobody makes it like you do."

"You won't get around me that way."

"Maybe I will."

She shot a look over her shoulder that Brian recognized as one only a mother could conjure to wither a child.

"And maybe I won't," Patrick muttered, then brightened when he saw Brian at the door. "Ma, we've got company. Have a seat, Brian. Had breakfast? My mother makes world-famous French toast."

"Witnesses won't save you," Adelia said mildly, but turned to smile at Brian. "Come in and sit. Patrick, get Brian and your father plates."

"No, thank you. There's no need to trouble."

"Ma, I can't find my brown shoes." Sarah came bursting in. "Hello, Brian, morning, Dad."

"Sure I had my eyes right on them for weeks," Adelia said as she flipped sizzling bread in the pan. "I can't think how those shoes slipped out of my sight."

Sarah rolled her eyes and yanked open the refrigerator. "I'm going to be late."

"You could wear one of the other six thousand pairs of shoes jammed in your closet," her brother suggested.

Sarah rapped him on the back with the carton of juice she held and otherwise ignored him. "I don't have time for breakfast." She poured juice, glugged it down. "I'll be home by five."

"Take a muffin," Adelia ordered.

"We don't have any blueberry."

"Take what we do have."

"Okay, okay." She grabbed a muffin off a plate, gave

her mother a smacking kiss on the cheek, rounded the table to give her father one in turn, crossed her eyes at her brother, then dashed out again.

"Sarah works at the vet's office during the summer," Adelia explained. "The pair of you wash up here now, and we'll get you something hot to eat."

Since the scent of that fried bread was impossible to resist, Brian started toward the sink. And saw the huge old dog stretched out by the stove. He resembled a long, black and outrageously shaggy floor mat.

"And who's this?" Automatically Brian crouched down.

"That's our Sheamus. He's an old man now, and likes to tuck himself at my feet while I'm cooking."

"My wife's fond of mutts," Travis said as he ran water in the sink.

"And they of me. He spends most of his time sleeping," she told Brian. "And isn't much for anyone but family now." Even as she said it her brows rose up. Brian had no more than stroked the old dog's head before Sheamus opened his eyes, thumped his ragged tail, and with a moan rolled over onto his back for a belly rub.

"Would you look at that? He's taken to you."

"Well mutts and I, we understand each other. You're a good old boy, aren't you? Fat and happy."

"Someone feeds him table scraps." Adelia slanted a look at her husband.

"I don't know what you're talking about." All innocence, Travis held out the soap when Brian stood up again.

"Hah" was all she said to that. "Would you have coffee, Brian, or tea?"

"Tea, thank you."

"Sit." She pointed to a chair, then shifted the finger to her son. "You, go. I'll finish with you later."

"I'll be at the stables, doing penance." With a heavy sigh, Patrick rose, then he wrapped his arms around his mother's waist, laid his chin on top of her head. "Sorry."

"Get."

But Brian saw her lay a hand over Patrick's, and squeeze. With a quick grin tossed to the room in general, he bolted.

"That boy's responsible for every other line on my face," Adelia muttered.

"What lines?" Travis asked, and made her laugh.

"That's the right answer. So, Brian, does Royal Meadows suit you?"

After drying his hands, he crossed to the table to sit. "Yes, ma'am."

"Oh, we're not so very formal around here. You don't have to ma'am me. Unless you're in trouble." She poured tea for him, and coffee for Travis, then stayed where she was, her free hand resting on her husband's shoulder.

"How did Zeus do this morning?"

"Took the oval in a minute-fifty flat."

"I'm sorry I missed it." She turned back to the stove to heap golden bread onto a platter.

"I'll offer you a one-year contract," Travis began.

"Can't you let the boy eat before you talk business?"

"The boy wants to know."

Brian took the platter, transferred three slices to his plate. "Yes, he does."

"You'll have a guaranteed annual salary." Travis named an amount that had Brian struggling not to bobble the syrup. "And, after two months, a two-percent share of each purse. In six months, we'll re-negotiate that percentage."

"We'll negotiate it up." Steady again, Brian cut into his breakfast. "Because I promise you, I'll have earned it."

They discussed—haggled a bit for form sake—responsibilities, benefits, bonuses, duties.

Brian was on his second serving of toast, and Travis the last of his coffee, when Keeley came in.

She wore buff colored jodhpurs. Elegant and form-fitting. Her high black boots were shined like dark mirrors. Her white blouse draped soft with its wide collar buttoned high. She had tamed her hair into a sleek twist that left her face unframed. Small, complicated twists of gold glinted at her ears.

Her brow lifted at the sight of Brian eating breakfast

in her kitchen, and her mouth thinned before it moved into a cool, practiced smile. "Good morning, Mr. Donnelly."

"Miss Grant."

"I'm pressed for time this morning." She walked to her father, bent down, rubbed her cheek against his.

"You should eat," her mother told her.

"I'll get something later." She went to the refrigerator, took out a soft drink. "I'll be done in a couple of hours." She went to her mother, bending first to scratch Sheamus on the top of the head, then in the same manner she'd used with her father, rubbed cheeks with Adelia before she headed out the back door.

"I'll come down in a bit," Adelia called after her. "I'd like to watch."

Twenty minutes later, Brian walked from the house toward the trainer's quarters. He saw Keeley in the paddock in front of the small building. She sat astride a black gelding. As she walked the horse, a man photographed her from various angles.

Brian paused to watch, hands on hips. She was getting her picture in some fancy magazine, he imagined. Royal Meadows Princess. No doubt she'd look fine and glossy in it.

She set the horse into a trot, then a canter, swinging in to sail over a jump. Brian's lips pursed. She had good form, he had to admit it. When she repeated that jump, then another, for the camera, he heard her laugh float out over the air.

He turned away, dismissing her. Trying to.

He climbed the stairs to the trainer's quarters, knocked.

"Come in, and welcome. In here," Paddy called out.

He sat at a desk in a room set up as an office. File cabinets lined one wall, and photographs of horses lined them all. The window was open, and on a shelf beside it sat a computer. If the dust on its cover was any indication, it was rarely, if ever, used.

Paddy's glasses balanced on the end of his nose as he gestured to a chair. "You and Travis worked out your details."

"We did. He's a fair man."

"Did you expect otherwise?"

"I don't expect anything from owners, and that way they don't often surprise me."

With a chuckle Paddy shoved up his glasses, scratched his nose. "This one might."

"I want to thank you for putting my name in so Mr. Grant would consider me."

"I've kept my eye and ear on things, though I've retired. Well, retired twice now, if the truth be known, and come out of it again as Travis and Dee haven't been satisfied with the trainers who've come along. This time I mean it to stick. I mean you to stick, boy."

When his glasses slid down again, Paddy grunted

in annoyance and took them off. "We'll be bunking here together, if you have no objection, for the next week. After that, I'll be off, and the place is yours."

"Where are you going?"

"Home. Back to Ireland."

"After all these years?"

"I was born there. I've a mind to die there—though I've life left in me, no mistake. I've a yearning to spend the last years of it at home."

"What'll you do there?"

"Oh, go to the pub to tell lies," Paddy said with a twinkling grin. "Drink a pint of decent Guinness. You'll miss that here, I can tell you. It's just not the same built out of a Yank tap."

Brian had to laugh. "It's a long way to go for a pint, even for Guinness."

"Well now, there's a little farm in the south of Cork, not far from Skibbereen. Do you know Skibbereen, Brian?"

"Aye. It's a pretty town."

"Sloping streets and painted doorways," Paddy said, a bit dreamily. "Well, the farm's a bit of a ways from that pretty town. My Dee was raised there, by my sister after Dee's parents died. When my sister got sickly, the farm fell on hard times with Dee trying to run it and tend to her aunt Lettie. In the end, Lettie passed and the farm was lost, and Dee came here to me. A few years ago, the farm came up for sale, and though she told him not to, Travis bought it for her. The man knows her heart."

"So that's where you're going?" Brian asked, though he didn't have a clue why Paddy was telling him. "To be a farmer?"

"That's where I'm going, but I don't think I'll make much of a farmer. I'll have myself a few horses for company."

He shifted, turned his gaze to the window and the hills beyond where horses grazed in the late-morning sunshine.

"I'll miss my little Dee, and Travis, and the children. The friends I've made here. But I've a need to go. An itch, if you follow me."

"I do." There was little Brian understood more than an itch to be going.

"I imagine I'll be flying back and forth across the pond quite a bit—and they'll come to me as well. I've seen Dee married to a man I respect, and love like my own son. I've watched her children grow into fine young men and women. That's a rare thing. And I've had a hand in turning out champions. A man who has a thoroughbred put into his hands is a fortunate man."

"Have you no wish for your own place, your own champions?"

"I toyed with it—but in the end no, it wasn't for me." He turned his attention back to Brian. "Is that what you're after in the end?"

"No. Your own place means you're rooted, doesn't it? And there's no moving on if moving on strikes you. In any case, most owners leave the work and the decisions to the trainer, so you don't own, but you run."

"Travis Grant knows how to work." Paddy inclined his head. "He knows his horses. He loves them. If you earn his trust, he'll trust you, but he'll know every move you make. He's not one for strolling into the winner's circle after the day is done. Shedrow business will be his business, and Dee's, as much as it is yours. Whether you like it or not."

"His wife?"

Amused now, Paddy sat back. "You met her last night when she was done up fancy. I like seeing her looking fine that way. You're more like to see her down in the stables lancing an abscess or soothing a colicky mare. She's no delicate flower. My Dee's a thoroughbred. And she's bred true. Not one of her children would back away from a hard day's work when it's needed. You'll learn for yourself how things go around here, and you'll find it's not such a far distance from main house to shedrow as it is in some places."

"It's usually better all around if it is," Brian muttered, and Paddy cackled with laughter.

"Right you are, lad, in most cases. Owners can be a fly in your ointment without a doubt. You'll make up your own mind about this place, and these owners. And I hope you'll let me know what you think after a bit of time's passed. Now, let's take a look at the condition book to start off."

When Brian left Paddy, he was satisfied with the world in general. Or what, he thought as he trooped down the stairs, was soon to become his world in general. He'd make his mark at Royal Meadows, and live well doing it. His quarters were first-rate. The truth was, he'd have been willing to live in a hovel for the chance to work with Travis Grant's stable.

Everything he'd ever wanted was at his fingertips. He didn't intend to let it slip through.

He turned toward the stables where he'd parked his rental car. Paddy had told him to have a look at the little red lorry down that way, as he'd be selling it before leaving for Ireland. If the thing ran, it would do, Brian thought. He didn't require anything but the most elemental means of transportation. And time to get used to driving on the wrong damn side of the road.

As he rounded the garage he was scowling over that one sticking point, and nearly ran into Keeley.

She looked as fresh and perfect as she had that morning. Not a hair out of place, not a speck of dust on her boots. He wondered how the hell she managed it.

"Good day to you, Miss Grant. I saw you in the paddock earlier. That's a fine horse."

She was hot, irritable and very close to flash point since the photographer had hit on her. The photo shoot had been necessary. She needed the exposure, the publicity, but she damn well didn't need the hassle.

"Yes, he is." She made to move by, and Brian shifted to block her.

"Begging your pardon, princess. Did I neglect to pull my forelock?"

She held up a hand. Her temper was a vile thing when loose, and the drumming in her head warned her it was very close to springing free.

"I'm already annoyed. It won't take much to push me to furious." But she drew a deep breath. If the scene in the kitchen earlier meant anything, Brian Donnelly was now part of Royal Meadows. She didn't make a habit of sniping at a member of the team.

"Sam's a nine-year-old. Hunter. A thoroughbred, Irish Draught horse cross. I've had him since he was four." She lifted the bottle she carried and sipped her soft drink.

"Is that all you put in you?" He tapped a finger on the bottle. "Bubbles and chemicals?"

"You sound like my mother."

"Maybe that's why you have a headache."

Keeley dropped the hand she'd pressed to her temple. Those eyes of his, she thought, were entirely too keen. "I'm fine."

"Turn around."

"I beg your pardon."

Brian merely stepped around her, laid his hands

on the nape of her neck. Her already stiff shoulders jerked in protest. "Relax. I'm not after grabbing you in a fit of passion when any member of your family might come along. I'd like to put in at least one day on the job before I get the boot."

As he spoke he was kneading, pressing, running those strong fingers over the knots. He hated seeing anything in pain. "Blow out a breath," he ordered when she stood rigid as stone. "Come on, *maverneen,* don't be so hardheaded. Blow out a nice long breath for me."

Out of curiosity she obeyed and tried not to think how marvelous his hands felt on her skin.

"Now another."

His voice had gone to croon, lulling her. As he worked, murmured, her eyes fluttered closed. Her muscles loosened, the knots untied. The threatening throbbing in her head faded away. She all but slid into a trance.

She arched against his hands, just a little. Moaned in pleasure. Just a little. He kept his hands firm, professional, even as he imagined skimming them down over her, slipping them under that soft white blouse. He wanted to touch his lips to her nape, just where his thumb was pressing. To taste her there.

And that, he knew, would end things before they'd begun. Wanting a woman was natural. Taking one, where the taking held such risks, was suicide.

So he let his hands drop away, stepped back. She

nearly swayed before she caught herself. When she turned toward him, it felt almost like floating. "Thank you. You're very good at that."

Magic hands, she thought. The man had magic in his hands.

"So I've been told." He shot her a cocky grin. "I've a feeling you need regular loosening up." He snatched the bottle out of her hand. "Go drink some water, and change. You're dressed too warmly for the heat of the day."

She angled her head and was just annoyed enough now to give him a long, thorough look. His hair, all that mass of gold streaked brown was windblown. That wonderfully sculpted mouth just quirked at the corners.

"Any other orders?"

"No, but an observation."

"I'm fascinated."

"No, you're irritated again, but I'll tell you anyway. Your mouth's more appealing naked as it is now than when it's painted as it was this morning."

"So you don't approve of lipstick?"

"Not at all. Some women need it. You don't, so it's just a distraction."

Baffled, nearly amused, she shook her head. "Thanks so much for the advice." She started for the house—where she'd been going to change into something cooler in the first place.

"Keeley."

She stopped, but instead of turning merely glanced over her shoulder to where he stood, thumbs in the pockets of ancient jeans. "Yes?"

"It's nothing. I just wanted to try out your name. I like it."

"So do I. Isn't that handy?"

This time he blew out a breath as she strode off— long legs in tight pants and tall boots. He lifted her soft drink, took a deep sip. Playing with fire with that one, Donnelly, he warned himself. Since he was damned sure singed fingers wouldn't be all he would get if he risked a touch, it was best to back away before the heat became too tempting to resist.

Chapter 3

"Heels down, Lynn. Good. Hands, Shelly. Willy, pay attention." Keeley scanned each one of her afternoon students' form. They were coming along.

Six horses mounted with six children circled the paddock at a sedate walk. Two months before three of those children had never seen a horse firsthand, much less ridden one. Royal Meadows Riding Academy had changed that. It was making a difference.

"All right. Trot. Heads up," she ordered, hands on hips as she watched her students change gaits with varying degrees of success. "Heels down. Knees, Joey. That's the way. You're a team, remember. Looking good. Much better."

She moved closer, tapped the heels of one of her

two boys. He grinned and turned them down. Oh, yes, much better, she thought. A month before Willy had jerked like a puppet every time she'd touched him.

It was all about trust.

She had them change leads, reverse, then attempt a wide figure eight.

It was a little messy, but she let them giggle their way through it.

It was also all about fun.

Brian watched her from a distance. He hadn't seen her for a couple of days. Nearly all of his time had been spent at the stables, or at one of the tracks where the Grants' horses ran. Apparently Keeley didn't spend much time at any of those locations.

He'd looked for her.

And had assumed she whiled away her time having lunch in some trendy spot, or shopping. Having her hair done or her fingernails painted. Whatever it was rich daughters did with their days.

But here she was, circling the paddock with a bunch of kids, obviously instructing them. He supposed it was a kind of hobby, teaching the privileged children of country club parents how to ride in proper English style.

Hobby or not, she looked good doing it. She'd chosen an informal look of jeans and a cotton shirt the color of blueberries. She'd pulled her hair back in some sort of band so that it fell in a wildly curling ponytail. Her boots appeared old, scuffed and serviceable.

She seemed to be enjoying herself. He didn't believe he'd seen her smile like that before. Not so quick and open and warm. Unable to resist, he walked closer as she stopped one of her students, stroked a hand over the horse's neck as she and the little girl had what appeared to be an earnest conversation.

By the time he'd reached the fence, Keeley had lined up all but the girl. Teaching them to control their mounts, he decided, to keep them quiet while something was going on around them.

The single rider posted prettily around the paddock, while Keeley turned a circle to keep her in sight. And circling, she saw Brian leaning on the fence.

The smile vanished, and he thought that was a true shame. But there was something almost as appealing about that cool, suspicious look she often aimed in his direction. He answered it with a grin, and settled in to watch the rest of the lesson.

Keeley didn't mind an audience. Often her parents or one of her siblings or one of the hands stopped by to watch. She'd certainly carried on her lessons with a parent or two of a student looking on. But since she didn't care for this particular observer, she ignored him.

One by one she selected a student to go through the day's routine solo. She corrected form, encouraged, pushed a little when it was needed for more effort or concentration. When she called for dismount, every one of them groaned.

"Five more minutes, Miss Keeley. Can't we ride for five more minutes?"

"I already let you ride five more minutes." She patted Shelly's knee. "Next week we're going to try a canter."

"I'm getting a horse for Christmas," Lynn announced. "And next spring, my mother says we'll enter shows."

"Then you'll have to work very hard. Cool off your mounts."

"That's a fine-looking group you have there. Miss Keeley."

Ingrained manners had her acknowledging Brian, walking over to the fence as she kept her eye on her students. "I like to think so."

"That boy there?" He nodded toward the dark-eyed, thin-faced Willy. "He's in love with that horse. Dreams of him at night, of racing over fields and hills and adventuring."

It made her smile again. "Teddy loves him, too. Teddy Bear," she explained. "A big, gentle sweetheart."

"This lot's lucky to have the wherewithal for lessons with a good instructor, and smart mounts. You stable them here? I haven't seen any of these down in my area."

"They're mine. I stable them here." Her horses, her school, her responsibility. "Excuse me. The lesson's not over until the horses are groomed."

Here's your hat, what's your hurry? Brian thought. Well, he had a few things to see to. But that didn't mean he couldn't wander back this way in a bit.

He bothered her. There was no real explanation for it, Keeley thought. It just was. She didn't like the way he looked at her. And why was she the only one who seemed to notice that edge in his eyes when they landed on her.

She didn't like the way he talked to her. And again, she seemed to be the only one aware of that sly little lilt in his voice when he said her name.

Everyone else thought Brian Donnelly was just dandy, she mused as she ran her hands up a gelding's legs to check for heat. Her parents considered him the perfect man to replace Uncle Paddy—and Uncle Paddy had nothing but praise for him.

Sarah thought he was hot. Patrick thought he was cool. And Brendon thought he was smart.

"Outnumbered," she muttered, and lifted the horse's foreleg to check the hoof.

Maybe it was some chemical reaction. Something that caused her hackles to rise when he was in the vicinity. After all, he appeared to be perfectly competent in his work. More than, she admitted, from what she'd heard. And as they were both busy, they would rarely bump up against each other. So it shouldn't matter.

But she didn't like the fact that she was avoiding the

stables and shedrow. That she was deliberately fore-going the pleasure of wandering down that way and watching the workouts, or lending a hand in groom-ing. She didn't like knowing that about herself.

She certainly didn't care for the fact that she sus-pected *he* knew it. Which gave him entirely too much importance.

Which, she admitted, she was doing even now just by thinking of him.

The horse wickered. Keeley's shoulders stiffened.

"You've a good eye for horses," Brian said.

It didn't surprise her that she hadn't heard him come in. And it didn't surprise her that despite not hear-ing she'd known he was there. The air changed, she thought, when he was in it.

"I come by it naturally."

"You do. Teddy Bear." He murmured it, causing her to look up as she lowered the gelding's leg. His eyes were on the horse's, his skilled and clever hands al-ready moving over head and throat. Keeley heard the gelding blow out a soft breath. Pure pleasure.

"You've a kind and patient heart, don't you?" Brian moved into the box, those wide palmed hands still skimming, stroking, checking. "And a fine broad back for carrying small, dreamy boys. How long have you had him?"

She blinked, nearly flushed. There was something

hypnotic about those hands, about that voice. "Nearly two years."

Brian ran his hands down the flank. Stopped. His eyes narrowed as he stepped closer and examined a crosshatch of scarring. "What's this?" But he knew, and turned on Keeley so quickly she backed up to the wall before she could stop herself. "This horse has been whipped, and whipped bloody."

"His previous owner," she said, icily as a defense against that first spurt of alarm, "had a heavy hand with a whip. He wanted to show Teddy, but Teddy shied at the jumps. This was his way of showing he was the boss."

"Bloody bastard." And though his eyes still glinted with heat, his voice went soft again. "You're in a better place now, aren't you, boy. A fine home with a pretty woman to rub you down. Rescued him, did you?" he said to Keeley.

"I wouldn't go that far. There are different methods of breaking a horse. I don't happen to—"

"I don't break horses." Brian ducked under Teddy's belly, then his eyes met Keeley's over the wide back. "I make them. Any idiot can use a bat or a whip and break both spirit and heart. It takes skill and patience and a gentle hand to make a champion, or even just a friend."

She waited a moment, surprised her knees wanted to shake. "Why do you expect me to disagree with you?" she wondered aloud. She stepped out of the box, moved to the next.

The aging mare greeted her with a snort and a bump of head on shoulder. Keeley snatched up a body brush to finish off her student's sketchy grooming.

"I can't stand seeing anything mistreated." Brian spoke quietly from behind her. Keeley didn't turn, didn't answer. Now that the first spurt of anger had passed, he had just enough room for shame at the way he'd turned on her. "Especially something that has so little choice. It makes me sick, and angry."

"And you expect me to disagree, again?"

"I snapped at you. I'm sorry." He touched a hand to her shoulder, left it there even when she stiffened— as he would with a nervous horse. "You look into eyes like that one has over there, and you see inside them that huge, generous heart. Then the scars where someone beat him—because he could. It scrambles my brain."

With an effort she relaxed her shoulders. "It took me three months to get him to trust me enough not to shy every time I lifted my hand. One day, he stuck his head out when I came in and called to me the way they do when they're happy to see you. I fed him carrots and cried like a baby. Don't tell me about mistreatment and scrambled brains."

Shame wasn't something he felt often, but it was

easy to recognize. He took a deep breath and hoped to start again. "What's this pretty mare's story?"

"Why do you think there's a story? She's a horse. You ride her."

"Keeley." He laid a hand over hers on the brush. "I'm sorry."

She moved her hand, but gave in and rested her cheek on the mare's neck. Rubbing, Brian noted, as she did when she hugged her parents.

"Her crime was age. She's nearly twenty. She'd been left stabled, and neglected. She was covered with nettle rash and lice. Her people just got bored with her, I suppose."

He didn't think when he stroked her hair. His hands were as much a part of his way of communicating as his voice. "How many do you have?"

"Eight, counting Sam, but he's too much for the students at this point."

"And did you save them all?"

"Sam was a gift for my twenty-first birthday. The others…well, when you're in the center of the horse world, you hear about horses. Besides, I needed them for the school."

"Some would expect you to stock thoroughbreds."

"Yes." She shifted. "Some would. Sorry, I have to feed the horses, then I have paperwork."

"I'll give you a hand with the feeding."

"I don't need it."

"I'll give you one anyway."

Keeley moved out of the box, rested a hand on the door. Best, she decided, to deal with this clean and simple. "Brian, you're working for my family, in a vital and essential role, so I think I should be straight with you."

"By all means." The serious tone didn't match the glint in his eye as she leaned back.

"You bother me," she told him. "On some level, you just bother me. It's probably because I just don't care for cocky, intense men who smirk at me, but that's neither here nor there."

"No, that's here and it's there. What kind do you care for?"

"You see—that's just the sort of thing that annoys me."

"I know. It's interesting, isn't it, that I find myself compelled to do just the thing that gets a rise out of you? You bother me as well. Perhaps it's that I don't care for regal, cool-eyed women who look down their lovely noses at me. But here we are, so we should try getting on as best we can."

"I don't look down my nose at you, or anyone."

"Depends on your point of view, doesn't it?"

She turned on her heel and marched away, focusing intensely on measuring out grain.

"Why don't we talk of something safe?" he suggested. "Like what I think about Royal Meadows. I've worked on farms and around tracks since I was ten. Stableboy, exercise boy, groom. Working my way up, hustling my way through. Twenty years means I've seen all sides of training, racing and breeding. The bright and the dark. And in twenty years, I've never seen brighter than Royal Meadows."

She paused, and her gaze shifted to his face before she began to add supplements to the grain.

"To my way of thinking, there aren't many people as worthy as one good horse. Your parents are admirable people. Not just for what they have, but much more for what they've done, and what they do with it. I'm honored to work for them. And," he said when she turned to him again, "they're lucky to have me."

She laughed. "Apparently they agree with you." Shaking her head, she moved by to start the feeding, and as she passed him he breathed in the scent of her hair, of her skin.

"But you're not sure you do. Though you don't seem to have much interest in the workings of the farm itself."

"Don't I?"

He studied the neatly typed list on the wall that indicated which supplements in what amounts were added for each particular horse for the evening feed. "I see your sisters and your brothers on a daily basis," he commented as he began to fix Teddy's meal. "Everyone in your family, down at the shedrow, or at the track, but you."

She could have told him the time and placement of every horse they'd run that past week. Which were being medicated, which mares were breeding. Pride kept her silent. She preferred thinking of it as pride, and not sheer stubbornness.

"I suppose your little school keeps you busy."

Her teeth clamped together, wanted to grind, but she spoke through them. "Oh, yes, my little school keeps me busy."

"You're a good teacher." He moved to Teddy's box.

"Thank you so much."

"No need to be snotty about it. You are a good teacher. And one of those rich kids might stick it out, rather than getting bored once horse fever's passed."

"One of my rich kids," she murmured.

"It takes skill, endurance, and money, doesn't it, to compete in horse shows. I don't follow show jumping myself, though I've found it pretty enough to watch. You might be training yourself a champion. The Royal International or Dublin Grand Prix. Maybe the Olympics."

"So, let's see if I get this. Rich kids compete in horse shows and win blue ribbons and those who aren't so privileged do what? Become grooms?"

"That's how the world works, doesn't it?"

"That's how it can work. You're a snob, Brian."

He looked up, flabbergasted. "What?"

"You're a snob, and the worst kind of snob—the kind who thinks he's broad-minded. Now that I know that, you don't bother me at all."

The stable phone rang, delighting her. Whoever was on the other end not only had perfect timing but they had her gratitude. It gave her great pleasure to see the absolute shock on Brian's face as she walked to the phone.

"Royal Meadows Riding Academy. Would you hold one moment, please." With a friendly smile, she laid a hand over the receiver. "Really, I can finish up here. I'm keeping you from your work."

"I'm not a snob," he finally managed to say.

"Of course you wouldn't see it that way. Can we discuss this another time? I need to take this call."

Irked, he shoved the scoop back in the grain. "I'm not the one wearing bloody diamonds in my ears," he muttered as he stalked out.

It put him out of humor for the rest of the day. It stuck in his craw and festered there. A nasty little canker sore on the ego.

Snob? Where did the woman get off calling him a snob? And after he'd made the effort to be friendly, even compliment her on her snooty little riding academy.

He did the evening check himself, as was his habit,

and spent considerable time going over the prime filly who was to head down to Hialeah to race there. Travis wanted Brian to go along for this one, and he was more than happy to oblige.

It would do him a world of good to put a thousand miles or so between himself and Keeley.

"Shouldn't be looking in that direction, even for a blink," he muttered, then nuzzled the filly. "Especially when I've got a darling like you in hand. We'll have us a time in Florida, won't we, you and me?"

"Poker game tonight," one of the grooms called out as Brian left the stables. He added an eyebrow wiggle and a grin to the announcement.

"I'll be back then. And it'll be my pleasure to empty your pockets." But for now, he thought, he had paperwork of his own.

When he returned from Florida they'd separate the foals from their mothers. The weanlings would cause a commotion the first day or so. And the yearling training would begin in earnest. He had charts to make, schedules to outline, plans to ponder.

And he wanted to put a great deal of personal time into the forming of Bad Betty.

He had no business detouring toward Keeley's stable. Still it would only take a minute, Brian told himself, to set the woman straight.

But instead of Keeley, he found her sister. Sarah stopped her dash past him and waved. "Hi. Wonderful evening, isn't it? I'm going to take advantage of it and sneak in a ride before sunset. Want to join me?"

It was tempting. She was good company, and he hadn't felt a horse under him in weeks. But there was work. "I'd love to, another time. You riding one of Keeley's?"

"Yeah. She's always up for someone to exercise one of her babies. The kids don't give them much of a workout, so they can get stale. Or bored. Her Saturday class is a little more advanced, but still."

He fell into step beside her. "I don't suppose an hour of posture and posting does much for the horses."

"Oh, she lets them out to pasture, and rides herself whenever she can fit it in. Which isn't as much as she'd like, but the kids are the priority. And that hour of posture and posting does a lot for them."

He made a noncommittal sound as they rounded the building. He hoped Keeley was still inside what he supposed was an office. He wanted a word with her. "I saw part of her class today."

"Did you? Aren't they cute? Today's what…oh, yeah, Willy. Did you notice the little guy, dark hair and eyes? He rides Teddy."

"Aye. He has good form, and he's cheerful about it."

"He is now. He was a scared little rabbit when Keeley took him on." Sarah swung into the stables, headed directly for the tack room.

"Afraid of horses?"

"Of everything. I don't know how people can do that to a child. I'll never understand it."

"Do what?"

She chose her tack, murmuring a thanks when Brian took the saddle from her. "Hurt them." She glanced back. "Oh, I thought since you'd seen the class, Keeley would have told you the whole deal about the school."

"No." He took the saddle blanket as well. "We didn't get to that. Why don't you tell me the whole deal?"

"Sure." She went to the old mare, cooed. "There's my girl. Want to go for a ride? Sure you do." She slipped the bridle on, fixed the bit, then led the mare out. "I don't know if it started with the horses or the kids. It all seemed to happen at the same time. She bought Eastern Star first. He was a thoroughbred, five years old, and he hadn't lived up to his potential. According to the owners. They pumped him up before a race."

"Drugged him."

"Amphetamines." Her pretty face went hard. "They got caught, but they'd damaged Star's heart and kidneys in the process. She bought him. We nursed him, did everything we could. He didn't last a year. It still gets me," Sarah murmured.

She shook her head and began to saddle her mount. "After that it was like a mission to Keeley. So I guess the horses came first. She put this place together, and got the word out that she was opening a small academy. The ones who can pay, pay a very stiff fee to have her teach their kids—and she's worth it. Those stiff fees help subsidize the other students."

"What other students?"

"Ones like Willy." Sarah cinched the saddle, checked the stirrups. "Underprivileged, abused, circling the system kids. She takes them for nothing— no, she hunts them up, sponsors them, outfits them, works with a child psychologist. It's why she doesn't have as much time to ride as she used to. Our Keeley doesn't do anything halfway. She'd take more on, but she wants to keep the classes small so each kid gets plenty of attention. So she's campaigning for other academies, other owners to start similar programs."

Sarah patted the mare's neck. "I'm surprised she didn't mention it. She rarely misses an opportunity to talk someone into getting involved."

With a cheerful smile, she vaulted into the saddle. "Listen, would you like to come up for dinner? I hear Dad's grilling chicken."

"Thanks all the same, but I've plans. Enjoy your ride."

He had plans all right, he thought as Sarah trotted off. To eat crow. He wasn't sure what it tasted like, but he already knew he wasn't going to enjoy it.

He walked around to the office, knocked. He supposed if he'd been wearing a hat, he'd have held it in his hands. When she didn't answer, he opened the door, glanced in.

Neat, organized, as expected. The air smelled of her—just the faintest echo of scent.

But everything inside was designed for business. A desk—with a computer he imagined was a great deal more in use than Paddy's—a two-line telephone and a little fax machine. File cabinets, two trim chairs and a small fridge. Curious, he walked in and opened it. Then had to grin when he saw it was stocked with bottles of the soft drink she seemed to live on.

A scan of the walls had the grin turning to a wince. Blue ribbons, medals, awards were all neatly framed and displayed. There were photographs of her in formal riding gear flying over jumps, smiling from the back of a horse or standing with her cheek pressed to her mount's neck.

And in a thick frame was an Olympic medal. A silver.

"Well, hell. We'll make that two portions of crow," he murmured.

Chapter 4

It was his fault. She could put the blame for this entirely on Brian Donnelly's shoulders. If he hadn't been so insufferable, if he hadn't been there *being* insufferable when Chad had called, she wouldn't have agreed to go out to dinner. And she wouldn't have spent nearly four hours being bored brainless when she could've been doing something more useful.

Like watching paint dry.

There was nothing wrong with Chad, really. If you only had, say, half a brain, no real interest outside of the cut of this year's designer jacket and were thrilled by a rip-roaring debate over the proper way to serve a triple latte, he was the perfect companion.

Unfortunately, she didn't qualify on any of those levels.

Right now he was droning on about the painting he'd bought at a recent art show. No, not the painting, Keeley thought wearily. A discussion of the painting, of art, might have been the medical miracle that prevented her from slipping into a coma. But Chad was discoursing—no other word for it—on The Investment.

He had the windows up and the air conditioning blasting as they drove. It was a perfectly beautiful night, she mused, but putting the windows down meant Chad's hair would be mussed. Couldn't have that.

At least she didn't have to attempt conversation. Chad preferred monologues.

What he wanted was an attractive companion of the right family and tax bracket who dressed well and would sit quietly while he pontificated on the narrow areas of his interest.

Keeley was fully aware he'd decided she fit the bill, and now she'd only encouraged him by agreeing to this endlessly tedious date.

"The broker assured me that within three years the piece will be worth five times what I paid for it. Normally I would have hesitated as the artist is young and relatively unknown, but the show was quite successful. I noticed T.D. Giles considering two of the pieces personally. And you know how astute T.D. is about such things. Did I tell you I ran into his wife, Sissy, the other day? She looks absolutely marvelous. The eye tuck did wonders for her, and she tells me she's found the most amazing new stylist."

Oh God, was all Keeley could think. Oh God, get me out of here.

When they swung through the stone pillars at Royal Meadows, she had to fight the urge to cheer.

"I'm so glad our schedules finally clicked. Life gets much too demanding and complicated, doesn't it? There's nothing more relaxing than a quiet dinner for two."

Any more relaxed, Keeley thought, and unconsciousness would claim her. "It was nice of you to ask me, Chad." She wondered how rude it would be to spring out of the car before it stopped, race to the house and do a little dance of relief on the front porch.

Pretty rude, she decided. Okay, she'd skip the dance.

"Drake and Pamela—you know the Larkens of course—are having a little soirée next Saturday evening. Why don't I pick you up at eightish?"

It took her a minute to get over the fact he'd actually used the word soirée in a sentence. "I really can't, Chad. I have a full day of lessons on Saturday. By the time it's done I'm not fit for socializing. But thanks." She slid her hand to the door handle, anticipating escape.

"Keeley, you can't let your little school eclipse so much of your life."

Her hand stiffened, and though she could see the lights of home, she turned her head and studied his perfect profile. One day, someone was going to refer to the academy as *her little school,* and she was going to be very rude. And rip their throat out. "Can't I?"

"I'm sure it amuses you. Hobbies are very satisfying."

"Hobbies." She bared her teeth.

"Everyone needs an outlet, I suppose." He lifted a hand from the wheel and gracefully waved away over two years of hard work. "But you must take time for yourself. Just the other day Renny mentioned she hadn't seen you in ages. After all, when the novelty wears off, you'll wonder where all this time has gone."

"My school is not a hobby, an amusement, or a novelty. And it is completely my business."

"Naturally. Of course." He gave her a patronizing little pat on the knee as he stopped the car, shifted toward her. "But you must admit, it's taking up an inordinate amount of your time. Why it's taken us six months to have dinner together."

"Is that all?"

He misinterpreted the quiet response, and the gleam in her eyes. And leaned toward her.

She slapped a hand on his chest. "Don't even think about it. Let me tell you something, pal. I do more in one day with my school than you do in a week of pushing papers in that office your grandfather gave you between your manicures and amaretto lattes and soirées. Men like you hold no interest for me whatsoever, which is why it's taken six months for this tedious little date. And the next time I have dinner with you, we'll be slurping Popsicles in hell. So take your French tie and your Italian shoes and stuff them."

Utter shock had him speechless as she shoved open her door. As insult trickled in, his lips thinned. "Obviously spending so much time in the stables has eroded your manners, and your outlook."

"That's right, Chad." She leaned back in the door. "You're too good for me. I'm about to go up and weep into my pillow over it."

"Rumor is you're cold," he said in a quiet, stabbing voice. "But I had to find out for myself."

It stung, but she wasn't about to let it show. "Rumor is you're a moron. Now we've both confirmed the local gossip."

He gunned the engine once, and she would have sworn she saw him vibrate. "And it's a British tie."

She slammed the car door, then watched narrow-eyed as he drove away. "A British tie." A laugh gurgled up, deep from the belly and up into the throat so she had to stand, hugging herself, all but howling at the moon. "That sure told me."

Indulging herself in a long sigh, she tipped her head

back, looked up at the sweep of stars. "Moron," she murmured. "And that goes for both of us."

She heard a faint *click,* spun around and saw Brian lighting a slim cigar. "Lover's spat?"

"Why yes." The temper Chad had roused stirred again. "He wants to take me to Antigua and I simply have my heart set on Mozambique. Antigua's been done to death."

Brian took a contemplative puff of his cigar. She looked so damn beautiful standing there in the moonlight in that little excuse of a black dress, her hair spilling down her back like fire on silk. Hearing her long, gorgeous roll of laughter had been like discovering a treasure. Now the temper was back in her eyes, and spitting at him.

It was almost as good.

He took another lazy puff, blew out a cloud of smoke. "You're winding me up, Keeley."

"I'd like to wind you up, then twist you into small pieces and ship them all back to Ireland."

"I figured as much." He disposed of the cigar and walked to her. Unlike Chad, he didn't misinterpret the glint in her eye. "You want to have a pop at someone." He closed his hand over the one she'd balled into a fist, lifted it to tap on his own chin. "Go ahead."

"As delightful as I find that invitation, I don't solve my disputes that way." When she started to walk away, he tightened his grip. "But," she said slowly, "I could make an exception."

"I don't like apologizing, and I wouldn't have to—again—if you'd set me straight right off."

She lifted an eyebrow. Trying to free herself from that big, hard hand would only be undignified. "And are you referring to my little school?"

"It's a fine thing you're doing. An admirable thing, and not a little one at all. I'd like to help you."

"Excuse me?"

"I'd like to give you a hand with it when I can. Give you some of my time."

Off balance, she shook her head. "I don't need any help."

"I don't imagine you do. But it couldn't hurt, could it?"

She studied him with equal parts suspicion and interest. "Why?"

"Why not. You'll admit I know horses. I have a strong back. And I believe in what you're doing."

It was the last that cut through her defenses. No one outside of family had understood what she wanted to do as easily. She flexed her hand in his, and when he released her, stepped back. "Are you offering because you feel guilty?"

"I'm offering because I'm interested. Feeling guilty made me apologize."

"You haven't apologized yet." But she smiled a little

as she began to walk. "Never mind. I might be able to use a strong back from time to time." She glanced over as he fell into step beside her. It looked like he had one, she mused, skimming her gaze over the rough jeans and plain white T-shirt he wore.

A strong, healthy body, good hands and an innate understanding of horses. She could do a great deal worse, she supposed. "Do you ride?"

"Well, of course I ride," he began, then caught her smirky little smile. "Having me on again, are you?"

"That one was easy." She turned to wander along a path that meandered through late-blooming shrubs and an arbor of gleaming moonflowers. "I won't pay you."

"I've a job, thanks."

"The kids handle a lot of the chores," she told him. "It's part of the package. This isn't just about teaching them to post and change leads at a canter. It's about trust—in themselves, in their horse, in me. Making a connection with their horse. Shoveling manure makes quite a connection."

He grinned. "I can't argue with that."

"Still they're kids, so fun is a big part of the program. And they're learning so they don't always do the best job mucking out or grooming. And there isn't always enough time to have them deal properly with the tack."

"I started my illustrious career with a pitchfork in my hand and saddle soap in my pocket."

Idly he tugged a white blossom from the vine, tucked it into her hair. The gesture flustered her— the easy charm of it—and made her remember they were walking in the moonlight, among the flowers.

Not, she reminded herself, a good idea.

"All right then. If and when you've time to spare, I've got an extra pitchfork."

When she veered toward the house he took her hand again. "Don't go in yet. It's a pretty night and a shame to waste it with sleeping."

His voice was lovely, with a soothing lilt. There was no reason she could think of why it made her want to shiver. "We both have to be up early."

"True enough, but we're young, aren't we? I saw your medal."

Distracted, she forgot to pull her hand away. "My medal?"

"Your Olympic medal. I went looking for you in your office."

"The medal lures parents who can afford the tuition."

"It's something to be proud of."

"I am proud of it." With her free hand she brushed her hair as the breeze teased it. Her fingertips skimmed over the soft petals of the flower. "But it doesn't define me."

"Not like, what was it? A British tie?"

The laugh got away from her, and eased the odd tension that had been building inside her. "Here's a surprise. With a great deal of time and some effort, I might begin to like you."

"I've plenty of time." He released her hand to toy with the ends of her hair. She jerked back. "You're a skittish one," he murmured.

"No, not particularly." Usually, she thought. With most people.

"The thing is, I like to touch," he told her and deliberately skimmed his fingers over her hair again. "It's that…connection. You learn by touching."

"I don't…" She trailed off when those fingers ran firmly down the back of her neck.

"I've learned you carry your worries right there, right at the base there. More worries than show on your face. It's a staggering face you have, Keeley. Throws a man off."

The tension was slipping away from under his fingers as he touched her, and building everywhere else. A kind of gathering inside her, a concentration of heat. The pressure in her chest was so sudden and strong it made her breath short. The muscles in her stomach began to twist, tighten. Ache.

"My face doesn't have anything to do with what I am."

"Maybe not, but that doesn't take away the pure pleasure of looking at it."

If she hadn't trembled, he might have resisted. It was a mistake. But he'd made them before, would make them again. There was moonlight, and the scent of the last of summer's roses in the air. Was a man supposed to walk away from a beautiful woman who trembled under his hand?

Not this man, he thought.

"Too pretty a night to waste it," he said again, and bent toward her.

She jerked back when his mouth was a whisper from hers, but his fingers continued to play over her neck, keeping her close. His gaze dropped to her lips, lingered, then came back to hers.

And he smiled. *"Cushla machree,"* he murmured, and as if it were an incantation, she slid under the spell.

His lips brushed hers, wing-soft. Everything inside her fluttered in response. He drew her closer, gradually luring her body to fit against his, curves to angles, as his hand played rhythmically up and down her spine.

A light scrape of teeth, and her lips parted for him.

Her head went light, her blood hot, and her body seemed balanced on the brink of something high and thin. It was lovely, lovely to feel this soft, this female, this open. She brought her hands to his shoulders, clung there while she let herself teeter on that delicious edge.

He knew how to be gentle, there had always been gentleness inside him for the fragile. But her sudden and utter surrender to him, to herself, had him forcing back the need to grab and plunder. Resistance was what he'd expected. Anything from cool disdain to impulsive passion he would have understood. But this... giving destroyed him.

"More," he murmured against her mouth. "Just a little more." And deepened the kiss.

She made a sound in her throat, a low purr that slipped into his system like silk. His heart shook, then it stumbled, then God help him, it fell.

The shock of it had him yanking her back, staring at her with the edgy caution of a man suddenly finding himself holding a tiger instead of a kitten.

Had he actually thought it a mistake? Nothing more than a simple mistake? He'd just put the power to crush him into her hands.

"Damn it."

She blinked at him, struggling to catch up with the abrupt change. His face was fierce, and the hands that had shifted to her arms no longer gentle. She wanted to shiver, but wouldn't permit another show of weakness.

"Let me go."

"I didn't force you."

"I didn't say you did."

Her lips still throbbed from the pressure of his, and

her stomach quaked. Rumor was she was cold, she thought dimly. And she'd believed it herself. Finding out differently wasn't cause for celebration. But for panic.

"I don't want this." This vulnerability, this need.

"Neither do I." He released her to jam his hands into his pockets. "That makes this quite the situation."

"It's not a situation if we don't let it be one." She wanted to rub a hand over her heart, to hold it there. It amazed her that he couldn't hear it hammering. "We're both grown-ups, able to take responsibility for our own actions. That was a momentary lapse on both our parts. It won't happen again."

"And if it does?"

"It won't, because each of us have priorities and a…situation would complicate matters. We'll forget it. Good night."

She walked to the house. She didn't run, though part of her wanted to. And another part, a part that brought her no pride, simply wanted him to stop her.

He'd hoped the time away in Florida with work at the center of his world would help him do just what she'd said to do. Forget it.

But he hadn't, and couldn't, and finally decided it had been a ridiculous thing for her to expect. Since he was suffering, he saw no reason why he should let her off so damn easy.

He knew how to handle women, he reminded himself. And princess or not, Keeley was a woman under it all. She was going to discover she couldn't swat Brian Donnelly aside like a pesky fly.

He walked up from the stables, his bag slung over his shoulder. He'd yet to go to his quarters, and had slept very little on the drive back from Hialeah. He could have flown back, but the choice to stay with the horses and make the drive had been his.

His horses had done all he'd asked of them, made him proud at heart and plumper in the pocket. Seeing that they were delivered home and settled back again was the least he could do.

But right now he wanted nothing more than a hot shower, a shave and a decent cup of tea.

Though he'd have traded all of that for one more taste of Keeley.

Knowing it irritated him had him scowling in the direction of her paddock. The minute he was cleaned up, he promised himself, the two of them would have a little conversation. Very little, he decided, before he got his hands on her again. And when he did, he was going to—

The erotic image he conjured in his head burst like a bubble when he rounded the house and saw Keeley's mother kneeling at the flower bed.

It was not the most comfortable thing to come across the mother when you'd been picturing the daughter naked. Then Adelia looked over at him, and he saw the tears on her cheeks. And his mind went blank.

"Ah...Mrs. Grant."

"Brian." Sniffling, she wiped her cheeks with the back of her hand. "I was doing some weeding. Just tidying up the beds here." She tugged at the cap on her head, then she lowered her hands, dropped back on her heels. "I'm sorry."

"Ah..." Said that already, he thought, panicked. Say something else. He was never so helpless as he was with female tears.

"I'm missing Uncle Paddy. He left yesterday." She didn't quite muffle a sob. "I thought if I came by here and fiddled, I'd feel some better, but it's knowing he's not down at the stables, or up there. I know he had to go. I know he wanted to go. But..."

"Ah..." Oh hell. Frantic, Brian dug in his back pocket for his bandanna. "Maybe you should..."

"Thanks." She took the cloth as he crouched beside her. "You'll know what it's like, I think, being away from family."

"Well, mine's not close, so to speak."

"Family's family." She dried her face, blew out a breath.

She looked so young, he thought, and not like a mother at all, with her cap crooked on her head and her eyes drenched. He did what came natural for him, and took her hand.

For a moment, she leaned her head on his shoulder, sighed. "He changed everything for me, Paddy did, when he brought me here. I was so nervous coming all this way. New place, new people. A new country. And I hadn't seen Paddy outside pictures for years, or even been face-to-face since I was a baby, but as soon as I saw him, it was all right again. I don't know what I'd have done without him."

It loosened the fist around her heart to talk. Soothed her that he gave her the quiet that was an offer to listen.

"I didn't want to blubber in front of Travis and the children because they're missing him, too. And I was holding on pretty well until I came down here. This is where I lived when I first came to Royal Meadows. In a pretty room with green walls and white curtains. I was so young."

"I guess you're old and decrepit now," Brian said and was relieved when she laughed.

"Well, perhaps not quite decrepit, but I was greener then. I'd never seen a place like this in all my life, and I was going to be living right in the middle of it thanks to Paddy. If it hadn't been for him, I don't think Travis would ever have taken the likes of me on as a groom."

"A groom." Brian's brows lifted. "I thought that was a made-up story."

"Indeed it's not," she said with some heat—and an

unmistakable touch of pride. "I earned my keep around here, make no mistake. I was a damn fine groom in my time. Majesty was mine."

Brian lowered himself until he was sitting on the ground beside her. "You groomed Majesty?"

"That I did, and was there to watch him take the Derby. Oh, I loved that horse. You know what it's like."

"I do, yes."

"We lost him only last year. A fine long life he had. I think that was when Paddy decided it was time for him to go home again. He's there by now, and I know what he sees when he stands out in front of the house, and that's a comfort. As you've been just now, Brian. Thank you."

"I didn't do anything. I fumble with tears."

"You listened." She handed him back his bandanna.

"Mostly because tears render me speechless. You've a bit of garden dirt here."

Keeley came down the path just in time to see Brian gently wipe her mother's face with a blue bandanna. The tearstains had her leaping forward like a mama bear to her threatened cub.

"What is it? What did you do?" Hissing at Brian, she wrapped an arm around Adelia's shoulder.

"Nothing. I just knocked your mother down and kicked her a few times."

"Keeley." With a surprised laugh, Adelia patted her daughter's hand. "Brian's done nothing but lend me his hankie and his shoulder while I had a little cry over Uncle Paddy."

"Oh, Mama." Keeley pressed her cheek to Adelia's, rubbed. "Don't be sad."

"I have to be, a little. But I'm better now." She leaned over, surprising Brian with a kiss on the cheek. "You're a nice young man, and a patient one."

He got to his feet to help her up. "I don't have much of a reputation for either, Mrs. Grant."

"That's because not everyone looks close enough. You should be able to call me Dee easy enough now that I've cried on you. I'm going down to the stables, do some work."

"She never cries," Keeley murmured when her mother walked away. "Not unless she's very happy or very sad. I'm sorry I jumped at you that way, but when I saw she'd been crying, I stopped thinking."

"Tears affect me much the same way, so we'll let it be."

She nodded, then cast around for something to say that would help relieve the awkwardness. She'd been so sure she'd be controlled and composed when she saw him again. "So, I heard you did well at Hialeah."

"We did. Your Hero runs particularly well in a crowd."

"Yes, I've seen him. He lives to run." She noted the bag Brian had set down. "And here you are not even really back yet, and you've had one woman crying on your shoulder and another swiping at you. I really am sorry."

"Sorry enough to make me some tea while I clean up?"

"I...all right, but I've got less than an hour."

"Takes a good deal less to brew a pot of tea." Satisfied, he started up the steps. "You've a class this afternoon then?"

"Yes." Trapped, Keeley shrugged and followed him up and inside. He'd been kind to her mother, she reminded herself. She was obliged to repay that. "At three-thirty. I have some things to do before the students arrive."

"Well, I won't be long. You know where the kitchen is, I expect."

She frowned after him as he strolled off into the bedroom.

Making him cozy pots of tea wasn't how she'd expected to handle the situation, she thought. She'd given it a great deal of consideration and had decided the best thing all around would be to maintain a polite, marginally friendly distance. That business the other night had been nothing but a moment's foolishness. Harmless.

Incredible.

She gave herself a shake and got down the old teapot Paddy had favored. No, it was nothing to worry about. In fact, on one level she really should be grateful to Brian. He'd shown her she wasn't as indifferent to men as she'd believed. It had bothered her a little that she'd never felt that spark so many of her friends had spoken of.

Well, she'd certainly felt a whole firestorm of sparks when he'd put his hands on her. And that was good, that was healthy. Someone had finally caught her at the right time and the right place and the right mood. If it could happen once, it could happen again.

With someone else, of course. When she decided it was time.

She set the tea aside to steep, then opening a cupboard stretched high for a cup.

"I'll get that." He moved in behind her, handily trapping her between his body and the counter. Closed his hand over hers on the cup.

She could smell the shower on him, feel the heat of it. And her mouth went dry.

"I decided I don't care to forget it."

She had to concentrate on regulating her breathing. "I beg your pardon?"

"And that I'm not going to let you forget it, either."

She needed to swallow, but her throat wouldn't cooperate. "We agreed—"

"No, we didn't." He brought the cup down, set it aside. "We agreed we didn't want this." The ponytail she wore left a lovely curve of her neck bare. He nuzzled there. "And I'd say there's been an unspoken agreement that despite that, we want each other."

The firestorm was back, a burst at the base of her neck that showered heat down her spine. "We don't know each other."

"I know how you taste." He nipped lightly at flesh. "And feel, and smell. I see your face in my mind whether I want to or not." He spun her around, and his eyes were dark and restless. "Why should you have a choice when I don't?"

His mouth crushed down on hers, a hot and dangerous thrill. With his hands gripped in her hair, he pressed his body to hers.

And this time she felt as much anger as passion in the embrace. Now, wrapped around the thrill, was a thin snake of fear. The combination was unbearably exciting.

"I'm not ready for this." She struggled back. "I'm not ready for this. Can you understand?"

"No." But he understood what he saw in her eyes. He'd frightened her, and he'd no right to do so. "But then again, I don't want to." So he backed away. "Your mother said I was a patient man. I can be, under some circumstances. I'll wait, because you'll come to me. There's something alive between us, so when you're ready, you'll come to me."

"There's a thin line between confidence and arrogance, Brian. Watch your step," she suggested as she started for the door.

"I missed you."

Her hand closed over the knob, but she couldn't turn it. "You know all the angles," she murmured.

"That may be true. But still I missed you. Thanks for the tea."

She sighed. "You're welcome," she said, and left him.

Chapter 5

Bad Betty had more than earned her name. She didn't just make trouble, she looked for it. Nothing seemed to please her more than nipping at grooms. Unless it was kicking exercise boys. She chased other yearlings when out in pasture, then reared and kicked and snorted bad-temperedly when it was time to be stabled for the night.

For all those reasons, and more, Brian adored her.

There was a communal sigh of relief in the shedrow when he opted to deal with her personally. She tested him, and though she rarely got by Brian's guard he had an impressive rainbow of bruises with her name on them.

There were mutters that she was a man-eater, but

Brian knew better. She was a rebel. And she was a winner. It was only a matter of teaching her how to start winning without damaging that wild spirit.

On the longe line he circled her into a walk while she pretended to ignore him. Still, when he spoke to her, her ears twitched, and now and then she sent him a sidelong glance. And days of hard work were rewarded when he lengthened the line and she broke into a canter.

"Ah, that's the way. What a beauty you are." He'd liked to have captured that moment—the gorgeous filly cantering gracefully in a circle, while green hills rolled up to a blue sky.

It would make a picture, and look to some like a frolic. But those who knew would see this moment— a racehorse learning to take commands from signals transmitted through her mouth—was another step toward the finish line.

He saw one more thing as he looked at her, as he studied lines and form and that unmistakable gleam in her eyes.

He saw his destiny.

"We'll go, you and I," he said quietly. "We were meant to go together. Rebels we are, or so people say who can't see where we're headed. We've races to win, don't we?"

He shortened the line, and she dropped into a trot. Shortened it still further and her gait changed to a walk. Sweat gleamed on her coat, trickled down his back. Summer wasn't just clinging to September. It was pummeling it.

They ignored the heat, and watched each other.

Again and again he used the line to signal her as she circled, and all the while he praised her.

Watching was irresistible. She had work to do, chores piled up. But if she couldn't take a few moments out on a brilliant September day to watch a little magic, what was the point?

She leaned on the paddock fence, enjoying the view as Brian put Betty through her paces. Her father had been right in hiring him, she thought. There was a connection between man and horse that was stronger, and even more tangible than the line between them. She could feel it. Amusement, affection, challenge.

This wasn't something that could be taught. It simply was.

She knew Brian took time for every weanling on the farm when he wasn't out of town at a race. That wasn't an easy task in an operation as large as Royal Meadows. But it was the kind of touch that made a difference. A smart and caring horseman knew that the more a horse was handled, touched, communicated with during its youth, the better it would respond to later training.

"Looks good, doesn't she?" Brian said as he let out the line for one last canter.

"Very. You've made considerable progress with her."

"We've made progress with each other, haven't we *a ghra*. She's ready to feel a rider on her."

Knowing Betty's reputation, Keeley tucked her tongue in her cheek. "And who are you bribing—or threatening—to get up on her?"

Gradually Brian shortened the line, and Betty moved into an even trot. "Want the job?"

"I have a job, thanks." But it was tempting.

Brian knew when a seed planted needed to be left alone to sprout. "Well, she'll have her first weight on her tomorrow morning." He shortened the line again, moving Betty toward him, and both of them toward Keeley.

He liked the look of her there against the fence, with her hair as glossy as the filly's coat, and her eyes as cautious. "This one won't be placid and eager to please. But she'll come round, won't you, *maverneen?*"

He stroked the filly's neck, and she sniffed at the pouch on his belt, then turned her head away.

"She wants to let me know she doesn't care that I've apples in here. No, doesn't matter a bit to her." He looped the line around the fence and took an apple and his knife from his pocket. Idly he cut it in half. "Maybe I'll just offer this token to this other pretty lady here."

He held out the apple to Keeley, and Betty gave him

a solid rap with her head that rammed him into the fence. "Now she wants my attention. Would you like some of this then?"

He shifted, held the apple out. Betty nipped it from his palm with dignified delicacy. "She loves me."

"She loves your apples," Keeley commented.

"Oh, it's not just that. See here." Before Keeley could evade—could think to—he cupped a hand at the back of her neck, pulled her close and rubbed his lips provocatively over hers.

Betty huffed out a breath and butted him.

"You see?" Brian let his teeth graze lightly before he released Keeley. "Jealous. She doesn't care to have me give my affection to another woman."

"Next time kiss her and save yourself a bruise."

"It was worth it. On both counts."

"Horses are more easily charmed than women, Donnelly." She plucked the apple out of his hand, bit in. "I just like your apples," she told him, and strolled away.

"That one's as contrary as you are." He nuzzled Betty's cheek as he watched Keeley walk to her stables. "What is it that makes me find contrary females so appealing?"

She hadn't meant to go down to the yearling stalls. Really. It was just that she was up early, her own morning chores were done. And she was curious. When she stepped inside the stables, out of the soft gray dawn, the first thing she heard was Brian's voice.

It made her smile. At least the exasperation in it made her smile.

"Come on now, Jim, you lost the draw. You can't be welshing on me."

"I'm not. I'm gearing up."

The young exercise boy was gritting his teeth and rolling his shoulders when Keeley stepped up to the box. "Good morning. I heard you drew the short straw, Jim."

"Yeah, just my luck." He shot a mournful look at Betty. "This one wants to eat me."

"Chew you up and spit you out more like," Brian said in disgust. "You're just giving her cause now by letting her know she intimidates you. You'll go down in history today—the first weight the next winner of the Triple Crown feels on her back."

As if reacting to the prediction, Betty snorted, tried to dance as Brian firmed his grip on the shortened reins. And Jim's eyes went big as moons in a pale face.

"I'll do it." Keeley wasn't sure if it was the challenge of it, or compassion for the terrified boy. "If it's an historic moment, it should be a Grant up on a Royal Meadows champion." She smiled at Jim as she said it. "Let me have the jacket and hat."

"You sure?" With more hope than shame, Jim looked from Keeley to Brian.

"She's the boss. In a manner of speaking," Brian told him. "Your loss here, Jim."

"I'll take the loss and save all my skin." A little too eagerly, he started out of the box. As if sensing her opening, Betty bunched, kicked out. Swearing, Brian shoved Jim aside with his shoulder and took the hoof in the ribs.

The air went blue, and every curse was in an undertone that only added impact. Without a second thought, Keeley moved into the box and laid her hand over his on the reins to help control the filly.

A thousand pounds of horse fought to plunge. Keeley felt the heat from her, and from Brian when their bodies bumped together. "How bad did she get you?"

"Not as bad as she'd like." But enough, he thought, to steal his breath and have the pain shooting up until he saw stars dancing.

He tossed the hair out of his eyes, blinked at the sweat stinging in them and muscled the filly down.

"Man, Bri, I'm sorry."

"You should have more sense than to turn your back on a skittish filly," Brian snapped out. "Next time I'll let her take a shot at your head. Go on out. She knows she's bested you. Stand back," he ordered Keeley in the same cold tone of command, then he jerked the reins just enough to bring Betty's head down.

"So this is how it's to be? You want all the temper

and none of the glory? Am I wasting my time with you? Maybe you don't want to run. We'll just wait until you come into season and bring a stallion in to mount you, and set you out to pasture to breed. Then you'll never know, will you, what it is to win."

Just outside the box, Keeley slipped on the padded jacket and hat. And waited. There was a line of damp down the back of his shirt, his hair was a wild tangle of brown and gold. Muscles rippled in his arms, and his boots were scarred and filthy.

He looked, she decided, exactly how a horseman should look. Powerful. Confident. And just arrogant enough to believe he could win over an animal more than five times his weight.

He kept talking, but he'd switched to Gaelic now. Slowly, the rhythm of the words smoothed out, and warmed. Almost like a song, they played in the air, rising, falling. Mesmerizing.

The filly stood quiet now, her dark brown eyes focused on Brian's green ones.

Seduced, Keeley thought. She was watching a kind of seduction. She'll do anything for him, Keeley realized. Who wouldn't if he touched you that way, looked at you that way, used his voice on you that way?

"Come in here," he told Keeley. "Let her get your scent. Touch her so she can feel you."

"I know how it's done," she murmured. Though she'd never seen it done quite like this.

She slipped into the stall, ran her hands gently over Betty's neck, her side. She felt the muscles quiver under her hand, but the filly looked at nothing and no one but Brian.

"I've seen countless people work in countless ways with countless horses." Keeley spoke quietly as she stroked Betty. But like the horse, her eyes were on Brian. "I've never seen anyone like you. You have a gift."

His eyes shifted, met hers, held for a moment. One timeless moment. "She has the gift. Talk to her."

"Betty. Not-so-bad Betty. You scared poor Jim, didn't you, but you don't scare me. I think you're beautiful." She saw the filly's ears lay back, felt the slight shift under her hands, but kept talking. "You want to race, don't you? Well, you can't do it alone. I'd tell you this isn't going to hurt, but you don't care about that anyway. It's all pride with you."

Once again she looked at Brian. "It's all pride," she repeated, understanding both horse and man. "But you can't have the pride of winning without this step."

When Brian tightened the saddle, everyone seemed to hold their breath. Then Keeley let hers out, and put her knee in Brian's hands for a leg up.

She bellied over the saddle, lay still as Betty shied. She knew just what could happen if the filly wasn't controlled. A wrong move on anyone's part and she could find herself under several hundred pounds of agitated horse.

But Brian's voice whispered, soft and dreamy, and the light began to go pale gold. Slowly Keeley eased herself up until she sat, her feet sliding into the stirrups.

The new sensation had Betty fighting to toss her head, dancing back and kicking out. Now Keeley leaned forward, stroking, and added her voice to Brian's.

"Get used to it," she ordered in a no-nonsense tone directly opposed to his crooning. "You were born for this."

"There now, *cushla.*" His lips twitched at the corners as he soothed Betty. "She's not so scary now, is she? She's hardly much of a thing at all up there on your big, beautiful back. She's only a princess, but you, you're a queen, aren't you?"

"So, I'm outranked?" Keeley wasn't sure if she was amused or insulted.

Gradually the restless movements stilled. Brian took a chunk of apple from his pocket, fed it to Betty with murmured praise and reassurance. "She's doing well."

"She'd like to bounce me off the ceiling."

"Oh aye, that she would, but she's not trying it at the moment. You're doing well, too." His gaze lifted until his eyes met Keeley's. "As natural at this as she is. Blue bloods, both of you."

"Are we making history, Brian?"

"Bet on it," he told her and kissed Betty just above the nose.

She gave him most of the morning. Dismounting, remounting, sitting quietly while he led them around the stall. Betty gave a couple of bucks, but everyone knew it was only for show.

"Will you try the walking ring with her?"

Keeley started to decline. She had work, and was already behind for the day. But the feel of the young, fresh horse under her was too much of a pleasure, too much of a challenge. She'd put in a few hours on paperwork that night.

"If you think she's ready."

"Oh, she's ready. It's the rest of us who have to catch up." He opened the box and led them out.

The walking ring was surrounded by a high wall, to give the student privacy and prevent distractions as she took her first steps under the control of a rider. As Brian led them toward it, several of the hands stopped work to watch. Money changed hands.

"Some of them bet we wouldn't manage her this morning," Brian said casually. "You just earned me fifty dollars."

"If I'd known there was a pool, I'd have bet myself."

He glanced up. "Which way?"

"I always bet to win."

He stopped inside the ring, handed Keeley the reins. "She's yours now."

Keeley angled her head. "In a manner of speaking," she said and nudged Betty into a walk.

They made a picture, Brian mused. A stunning one. The long-legged thoroughbred with her regal head and gleaming coat, and the delicate woman riding her.

If he'd ever wanted one horse for his own—and he didn't, hadn't—it would be this one.

If he'd ever wanted one woman for his own...

Well, that was the same. He'd never wanted the responsibilities that came from having. And neither of these could ever be his in any case. But he'd have something of each of them, and that was better all around.

For the horse, he'd have the knowledge that part of what he was went into the making of a champion. And the woman, before long he'd have the pleasure of knowing what it was to have her wrapped around him in the night. Maybe only once, but once would be enough.

Whatever the risks of that were, there was no stopping it. They came a bit closer to it every time they looked at each other. Today, he'd come to understand she knew it, too. Now it was only a matter of the time and place. And that would be up to her.

"They look good."

Brian didn't wince, but he wanted to. It was definitely inconvenient to have the father of the woman you were fantasizing about interrupt that particular image. Especially inconvenient when the man was also your employer.

"That they do. Betty needs a steady hand, and your daughter has one."

"Always has." Travis slapped a hand on Brian's shoulder and brought on instantaneous guilt. "I ran into Jim, who confessed all. You took a kick."

"It's nothing." He imagined his ribs would be sore for weeks.

"Have it looked at." The tone was casual, and carried command.

"I will shortly. Jim was spooked. I shouldn't have pushed him into it."

"He's young," Travis agreed. "But this is part of his job. At the moment, he feels bad enough that you could ask him to let Betty sit on him. I'd take advantage of it."

"And so I will. He's a good lad, Travis. Just a bit green yet. I'm thinking of taking him with me to the track more, letting him get some seasoning."

"That's a good idea. You have a number of them. Good ideas," Travis added.

"That's what you pay me for." Brian hesitated, then plunged. "Betty's not just your best shot at your Derby, she's the one who'll do it for you. And I'll wager my full year's contract pay she'll wear the Triple Crown."

"That's a leap, Brian."

"Not for her. I say she'll break records, smash them to bits. And when it comes time to breed her, it should be Zeus. I've done the charts," Brian continued. "I know you and Brendon manage the breeding end of the farm yourselves, but—"

"I'll look at your charts, Brian."

Brian nodded, shifted to watch Betty. "It's not the charts so much, though they'll bear me out. It's that I know her. Sometimes…" Despite himself, he found himself staring at Keeley. "You just recognize it all."

"I know it." Eyes narrowed in consideration, Travis scanned Betty's form. "Work out the race schedule you think will work for her—once she's ready. We'll talk about it."

Keeley walked Betty toward them, pulling her up with a tug of the reins and a quiet vocal command. "She's decided to tolerate me."

"What do you think?" Travis stroked the filly's neck, ignoring her first instinctive feint at nipping.

"She's not common," Keeley began, "though she has some behavioral problems that would make her so if they aren't corrected. She's smart. A fast learner. Which means you have to stay a step ahead of her. It's early days yet, of course, but I'd say this isn't a horse that's going to loaf. She'll work hard, and she'll race hard, under the right hand. If I were still competing, I'd want her."

"She's not meant for the show ring." Brian took out another chunk of apple. "She's for the oval."

Betty took the reward, then as if to show he was the only one of the three humans who mattered, bumped her head lightly against his shoulder.

"She still has to prove she can run in a crowd," Keeley pointed out. "You might want to put blinders on her."

"Not with this one, I'm thinking. The other horses won't be distractions to her. They'll be competitors."

"We'll see." Keeley dismounted, started to hand Brian the reins, but her father took them.

"I'll walk her back."

And that, Brian thought, absurdly bereft, was the difference between training and owning.

"No need to look so annoyed." Keeley cocked her head as Brian scowled after Betty. "She did very well. Better than I'd expected."

"Hmm? Oh, so she did, yes. I was thinking of something else."

"Ribs hurting?" When he only shrugged, she shook her head. "Let me take a look."

"She barely caught me."

"Oh, for heaven's sake." Impatient, Keeley did what she would have done with one of her brothers: She tugged Brian's T-shirt out of his jeans.

"Well, darling, if I'd known you were so anxious

to get me undressed, I'd have cooperated fully, and in private."

"Shut up. God, Brian, you said it was nothing."

"It's not much."

His definition of not much was a softball-size bruise over the ribs in a burst of ugly red and black. "Macho is tedious, so just shut up."

He started to grin, then yelped when she pressed her fingers to the bruise. "Hell, woman, if that's your idea of tender mercies, keep them."

"You could have a cracked rib. You need an X ray."

"I don't need a damned—ouch! Bollocks and bloody hell, stop poking." He tried to pull his shirt down, but she simply yanked it up again.

"Stand still, and don't be a baby."

"A minute ago it was don't be macho, now it's don't be a baby. What do you want?"

"For you to behave sensibly."

"It's difficult for a man to behave sensibly when a woman's taking his clothes off in broad daylight. If you're going to kiss it and make it better, I've several other bruises. I've a dandy one on my ass as it happens."

"I'm sure that's terribly amusing. One of the men can drive you to the emergency room."

"No one's driving me anywhere. I'd know if my ribs are cracked as I've had a few in my time. It's a bruise, and it's throbbing like a bitch now that you've been playing with it."

She spotted another, riding high on his hip, and gave that a poke. This time he groaned.

"Keeley, you're torturing me here."

"I'm just trying…" She trailed off as she lifted her head and saw his eyes. It wasn't pain or annoyance in them now. It was heat, and it was frustration. And it was surprisingly gratifying. "Really?"

It was wrong, and it was foolish, but a sip of power was a heady thing. She trailed her fingers along his hip, up his ribs and down again, and felt his muscles quiver. "Why don't you stop me?"

His throat hurt. "You make my head swim. And you know it."

"Maybe I do. Now. Maybe I like it." She'd never been deliberately provocative before. Had never wanted to be. And she'd never known the thrill of having a strong man turn to putty under her hands. "Maybe I've thought about you, Brian, the way you said I would."

"You pick a fine time to tell me when there's people everywhere, and your father one of them."

"Yeah, maybe that's true, too. I need that buffer, I guess."

"You're a killer, Keeley. You'd tease a man to death."

He didn't mean it as a compliment, but to her it was

a revelation. "I've never tried it before. No one's ever attracted me enough. You do, and I don't even know why."

When she dropped her hand, he took her wrist. It surprised him to feel the gallop of her pulse there, when her eyes, her voice had been so cool, so steady. "Then you're a quick learner."

"I'd like to think so. If I come to you, you'd be the first."

"The first what?" Temper wanted to stir, especially when she laughed. Then his mind cleared and the meaning flashed through like a thunderbolt. His hand tightened on her wrist, then dropped it as though she had turned to fire.

"That scared you enough to shut you up," she observed. "I'm surprised anything could render you speechless."

"I've..." But he couldn't think.

"No, don't fumble around for words. You'll spoil your image." She couldn't think just why his dazed expression struck her as so funny, or why the shock in his eyes was endearing somehow.

"We'll just say that, under these circumstances, we both have a lot to consider. And now, I'm way behind in my work, and have to get ready for my afternoon class."

She walked away, as easily, as casually, Brian thought numbly, as she might have if they'd just finished discussing the proper treatment for windgalls. She left him reeling.

He'd gone and fallen in love with the gentry, and the gentry was his boss's daughter. And his boss's daughter was innocent.

He'd have to be mad to lay a hand on her after this.

He began to wish Betty had just kicked him in the head and gotten it all over with.

Served her right, Keeley decided. Spend the morning indulging herself, spend half the night doing the books. And she hated doing the books.

Sighing, she tipped back in her chair and rubbed her eyes. In another year, maybe two, the school would generate enough income to justify hiring a bookkeeper. But for now, she just couldn't toss the money away for something she could do herself. Not when she could use it to subsidize another student, or buy one of them a pair of riding boots.

It was tempting, particularly at times like these, to dip into her own bank account. But it was a matter of pride to keep the school going on its own merit, as much as she possibly could.

Ledgers and forms and bills and accounts, she thought, were her responsibility. You didn't have to like your responsibilities, you just had to deal with them.

She had two full-tuition students on her waiting list.

One more, she calculated—two would be better—but one more and she could justify opening another class. Sunday afternoons.

That would give her eighteen full tuitions. Two years before, she'd had only three. It was working. And so, now, should she.

She swiveled back to the computer and focused on her spreadsheet program. Her eyes were starting to blur again when the door behind her opened.

She caught the scent of hot tea before she turned and saw her mother.

"Ma, what are you doing out here? It's midnight."

"Well, I was up, and I saw your light. I thought to myself, that girl needs some fuel if she's going to run half the night." Adelia set a thermos and a bag on the desk. "Tea and cookies."

"I love you."

"So you'd better. Darling, your eyes are half shut. Why don't you turn this off and come to bed?"

"I'm nearly done, but I can use the break—and the fuel." She ate a cookie before she poured the tea. "I'm only behind because I played this morning."

"From what your father tells me you weren't playing." Adelia took a chair, nudged it closer to the desk. "He's awfully pleased with how Brian's bringing Betty along. Well, he's pleased with Brian altogether, and so am I from what I've seen. But Betty's quite the challenge."

"Hmm." So was Brian, Keeley thought. "He has his own way of doing things, but it seems to work." Considering, she drummed her fingers on the desk. She'd always been able to discuss anything with her mother. Why should that change now?

"I'm attracted to him."

"I'd worry about you if you weren't. He's a fine-looking young man."

"Ma." Keeley laid a hand over her mother's. "I'm very attracted to him."

The amusement faded from Adelia's eyes. "Oh. Well."

"And he's very attracted to me."

"I see."

"I don't want to mention this to Dad. Men don't look at this sort of thing the way we do."

"Darling." At a loss, Adelia sighed out a breath. "Mothers aren't likely to look at this sort of thing the same way their daughters do. You're grown up, and you're a woman who answers to herself first. But you're still my little girl, aren't you?"

"I haven't been with a man before."

"I know it." Adelia's smile was soft, almost wistful. "Do you think I wouldn't know if that had changed for you? You think too much of yourself to give what you are to something unless it matters. No one's mattered before."

Here the ground was boggy, Keeley thought. "I

don't know if Brian matters in the way you mean. But I feel different with him. I want him. I haven't wanted anyone before. It's exciting, and a little scary."

Adelia rose, wandered around the little office looking at the ribbons, the medals. The steps and the stages. "We've talked about such matters before, you and I. About the meaning and the precautions, the responsibilities."

"I know about being responsible and sensible."

"Keeley, while it is true that all that is important, it doesn't tell you—it can't tell you—what it is to be with a man. There's such heat." She turned back. "There's such a force you make between you. It's not just an act, though I know it can be for some. But even then it's more than just that. I won't tell you that giving your innocence is a loss, for it shouldn't be, it doesn't need to be. For me it was an opening. Your father was my first," she murmured. "And my only."

"Mama." Moved, Keeley reached for her hands. Her mother's hands were so strong, she thought. Everything about her mother was strong. "That's so lovely."

"I only ask you to be sure, so that if you give yourself to him, you take away a memory that's warm and has heart, not just heat. Heat can chill after time passes."

"I am sure." Smiling now, Keeley brought her

mother's hand to her cheek. "But he's not. And, Ma, it's so odd, but the way he backed off when I told him he'd be the first is why I'm sure. You see, I matter to him, too."

Chapter 6

It was amazing, really, how two people could live and work in basically the same place, and one could completely avoid the other. It just took setting your mind to it.

Brian set his mind to it for several days. There was plenty of work to keep him occupied and more than enough reason for him to spend time away from the farm and on the tracks. But he found avoidance scraped his pride. It was too close a kin to cowardice.

Added to that, he'd told Keeley he wanted to help her at the school and had done nothing about it. He wasn't a man to break his word, no matter what it cost him. And, he reminded himself as he walked to Keeley's stables, he was also a man of some self-control. He had no intention of seducing or taking advantage of innocence.

He'd made up his mind on it.

Then he stepped into the stables and saw her. He wouldn't have said his mouth watered, but it was a very close thing.

She was wearing one of those fancy rigs again—jodhpurs the color of dark chocolate and a cream sort of blouse that looked somehow fluid. Her hair was down, all tumbled and wild as if she'd just pulled the pins from it. And indeed, as he watched she flipped it back and looped it through a wide elastic band.

He decided the best place in the universe for his hands to be were in his pockets.

"Lessons over?"

She glanced back, her hands still up in her hair. Ah, she thought. She'd wondered how long it would take him to wander her way again. "Why? Did you want one?"

He frowned, but caught himself before he shifted his feet. "I said I'd give you a hand over here."

"So you did. As it happens I could use one. You did say you could ride, didn't you?"

"I did, and I do."

"Good." Perfect. She gestured toward a big bay. "Mule really needs a workout. If you take him, I'll be able to give Sam some exercise, too. Neither of them has had enough the last couple of days. I'm sure I have tack that'll suit you." She opened a box door and led out the already saddled Sam. "We'll wait in the paddock."

As they clipped out, Brian eyed Mule, Mule eyed Brian. "She's a bossy one, isn't she now?" Then with a shrug, Brian headed to the tack room to find a saddle that suited him.

She was cantering around the paddock when he came out, her body so tuned to the horse they might have been one figure. With the slightest shift in rhythm and angle, she took her mount over three jumps. Cantering still, she started the next circle, then spotted Brian. She slowed, stopped.

"Ready?"

For an answer, he swung into the saddle. "Why are you all done up today?"

"It was picture day. We take photographs of the classes. The kids and the parents like it. Mule's up for a good run, if you are."

"Then let's have at it." With a tap of his heels he sent the horse out of the open gate at an easy trot.

"How are the ribs?" she asked as she came up beside him.

"They're all right." They were driving him mad, because every time he felt a twinge he remembered her hands on him.

"I'm told the yearling training's coming along well, and Betty's one of the star pupils—as predicted."

"She has the thirst. All the training in the world can't give a horse the thirst to race. We'll be giving her a taste of the starting gate shortly, see how she does with it."

Keeley headed up a gentle slope where trees were still lush and green despite the encroaching fall. "I'd use Foxfire with her," she said casually. "He's a sturdy one, with lots of experience. He loves to charge out of the gate. She sees him do it a couple of times, she won't want to be left behind."

He'd already decided on Foxfire as Betty's gate tutor, but shrugged. "I'm thinking about it. So... have I passed the audition here, Miss Grant?"

Keeley lifted a brow, and a smile ghosted around her mouth as she looked Brian over. She'd been checking his form, naturally. "Well, you're competent enough at a trot." With a light tap, she sent Sam into a canter. The minute Brian matched her pace, she headed into a gallop.

Oh, she missed this. Every day she couldn't fly out across the fields, over the hills, was a sacrifice. There was nothing to match it—the thrill of speed, the power soaring under her, through her, the thunder of hooves and the whip of wind.

She laughed as Brian edged by her. She'd seen the quick grin of challenge, and answered it by letting Sam have his head.

It was like watching magic take wing, Brian thought.

The muscular black horse soared over the ground with the woman on his back. They streaked over another rise, moving west, into the dying sun. The sky was a riot of color, a painting slashed with reds and golds. It seemed to him she would ride straight into it, through it.

And he'd have no choice but to follow her.

When she pulled up, turned to wait for him, her face flushed with pleasure, her eyes gleaming with it, he knew he'd never seen the like.

And wanting her was apt to kill him.

"I should've given you a handicap," she called out. "Mule runs like a demon, but he's no match for this one." She leaned over the saddle to pat Sam's neck. She straightened, shook her hair back. "Gorgeous out, isn't it?"

"Hot as blazes," Brian corrected. "How long does summer last around here?"

"As long as it likes. Mornings are getting chilly, though, and once the sun dips down behind the hills, it'll cool off quickly enough. I like the heat. Your Irish blood's not used to it yet."

She turned Sam so she could look down at Royal Meadows. "It's beautiful from up here, isn't it?"

The buildings spread out, neat, elegant, with the white fences of the paddocks, the brown oval, the horses being led to the stable. A trio of weanlings, all legs and energy, raced in the near pasture.

"From down there, too. It's the best I've ever seen."

That made her smile. "Wait till you see it in winter, with snow on the hills and the sky thick and gray with more—or so blue it hurts your eyes to look at it. And the foalings start and there are babies trying out their legs. When I was little, I couldn't wait to run down and see them in the morning."

They began to walk again, companionably now, as the light edged toward dusk. She hadn't expected to be so comfortable with him. Aware, yes, she always seemed aware of him now. But this simple connection, a quiet evening ride, was a pleasure.

"Did you have horses when you were a boy?"

"No, we never owned them. But it wasn't so far to the track, and my father's a wagering man."

"And are you?"

He tilted his face toward her. "I like playing the odds, and fortunately, have a better feel for them than my father. He loved the look of them, and the rush of a race, but never did he gain any understanding of horses."

"You didn't gain any, either," Keeley said and had him frowning at her. "What you've got you were born with. Just like them," she added, gesturing toward the weanlings.

"I think that's a compliment."

"I don't mind giving them when they're fact."

"Well, fact or fiction, horses have been the biggest

part of my life. I remember going along with my da and seeing the horses. When he could manage it, he liked to go early, check out the field, talk with the clockers and the grooms, get himself a feel for things—or so he said. He lost his money more often as not. It was the process that appealed to him."

That, and the flask in his pocket, Brian thought, but with tolerance. His father had loved the horses and the whiskey. And his mother had understood neither.

"One of the first times I went along, I saw an exercise boy, very young lad, ponying a sorrel around the track. And I thought, there, that's it. That's what I want to do, for there can't be anything better than doing that for your life and your living. And while I was still young enough, and small enough, I slid out of going to school as often as it could be managed and hitched rides to the track to hustle myself. Walk hots, muck stalls, whatever."

"It's romantic."

He caught himself. He hadn't meant to ramble on that way, but the ride, the evening, the whole of it made him sentimental. When he started to laugh at her statement, she shook her head.

"No, it is. People who aren't a part of the world of it don't understand, really. The hard work, the disappointments, the sweat and blood. Freezing predawn workouts, bruises and pulled muscles."

"And that's romantic."

"You know it is."

This time he did laugh, because she'd pegged him. "As a boy, when I hung around the shedrow, I'd see the horses come back through the mist of morning, steam rising off their backs, the sound of them growing louder, coming at you before ever you could see them. They'd slip out of the fog like something out of a dream. Then, I thought it the most romantic thing in the world."

"And now?"

"Now, I know it is."

He broke into a canter, riding with her until the lights of Royal Meadows began to flicker on and glow. He hadn't expected to spend a comfortable, contented hour in her company, and found it odd that underlying all the rest that buzzed between them they'd seemed to have formed a kind of friendship.

He'd been friends with women before, and was well on the way to being convinced he'd do just fine keeping it all on a friendly level with Keeley. He was the one who'd initiated the sexual charge, so it seemed reasonable and right that he be the one to dampen it again.

The logic of it, and the ride, relaxed him. By the time they reached the stables to cool down the horses, he was in an easy mood and thinking about his supper.

Since she was interested, he told her of the yearling training, the progress, the five-year-old mare with colic, and the weanling with ringbone.

Together they watered the horses, and while Brian took the saddles and bridles to the tack room, Keeley set up the small hay nets and set out the grooming kits.

They worked across from each other, in opposite boxes.

"I heard you and Brendon are heading off to Saratoga next week," she commented.

"Zeus is running. And I think Red Duke is a contender, and your brother agrees. Though I've only seen that track on paper and in pictures. We're off to Louisville as well. I want to be well familiar with that course before the first Saturday in May."

"You want Betty to run the Derby."

"She will run it. And win it." He picked up the curry comb to scrape out the body brush. "We've conversed about it."

"You've talked to Brendon about the Derby?"

"No, Betty. And your father as well. I expect Brendon and I will talk it through while we're away."

"What does Betty have to say?"

"Let's get on with it." He glanced over, saw she was running her fingers over Sam's coat, checking for lumps or irregularities. "Why aren't you still competing? With that one under you you'd need a vault for all your medals."

"I'm not interested in medals."

"Why not? Don't you like to win?"

"I love to win." She leaned gently against Sam, lifted his leg and sent Brian a long look that had his stomach jittering before she gave her attention to picking out the hoof. "But I've done it, enjoyed it, finished with it. Competing can take over your life. I wanted the Olympics, and I got it."

She shifted to clean out the next hoof. "Once I had, I realized that so much of what I was, what I felt and thought had been focused on that single goal. And then it was over. So I wanted to see what else there was out there, and what else I had in me. I like to compete, but I found out it doesn't always have to be done, and won, in the show ring."

"With the kind of school you've got going here, you should have someone working with you."

She shrugged and began to rub in hoof oil. "Up until now I'd been able to draft Sarah or Patrick into giving me a hand. Ma helps out when she can, and so does Dad. Brendon and Uncle Paddy put in hours with each one of my horses as I got them. And the cousins—Burke and Erin's kids from Three Aces—they're always willing to pitch in if I need extra hands."

"I haven't seen anyone working here but you."

"Well, that's very simple. Patrick and Sarah are off to college—and Brady, who's another I can browbeat into shoveling boxes when he's here. Brendon's doing a lot more traveling now than he used to. Uncle

Paddy's in Ireland, and the cousins are just back from a holiday and in school. Either my mother or father, sometimes both, show up here at dawn half the time. Whether I ask them or not."

She got to her feet. "And now that I've got you interested, I've come up with a part-time groom/exercise boy/stablehand. That's a pretty good deal for a small riding academy."

She strolled out to start the evening feeding.

"You could get an eager young boy or girl to come in before and after school—pay them in lessons."

"Before school, eager young boys and girls should be eating breakfast, and after they should be playing with friends and doing homework."

"That's very strict."

She chuckled and mixed some sliced carrots into the feed as an extra treat. "That's what all my students say. I want them well-rounded. My family saw to it that I had interests and friendships outside the stable, that I got an education, that I saw something of the world besides the track and the barn. It matters."

They divvied up the horses, and the stables filled with the sounds of whickers and whinnies as the meal was served.

"If you don't mind my saying so, you don't seem to be getting out and about much now."

"I'm compulsive. Goal oriented. I see what I want

and well, it's like putting on blinders and heading down the backstretch. All I see is the finish line."

She leaned in to rub a gelding's neck as if he were a pet dog. "Which is why my parents wouldn't let me spend my entire childhood around or on a horse. I took piano lessons, and as soon as I started I was determined to be the best student at the recital. If it was my job to clean the kitchen after dinner, then that damn kitchen was going to sparkle so bright you'd need sunglasses for your midnight snack."

"That's frightening."

Responding to the humor in his eyes, she nodded. "It can be. Focusing on the school means, even though it's still a single goal, that my compulsion to succeed is spread out to encompass so many elements—the kids, the horses as well as the academy itself. Once it's firmly established, I can delegate a bit more, but I need to learn from the ground up. I don't like to make mistakes. Which is why I haven't been with a man before now."

He was thrown off balance so quickly and completely, he could hear his own brain stumble. "Well, that's…that's wise."

He took one definite step back, like a chessman going from square to square.

"It's interesting that makes you nervous," she said, countering his move.

"I'm not nervous, I'm...finished up here, it seems." He tried another tactic, stepped to the side.

"Interesting," she continued, mirroring his move, "that it would make you nervous, or uneasy if you prefer, when you've been...I think it's safe to use the term 'hitting on me' since we met."

"I don't think that's the proper term at all." Since he seemed to be boxed into a corner, he decided he was really only standing his ground. "I acted in a natural way regarding a physical attraction. But—"

"And now that I've reacted in a natural way, you've felt the reins slip out of your hands and you're panicked."

"I'm certainly not panicked." He ignored the terror gripping claws into his belly and concentrated on annoyance. "Back off, Keeley."

"No." With her eyes locked on his, she stepped in. Checkmate.

His back was hard up against a stall door and he'd been maneuvered there by a woman half his weight. It was mortifying. "This isn't doing either of us any credit." It took a lot of effort when the blood was rapidly draining out of his head, but he made his voice cool and firm. "The fact is I've rethought the matter."

"Have you?"

"I have, yes, and—stop it," he ordered when she ran the palms of her hands up over his chest.

"Your heart's pounding," she murmured. "So's

mine. Should I tell you what goes on inside my head, inside my body when you kiss me?"

"No." He barely managed a croak this time. "And it's not going to happen again."

"Bet?" She laughed, rising up just enough to nip his chin. How could she have known how much *fun* it was to twist a man into aroused knots? "Why don't you tell me about this rethinking?"

"I'm not going to take advantage of your—of the situation."

That, she thought, was wonderfully sweet. "At the moment, I seem to have the advantage. This time you're trembling, Brian."

The hell he was. How could he be trembling when he couldn't feel his own legs? "I won't be responsible. I won't use your inexperience. I *won't* do this." The last was said on a note of desperation and he pushed her aside.

"I'm responsible for myself. And I think I've just proven to both of us, that if and when I decide you'll be the one, you won't have a prayer." She drew a deep, satisfied breath. "Knowing that's incredibly flattering."

"Arousing a man doesn't take much skill, Keeley. We're cooperative creatures in that area."

If he'd expected that to scratch at her pride and cut into her power, he was mistaken. She only smiled, and the smile was full of secret female knowledge. "If that was true between us, if that were all that's between us, we'd be naked on the tack room floor right now."

She saw the change in his eyes and laughed delightedly. "Already thought of that one, have you? We'll just hold that thought for another time."

He swore, raked his hands through his hair and tried to pinpoint the moment she'd so neatly turned the tables on him, when the pursued had become the pursuer. "I don't like forward women."

The sound she made was something between a snort and a giggle, and was girlish and full of fun. It made him want to grin. "Now that's a lie, and you don't do it well. I've noticed you're an honest sort of man, Brian. When you don't want to speak your mind, you say nothing—and that's not often. I like that about you, even if it did irritate me initially. I even like your slightly overwide streak of confidence. I admire your patience and dedication to the horses, your understanding and affection for them. I've never been involved with a man who's shared that interest with me."

"You've never been involved with a man at all."

"Exactly. That's just one reason why. And to continue, I appreciate the kindness you showed my mother when she was sad, and I appreciate the part of you that's struggling to back away right now instead of taking what I've never offered anyone before."

She laid a hand on his arm as he stared at her with baffled frustration. "If I didn't have that respect and that liking for you, Brian, we wouldn't be having this conversation no matter how attracted I might be to you."

"Sex complicates things, Keeley."

"I know."

"How would you know? You've never had any."

She gave his arm a quick squeeze. "Good point. So, you want to try the tack room?" When his mouth fell open, she laughed and threw her arms around him for a noisy kiss on his cheek. "Just kidding. Let's go up to the main house and have some dinner instead."

"I've work yet."

She drew back. She couldn't read his eyes now. "Brian, neither of us have eaten. We can have a simple meal in the kitchen—and if you're worried, we won't be alone in the house so I'll have to keep my hands off you. Temporarily."

"There's that." He couldn't stand it. How could he be expected to? She'd thrown her arms around him with such easy affection. And his heart was balanced on a very thin wire. Trying to keep the movement casual, he set her aside. "Well, I could eat."

"Good."

She would have taken his hand, but his were already in his pockets. It amused and touched her how restrained he was determined to be. And if it made her naturally competitive spirit kick in, well, she couldn't help it, now could she?

"I'm hoping to get down to Charles Town and watch some of the workouts once you take Betty and some of the other yearlings to the track."

"She'll be ready for it soon enough." Relief was like a cool wave through his blood. Talking of horses would make it all easier. "I'd say she'll surprise you, but you've been up on her. You know what she's made of."

"Yeah, good stock, good breeding, a hard head and a hunger to win." She flashed him a smile as they approached the kitchen door. "I've been told that describes me. I'm half Irish, Brian, I was born stubborn."

"No arguing with that. A person might make the world a calmer place for others by being passive, but you don't get very far in it yourself, do you?"

"Look at that. We have a foundation of agreement. Now tell me you like spaghetti and meatballs."

"It happens to be a favorite of mine."

"That's handy. Mine, too. And I heard a rumor that's what's for dinner." She reached for the doorknob, then caught him off guard by brushing a light kiss over his lips. "And since we'll be joining my parents, it would probably be best if you didn't imagine me naked for the next couple of hours."

She sailed in ahead of him, leaving Brian helplessly and utterly aroused.

There was nothing like an extra helping of guilt to cool a man's blood. And it was guilt as much as the

hot food and the glass of good wine that got Brian
through the evening in the Grant kitchen. The size of
it left little room for lust, considering.

There was Adelia Grant giving him a warm greeting as if he was welcome to swing in for dinner anytime he had the whim, and Travis getting out an extra
plate himself—as if he waited on employees five days
a week—and saying that there was plenty to go around
as Brendon had other plans for dinner.

Before he knew it, he was sitting down, having food
heaped in front of him and being asked how his day
had been. And not in a way that expected a report.

He didn't know what to do about it. He liked these
people, genuinely liked them. And there he was lusting after their daughter. An alley mutt after a registered purebred.

And the hell of it was, he liked her as well. It had
been so simple at first, when there'd been only heat.
Or he'd been able to tell himself that's all there was.
For a time it had been possible to tolerate being in love
with her—or at least talking himself out of believing
it. But *caring* for her made it all a study in frustration.

He could certainly convince himself that he was in
love with the *idea* of her rather than the woman. The
physical beauty, the class, the sheer inaccessibility of
her. That was all a kind of challenge, a risk he enjoyed
taking. But she'd gone and opened herself up to him,

so every time he was around her, she showed him more of herself.

The kindness, the humor, the strength of purpose and sense of self he admired.

And now this teasing, this sexual flirt in an innocent's body was driving him mad. And God help him, he liked it.

"Have some more, Brian."

"I'll be sorry if I do." But he took the big bowl Adelia offered him. "Sorrier if I don't. You're a rare cook, Mrs. Grant."

"Dee, I told you. And rare was just what I was for a number of years. Before Hannah retired—that was our housekeeper. She was with Travis longer than I've been with him. When she retired a few years back I just didn't want another woman, a stranger, you know, in the house day and night and so on. I figured I'd better learn to cook something more than fish and chips or we'd all starve to death."

"Nearly did the first six months," Travis commented and earned a narrow-eyed stare from his wife.

"Well, sure and the experience made you get a handle on that fancy grill outside, didn't it? The man was spoiled rotten. I wager you could even put a meal together for yourself, Brian."

Idly he rubbed Sheamus—who was snoring under the table—with the side of his boot. "If I've no choice in the matter."

Brian caught the lazy look Keeley sent him as she sipped her wine. Heat balled in his belly. In defense he turned to Travis. "I'm told you enjoy a hand or two of poker from time to time."

"I've been known to."

"The lads're talking about a game tomorrow night."

"I might come down—I've heard you're a hard man to beat."

"If you're going to play cards, you should ask Burke to join you," Adelia put in. "Then maybe Keeley, Erin and I can find something equally foolish to do with our evening."

"Good idea. More wine, Brian?" Keeley lifted the bottle, cocked a brow. The purr in her voice was subtle, but he heard it. And suffered.

"No, thanks. I've work yet."

"I'll walk down with you when you're ready," Travis told him. "I'd like a look at that colicky mare."

"The two of you go ahead. We'll see to the dishes."

Travis grinned like a boy. "No KP?"

"There's not that much to be done, and you can make up for it tomorrow." She got up to clear, and kissed his temple. "Go on, I know you've been worrying about her."

"Thank you for the fine meal, Dee," Brian added when she angled her head.

"And you're very welcome."

"Good night, Keeley."

"Good night, Brian. Thanks for the ride."

Adelia waited until the men were out, then turned to her daughter. "Keeley, I never would've thought it of you. You're tormenting the poor man."

"There's nothing poor about that man." Delighted with herself, Keeley broke off a piece of bread and crunched down on it. "And tormenting him is so rewarding."

"Well, there's not a woman with blood in her could argue with that. Mind you don't hurt him, darling."

"Hurt him?" Seriously shocked, Keeley rose to help with the dishes. "Of course I won't. I couldn't."

"You never know what you will or you can do." Adelia patted her daughter's cheek. "You've a lot to learn yet. And however much you learn you'll never really understand everything that goes on inside a man."

"I've good a pretty good idea about this one."

Adelia opened her mouth, then shut it again. Some things, she knew, couldn't be explained. They had to be lived.

Chapter 7

Brian came to know the roads leading from Maryland into West Virginia as well as he knew those in the county of Kerry. The highways where cars flashed by like little rockets, and the curving back roads where everything meandered were all part of his life now, and what some people would say led to a feeling of home.

There were times the green of the hills, the rise of them, reminded him of Ireland. The pang he felt at those moments surprised him as he didn't consider himself a sentimental man. At others, he'd drive along a winding road that followed a winding creek and the land was all so very different with its thick woods and walls of rock. Almost exotic. Then he'd feel a sense of contentment that surprised him nearly as much.

He didn't mind contentment. It just wasn't what he was looking for.

He liked to move. To travel from place to place. It was all to the good that his position at Royal Meadows gave him that opportunity. He figured in a couple of years, he'd have seen a great deal of America—even if the oval was in the foreground of each view.

He told himself he didn't think of Ireland as home— or Maryland as home, either. Home was the shedrow, wherever it might be.

Still, he felt a sense of welcome and ease when he drove between the stone pillars at Royal Meadows. And he felt pleasure when he saw Keeley in her paddock with one of her classes. He stopped to watch as she took her group from trot to canter.

It was a pretty sight, not despite the clumsiness and caution of some of the children, but because of it. This was no slick and choreographed competition but the first steps of a new adventure. Fun, she'd said, he remembered. They would learn, take responsibility, but she didn't forget they were children.

And some of them had been hurt.

Seeing her with them, looking at what she'd built herself when she could have spent her days exactly as he'd once imagined she did, brought him more than respect for what she was. It brought admiration that was a little too bright for comfort.

He could hear the squeals, and Keeley's calm, firm

voice—a pretty sight and a pretty sound. He climbed out of the truck and walked over for a closer view.

There were grins miles wide, and eyes big as platters. There were giggles and there were gasps. As far as Brian could see, the mood ran from screaming nerves to wild delight. Through it all, Keeley gave orders, instruction, encouragement, and used each child's name.

Her long fire-fall of hair was roped back again. Her jeans were faded to a soft blue-gray like the many-pocketed vest she topped over it. Under that she wore a slim sweater the color of spring daffodils. She liked her bright tones, Keeley did, Brian mused. And her glitters as well, he mused as the light caught the dangle of little stones at her ears.

She'd be wearing perfume. She always had some cagey female scent about her. Sometimes just a drift that you had to get right up beside her to catch. And other times it was a siren call that beckoned you from a distance.

Never knowing which it would be was enough to drive a man mad.

He should stay away from her, Brian told himself. God knew he should stay away from her. And he figured he had as much chance of doing so as one of her riding hacks had of winning the Breeder's Cup.

She knew he was there. The ripple of heat over her skin told her so. She couldn't afford to be distracted with six children depending on her full attention. But oh, the awareness of him, of herself and that quick trip of the pulse, was a glorious sensation.

She began to understand why women so often made fools of themselves for men.

When she ordered the class to switch back to a trot, there were a few groans of disappointment. She had them change directions, then took them through all their paces, and back down to walk. Brian waited until she instructed them to stop, then applauded.

"Nicely done," he said. "Anyone here looking for a job, you just come see me."

"We have an audience today. This is Mr. Donnelly. He's head trainer at Royal Meadows. He's in charge of the racehorses."

"Indeed I am, and I've always got my eyes open for a new jockey."

"He talks pretty," one of the girls whispered, but Brian's ears were keen. He shot her a grin and had her blushing like a rosebud.

"Do you think so?"

"Mr. Donnelly's from Ireland," Keeley explained. Amazing, she thought, he even makes ten-year-old girls moon.

"Miss Keeley's mother's from Ireland. She talks pretty, too."

Brian glanced up and saw the boy he remembered as Willy studying him. "No one talks prettier than those from Ireland, lad. It's because we've all been kissed by the fairies."

"You're supposed to get money from the Tooth Fairy when you lose a tooth, but I never did."

"That's just your mother." The girl behind Willy rolled her eyes. "There aren't real fairies."

"Maybe they don't live here in America, but we've plenty where I come from. I'll put a word in for you, Willy, next time you lose a tooth."

His eyes rounded. "How did you know my name?"

"A fairy must've told me."

Keeley struggled to compose her features as Willy goggled. "Class. Dismount. Cool and water your mounts."

There was a great deal of chatter and movement now. Though Willy dismounted, he stood, holding the reins and studying Brian. Too cautious a look for one so young, Brian thought. And it tugged at his heart.

Willy took a breath, seemed to hold it. "I have one that's loose. A tooth."

"Do you?" Unable to resist, Brian climbed over the fence, hunched down. "Let's have a look."

Willy obliged by baring his teeth and poking his tongue against a wobbly incisor. "That's a good one. You'll be able to spit through where that was in a day or two."

"You're not supposed to spit." Willy slanted a look up at Brian as he began to walk.

"Who says?"

"Ladies." Bobby added a shrug. "They don't like you to burp, either."

"Ladies can be fussy about certain things. It's best to spit and burp among the men, I suppose."

"You're not supposed to run like a wild animal, either." Peeking around to make certain Keeley wasn't frowning in his direction, Willy shoved up the sleeve of his shirt. "This is from running like a wild animal on the playground at school. I skidded for*ever* and scraped lots of skin right off so it got really bloody."

Understanding his role, Brian pursed his lips, nodded. "That's very impressive, that is."

"I've got an even better one on my knee. Have you got any?"

"I've got a pretty good bruise." To play the game properly, Brian glanced around first, then tugged his shirt up to display the yellowing bruise on his ribs.

"Wow! That musta really hurt. Did you cry?"

"I couldn't. Miss Keeley was watching. Here she comes," he added in a conspirator's whisper and pulled his shirt down, whistled idly.

"Willy, you need to water Teddy."

"Yes, ma'am. I had a dream about Teddy last night."

"You tell me about it when we're grooming him, okay?"

"Okay. Bye, mister."

"Now that's a taking little creature," Brian murmured as Willy led his horse out to the water trough.

"Yes, he is. What were you talking about?"

"Man business." Brian hooked his thumbs in his pockets. "I've got to get down to the shedrow or I'd help you with the grooming. I could send you up a hand if you like."

"Thanks, but it's not necessary."

"Just ring down if you change your mind." He needed to go, let them both get on with work. But it was so nice to stand here and smell her. Today, the scent was subtle, just a hint of heat. "They looked good at the canter."

"They'll look better in a few weeks." It was time to get the horses inside, start the grooming session. But... What would another minute hurt? "I heard you took a few pots in the poker game last night."

"I came away about fifty ahead. Your cousin Burke's a slick one. I'd say he whistled home with double that."

"And my father?"

Brian's grin flashed. "I like thinking that's where I got the fifty. I told him he's better off sticking with the horses."

Keeley's brow rose. "And his response to that?"

"Isn't something I can repeat in polite company."

She laughed. "That's what I thought. I've got to get the horses inside. Parents will be trickling along soon."

"Don't they ever come to watch?"

"Sometimes. Actually I've asked them to give us a few weeks so the kids aren't distracted or tempted to show off. You were a good test audience."

"Keeley." He touched her arm as she turned away. "The little boy. Willy. He's got a tooth he'll be losing in a couple of days. It'd be nice if someone remembered to put a coin under his pillow."

Her heart, which had leaped at his touch, quieted. Melted. "He's with a very good foster family right now. Very nice and caring people. They won't forget."

"All right then."

"Brian." This time it was her hand on his arm. Despite the curious eyes of her students, she rose to her toes to brush her lips over his cheek. "I have a soft spot for a man who believes in fairies," she murmured, then walked away to gather her students.

A very soft spot, she thought, for a man with a cocky grin and a kind heart. She opened the terrace doors of her room, stepped out into the night. There was a chill in the air, and a sky so clear the stars flamed like torches. She could smell the flowers, the spice of the first mums, the poignancy of the last of the roses.

A breeze had the leaves whispering.

The three-quarter moon was pale gold, shedding light that gilded the gardens and shimmered over the fields. It seemed she could cup her hands, let that light pour into them and drink it like wine.

How could anyone sleep on so perfect a night?

Slowly she shifted and looked toward Brian's quarters. Light gleamed in his windows. And her pulse fluttered in her throat.

She told herself if his lights were off, she would close the doors again and try to sleep. But there they were, bright against dark, beckoning.

She closed her eyes on a shiver of anticipation and nerves. She'd prepared herself for this step, this change in her life, in her body. It wasn't an impulse, it wasn't reckless. But she felt impulsive. She felt reckless.

She was a grown woman, and the decision was hers.

Quietly she stepped back and closed the doors.

Brian closed the condition book, pressed his fingers to his tired eyes. Like Paddy, he wasn't quite sure he trusted the computer, but he was willing to fiddle with it a bit. Three times a week he spent an hour trying to figure the damn thing out with the notion that eventually he could use it to generate his charts.

Graphics, they called it, he thought, shifting to give the machine a suspicious glare. Timesaving and efficient, if you believed all the hype. Well, tonight he was too damn tired to spend an hour trying to be timesaving and efficient.

He hadn't had a decent night's sleep in a week.

Which had nothing to do with his job, he admitted. And everything to do with his boss's daughter.

It was a good thing he had that trip to Saratoga coming up, he decided as he pushed away from his desk and rose. A little distance was just what was needed. He didn't care for this unsteady sensation or this worrying ache around the heart.

He wasn't the type to fret over a woman, he thought. He enjoyed them, and was happy for them to enjoy him, then each moved on without regrets.

Moving on was always the end plan.

New York, he remembered, was a fair distance away. It should be far enough. As for tonight, he was going to have a shot of whiskey in his tea to help smooth out the edges. Then by God, he was going to sleep if he had to bash himself over the head to accomplish it.

And he wasn't going to give Keeley another thought.

The knock on the door had him cursing under his breath. Though she'd been doing well, his first worry was that the mare with bronchitis had taken a bad turn. He was already reaching for the boots he'd shed when he called out.

"Come in, it's open. Is it Lucy then?"

"No, it's Keeley." One brow lifted, she stood framed in the door. "But if you're expecting Lucy, I can go."

The boots dangled from his fingertips, and those fingertips had gone numb. "Lucy's a horse," he managed to say. "She doesn't often come knocking on my door."

"Ah, the bronchitis. I thought she was better."

"She is. Considerably." She'd gone and let her hair loose, he thought. Why did she have to do that? It made his hands hurt, actually hurt with wanting to slide into it.

"That's good." She stepped in, shut the door. And because it seemed too perfect not to, audibly flipped the lock. Seeing a muscle twitch in his jaw was incredibly satisfying.

He was a drowning man, and had just gone under the first time. "Keeley, I've had a long day here. I was just about to—"

"Have a nightcap," she finished. She'd spotted the teapot and the bottle of whiskey on the kitchen counter. "I wouldn't mind one myself." She breezed past him to flip off the burner under the now sputtering kettle.

She'd put on different perfume, he thought viciously. Put it on fresh, too, just to torment him. He was damn sure of it. It snagged his libido like a fishhook.

"I'm not really fixed for company just now."

"I don't think I qualify as company." Competently she warmed the pot, measured out the tea and poured the boiling water in. "I certainly won't be after we're lovers."

He went under the second time without even the chance to gulp in air. "We're not lovers."

"That's about to change." She set the lid on the pot, turned. "How long do you like it to steep?"

"I like it strong, so it'll take some time. You should go on home now."

"I like it strong, too." Amazing, she thought, she didn't feel nervous at all. "And if it's going to take some time, we can have it afterward."

"This isn't the way for this." He said it more to himself than her. "This is backward, or twisted. I can't get my mind around it. No, just stay back over there and let me think a minute."

But she was already moving toward him, a siren's smile on her lips. "If you'd rather seduce me, go ahead."

"That's exactly what I'm not going to do." Though the night was cool and his windows were open to it, he felt sweat slither down his back. "If I'd known the way things were, I'd never have started this."

That mouth of his, she thought. She really had to have that mouth. "Now we both know the way things are, and I intend to finish it. It's my choice."

His blood was already swimming. Hot and fast. "You don't know anything, which is the whole flaming problem."

"Are you afraid of innocence?"

"Damn right."

"It doesn't stop you from wanting me. Put your hands on me, Brian." She took his wrist, pressed his hand to her breast. "I want your hands on me."

The boots clattered to the floor as he went under for the third time. "It's a mistake."

"I don't think so. Touch me."

His hand closed over her. She was small, delicate, and through some momentary miracle, his. "Doesn't matter if it's a mistake," he said, giving up entirely.

"We won't let it be one." Her head fell back as his hands began to move.

"Doesn't matter. But I'll be careful with you."

Her eyes were blue and brilliant as she lifted her arms, slid her hands into his wildly waving hair. "Not too careful, I hope."

When he swept her up in his arms she let out a shuddering sigh. "Oh, I was hoping you'd do that." Thrilled, she pressed her lips to the side of his neck. "I was really hoping you'd do that."

He turned his face into her hair, drew in the scent, held it inside him. "You've only to tell me what you like."

She tipped her head back to look at him as he carried her into the bedroom. "Show me what I like."

With moonlight and cool breezes shimmering through the open windows, he laid her on the bed. There had been moonlight the first time he'd kissed her, soft fingers of it then, as there were now. He'd never forget the look of it, or of her.

There had been few gifts in his life that had mattered, that had stayed in him, in his heart and memory. She would, he knew. She was a gift he would cherish.

"This," he murmured, nibbling at her lips till they parted for him.

She opened, willing, wanting to be touched and tasted and taken. Even as he sensed her eagerness he led her slowly, patiently, thoroughly through the layers of sensations.

He caressed, his fingertips, palms, light as the air, then lingering at some secret place that had her breath catching on little jolts of pleasure. His mouth cruised lazily over her skin, sliding her into warmth, then it would come back to hers again, with a hungry bite that shot her into the heat.

Instinctively, avidly, she arched against him.

He was murmuring to her, lovely, stirring words in the old tongue, each like a tender kiss on the soul. Her heart fluttered, wings spreading wide for flight.

There were no nerves, no doubts as she raised herself to him, wrapped herself around him. When he slipped off her shirt, the breeze and his fingertips whispered over her. She felt beautiful.

Her skin was white silk, her hair rich flame. Every tremble was a gift, every sigh a treasure. In his life he'd never held anything as lovely as Keeley discovering herself.

She never shied when he undressed her, but embraced each new moment, welcomed each fresh sensation. Her curious hands moved over him, undressing him in turn. He'd never known how arousing it could be to be someone's first.

Her heart hammered under his mouth, and the scent she'd dabbed on that fragile flesh swirled into his senses until they were as clouded as hers. He took more, just a little more, and she began to move under him in mindless invitation.

So much. There was so much, was all she could think. Her body was flooded with sensations, her flesh quivering from them. She could hear her own moans, her own ragged breaths but could do nothing to control them. The very loss of control was thrilling.

Everything inside her was tangled and straining. And desperate. Her nails bit into his back, her teeth found his shoulder. Then his hand closed over her.

She cried out from the shock of it, all that pulsing, pumping pleasure, the sheer heat of it that washed in one huge wave that crashed over her, inside her, and left her shuddering. She reared up, eyes blind, her fingers diving into his hair.

Then his mouth was on hers again, hotter now, hungrier, giving her no chance to catch her breath or her sanity.

"Give yourself to me," he whispered, the blood pounding in his head as her eyes, heavy, stunned, looked into his. "Take me in."

With her eyes on his, she opened and arched, and gave.

It was like rising into the air, each stroke another beat of wings. Pleasure climbed higher and higher still, lifting through her body, sweeping through her mind. All she could see were his eyes, dark and green and focused on her, even as his body was focused on hers. Mated and matched and moving with her.

Staggered by the beauty of it, she lifted a hand to his cheek, murmured his name.

And he was lost. Love and passion, dreams and desire stabbed through his heart. Helpless, he buried his face in her hair and let himself go.

With her eyes closed she absorbed the delights of being a well-loved woman. Her body felt gloriously heavy, her mind wonderfully muffled. There was no need to wonder or worry if she had given Brian the same pleasure. She had seen it in his face, and felt it as he lay over her with his heart still thundering.

There was a change inside her, she thought. Awareness, understanding. And a soaring kind of triumph.

Smiling to herself, she traced a finger down his back. "How are the ribs?"

"What?"

And didn't it feel grand to hear that sleepy slur in his voice? "Your ribs. That's still a nasty bruise you have there."

"I can't feel anything." His head was still spinning. "What's this scent you've put on? It's devious."

"Just one of my many secrets."

He lifted his head, started to grin at her, then it swamped him again. The look of her, the love of her. Lowering his head he brought his lips to hers in a long, dreamy kiss that came out of his soul and stirred hers.

Her hand slid limply to the mattress. "Brian."

"I'm crushing you." He said it briskly. He'd terrified himself.

He shifted away and shattered the moment. "There's not really very much of you." Suddenly aware that the breeze fluttering in the windows he left open was cold, he tugged at the bedspread until he could wrap it around her. "Are you all right then?"

"I'm fabulous, thank you." Laughing, she sat up, without a shrug for modesty as the spread slid to her waist. She caught his face in her hands and gave him a quick, affectionate kiss. "Are you all right then?" she said, mimicking his brogue.

"That I am, but I've had a bit of practice."

"I'll bet. But let's not bring up all your conquests just now. I'd hate to be obliged to punch you when I'm feeling so friendly."

"I wouldn't say they were conquests precisely. But we'll let that be."

"Wise choice."

"Let me close the windows. You're cold."

She angled her head as he rose. "There's nurturing in that bruised body of yours, Donnelly."

"I beg your pardon?"

"I'd say it comes from the horses." She pursed her lips, considered while he *thunked* a window down and scowled. "You look after them, worry about them, make plans for them, see to their needs and their comfort—oh and their training, of course. Then if you don't watch yourself you start to do it with people, too."

"I don't nurture people." He found the idea mildly insulting. "People can look after themselves. I don't even like people very much." He stalked over and shut the other window. "Present company excepted, as you're sitting naked in my bed and it would be rude to say otherwise."

"You didn't phrase that quite right. You don't like very many people. Do you have a robe?"

"No." He wasn't sure if it was the truth in what she said, or her understanding of him that irked him.

"Figures." She spied one of his work shirts tossed over a chair, and though it smelled of horses, slipped it on. "I'd say that tea's probably strong enough to hammer nails by now. Do you still want it?"

She looked…interesting in his shirt. Interesting enough that his blood began to churn again. "What are my options?"

"On my schedule, we have a cup of tea, a little conversation, then you get to seduce me back into bed and make love to me again before I go home."

"That's not bad, but I think it bears improving."

"Oh, and how's that?"

"We cut out the tea and conversation."

She ran her tongue over her top lip—his taste was still there—as he walked toward her. "That would take us straight to you seducing me? Correct?"

"That's my plan."

"I can be flexible."

His grin flashed. "I'd like to test that out."

They never got around to the tea.

And when she'd left him, he stood at the door and watched her run along the path. Love-struck idiot, he told himself. You can't keep her. You've never kept anything in your life that you couldn't fit in the bag you toss over your shoulder.

It was a bad turn of luck, that was all, that he would slip up and fall in love. It was bound to hurt like blazes before it was done. He'd get over it, of course. Over her and over this slippery feeling inside his heart. He wasn't so far gone as to believe this sort of madness lasted.

So best to enjoy it, he decided, and turned away when Keeley disappeared in the dark.

When he climbed into bed, her scent was on his pillow. For the first time in a week he slept deep and slept well.

Chapter 8

She missed him. It was the oddest thing to find herself thinking about Brian off and on during the day, and thinking of a dozen things she wanted to tell him, or show him when he got back from Saratoga.

She wasn't the only one.

During his next lesson Willy asked if Mr. Donnelly was coming so he could show off the fresh gap in his teeth. The man, Keeley mused, made an impression and made it fast.

It wasn't as if she didn't have enough to occupy her mind or her time. She'd found enough tuition students to add another class and was even now snaking her way through the maze of bureaucracy to arrange for three additional subsidized students.

She'd had meetings with the psychologist, the social worker, the parents and the children. The paperwork alone was enough to, well, choke a horse, she admitted. But it would be worth it in the end.

With some amusement, she flipped through the article in *Washingtonian Magazine*. She knew the exposure was responsible for netting her the new full tuition students. The photographs were gorgeous and the text made full use of her background, her Olympic medal and her social standing.

No problem there, she decided, particularly since the academy was mentioned several times.

She glanced at the phone with a little sigh as it rang. It hadn't stopped since the article had been published. The time was coming, Keeley thought, when she was going to have to break down and hire an assistant.

But for now, the school was all hers.

"Good morning, Royal Meadows Riding Academy." Her coolly professional tone warmed when she heard her cousin Maureen's voice.

Fifteen minutes later, she was hanging up and shaking her head. It appeared she was going to dinner and the races that evening. She'd said no—at least Keeley was fairly certain she'd said no five or six times. But nobody held out against Mo for long. She just rolled over you.

Keeley eyed the piles of paperwork on her desk, huffed out a breath when the phone rang again. Just do the first thing, she reminded herself, then do the second, and keep going until it was done.

She'd done the first, the second and the third, when her father came in.

He stopped in the doorway, held up a hand. "Wait, don't tell me. I know you. The face is very familiar." He narrowed his eyes as she rolled hers. "I'm sure I've seen you before, somewhere. Tibet? Mazetlan? At the dinner table a year or two ago."

"It hasn't been more than a week." She reached up as he bent to kiss her. "But I've missed you, too. I've been swamped here."

"So I've heard." He flipped open the magazine to her article. "Pretty girl. I bet her parents are proud of her."

"I hope so." When the phone rang, she muffled a shriek, waved her hands. "Let the machine get it. It's been ringing off the hook since Sunday. Half the parents who call in to inquire about lessons haven't even asked their kids if they want to ride."

She scooted her chair to the little fridge and took out two bottles of soda. "So thanks."

"For?" Travis prompted as he took the soft drink.

"For always asking."

"Then you're welcome. I hear I'm escorting two lovely women to dinner tonight."

"Mo caught you?"

He chuckled before he tipped back the bottle to

drink. "'We haven't had an inter-family gathering in weeks'," he mimicked, "'Don't you love me anymore?'"

"She always pushes the right button." Keeley studied the toe of her oldest boots. "So...have you heard from Brendon?"

"Late yesterday. They should be home tonight."

"That's good." You'd think the man could have called her once, she thought, scowling at her boots. Sent a telegram, a damn smoke signal.

"I imagine Brian's anxious to get back."

Her head jerked up. "Really?"

"Betty's making progress—as are several of the other yearlings. She's doing particularly well on the practice oval. She's ready for Brian to take her over full-time."

"I caught one of her morning workouts. She looks strong."

"We breed true at Royal Meadows." There was something wistful in his tone that had Keeley lifting her brows.

"What's the matter?"

"Nothing." Travis shrugged it off and rose. "Getting old."

"Don't be ridiculous."

"Yesterday you were riding on my shoulders," he murmured. "The house was full of noise. Clomping up and down the steps, doors slamming. Scattered toys. I don't know how many times I stepped on one of those damned little cars of Brady's."

Turning back, he ran a hand over her hair. "I miss that. I miss all of you."

"Daddy." In one fluid movement she rose and slid her arms around him.

"It's the way it's supposed to work. Three of you off at college, Brendon moving around to get a handle on the business of things. It's what he wants. And you, building your own. But...I miss the crowd of you."

"I promise to slam the door the very first chance I get."

"That might help."

"Sentimental softie. I love that about you."

"Lucky for me." He gave her a quick, hard squeeze, then glanced over as the phone rang again. "Actually I didn't stop in for sentiment, but to give you some business advice." He drew her back. "You need help around here."

"I'm thinking about it. Really," she added when he angled his head. "As soon as I straighten things out I'll look into it."

"I seem to recall you saying the same thing six months ago."

"It just hasn't been the right time. I've got it all under control." Even as she said it, the phone rang again.

"Keeley, getting help doesn't mean you won't be in charge, doesn't mean it won't be your school."

"I know, but...it won't be the same."

"I'm here to tell you nothing stays the same. The farm's more than it was when it passed to me, and less than it will be when it passes to you and your brothers and sisters. But I've put my mark on it. Nothing can change that."

"I guess I just don't want it to get away from me."

"You've already proven you can do it."

"You're right. Of course, you're right. But it isn't easy to find the right person. It would have to be someone good with kids and horses, and who'd be able to pitch in with the administrating to some extent and wouldn't quibble about shoveling manure. Plus I'd have to be able to depend on them, and get along with them. And they'd have to be diplomatic with parents, which is often the trickiest part."

Travis picked up his soft drink again. "I might be able to point you in the right direction there."

"Oh? Listen, Dad, I appreciate it, but you know, a friend of a friend or the son or daughter of an acquaintance. That kind of thing gets very sticky if it doesn't work out."

"Actually, I was thinking of someone a little closer to home. Your mother."

"Ma?" With a half laugh Keeley sat again. "Ma doesn't want this headache, even if she had time for it."

"Shows what you know." Smug now, he drank. "Just mention it to her, casually. I won't say a word about it."

By the time the day's lesson was over, and the last horse groomed and fed, Keeley dragged herself into the house. She wanted nothing more than a long bath and a quiet night. And if she ducked the evening plans, her cousin Mo would dog her like a hound. Better to face an evening out than weeks of nagging.

She moved through the kitchen, into the hall. Her father was right, she realized. How would any of them get used to the quiet? No one was shouting down the stairs or rushing in the door or playing music so loud it vibrated the eardrums.

She paused at the top of the steps, looking right. There was the room Brady and Patrick shared. She still remembered that during one spat Brady had run a line of black tape from the ceiling, down the wall, across the floor, and up again, cutting the room in half.

One had been marked Brady's Territory. The other he'd dubbed No Man's Land.

And how many times had she heard Brendon pound a fist on the wall between his room and theirs ordering them to keep it down before he came in and knocked their heads together?

When she passed Sarah's room, she saw her mother sitting on the bed, stroking a red sweater.

"Ma?"

"Oh." Adelia looked up. Her eyes were damp, but she shook her head and smiled. "You startled me. It's so bloody quiet in this house."

Keeley stepped in. The room had bright blue walls. The curtains and spread picked up that bold hue and matched it with an equally vivid green in wide stripes. It should have been horrible, Keeley mused, as she often did. But it worked.

And it was completely Sarah.

"Do you and Dad share the same brain?" Keeping her voice light, Keeley sat on the bed. "He was feeling sad this morning over the same thing."

"I suppose after all these years together, you pick up the same vibrations or whatever. And Sarah called just a bit ago. She's desperately in need for this particular red sweater, which she can't think how she forgot to take with her. She sounds so happy and busy and grown up."

"They'll all be home next month for Thanksgiving, then again for Christmas."

"I know. Still, if I could think of a way to get away with it, I'd deliver this sweater myself instead of shipping it. Lord, look at the time. I've got to get myself cleaned up and changed for dinner. And so do you."

"Yeah." Keeley pursed her lips in thought while her mother smoothed the sweater one more time and rose. "I'm running behind today," she began. "I seem to be running behind a lot lately."

"That's what happens to successful people."

"I suppose so. And adding on this class is going to crowd my time and energy even more."

"You know I'll give you a hand when you need it, and so will your father." Adelia walked out of the room and into her own to lay Sarah's sweater aside.

"Yes, I appreciate that. I guess I'm going to have to seriously consider something more formal and permanent, though. I really hate to. I mean, taking on an outsider, it's difficult for me. But…"

Keeley let the word hang, surprised when her mother—who usually had something to say—remained silent.

"I don't suppose you'd be interested in working part-time at the school?"

Adelia turned her head, met Keeley's eyes in the mirror over the bureau. "Are you offering me a job?"

"It sounds awfully strange when you put it that way, but yes. But don't do it because you feel obliged. Only if you think you'd have the time or the inclination."

Adelia spun around, her face brilliant. "What the devil's taken you so long? I'll start tomorrow."

"Really? You really want to?"

"I've been *dying* to. Oh, it's taken every bit of my willpower not to come down there every day until you just got so used to me being around you didn't realize I *was* working there. This is exciting!" She rushed over to give Keeley a hug. "I can't wait to tell your father."

Keeping her arms tight around her daughter, Adelia did a quick dance. "I'm a groom again."

"If I'd known you were available, Dee, and looking for work, I'd've hired you." Burke Logan, settled back in his chair and winked at his wife's cousin.

"We like to keep the best on at Royal Meadows." Adelia twinkled at him across the table in the track's dining room. He was as handsome and as dangerous to look at as he'd been nearly twenty years before when she'd first met him.

"Oh, I don't know." Burke trailed a hand over his wife's shoulder. "We have the best bookkeeper around at Three Aces."

"In that case, I want a raise." Erin picked up her wine and sent Burke a challenging look. "A big one. Trevor?" Her voice was smooth, shimmering with Ireland as she addressed her son. "Do you have in mind to eat that pork chop or just use it for decoration?"

"I'm reading the *Racing Form*, Ma."

"His father's son," Erin muttered and snagged the paper from him. "Eat your dinner."

He heaved a sigh as only a twelve-year-old boy could. "I think Topeka in the third, with Lonesome in the fifth and Hennessy in the sixth for the trifecta. Dad says Topeka's generous and a cinch tip."

At his wife's long stare, Burke cleared his throat.

"Stuff that pork chop in your mouth, Trev. Where's Jena?"

"She's fussing with her hair," Mo announced, and snatched a French fry from Travis's plate. "As usual," she added with the worldly air only an older sister could achieve, "the minute she turned fourteen she decided her hair was the bane of her existence. Huh. Like having long, thick, straight-as-a-pin black hair is a problem. This—" she tugged on one of the hundreds of wild red curls that spiraled around her face "—is a problem. If you're going to worry about something as stupid as hair, which I don't. Anyway, you guys have to come over and see this weanling I have my eye on. He's going to be amazing. And if Dad lets me train him…"

She trailed off, slanting a look at her father across the table.

"You'll be in college this time next year," Burke reminded her.

"Not if I can help it," Mo said under her breath.

Recognizing the mutinous look, Erin changed the subject. "Keeley, Burke tells me your new trainer is a natural with the horses, with Travis and with cards as well."

"And I hear he's gorgeous, too," Mo added.

"Where'd you hear that?" Keeley demanded before she could bite her tongue in two.

"Oh, word gets around in our snug little world," Mo

said grandly. "And Shelley Mason—one of your kids? Her sister Lorna's in my World History class, a *huge* bore by the way. The class, that is, not Lorna, who's only a small bore. Anyway, she picked Shelley up last week from your place and got a load of the Irish hunk, so I heard all about it. Which is why I'm planning on coming over as soon as I can and getting a load of him myself."

"Trevor, give your sister your pork chop so she can stuff it in her mouth."

"Dad." Giggling, Mo snatched another fry. "I'm just going to look. So, Keeley, is he gorgeous? I respect your opinion more than Lorna Mason's."

"He's too old for you," Keeley said, a bit more sharply than she intended and had Mo rolling her eyes.

"Jeez. I don't want to marry him and have his children."

Travis's laugh prevented Keeley from snapping back with something foolish. "Good thing. Now that I've found someone who comes close to replacing Paddy, I don't intend to lose him to Three Aces."

"Okay." Mo licked salt from her fingertip. "I'll just ogle him."

Annoyed, and feeling ridiculous at the reaction, Keeley pushed back her chair. "I think I'll go down and take a look at the field, and check on Lonesome. He's always a little sulky before a race."

"Cool." Mo sprang up. "I'll go down with you."

Mo rushed out of the dining room, heading out past the betting windows at a fast clip, so that Keeley was forced to step lively to keep pace. "It's going to be so much fun for you, having your mom work at the school. There's nothing like a family operation, you know. Which is all I want. I mean, come on, I don't have to go to college to be a trainer. If I already know what I want to do, and I'm learning how to do it every day right at home, what's college going to do for me?"

"Expand your brain?" Keeley suggested.

Ignoring that, Mo hurried outside where the air had turned crisp. "I know horses, Keeley. You understand what it's like. It's instinct and experience and it's *doing*." She gestured widely. "Well, I've got time to nag my parents into submission."

"No one does it better."

With a laugh, Mo hooked her arm through her cousin's. "I'm so glad to see you. The summer just winged by, you know, with all of us so busy with stuff."

"I know."

They made the turn for the shedrow and the world was suddenly horses.

Some were being prepped for the next race. In the boxes, grooms wrapped long, thin legs that would carry those huge bodies in a blur of speed and power. Trainers with keen eyes and gentle hands moved among the horses to pamper a skittish ride or rev up another.

The hot walkers cooled down horses who'd already run. Legs were examined, iced down. Through the sharp air came the hoofbeats that signaled another field was coming back from the race. Steam rose off the horses' backs, turning into a fine and magical mist.

"Of all the shedrows in all the world." Brendon came out of the stables, grinning.

"You're back."

"Just." He strolled over to rub a hand over Mo's hair. "I talked to Ma a couple of hours ago from the road and she said you were all coming here tonight. So we swung by on the way home."

"We?"

"Yeah, Bri's taking a look at Lonesome, giving him a pep talk. Moodiest damn horse. Figured we might as well catch the race, then I can hook a ride back with you guys and Brian can trailer Zeus back home."

"Sounds like a plan." It pleased her to hear the calm of her own voice while her heart was galloping. "Actually I came down to take a look at Lonesome myself."

"He's all yours—and Bri's. Hey, I've got time to get some dinner. See you up there."

"Now you can introduce me to the hunk." Mo fell into step beside Keeley.

"I will if you can behave like you have a brain as well as glands."

"It has nothing to do with glands, I'm just curious.

Don't worry, I'm taking a page out of your book there when it comes to men."

Keeley stopped at the door to the stables. "Excuse me?"

"You know, guys are fine to look at, or to hang around with occasionally. But there are lots more important things. I'm not going to get involved with one until I'm thirty, soonest."

Keeley wasn't certain whether to be amused or appalled. Then she heard Brian's voice, the lilt of it. And she forgot everything else.

He was in the box with Lonesome, a temperamental roan gelding. The horse moped, as was his habit before a race.

"They ask too much of you, there's no doubt about it," Brian was saying as he checked the wrappings on Lonesome's legs. "It's a terrible cross you have to bear, and you show great courage and fortitude day after day. Perhaps if you win this one I can put a word in for you. You know, extra carrots and that sort of thing, a bit of molasses in the evening. A bigger brass plaque for your box at home."

"That's bribery," Keeley murmured.

Brian turned, his eyes going warm. "That's bargaining," he corrected. "But if I can interest you in a bribe," he began and opened the box door intending to snatch Keeley inside for a much anticipated welcome back kiss.

He nearly stepped over Mo. "Sorry. Didn't see you there."

"I'm short. That's my cross to bear. I'm Mo Logan." She stuck out a friendly hand. "Keeley's cousin from Three Aces."

"Pleased to meet you. You've a horse running tonight, Ms. Logan?"

"Mo. Hennessy. Sixth race. My money says he'll win laughing."

"I'll keep that in mind if I get up to the betting window."

"I want to take a look at Hennessy before his race. Come up to the dining room if you have time, Brian, for food or a drink. The family's all there."

"Thank you for that. Pretty thing," Brian murmured when Mo dashed off.

"She wanted to take a look at you, too. She heard you were a hunk."

"Is that so?" Amused, Brian shifted. "Did you tell her that?"

"I certainly did not. I have more respect for you than to speak of you in such a sexist way."

"Respect's a good thing." He yanked her into the box, crushing his mouth to hers before she could laugh. "But I'm banking on passion just at the moment. Have you passion for me, Keeley?" he murmured against her mouth.

"Apparently." Her ears were ringing. "Oh, Brian, I

want—" She strained against him until they bumped into the horse. "You. Now. Somewhere. Can't we...it's been days."

"Four." He wanted to tear off the long slim dress she wore and mount her like a stallion, all blinding heat and primitive need.

He'd thought, convinced himself, that he'd be sensible about her, kept his wants and wishes under control. And all it had taken was seeing her. Just seeing her. It was exactly as it had been that first time he'd laid his eyes on her. A lightning strike in heart and blood.

"Keeley." He ran kisses over her face, buried his in her hair, then started all over again. "I've such a need for you. It's like burning from the inside out. Come with me, out to the lorry."

"Yes." At that moment, she'd have gone anywhere. It seemed he would swallow her whole. "Hurry. Let's hurry."

She took his hand, fumbled with the door herself. Breathless, she would have stumbled if he hadn't caught her. "Teach me to wear heels in the damn stable," she muttered. "My legs are shaking."

With a nervous laugh she turned back to him. Her legs stopped trembling. At least she couldn't feel them. All she could feel now was the unsteady skipping of her heart.

He was staring at her, his eyes intense. When she'd

turned his hands had reached up to frame her face. "You're so beautiful."

She'd never believed words like that mattered. They were so easily, and so often carelessly, said. But they didn't seem easy from him. And there was nothing careless about the tone of his voice. Before she could speak, before she could think of what could be said, there was a shout and the sound of running feet.

"Keeley, hurry, come with me." Oblivious to the intimacy of the scene she'd burst in on, Mo grabbed her hand. "I need back up. The bastard."

"What? What's happened?"

"If he thinks he's going to get away with it, he's got another think coming." Dragging Keeley, Mo barreled through the stables, turned and charged toward a stall.

Keeley could already hear the voices raised in argument. She saw the man first. She recognized him. Peter Tarmack with his oiled hair and cheap pinkie ring made a habit of picking up horses in claiming races, then running them into the ground.

The jockey was a familiar face as well. He was past his prime and, like Tarmack, was known to enjoy a few too many nips from the bottle at the track. Still, he picked up rides now and again when a regular jockey was sick or injured.

"I tell you, Tarmack, I won't ride him. And you won't get anyone else to. He's not fit to run."

"Don't you tell me what's fit. You'll get up and you'll ride, and you'll damn well place. You've been paid."

"Not to ride a sick and injured horse. You'll get your money back."

"What you haven't already put in a bottle."

Because Mo was quivering and had sucked in a breath to speak, Keeley squeezed her hand hard enough to grind bone. "Is there a problem, Larry?"

"Miss Keeley." The jockey yanked off his cap and turned his wrinkled, flustered face to hers. "I'm trying to tell Mr. Tarmack here that his horse isn't fit to race tonight. He's not fit."

"It's not your place to tell me anything. And I don't need one of the almighty Grant's damn whelps interfering in my business."

Before Keeley could respond, Brian had moved in. She blinked and he had hauled Tarmack up to his toes. "That's no way to be speaking to a lady." His voice was quiet, the eye of a storm. And the storm, with all its vengeance, was in his eyes. "You'll want to apologize for that, while you still have teeth to help you form the words."

"Brian, I can handle this."

"You'll handle what you like." He kept his eyes on Tarmack's now bulging ones. "But he'll by God apologize with his very next breath."

"I beg your pardon." Tarmack choked it out, wheezed

in air as Brian relaxed his grip a little. "I'm simply trying to deal with a washed-up jockey—and one I've paid in advance."

"You'll get your money back," the jockey replied, then turned to Keeley. "Miss Keeley, I'm not getting up on this ride. He's half lame from a knee spavin, and anybody with eyes can see he's hidebound. He ain't fit to race."

"Excuse me." Her voice viciously cold, she pushed past Tarmack and moved into the box to examine the horse for herself. Within moments, her hands were shaking with rage.

"Mr. Tarmack, if you try to put a jockey on this horse, I'll have you up on charges. In fact, I'm damn well having you up on charges regardless. This gelding's sick, injured and neglected."

"Don't hang that on me. I've only had him a couple weeks."

"And in a couple weeks you haven't noticed his condition? You've been working him despite it?"

"Now you look." He started to take a step forward and found himself looking eye to eye with Brian again. "Listen," he said, his tone shifting to a whine. "Maybe you can be sentimental when you've got money. Me, I make my living moving horses. They don't run, I go in the red."

"How much?" Keeley laid a hand on the gelding's

cheek. In her heart, he was already hers. "How much did he cost you?"

"Ah…ten grand."

Brian merely shoved a finger into Tarmack's breastbone. "Pull the other one. It has bells on it."

Tarmack shifted his shoulders. "Maybe it was five thousand. I'd have to check my books."

"You'll have a check for five thousand tomorrow. I'm taking the horse tonight. Brian, would you take a look at him, please?"

"Wait just a minute."

This time it was Keeley who turned and she who shoved Tarmack aside. "Be smart. Take the money. Because whether you do or don't I'm taking this horse with me."

"The knee needs treatment," Brian said after a quick look. It burned his blood to see how the injury had been neglected. "We can deal with that. From the look of him, I'd say he has a good case of bots. He needs tending."

"He'll get tending."

Keeley merely glanced over her shoulder at Tarmack. "You can go." Her voice held the regal ring of dismissal—princess to peasant. "Someone will deliver the check to you in the morning."

The tone burned in Tarmack's gut. She wouldn't be so hoity-toity without her damn bodyguard, he thought. He'd have taught her a little respect if the Irish bastard hadn't been around.

He bunched a fist impotently in his pocket and tried to save face. "I'm not just letting you take the horse and leave me with nothing but your say-so. I don't give a damn who you are."

Brian straightened again, blood in his eye, but Keeley merely held up a hand. "Mo, would you please take Mr. Tarmack to the dining room. If you'd ask my father to write him a check for the five thousand, and I'll straighten it out later."

"Happy to." She grabbed Keeley by the shoulders, kissed her. "I knew you'd do it." Then with a sniff she turned away. "Come with me, Tarmack. You'll get your money."

"I'm sorry, Miss Keeley." Larry ran his cap through his hands. "I didn't know how bad it was till I saw the ride here. I couldn't get up on him seeing how he was."

"You did the right thing. Don't worry."

"He did pay me ahead, like he said."

She nodded, stepped out of the box again, gesturing to him. "How much do you have left?"

"'Bout twenty."

"Come and see me tomorrow. We'll take care of it."

"'Preciate it, Miss Keeley. That horse there, he ain't worth no five, you know."

She studied the gelding. His color was muddy, his face too square for elegance and made homelier still by an off-center blaze of dirty white. And his eyes were unbearably sad.

"Sure he is, Larry. He's worth it to me."

Chapter 9

"You don't have to help with this."

Brian said nothing, simply continued to clip the gelding's legs. Bots were a common enough problem, especially with horses at grass. But this one had been sadly neglected. He had no doubt the eggs the botfly had laid on the gelding's legs had been transferred to the stomach.

"Brian, really." Keeley continued to mix the blister for the knee spavin. "You've had a really long day. I can handle this."

"Sure you can. You can handle this, morons like Tarmack, washed-up jockeys and everything else that comes along before breakfast. Nobody's saying different."

Since the statement wasn't delivered in what could be mistaken for a complimentary tone, Keeley turned to frown at him. "What's wrong with you?"

"There's not a bloody thing wrong with me. But you could use some work. Do you have to do everything yourself, every flaming step and stage of it? Can't you just take help when help's offered and shut the hell up?"

She did shut the hell up, for ten shocked seconds. "I simply assumed that you'd be tired after your trip."

"I'll let you know when I'm tired."

"The gelding here doesn't seem to be the only one with something nasty in his system."

"Well, it's you in my system, princess, and it feels a bit nasty at the moment."

Hurt came first, a quick short-armed jab. Pride sprang in to defend. "I'll be happy to purge you, just like I'll purge this horse tomorrow."

"If I thought it would work," he muttered, "I'd purge myself. You'll want to wait until at least midday," Brian told her. "You can't be sure the last time he was fed."

"I know how to treat stomach-bots, thank you." Gently she began to apply the blister to the injured knee.

"Here, you'll get that all over your clothes."

Keeley jerked away bad-temperedly when Brian reached for the pot of blister. "They're my clothes."

"So you should have more respect for them. You've no business treating a horse in clothes like that. Silk dresses for God's sake."

"I've got a closetful. We princesses tend to."

"Nevertheless." He curled his fingers around the lip of the pot, and under the sick gelding they began a vicious little tug-of-war. He would have laughed, was on the point of it, when he looked at her face and saw that her eyes were wet.

He let go of the pot so abruptly, Keeley fell back on her butt. "What are you doing?" he demanded.

"I'm applying a non-irritating blister to a knee spavin. Now go away and let me get on with it."

"There's no reason to start that up. None at all." Panic jingled straight to his head, nearly made him dizzy. "This is no place for crying."

"I'm upset. It's my stable. I can cry when and where I choose."

"All right, all right, all right." Desperately he dug into his pocket for a bandanna. "Here, just blow your nose or something."

"Just go to hell or something." Rather grandly, she turned her shoulder on him and continued to apply the blister.

"Keeley, I'm sorry." He wasn't sure for exactly what, but that wasn't here nor there. "Dry your eyes now, *a grha,* and we'll make this lad comfortable for the night."

"Don't take that placating tone with me. I'm not a child or a sick horse."

Brian dragged his hands through his hair, gave it one good yank. "Which tone would you prefer?"

"An honest one." Satisfied the blister was properly applied, she rose. "But I'm afraid the derisive one you've used since we got here fits that category. In your opinion, I'm spoiled, stubborn and too proud to accept help."

Though the tears appeared to have passed, he thought it wise to be cautious. "That's pretty close to the truth," he agreed, getting to his feet. "But it's an interesting mixture, and I've grown fond of it."

"I'm not spoiled."

Brian raised his eyebrows, cocked his head. "Perhaps the word means something different to you Yanks. Seems to me it's not everyone who could casually ask their father to write a check for five thousand dollars for a sick horse."

"I'll pay him back in the morning."

"I've no doubt of it."

Baffled now, she threw up her hands. "Should I have just left him there, walked away so that idiot Tarmack could find a jockey who would go up on him?"

"No, you did exactly right. But the fact's the same that you could toss around that kind of money without blinking an eye."

Brian walked to the gelding's head to examine his

eyes and teeth. It grated on him. He wished it didn't, as it said little for him that her easy dismissal of money scored his pride.

But it had, at that heated moment at the track, slammed the distance between them right in his face.

"You're a generous woman, Keeley."

"But I can afford to be," she finished.

"True enough." He ran his hands down the horse's neck, soothing. "But that doesn't take away from the fact that you are." Slowly he continued to work his way over the horse. "You'll have to forgive me—Irish of my class are generally a bit resentful of the gentry. It's in the blood."

"The class system's in your head, Brian."

That, he thought, wasn't even worth commenting on. What was, was. His fingers found a small knot. "He's a bit of an abscess here. We'll want to bring this to a head."

They'd bring something else to a head, she decided and moved in so they faced each other over the gelding's back. "So tell me, how do men of your class deal with taking women of mine to bed?"

His eyes flashed to hers, held. "I'd keep my hands off you if I could."

"Is that supposed to flatter me?"

"No. It just is, and doesn't flatter either of us." He moved out of the box to get flannel to heat for a hot fermentation.

No, she thought. She'd be damned if she'd leave it at that. "Is that all there is to it, Brian?" she demanded as she followed him out. "Just sex?"

He ran water, hot as his hand could bear, and soaked a large section of flannel in it. "No." He spoke without turning around. "I care about you. That just makes it more difficult."

"It should make it easier."

"It doesn't."

"I don't understand you. Would you be happier if we just jumped each other, without any connection, any understanding or feelings?"

He hauled up the bucket. "Infinitely. But it's too late for that, isn't it?"

Baffled, she walked back into the box behind him. "You're angry with me because you care about me. This water's too hot," she said when she tested it.

"No, it isn't. And I'm not angry with you at t'all." Murmuring to the gelding, he lay the heated flannel over the abscess. "A bit with myself, maybe, but it's more satisfying to take it out on you."

"That, at least, I can understand. Brian, why are we fighting?" She laid a hand over the one he held pressed to the flannel. "We're doing the right thing here tonight. The method of how we got the gelding here isn't as important as what happens to him now."

"You're right, of course." He studied the contrast of

their hands. His big, rough from work and hers small and elegant.

"And why we care for each other isn't as important as what we do about it."

About that he wasn't as sure, so he said nothing while she lifted another square of flannel and wrung it out.

Morning dawned misty and cool. As she'd slept poorly, Keeley's mind refused to click into gear. Her usual rush of morning adrenaline deserted her so that she began her daily chores with her body dragging and her brain fogged.

Brian's doing, she thought sulkily. This inconsistency of his, this off-and-on insistence to keep a distance between them was baffling. She'd never run into a problem she couldn't solve, an obstacle she couldn't overcome. But this one, this one man, might just be the exception.

He hurt her, and she hadn't been prepared for it. Could they have spent so much time together, been so intimate, and not understand each other? He cared about her, and that made it a problem. What kind of logic was that? she asked herself. Where was the sense in that kind of thinking?

Caring about someone made all the difference. She'd seen that constant well of compassion in him. It was, she admitted, as attractive, as appealing to her as that long, tough body, that thick, unkempt mane of sun-streaked hair.

The look of him, the face of planes and angles, the bold green eyes, might have stirred her blood—and had, though she'd been more annoyed than pleased initially. But it was the heart, the patience, the nurturing side he refused to acknowledge that had won her interest and respect.

Rather than being a problem, it had been, and was, the solution for her.

How could he look at her now, after all they'd shared, and see only the pampered daughter of a privileged home?

How could he, believing that, have feelings for her?

It was baffling, irritating and very close to infuriating. Or would be, she thought with a yawn, if she wasn't so damned tired.

The lack of energy struck unfairly keen when Mo bounced into the stables. "Just had to come by before I headed off to the eternal hell of school." She popped right into the box where Keeley was examining the injured knee. "How's he doing?"

"He's more comfortable." Testing, Keeley lifted the gelding's foot, bending the knee. He snorted, shied. "But you can see there's still pain."

"Poor guy. Poor big guy." Clucking, Mo patted his flank. "You were such a hero last night, Keel. I mean just stepping in and taking right over. I knew you would."

Keeley's brows drew together. "I didn't take over. I don't take over."

"Sure you did—you always do. The original take-charge gal. Very cool to watch. And this guy's grateful, aren't you, boy? Oh, and the hunk wasn't hard on the eyes, either." Grinning, she gave an obvious and deliberate shudder. "The real physical type. I thought he was going to punch that idiot Tarmack right in the face. Was kinda hoping he would. Anyway, the pair of you made a great team."

"I suppose."

"So, what about those smoldering looks?"

"What smoldering looks?"

"Get out." Mo cheerfully wiggled her eyebrows. "I got singed and I was only an innocent bystander. The guy looks at you like you were the last candy bar on the shelf and he'd die without a chocolate fix."

"That's a ridiculous analogy, and you're imagining things."

"He was going to pound Tarmack into dust for dissing you. Man, I just wanted to melt when he hauled the guy up by the collar. Too romantic."

"There's nothing romantic about a fight. And though I certainly could have handled Tarmack myself, I appreciated Brian's help."

Damn it, she thought. She hadn't even thanked him. Scowling, she stomped out of the box for a pitchfork.

"Yeah, you could have handled him. You handle everything. But not really needing to be rescued sort of makes *being* rescued more exciting, you know."

"No, I don't know," Keeley snapped. "Go to school, Mo. I've got mucking out to do."

"I'm going, I'm going. Sheesh. You must be low on the caffeine intake this morning. I'll come by later to see how the gelding's doing. I've got a kind of vested interest, you know? See you."

"Yeah, fine. Whatever." Keeley muttered to herself as she went to work on the stalls. There was nothing wrong with being able to handle things herself. Nothing wrong with wanting to. And she did appreciate Brian's help.

And she didn't need caffeine.

"I like caffeine," she grumbled. "I enjoy it, and that's entirely different from needing it. Entirely. I could give it up anytime I wanted, and I'd barely miss it."

Annoyed, she snagged the soft drink she'd left on a shelf and guzzled.

All right, so maybe she would miss it. But only because she liked the taste. It wasn't like a craving or an addiction or…

She couldn't say why Brian popped into her head just then. She was certain if he'd seen her staring in a kind of horror at a soft drink bottle, he'd have been amused. It was debatable what his reaction would be if he'd realized she wasn't actually seeing the bottle, but his face.

No, that wasn't a need, either, she thought quickly. She did not *need* Brian Donnelly. It was attraction. Affection—a cautious kind of affection. He was a man who interested her, and whom she admired in many ways. But it wasn't as if she needed...

"Oh God."

It had to be overreaction, she decided, and set the bottle aside as carefully as she would have a container of nitro. What she was going through was something as simple as overromanticizing an affair. That would be natural enough, she told herself, particularly since this was her first.

She didn't want to be in love with him. She began wielding the pitchfork vigorously now, as if to sweat out a fever. She didn't *choose* to be in love with him. That was even more important. When her hands trembled she ignored them and worked harder still.

By the time her mother joined her, Keeley had herself under control enough to casually ask Adelia to work in the office while she exercised Sam.

Keeley Grant had never run from a problem in her life, and she wasn't about to start now. She saddled her mount, then rode off to clear her head before she dealt with the problem at hand.

* * *

The portable starting gate was in place on the practice oval. The air was soft and cool. Brian had seen the blush of color coming onto the leaves, the hints of change. Though he imagined it would all be a sight in another week or two, his attention was narrowed onto the horses.

He was working in fields of five, using two yearlings and three experienced racers at a go. This last phase of schooling just prior to public racing would teach him every bit as much as it taught the yearlings.

He needed to watch their style, learn their preferences, their quirks, their strengths. Much of it would be guesses—educated ones to be sure, but guesses nonetheless, at least until they had a few solid races under their belts.

But Brian was very good at guessing.

"I want Tempest on the rail." He chewed on a cigar as it helped him think. "Then The Brooder, then Betty, Caramel and Giant on the outside."

He glanced around at the sound of hoofbeats, then lost his train of thought as Keeley trotted toward the oval. Irritated, he looked deliberately away and slammed the door on that increasingly wide area of his mind she insisted on occupying.

"I don't want the yearlings rated," he ordered, telling the exercise boys not to hold them back. "Nor punished, either. No more than a tap of the bat to signal. My horses don't need to be whipped to run."

Despite his concentration, he was aware when Keeley dismounted behind him. He took out his stopwatch, turning it over and over in his hand as the field was led to the gate.

"I don't know the yearling at the rail," Keeley said conversationally as she looped her reins around the top rung of the fence.

"Your father named him Tempest in a Teacup, as he's got a small build, but he's full of spirit. You don't often ride this way in the morning."

"No, but I wanted to see the progress. And my new assistant is handling things at the office."

He glanced over. She'd taken the band out of her hair. It flowed wild over her shoulders, but her face was cool and very serious. "Assistant is it? When did this happen?"

"Yesterday. My mother's working with me at the school now. Contrary to some beliefs, I don't insist on handling all the steps and stages by myself, when help is offered."

"Touchy still, are you?"

"Apparently."

"Well, you'll have to snarl at me later. I'm busy. Jim! Hold him steady now," Brian called out as Tempest shied a bit at the gate. "That one still objects a bit to being penned in. There, that's it," he murmured as the horses were loaded and the back gate shut. He held a finger over the timer, plunging when the gates sprang open.

The horses flew out.

He wondered if there was anything that gave his heart more of a knock than that instant, that first rush of speed, that blur of great bodies surging forward on the track.

But through the thrill of it, his eyes missed nothing. The stretch of legs, the clouds of dirt, the figures riding low over the necks.

"She wants the lead, right from the start," he murmured. "Wants the rest tasting her dust."

Caught up, Keeley leaned over the rail as the horses made the first turn. The thunder of hoofbeats drummed in her blood. "She runs well in a crowd. You were right about that. Tempest is a little nervy."

"We might try a shadow roll on him. He wants the outside. He's about endurance. The longer the race, the better he'll like it. There's Betty now. She wants the rail. Aye, she'll hug it like a lover."

Without thinking, he laid his hand over Keeley's on the rail. "Just look at her, will you? That's a champion. She doesn't need any of us. She knows it."

With his hand warm and firm over hers, Keeley watched the horses streak down the backstretch with Betty nearly a length in the lead. Pride and pleasure tangled inside her.

When Brian let out a shout, clicked his watch again, she started to turn, to indulge the giddy thrill by throwing her arms around him. But he was already drawing away.

"That's good time, damn good time. And she'll do better yet." He nodded, his eyes tracking as the riders rose high in their stirrups and slowed their mounts. "I'll find the right race for her, give her a taste of the real thing."

Giving Keeley an absent pat on the shoulder, he vaulted the fence.

She watched him go to the horses, to stroke and compliment Tempest, give the rider a few words before moving on to Betty.

The filly pranced flirtatiously, then lowered her head to nibble delicately on Brian's shoulder.

You're wrong, Keeley thought. Whatever she knows, whatever she is, she needs you.

And so, damn it, do I.

After he'd stroked, nuzzled, praised, and the horses were led away to be cooled down, Brian jumped over the fence again to pick up his clipboard.

"I'd hoped your father would be down to see her first run with a field."

"I'm sure he would have. He must be tied up with something."

With a grunt in response, Brian continued to scribble notes. "Well, I'm running more of the yearlings this morning, so he'll see plenty. How's the gelding?"

"Comfortable. The swelling's down a little. I want to wait until after my class today to drench him. It's a messy business and I don't need a half dozen kids coming around once it starts to work on him."

"Best to wait till late in the day anyway. You want a good twenty-four hours between his last feeding and the drenching. I can do that for you if you're busy."

The automatic refusal was on the tip of her tongue. She nipped it off, took a breath. "Actually, I was hoping you'd find time to take a look at him later."

"I can do that." He glanced up, saw how set and serious her face was. "What is it? Are you that worried?"

"No." She took another breath, ordered herself to relax. "I'm sure everything will be fine." She'd make sure of it, she told herself. One way or the other. "I'll feel better when things are under control, that's all."

She worked it out. She felt better when she had a situation defined and a goal in mind. This one wasn't really so complicated, after all. She wanted Brian. She was fairly certain she was in love with him. Being certain of that would take a little more time, she imagined, a little more consideration.

After all this was new territory and needed to be approached with caution and preparation.

But her feelings for him were strong, and not as one-dimensional as simple attraction.

If it was love, then she needed to make him fall in love with her. She was perfectly willing to work toward what she wanted, as long as she got it in the end.

Pleasantly tired after a long day's work, she gave her horses their evening meal. There was no question about it, she decided. Having her mother help had taken a huge burden of time and effort off her shoulders.

Was it stubbornness, she wondered, that caused her to pull back from a helping hand so often? She didn't think so. But it was something nearly as mulish. She wanted the people she loved and who loved her to be proud of her. And she equated that, foolishly, she admitted, with the need to be perfect.

But she preferred thinking of it as taking responsibility.

Just as she was doing now with Brian, she mused. If she was in love with him, she was responsible for her own feelings. And it was up to her to try to generate those same feelings in him.

If she failed... No, she wouldn't consider that. Once you considered failure you were one step farther away from success.

Moving into the gelding's box, she hung his hay bag and measured out his feed. "It's better tonight, isn't it?" Gently she checked the swelling on his knee.

When she heard the footsteps heading down on concrete, she smiled to herself.

"You're feeding him?" Brian stepped into the box. "I couldn't get up here any sooner."

"That's all right. He took the drenching without a quibble. And you can take my word for it, it worked." She straightened up, smiled. "You can see by the way he's eating, he's feeling better."

"Knows he's fallen into roses, he does." Brian examined the injury himself, nodded. "We have a stallion with the strangles, which is what held me up."

"Delicate creatures, aren't they?" She ran her hand over the gelding's withers. "Deceptive. The size of them, the speed and strength. It all shouts power. But under it all, there's the delicacy. You can be fooled by looking at something—at the face, at the form—and judging it without knowing what's inside."

"True enough."

"I'm not delicate, Brian. I have iron bred in me."

He looked at her. "I know you're strong, Keeley. And still, you've skin like a rosebud." Gently he ran his thumb over her cheek. "I have big hands, and they're hard, so I need to take care. It doesn't mean I think you're weak."

"All right."

He turned back to the horse. "Have you named him?"

"As a matter of fact, I have. We had a dog when I

was a girl. My mother found him, a very homely stray who started sneaking up to the house. She fed him, gained his confidence. And before my father knew it, he had a big, sloppy mutt on his hands. His name was Finnegan." She laid her cheek on the gelding's, rubbed. "And so now, is his."

"You've a sentimental streak along with that iron, Keeley."

"Yes, I do. And a latent romantic one."

"Is that so?" he murmured, a little surprised when she turned and ran her hands up his chest.

"Apparently. I didn't thank you for riding to my rescue last night."

"I don't recall riding anywhere." His lips twitched as she backed him out of the box.

"In a manner of speaking. You cut a bully down to size for me. I was upset and worried about the gelding, so I didn't really think about it at the time. But I did later, and I wanted to thank you."

"Well, you're welcome."

"I haven't finished thanking you." She bit lightly on his bottom lip, heard his quick indrawn breath.

"If that's what you have in mind, you could finish thanking me up in my bedroom."

"Why don't I just show you what I have in mind? Right here."

She had his shirt unbuttoned before he realized they were standing in an empty stall, freshly bedded with hay. "Here?" He laughed, taking both her hands to tug her out again. "I don't think so."

"Here." She countered his move by ramming his back against the side wall. "I know so."

"Don't be ridiculous." His lungs were clogged, and his mind insisted on following suit. "Anyone could come along."

"Live dangerously." She pulled the stall door shut behind them.

"I have been, since I first set eyes on you."

The thrum of the heart in her throat turned her voice husky. "Why stop now? Seduce me, Brian. I dare you."

"I've always found it hard to turn aside a dare." He reached out, tugged the band from her hair. "You cloud my senses, Keeley, like perfume. Before I know it, there's nothing there but you." He slid his hand around to cup the back of her neck, to draw her toward him. "And nothing that needs to be."

His mouth covered hers, soft, smooth in a kiss silky enough to have her gliding down on that alone. She'd asked for seduction knowing seduction wasn't needed.

"I want you, Brian. I wake up wanting you. Kiss me again."

And the way her body simply melted into his, the way her lips warmed and parted, inviting him in had every pulse in his body throbbing like a wound.

"I don't want to be gentle this time." He reversed their position until her back was against the wall, and his eyes, so suddenly dark, burned into hers. "I don't want to be so careful, just this once."

The thrill of it was a bolt through the heart. "Then don't. I'm not fragile like your horses, Brian. Don't be fooled."

"I'll frighten you." He couldn't have said if it was a threat or warning, but her answer was just another dare.

"Try it."

He tore her shirt open, sending buttons flying. He watched her eyes widen in shock even as he crushed his mouth to hers to swallow her gasp. Then his hands were on her, a rough scrape of callus over sensitive skin. Part of him expected her to object, to struggle away, but she only moaned against his savaging mouth, and held on.

When her knees gave like heated butter, he dragged her down to the mound of hay.

He used his mouth on her, his teeth, his tongue. A kind of wild fury. His hands raced over her, rough and possessive in their impatience to have more. To take all.

Her choked cries had the horses moving restlessly in their boxes. As he propelled her over that first breathless edge, she fisted her hands in his hair as if to anchor herself. Or to drag him with her.

He'd given her tenderness, shown her the beauty of lovemaking with patience and care. Now he showed her the dark glory of it with reckless demands and bruising hands.

Still she gave. Even with the whirlwind rushing inside him, he felt her give. Flesh dampened until it was slick, hearts pounded until the beat of them seemed to slap the air, but she rolled with him, accepting. Offering.

Even when her eyes were blind, the blue of them blurred as dark as midnight, she stayed with him. The sound of his name rushing through her lips seemed to sing in his blood.

She cried out, arching against his busy mouth when her world shattered into shards bright as glass. There was nothing to cling to, no thread to tie her to sanity, and still he drove her harder until the breath tearing from her lungs turned to harsh, primitive pants.

"It's me who has you." Wild to mate, he gripped her hips, jerked them high. "It's me who's in you." And plunged into her as if his life depended on it.

She heard a scream, high, thin, helpless. But it wasn't helplessness she felt. She felt power, outrageous power that pumped through her blood like a drug. Drunk on it, she reared up, her eyes locked on his as she fisted her hands in his hair once more.

She fixed her mouth on his, savaging it as he rode her, hard and fast. And she held on, held on, matching him beat for beat though she thought her body would burst, until she felt him fall.

"It's me," she said on a sob, "who has you." And still holding fast, let herself leap after him.

Chapter 10

As far as Keeley was concerned it was perfect. She'd fallen in love with a man who suited her. They had a strong foundation of common interests, enjoyed each other's company, respected each other's opinions.

He wasn't without flaws, of course. He tended to be moody and his confidence very often crossed the line into arrogance. But those qualities made him who he was.

The problem, as she saw it, was nudging him along from affair to commitment and commitment to marriage. She'd been raised to believe in permanency, in family, in the promise two people made to love for a lifetime.

She really had no choice but to marry Brian and

make a life with him. And she was going to see to it he had no choice, either.

It was a bit like training a horse, she supposed. There was a lot of repetition, rewards, patience and affection. And a firm hand under it all.

She thought it would be most sensible for them to become engaged at Christmas, and marry the following summer. Certainly it would be most convenient for them to build their life near Royal Meadows as both of them worked there. Nothing could be simpler.

All she had to do was lead Brian to the same conclusions.

Being the kind of man he was, she imagined he'd want to make the moves. It was a little galling, but she loved him enough to wait until he made his declaration. It wouldn't be with hearts and flowers, she mused as she walked Finnegan around the paddock. Knowing Brian there would be passion, and challenge and just a hint of temper.

She was looking forward to it.

She stopped to check the gelding's leg for any heat or swelling. Gently she picked up his foot to bend the knee. When he showed no signs of discomfort, she gave him a brisk rub on the neck.

"Yeah," she said when he blew affectionately on her shoulder, "feeling pretty good these days, aren't you? I think you're ready for some exercise."

His coat looked healthy again, she noted as she saddled him. Time, care and attention had turned the tide for him. Perhaps he'd never be a beauty, and certainly he was no champion, but he had a sweet nature and a willing spirit.

That was more than enough.

When she swung into the saddle, Finnegan tossed his head, then at her signal started out of the paddock in a dignified walk.

She went cautiously for a time, tuning herself to him, checking for any hitch in his gait that would indicate he was favoring his leg. It pleased her so much to feel him slide into a smooth rhythm that after a few moments she relaxed enough to enjoy the quiet ride.

Fall had used a rich and varied pallette this year to paint the trees in bold tones of golds and reds and orange. They swept over the hard blue canvas of sky and flamed under the strong slant of sunlight.

The fields held onto the deep green of high summer. Weanlings danced over the pastures, long legs reaching for speed as they charged their own shadows. Mares, their bellies swollen with the foals they carried, cropped lazily.

On the brown oval, colts and fillies raced in the majestic blur of power that brought thunder to the air.

This painting, Keeley thought, had been hers the whole of her life. The images that came back, repeating season after season. The beauty and strength of it, and the settled knowledge that it would go on year into year.

This she could, and would, pass on to her own children when the time came. The solidity of it, and the responsibilities, the joys and the sweat.

Sitting aside the healing gelding, she felt her throat ache with love. It wasn't just a place, it was a gift. One that had been treasured and tended by her parents. Her part in it, of it, would never be taken for granted.

When she saw Brian leaning on the fence, his attention riveted on the horses pounding down the backstretch, her aching throat seemed to snap shut.

For a moment she could only blink, stunned by the sudden, vicious pressure in her chest. Her skin tingled. There was no other word to describe how nerves swarmed over her in a wash of chills and heat.

As she fought to catch her breath, her heart pounded, a hammer on an anvil. The gelding shied under her, and had danced in a fretful half circle before she thought to control him.

And her hands trembled.

No, this was wrong. This wasn't acceptable at all. Where did this come from—how did she get this ball of terror in her stomach? She'd already accepted that she loved him, hadn't she? And it had been easy, a simple process of steps and study. Her mind was made up, her goals set. Damn it, she'd been pleased by the whole business.

So what was this shaky, dizzy, *painful* sensation, this clutch of panic that made her want to turn her mount sharply around and ride as far away as possible?

She'd been wrong, Keeley realized as she pressed an unsteady hand to her jumpy heart. She'd only been falling in love up to now. How foolish of her to be lulled by the smooth slide of it. This was the moment, she understood that now. This was the moment the bottom dropped away and sent her crashing.

Now the wind was knocked out of her, that same shock of sensation that came from losing your seat over a jump and finding yourself flipping through space until the ground reached up and smacked into you. Jolting bones and head and heart.

Love was an outrageous shock to the system, she thought. It was a wonder anyone survived it.

She was a Grant, Keeley reminded herself and straightened in the saddle. She knew how to take a tumble, just as she knew how to pick herself back up and focus mind and energy on the goal. She wouldn't just survive this knock to the heart. She'd thrive on it. And when she was done with Brian Donnelly, he wouldn't know what had hit him.

She steadied herself much as she had done before competitions. She took slow and deliberate breaths until her pulse rate slowed, focused her mind until it was calm as lake water, then she rode down to face her goal.

Brian turned when he heard her approach. The vague irritation at the interruption vanished when he saw Finnegan. He felt a keen interest there, and passing his clipboard and some instructions to the assistant trainer, moved toward the gelding.

"Well now, you're looking fit and fine, aren't you?" Automatically he bent down to check the injured leg. "No heat. That's good. How long have you had him out?"

"About fifteen minutes, at a walk."

"He could probably take a canter. He's looking good as new, no signs of swelling." Brian straightened, narrowing his eyes against the sun as he looked up at Keeley. "But you? Are you all right? You're a bit pale."

"Am I?" Small wonder, she thought, but smiled as she enjoyed the sensation of holding a secret inside her. "I don't feel pale. But you..." Swimming in the river of discovery, she leaned down. "You look wonderful. Rough and windblown and sexy."

His narrowed eyes flickered, and he stepped back, a little uneasy when she rubbed a hand over his cheek. There were a half a dozen men milling around, he thought. And every one of them had eyes.

"I was called down to the stables early this morning, didn't take time to shave."

She decided to take his evasive move as a challenge rather than an insult. "I like it. Just a little dangerous.

If you've got time later, I thought you might help me out."

"With what?"

"Take a ride with me."

"I could do that."

"Good. About five?" She leaned down again and this time took a fistful of his shirt to yank him a step closer. "And, Brian? Don't shave."

The woman threw him off balance, and he didn't care for it. Giving him those hot looks and intimate little strokes in the middle of the damn morning so he went through the whole of the day itchy.

Worse yet the man who was paying him to work through the day, not to be distracted by his glands, was the woman's father.

It was a situation, Brian thought, and he'd done a great deal to bring it on himself. Still how could he have known in the beginning that he'd become so involved with her on so many levels inside himself? Falling in love had been a hard knock, but he'd taken knocks before. You got bruised and you went on. A bit of attraction was all right, a little flirtation was harmless enough. And the truth was, he'd enjoyed the risk of it. To a point.

But he was well past that point now. Now he was all wrapped up in her and at the same time had become fond of her family. Travis wasn't just a good and fair boss, but was on the way to becoming a kind of friend.

And here he was finding ways to make love to his friend's daughter as often as humanly possible.

Worse than that, he admitted as he strode toward her stables, he was—from time to time—catching himself dreaming. These little fantasies would sneak into his head when he was busy doing something else. He'd find himself wondering how it would all be between Keeley and him if things were different, if they were on the same level, so to speak. And he thought— well, that is if he were the settling down sort—that she might be just the one to settle down with.

If he were interested in rooting in one place with one person, that is. Which of course, wasn't in his plans at all. Even if it was—which it wasn't—it wouldn't work.

She was clubhouse and he was shedrow, and that was that.

Keeley was just kicking up her heels a bit. He understood about that, couldn't hold it against her. For all the privilege, she'd had a sheltered life and now was taking a few whacks at the boundaries of it. He'd rebelled himself against the borders of his own upbringing by sliding his way out of school and into the stables when he'd still been a boy. Nothing had stopped him, not the arguments, the threats, the punishments.

As soon as he'd been able, he'd left home, moving from stable to stable, track to track. He'd kept loose, he'd kept free and unfettered. And had never looked back. His brothers and sisters married, raised children, planted gardens, worked in steady jobs. They owned things, he thought now, while he owned nothing that couldn't easily fit in his traveling bag or be disposed of when he took to the next road.

When you owned things you had to tend them. Before you knew it, you owned more. Then the weight of them kept your feet planted in one spot.

He flicked a glance up at the pretty stone building that was his quarters, and admired the way it stood out against the evening sky. Flowers in colors of rust and scarlet and gold ran along the foundation, and the truck he'd bought from Paddy was parked like it belonged.

He stopped and, much as Keeley had that morning, turned to survey the land. It was a place, he realized, that could hold a man if he wasn't careful. The openness of it could fool you into believing it wasn't confining, then it would tempt you to plant things—yourself included—until it had you, heart and soul.

It was smart to remember it wasn't his land, any more than the horses were his horses. Or Keeley was his woman.

But when he stepped over toward her paddock, that fantasy snuck up on him again. In the long, soft shadows and quiet light of evening she saddled the big buff-colored gelding he knew she called Honey. Her hair was pinned on top of her head in an absentminded, messy knot that was ridiculously sexy. She wore jeans and a sweater of Kelly green.

She looked…reachable, Brian realized. Like the kind of woman a man wanted with him after a long day's work. There'd be a lot to talk about with this woman, over dinner, in the privacy of bed. Shared loves, shared jokes.

A man could wake up in the morning with a woman like that and not feel trapped, or worry that she did.

Catching himself, Brian shook his head. That was foolish thinking.

"Look at this." Brian walked up to the fence, leaned on it. "You've done all the work already."

"You've caught me on a good day." Keeley checked the cinch, stepped back. She knew his stirrup length now, and his favored bit and bridle. "I had no idea how much time I'd free up by having Ma help out on a regular basis."

"And what do you intend to do with it?"

"Enjoy it." When he opened the gate she led both horses through. "I've been so focused on the work the last couple of years, I haven't stepped back often enough to appreciate the results." She handed him the reins. "I like results."

"Then maybe you'll use some of that free time to come by the track." He vaulted into the saddle once she was mounted. "I'm looking for results there. I have Betty entered in a baby race tomorrow."

"Her maiden race? I wouldn't want to miss that."

"Charles Town. Two o'clock."

"I'll ask my mother to take my afternoon class. I'll be there."

They kept it to a walk, skirting the paddock and heading toward the rise of land swept with trees gone brilliant in the softening slants of sunlight. Overhead a flock of Canada geese arrowed across the evening sky sending out their deep calls.

"Twice daily," Brian said, watching the flight. "Off they go on their travels, honking away, dawn and dusk."

"I've always liked the sound of them. I guess it's something else that says home this time of year." She kept her eyes on the sky until the last call echoed away.

"Uncle Paddy phoned today."

"And how's he doing?"

"More than well. He'd bought himself a pair of young mares. He's decided to try his hand at some breeding."

"Once a horseman," Brian said. "I didn't figure he could keep out of the game."

"You'd miss it, wouldn't you? The smell and the sound of them. Have you ever thought of starting your own place, your own line?"

"No, that's not for me. I'm happy making another

man's horses. Once you own, it's a business, isn't it? An enterprise. I've no yearning to be a businessman."

"Some own for the love of it," Keeley pointed out. "And even the business doesn't shadow the feelings."

"In the rare case." Brian looked over, scanning the outbuildings. Yes, this was a place, he thought, built on feelings. "Your father's one, and I knew another once in Cork. But ownership can get in the blood as well, until you lose touch with that feeling. Before you know it, it's all facts and figures and a thirst for profit. That sounds like bars to me."

Interesting, she thought. "Making a living is a prison?"

"The need to make one, and still a better one, first and foremost. That's a trap. My father found his leg caught there."

"Really?" He so rarely mentioned his family. "What does he do?"

"He's a bank clerk. Day after day sitting in a little cage counting other people's money. What a life."

"Well, it's not the life for you."

"Thank God for that. These lads want a bit of a run," he said and kicked Honey into a gallop.

Keeley hissed in frustration but clicked to her mount to match pace. They'd come back to it, she promised herself. She hadn't learned nearly enough about where the man she intended to marry came from.

They rode for an hour before heading back to stable

the horses and settle in the rest of her stock for the night. He was half hoping she'd ask him over to the house for dinner again, but she turned to him as they left the stables, lifted a brow.

"Why don't you ask me up for a drink?"

"A drink? There's not much of a variety, but you're welcome."

"It's nice to be asked occasionally." Before he could tuck his hand safely in his pocket, she took it, threaded their fingers together. "You have free time now and again yourself," she said easily. "I wonder if you've heard of the concept of dates. Dinner, movies, drives?"

"I've some experience with them." He glanced at his pickup as they turned toward his quarters. "If you've a yen for a drive, you can climb up into the lorry, but I'd need to shovel it out first."

She huffed out a breath. "That, Donnelly, wasn't the most romantic of invitations."

"Secondhand lorries aren't particularly romantic, and I've forgotten where I parked my glass coach."

"If that's another princess crack—" She broke off, set her teeth. Patience, she reminded herself. She wasn't going to spoil things with an argument. "Never mind. We'll forget the drive." She opened the door herself. "And move straight to dinner."

He caught the scent as soon as he stepped inside. Something aromatic and spicy that reminded him his stomach was about dead empty.

"What is it?"

"What is what?" Then she grinned and sniffed the air. "Oh, what is that? It's chili, one of my specialties. I put it on simmer before my last class."

"You cooked dinner?"

"Mmm." Amused, and very satisfied by his shock, she wandered off into the kitchen. "I didn't think you'd mind, and I knew we'd both be hungry by this time." She lifted the lid on a pot, gave it a quick stir while fragrant steam puffed out. "It's the kind of thing you can just leave and eat when you're ready, which is why it appeals to me. Oh, and I brought over a bottle of Merlot, though beer's never wrong with chili if you'd rather."

"I'm trying to remember the last time someone cooked for me—other than your mother and someone who was related to me."

Even more pleased, she turned to slide her arms around him. "Haven't any of your many women cooked for you?"

"Now and then perhaps, but not in recent memory." Because they were alone, he took her hips, brought her closer. "And I certainly remember none that smelled so appetizing."

"The women? Or the meal?"

"Both." He lowered his mouth to hers, allowed himself the luxury of sinking in. "And it reminds me I'm next to starving."

"What do you want first?" She grazed her teeth over his bottom lip. "Me, or the food?"

"I want you first. And last, it seems."

"That's handy, because I want you first, too." She drew back. "Why don't we clean up? I could use a shower." Laughing, her hands holding his, she pulled him out of the kitchen.

She'd brought over a change of clothes as well. It gave Brian a start to see her casually pulling on fresh jeans. Her hair was still wet from the shower they'd shared, her skin rosy from it. And, he noted a bit raw in places because he hadn't shaved.

But the wild love they'd made under the hot spray in the steamy room wasn't anywhere near as intimate, anywhere near as *personal* somehow as her having a clean sweater laying neatly folded on the foot of his bed.

She reached for it, then glanced over, catching him staring at her. "What is it?"

He shook his head. There wasn't a way to explain this sense of panic and delight that lived inside him while he watched her dress. "I've rubbed your skin raw." Reaching out, he traced his fingertips over her collarbone. "I should have shaved. You're so soft." He murmured it, trailing those fingers up over her shoulder. "I don't know how I manage to forget that."

When she trembled, he looked up into her face. For a moment she saw the need flash back into his eyes, glinting like the edge of a sword. "Now you're cold. Put your sweater on. I've got some ointment."

The hot edge faded as quickly as it came. It was frustrating, she thought as he rooted into a drawer, that the only time he really broke the tether on his control was when they made love.

He got out a tube and since she'd yet to put the sweater on, squeezed ointment onto his fingers and began to gently rub it on her abraded skin. She recognized the scent.

"That's for horses."

"So?"

She laughed and let him fuss. "Does this make me your mare now?"

"No, you're too young and delicate of bone for that. You're still a filly."

"Are you going to train me, Donnelly?"

"Oh, you're out of my league, Miss Grant." He glanced up, cocked a brow when he saw her grinning at him. "And what amuses you?"

"You can't help it can you? You have to tend."

"I put the marks on you," he muttered as he smoothed on the ointment. "It follows I should see to them."

She lifted a hand to toy with the ends of his damp, gold-tipped hair. "I like being seen to by a man with a tough mind and a soft heart."

That soft heart sighed a little, ached a little. But he

spoke lightly. "It's no hardship running my fingers over skin like yours." With his eyes on hers, he used the pad of his thumb to spread ointment over the gentle swell of her breast. "Particularly since you don't seem to have a qualm about standing here half naked and letting me."

"Should I blush and flutter?"

"You're not the fluttering sort. I like that about you." Satisfied, he capped the tube, then tugged the sweater over her head himself. "But I can't have such a fine piece of God's work catching a chill. There you are." He lifted her hair out of the neck.

"You don't have a hair dryer."

"There's air everywhere in here."

She laughed and dragged her fingers through her damp curls. "It'll have to do. Come on, let's have that wine while I finish up dinner."

He didn't know much about wine, but his first sip told him it was several steps up from what might be the usual accompaniment to so humble a meal as chili.

She seemed more at home in his kitchen than he was himself, finding things in drawers he'd yet to open. When she started to dress the salad, he set his glass aside.

"I'll be back in a minute."

"A minute's all you've got," she called out. "I'm putting the bread in to warm."

Since his answer was the slamming of the door,

she shrugged and lit the candles she'd set on the little kitchen table. Cozy, she decided. And just romantic enough to suit two practical-minded people who didn't go in for a lot of fussing.

It was the sort of relaxed, simple meal two people could prepare together at the end of a workday. She intended to see they had more of them, until the man got a clue this is exactly how it was going to be.

Satisfied, she picked up her wine, toasted herself. "To good strong starts," she murmured and drank.

Hearing the door open again, she took the bread out of the oven. "We're set in here, and I'm starving."

She turned to put the basket of bread on the table and saw Brian, and the clutch of mums and zinnias he held in his hand.

"It seemed to call for them," he said.

She stared at the cheerful fall blossoms, then up into his face. "You picked me flowers."

The sheer disbelief in her voice had him moving his shoulders restlessly. "Well, you made me dinner, with wine and candles and the whole of it. Besides, they're your flowers anyway."

"No, they're not." Drowning in love she set the basket down, waited. "Until you give them to me."

"I'll never understand why women are so sentimental over posies." He held them out.

"Thank you." She closed her eyes, buried her face in them. She wanted to remember the exact fragrance, the exact texture. Then lowering them again, she lifted her mouth to his for a kiss. Rubbed her cheek against his.

His arms came around her so suddenly, so tightly, she gasped. "Brian? What is it?"

That gesture, the simple and sweet gesture of cheek against cheek nearly destroyed him. "It's nothing. I just like the way you feel against me when I hold you."

"Hold me any tighter, I'll be through you."

"Sorry." He pressed his lips to her forehead to give himself a moment to compose. "I forget my own strength when I'm starving to death."

"Then sit down and get started. I'll put these in some water."

"I…" He had to say something and cast around for a topic where he wouldn't stutter or say something that would embarrass them both. "I meant to tell you earlier, I looked up Finnegan's records."

There, he thought as he sat and began to dish up salad for both of them. Safe ground. "Of course he's registered as Flight of Fancy."

"Yes, I knew that." She tucked the flowers in a vase, and set them on the table before joining Brian. "Finnegan suits him better, I think."

"He's yours to call what you like now. His record in his first year of racing was uneven. His blood stock is very decent, but he never came up to potential, and his owners sold him off as a three-year-old."

"I was going to look up his data. You've saved me the trouble." She broke a hunk of bread in half, offered it. "He has good lines, and he responds well. Even after the abuse he hasn't turned common."

"The thing is he did considerably better in his third year. Some of his match-ups were uneven, and in my mind he was a bit overraced. I'd have done things differently if I'd been working with him."

"You do things different, Brian, all around."

"Ah well. In any case, he went into that claiming race and that's how Tarmack got his hands on him."

"Bastard," Keeley said so coolly, Brian cocked his head.

"We won't argue there. I'm thinking you'd be wasting him in your school here. He was born for the track, and that's where he belongs."

Surprised, she frowned over her salad. "You think he should race?"

"I think you should consider it. Seriously. He's a thoroughbred, Keeley, bred to run. The need for it's in his blood. It's only that he's been misused and mismanaged. The atheletes inside him, and though your school's a fine thing, it's not enough for him."

"If he's prone to knee spavins—"

"You don't know that. It's not a hereditary thing. It was an injury a man was responsible for. You could have your father look him over if you don't think I've got the right of it."

She considered a moment, sipped her wine. "I certainly trust your judgment, Brian. It's not that. You and I both know that a horse can lose heart under mistreatment. Heart and spirit. I just wouldn't want to push him."

"Sure, it's up to you."

"Would you work with him?"

"I could." He ladled chili into bowls. "But so could you. You know what to do, what to look for."

She was already shaking her head. "Not for racing. I know my area, and it's not the track. If I consider running him again, I'd want him to have the best."

"That would be me," he said with such easy arrogance she grinned.

"Is that a yes?"

"If your father agrees to having me work your horse on the side, I'm happy to. We'll start him off easy, and see how he goes." He started to leave it at that, then because he thought she'd understand, hoped she would, finished. "It was in his eyes this morning, when you rode him down to the track. It was there. The yearning."

"I didn't see it." She reached over to touch his hand. "I'm glad you did."

"It's my job to see it."

"It's your gift," she corrected. "Your family must be proud of you." She spoke casually, began to eat again, then stared at him, baffled, when he laughed. "Why is that funny?"

"Pride wouldn't exactly be part of their general outlook to my way of thinking."

"Why?"

"People can't find pride in what they don't understand. Not all families, Keeley, are as cozy as yours."

"I'm sorry," she said, and meant it. Not only for whatever lack there was in his family feelings, but for deliberately prying.

"Sure it's not such a matter. We get on all right."

She meant to let it go, to change the subject, but the words burned inside her. "If they're not proud of you, then they're stupid." When he stared, his next bite of chili halfway to his mouth, she shrugged. "I'm sorry, but they are."

Watching her, he started to eat again. Her eyes were snapping, her cheeks flushed, her jaw set. Why the woman was fuming, he realized. "Darling, that's sweet of you to say, but—"

"It's not. It's rude, but I meant it." Snatching up the wine bottle, she topped off both of their glasses. "You have a real talent, and you've earned a strong reputation—or you damn well wouldn't be here at Royal Meadows. What's not to be proud of?" she demanded, with even more heat. "Your father, of all people, should understand."

"Why?"

Her mouth dropped open. "He's the one who introduced you to horses."

"To the track. It wasn't the horses for my father," Brian told her. He was so fascinated by her reaction it didn't occur to him that he was having an in-depth conversation about his family. Something he absolutely never did.

"They were a kind of vehicle. He admired them, certainly. But it was the wagering, the rush of gambling that called to him. Likely still does. That and the chance to take a few pulls from the flask in his pocket without my mother's silent and deadly disapproval. I told you, Keeley, he's a bank clerk."

"What difference does that make?"

All, was what Brian thought, but he struggled to find a more tangible explanation for her. "He stopped looking through the bars of his little cage years back. He and my mother, they married young, not quite the full nine months, you understand, before my oldest sister came along."

"That can be difficult, but still—"

"No, they were content with it. I think they love each other, in their way." He didn't think about those areas much, but since he was in it now, he did his best. "They made their home, raised their children. My father brought in the wage. Though he gambled, we never went hungry—and bills were paid sooner or later. My mother always set a decent table, and our

clothes were clean. But it seemed to me that the both
of them were just tired out at the end of the day, just
from doing."

Keeley remembered an expression of her mother's.
A child could starve with a full plate. She understood
that without love, affection, laughter, the spirit hun-
gered.

"Going your own way shouldn't stop them from
being happy for you."

"My brother and my sisters, they're clerks and parents and settled sort of people. I'm a puzzle, and sooner
or later when you can't solve a puzzle, you have to
think there's something wrong with it. Else there's
something wrong with you."

"You ran away," she murmured.

He wasn't sure he liked the phrase, but nodded. "In
a sense, I suppose, and as fast as I could. What's the
point in looking back?"

But he was looking back, Keeley thought. Looking
back over his shoulder, because he was still running
away.

Chapter 11

Keeley decided some men simply took longer than others to realize they wanted to go where you were leading them. It was hard to complain since she was having such a wonderful time. She was making it a habit to go to the track once a week, a pleasure she'd cut out of her life while she'd been organizing her academy.

There were still dozens of details that she needed to see to personally—the meetings, the reports and follow-ups on each individual child. She wanted to plan a kind of open house during the holidays, where all the parents, grandparents, foster families could come to the academy. Meet and mingle, and most importantly see the progress their children had made.

But now that her school was on course, and she'd expanded to seven days a week, she was more than happy to turn the classes over to her mother for one day.

She was thrilled to watch Betty's progress, to see for herself that Brian's instincts had been on target with the filly. Betty was, day after day and week after week, proving herself to be a top competitor and a potential champion.

But even more she was delighted to see Finnegan come to life under Brian's patient, unwavering hand.

Bundled against the chill of a frosty morning, Keeley stood at the fence of the practice oval and waited while Brian gave Larry his instructions on the workout run.

"He gets nervy in the gate, but he breaks clean. You'll need to rate him or he'll lose his wind. He likes a crowd so I want you to keep him in the pack till after the second turn. You let him know then, firm, that you want more. He'll give it to you. He doesn't like running in front, he misses the company."

"I'll keep his eye on the line, Mr. Donnelly. I appreciate you giving me the chance."

"It's Miss Grant's giving you the chance. I smell whiskey on your breath before post time tomorrow, and you won't get a second one."

"Not a drop. We'll run for you, if for nothing but

to show that son of a bitch Tarmack how you treat a thoroughbred."

"Fair enough. Let's see how she goes."

Brian walked back to the fence where Keeley stood sipping her soft drink. "I don't know if you made the best choice in jockeys, but he's sober and he's hungry, so it's a good gamble."

"It's not the winning this time, Brian."

He took her bottle, sipped, winced. How the woman could drink such a thing in the morning was beyond him. "It's always the winning."

"You've done a wonderful job with him."

"We won't know that until tomorrow at Pimlico."

"Stop it," she ordered when he slipped through the split rail fence. "Take credit when it's deserved. That's a horse that's found his pride again," she said as the practice field was led to the gate. "You gave it to him."

"For God's sake, Keeley, he's your horse. I just reminded him he could run."

You're wrong, she thought. You gave him back his pride, just the way you made him your own.

But Brian was already focused on the horse. He took out his stopwatch. "Let's see how well he remembers running this morning."

Mists swam along the ground, a shallow river over the oval. Shards of frost still glittered on the grass while the sun pulsed weakly through the layers of morning clouds. The air was gray and still.

With a ringing clang the gate sprang open. And the horses plunged.

Ground fog tore like thin silver ribbon at the powerful cut of legs. Bodies, glistening from the morning damp, surged past in one sleek blur.

"That's it," Brian murmured. "Keep him centered. That's the way."

"They're beautiful. All of them."

"Got to pace him." Brian watched them round the first turn while the clock in his head ticked off the time. "See, he'll match his rhythm to the leader. It's a game to him now. Out gallivanting with mates, that's all he's thinking."

Keeley laughed, leaned out as her heart began to bump. "How do you know what he's thinking?"

"He told me. Get ready now. Ready now. Aye, that's it. He's strong. He'll never be a beauty, but he's strong. See, he's moving up." Forgetting himself Brian laid a hand on her shoulder, squeezed. "He's got more heart than brains, and it's his heart that runs."

Brian clicked the watch when Finnegan came in, half a length behind the leader. "Well done. Yes, well done. I'd say he'll place for you tomorrow, Miss Grant."

"It doesn't matter."

Sincerely shocked more than offended, he goggled at her. "That's a hell of a thing to say. And what kind of luck is that going to bring us tomorrow, I'd like to know?"

"It's enough to watch him run. And better, to watch you watching him run. Brian." Touched, she laid a hand on his heart. "You've gone and fallen in love with him."

"I love all the horses I train."

"Yes, I've seen that, and understand that because it's the same with me. But you're in love with this one."

Embarrassed because it was true, Brian swung over the fence. "That's a woman for you, making sloppy sentiment out of a job."

She only smiled as Brian walked over to stroke and nuzzle his job.

"That's a fine thing. My daughter and my trainer grooming a competitor."

She glanced over her shoulder, held out a hand for her father as he strode toward her. "Did you see him run?"

"The last few seconds. You've brought him a long way in a short time." Travis pressed a kiss to the top of her head. "I'm proud of you."

She closed her eyes. How easily he said it, how lovely to know he meant it. It made her only more sad, more angry, that Brian had cause to laugh over the idea of his own father having any pride in him.

"You taught me to care, you and Ma. When I saw that horse, I cared because of what you put inside me."

She tilted her head up, kissed her father's cheek. "So thanks."

When his arm came around her, she leaned in, warm and comfortable. "Brian was right. The horse needs to race. It's what he is. I wanted to save him. But Brian knew that wasn't enough. For some it's not enough just to get by."

"You brought this off together."

"You're right." She laughed a little as realization dawned, so clear and bright she wondered how she'd missed it before. "Absolutely right."

She'd canceled classes for the day. It was, Keeley told herself, a kind of holiday. A celebration, she thought, in compassion, understanding and hard work. It wasn't only Finnegan's return to the track, but Betty's first important race. Her parents would be there, and Brendon.

If there was ever a day to close up shop, this was it.

She rode out to the track at dawn, to give herself the pleasure of watching the early workouts, of listening to the track rats, building anticipation.

"You'd think it was the Derby," Brendon said as he walked with her back to the shedrow. "You're hyped."

"I've never owned a racehorse before. And I'm pretty sure he's my first and last. I'm going to enjoy every moment of this, but... It's not my passion. Not like it's yours and Dad's. Even Ma's."

"You channeled your passions into the school. I never thought you'd give up competing, Keel."

"Neither did I. And I never thought I'd find anything that satisfied me as much, challenged me as much."

They stopped as horses were brought back from the early workouts.

Steam rose off their backs, out of the tubs of hot water set outside the stables. It fogged the air, cushioned the sound, blurred the colors.

Hot walkers hustled to cool off the runners, stable-hands and grooms loitered, waiting for their charges. Someone played a mournful little tune on a harmonica, with the ring of the farrier's anvil setting the beat.

"This is your deal here," she said, gesturing as Betty was led by. "Me, I'm happy just to watch."

"Yeah? Then what're you doing here so early?"

"Just carrying on a fine family tradition. I'm going to act as Finnegan's groom."

That was news to Brian, and he wasn't entirely pleased when she announced her intentions. "Owners don't groom. They sit in the grandstands, or up in the restaurant. They stay out of the way."

Keeley continued strapping Finnegan with straw. "How long have you worked at Royal Meadows now?"

His scowl only deepened. "Since midthrough of August."

"Well, that should be long enough for you to have noticed the Grants don't stay out of the way."

"Noticing doesn't mean approving." He studied the way she groomed Finnegan's neck and couldn't find fault. But that was beside the point. "Grooming a horse for showing or schooling or basic riding is a different matter than grooming before a race."

She let out a long-suffering sigh. "Does it look like I know what I'm doing?"

"His legs need to be wrapped."

Saying nothing, she gestured to the wrapping on the line, and the extra clothespins hooked to her jeans.

Not yet convinced, he studied her grooming kit and the other tools of a groomer's trade. The cotton batting, the blankets, the tack.

"The irons haven't been polished."

She glanced at the saddle. "I know how to polish irons."

Brian rocked back on his heels. He needed to see to Betty. She was racing in the second. "He needs to be talked to."

"This is funny, but I know how to talk, too."

Brian swore under his breath. "He prefers singing."

"Excuse me?"

"I said, he prefers singing."

"Oh." Keeley tucked her tongue in her cheek. "Any particular tune? Wait, let me guess. *Finnegan's Wake?*" Brian's steely-eyed stare had her laughing until she had to lean weakly against the gelding. The horse responded by twisting his head and trying to sniff her pockets for apples.

"It's a quick tune," Brian said coolly, "and he likes hearing his name."

"I know the chorus." Gamely Keeley struggled to swallow another giggle. "But I'm not sure I know all the words. There are several verses as I recall."

"Do the best you can," he muttered and strode off. His lips twitched as he heard her launch into the song about the Dubliner who had a tippling way.

When he reached Betty's box, he shook his head. "I should've known. If there's not a Grant one place, there's a Grant in another until you're tripping over them."

Travis gave Betty a last pat on the shoulder. "Is that Keeley I hear singing?"

"She's being sarcastic, but as long as the job's done. She's dug in her heels about grooming Finnegan."

"She comes by it naturally. The hard head as well as the skill."

"Never had so many owners breathing down my neck. We don't need them, do we, darling?" Brian laid his hands on Betty's cheek, and she shook her head, then nibbled his hair.

"Damn horse has a crush on you."

"She may be your lady, sir, but she's my own true love. Aren't you beautiful, my heart?" He stroked, sliding into the Gaelic that had Betty's ears pricked and her body shifting restlessly.

"She likes being excited before a race," Brian murmured. "What do you call it—pumped up like your American football players. Which is a sport that eludes me altogether as they're gathered into circles discussing things most of the time instead of getting on with it."

"I heard you won the pool on last Monday night's game," Travis commented.

"Betting's the only thing about your football I do understand." Brian gathered her reins. "I'll walk her around a bit before we take her down. She likes to parade. You and your missus will want to stay close to the winner's circle."

Travis grinned at him. "We'll be watching from the rail."

"Let's go show off." Brian led Betty out.

Keeley put the final polish on the saddle irons, rolled her now aching shoulders and decided she had enough time to hunt up a soft drink before giving Finnegan a last-minute pep talk.

She stepped outside and blinked in the sudden whitewash of light. The minute her eyes focused she saw Brian sitting near the stable door on an overturned bucket.

Alarm sprinted into her throat. He had his head in his hands and was still as stone.

"What is it? What's wrong?" She leaped forward to drop to the ground beside him. "Betty?" Her breath came short. "I thought Betty was racing."

"She was. She did. She won."

"God, Brian, I thought something was wrong."

He dropped his hands and she could see his eyes were dark, swarming with emotion. "Two and a half lengths," he said. "She won by two and a half lengths, and I swear I don't think she was half trying. Nothing could touch her, do you see? Nothing. Never in my life did I think to have a horse like that under my hands. She's a miracle."

Keeley laid her hands on his knees, sat back on her heels. Passion, she thought. She'd spoken to Brendon of it, but now she was looking at it. "You made her." Before he could speak, she shook her head. "That's what you said to me once. 'I don't break horses. I make them.'"

"I can't get my head round it just now. This field was strong. I put her in thinking now and then you need a lesson in humility. Time for her to grow up, you know what I mean. Face real competition."

Still staggered, he dragged his hands through his hair and laughed. "Well, she'll never learn a damn thing about humility."

"Why aren't you down with her?"

"That's for your parents. She's their horse."

"You've a lot to learn yourself." She got to her feet,

brushed off the knees of her jeans. "Well, Finnegan will be going down shortly. Why don't you come in and look him over?"

Brian blew out a breath, sucked in another, then rose. "I think he'll place for you," he told Keeley as he followed her in. "It wouldn't hurt to wager on it."

"I intend to wager on him." While Brian went in to check Finnegan's leg wrappings, she got papers out of the pocket of the jacket she'd laid aside.

"The wrappings look all right." He flicked a finger over the stirrups. "And you polished the irons well enough."

"Glad you approve. Next time you can do it." She held out the papers.

"What's this?"

"Papers giving you half interest in Flight of Fancy, also known as Finnegan."

"What are you talking about?"

"He was half yours anyway, Brian. This just makes it legal."

His palms went cold and damp. "Don't be ridiculous. I can't take that."

She'd expected him to refuse initially, but she hadn't expected him to go pale and snarl. "Why? You helped bring him back. You trained him."

"A couple of weeks work, on my off time. Now put those away and stop being foolish."

When he started to push by her, she simply shifted

to block his way. "First, he wouldn't be racing today if it wasn't for you. And second, you're as attached to him as I am. Probably more. If it's the money—"

"It's not the money." Though a part of him knew it was, to some extent. Because it was hers.

"Then what?"

"I don't own horses. I don't want to be an owner."

"That's a pity, because you are an owner. Or a half owner anyway."

"I said I'm not accepting it."

"We'll argue about it later."

"There's nothing to argue about."

She stepped out of the box, smiled sweetly. "You know, Brian, just because you can make a fifteen hundred pound horse do what you want, doesn't mean you can budge me one inch. I'm going to go bet on our horse. To win."

"He's not our—" He broke off, swore, as she'd already flounced out. "And you don't bet to win," he muttered. "It's nothing personal," he said to Finnegan who was watching him with soft, sad eyes. "I just can't be owning things. It's not that I don't have great affection and respect for you, for I do. But what happens if in a year or two down the road I move on? Even if I don't—as it's feeling more and more that I'd wonder why I would—I can't have the woman give me a horse. Even a half a horse. Well, not to worry. We'll straighten it all out later."

* * *

He shouldn't have been nervous. It was pitiful. It was just another horse, just another race. It wasn't, as Betty was, a shining gift. This was an apple-loving, sweet-natured gelding who'd already broken down once and had lost far more races than he'd won in his short career.

Brian was fond of him, of course, and wanted him to have his day in the sun. But he had no illusions about this one being a champion.

He was simply guiding the horse toward doing what he'd been born for. And that was run his best.

And still nerves danced in Brian's belly.

"The track's dry and fast," he told Larry as they walked past the backstretch. "That's good for him. The field's crowded, and he likes that, too. Blue Devil's the number six horse, and odds-on favorite. There's reason for that."

"I know Blue Devil." Larry nodded and gnashed a mouthful of gum. "He can slither through a pack like a snake. He gets in the lead, he sets a fast pace."

"I expect that's what he'll do today. I need you to feel what Finnegan's got in him. I don't want you over-racing him, but don't hold him back past the first turn. Let him test his legs."

"I'll take care of him, Mr. Donnelly. Here's Miss Grant come to see us off. He looks fine, Miss Grant. You done good with him."

"Yes." A little breathless from the run back from the betting window, she gave Finnegan a brisk rub. "We did."

When the call sounded for riders up, she stepped back. "Good luck."

"Talk to him." Brian gave Larry a leg up. "Don't forget to talk to him all the way. Don't let him forget what he's there for."

"They look good," Keeley decided. "Here."

"What now?"

"I put fifty down for you."

"You—damn it."

"You can pay me back out of your winnings," she said breezily. "We'd better get to the rail. I don't want to miss the start. Have you seen my family?"

"No. They're around. The lot of you's everywhere." Because she was moving through the crowd, he grabbed her hand. He could imagine her being trampled. "I don't know why you don't go up into the bar where you can watch in civilized surroundings."

"Snob."

"It's not a matter of—" He gave up. "I want you to tear up those papers."

"No. Look they're bringing them to the gate."

"I'm not taking a half interest in your horse."

"Our horse. Who's number three? I lost my *Racing Form*."

"Prime Target, eight to five, likes to come from behind. Keeley, it's a thoughtful gesture, but—"

"It's a sensible one. Okay, here we go." She shot him a brilliant smile. "Our first race."

The bell rang.

They shot out of the gate, ten muscular bodies with men clinging fiercely to their backs. Within seconds they were merged into one speeding form with legs reaching, flying, striking. Silks of red, white, gold, green streamed by in a shock of color. And the sound was huge.

Blindly Keeley groped for Brian's hand and clung. She lost her breath, and her sense, in the sheer thrill.

Clouds of dust spewed from the dry track, jockeys slanted forward like dolls, and the pack began to break apart at the second turn.

"He's holding onto fourth," Keeley shouted. "He's holding on."

The lead horse edged forward. A head, a half a length. Finnegan bulled up the line, nipping the distance, vying for third. Keeley heard the crowd around her, the solid roar of it, but her heart pounded to the rhythm of hoofbeats.

Those legs stretched, reached, lifted.

"He's gaining." She began to laugh, even as her hand clamped on Brian's, she laughed. From the joy bursting inside her, she might have been riding low on the gelding's back herself. "He's gaining. He's moving up, into second. Would you look at him?"

He was looking, and the grin on his face was wide. "I didn't give him enough credit for guts. Not nearly enough credit. He'll move on the backstretch. If he's still got it in him, he'll move."

And he moved, a big, unhandsome horse at twenty to one odds with a washed-up jockey in the irons. He moved like a bullet, streaking down the dirt, charging the leader, running neck-in-neck with the favorite while the crowd screamed.

Seconds before the finish line, he pulled ahead by a nose.

"He won." Keeley whirled to Brian. She wondered if the shock on his face mirrored her own. "My God, Brian, he won!"

"Two miracles in one day." He let out a short, baffled laugh, then another, longer. Riding on the thrill, he plucked Keeley off her feet and spun her in circles.

"I never expected it." She threw her arms in the air, then wrapped them around his neck and kissed him. "I never expected him to win."

"You bet on him."

"That was for love, not for reality. I never thought he'd win."

"He did." Brian gave her a last spin before setting her on her feet. "That's what counts."

"We're going to celebrate. Big time."

While Betty's win had left him shaken to the soul by that heady taste of destiny, this was sheer, stupefied delight. He snatched Keeley again and spun her into a quick waltz through the crowd.

"I'll buy you a bottle of champagne."

"Two," she corrected. "One for each of us. We have to get down to the winner's circle."

"You have to. I don't go to winner's circles."

He might behave like a mule, she mused, but he was a man. And she knew which button to push. "You don't have to go for me, or even for yourself. But you have to go for him." She held out a hand.

He wanted to swear but figured it a waste of breath. "I'll go, as his trainer. He's your horse. I don't own any part of him."

"Half," she corrected, trotting to keep up as Brian tugged her along. "But we can discuss which half."

Chapter 12

"Of course I'm seeing to him." Keeley bent to unwrap Finnegan's right foreleg.

"You should be up celebrating."

"This is part of it." She ran her hands carefully up the gelding's leg before pinning the wrapping to the line. "Finnegan and I are going to congratulate each other while I clean him up. But you could do me a favor." She pulled her ticket out of her pocket. "Cash in my winnings."

Brian shook his head. "At the moment I'm too pleased to be annoyed with you for betting my money." With one hand on the horse he leaned over to kiss her. "But I'm not taking half the horse."

Keeley hooked an arm around Finnegan's neck. "You hear that? He doesn't want you."

"Don't say things like that to him."

She laid her cheek against the gelding's. "You're the one hurting his feelings."

As two pairs of eyes studied him, Brian hissed out a breath. "We'll discuss this privately at some other time."

"He needs you. We both do."

The muscles in his belly twisted. "That's unfair."

"That's fact."

He looked so uncomfortable, she sighed. She wanted to throw up her hands, give the man a good thump. But it wasn't the time to rage or demand he take a good look at a woman who loved him.

"We will talk about it." They were going to talk about a great many things, she decided. Very soon. "But for now, we'll just be happy."

He hesitated while she went back to unwrapping Finnegan's legs. "I've been happier in the last few months than I've ever been."

"That doesn't have to change." She finished hanging the wrappings, picked up a dandy brush. "We're a good team, Brian. There's a lot we could do together."

Brian ran a hand down Finnegan's throat. "We've made quite a start here. Would you want to go out after a bit and have some fancy dinner and wine?"

Keeley slanted him a look. "Are you finally asking me for a date?"

"It seems appropriate under the circumstances." Grinning he fingered the betting ticket. "And it seems I've come in to some extra cash."

"Then I'd love to."

"I've got to go check on Betty, make sure she's transported back to the farm."

"If you run into any of my family, tell them where I am, will you?"

"I will. He's had his moment in the sun, hasn't he?" Brian murmured.

Keeley set the brush down, crossing over as Brian opened the stall door. "You've had quite a day, Donnelly."

"I have. I don't know when there's been another like it."

She put her arms around him, resting her head on his shoulder. "There'll be more." *For all of us.* She tipped back her head. "We'll make more," she promised as she raised her mouth to his.

He could have lost himself in her. It was so easy when he was holding her to slip away from the moment and into the dream.

"You're neglecting your horse." He rested his cheek against hers, closed his eyes. "I'll come back for you."

"I'll be waiting."

But he didn't move, only stood with her gathered

close while the love inside him pulsed like light. Then he drew back, taking both of her hands and bringing them to his lips. "Don't forget to give him apples. He's fond of them."

"Yes, I know." It felt as though her heart were shaking. "Brian—"

"I'll be back," he said and strode away before the words rising into his throat could be spoken.

"Something's changed," Keeley whispered. "I felt it." She pressed her hands, still warm from his, to her heart. "Oh, it's been a hell of a day. And it's not over yet." She swung back into the stall where Finnegan stood, watching her patiently. "He loves me. He just can't get his tongue around the words yet, but he loves me. I know it."

She picked up the dandy brush again. "We're going to cross another finish line before the day's over. I've got to make myself beautiful. We'll have candlelight and wine, and…"

She trailed off as she heard the stall door open again. Thinking it was Brian come back, she turned. Her brilliant smile faded into ice when she saw Tarmack.

"You think you pulled a fast one, don't you?"

"You're not welcome here."

"Snatched this horse out from under me. No better than a horse thief. Figure you can get away with it 'cause you're a Grant."

"You were paid your asking price." She spoke coolly. She caught the stink of too much whiskey on his breath. And so, she thought, did Finnegan. The horse was beginning to quiver. Calmly, she hooked her hand in his bridle. "If you have a complaint, take it up with the Racing Commission."

"So your father can pay them off?"

Her head came up. Her eyes went from ice to fire. "Be careful what you say about my father."

"I'll say what I want to say." He moved in, his eyes glazed and mean from drinking. "Cheats, all of you, looking down on those of us just trying to make a living. Stole this horse from me." He jabbed a finger into her shoulder. "Said he wasn't fit to run."

"And he wasn't." She wasn't afraid. There were people around, she thought quickly. She had only to call out. But a Grant didn't cry for help at the first tussle. She could deal with a drunk and pitiful bully.

"Fit to run for you, though. To run and win. That purse is mine by rights."

It was only the money, she thought. Just as Brian said, with some, it was all facts and figures, and no feeling. "You've got all the money out of me you'll get." She turned away to brush the gelding. "Now I suggest you leave before I file a complaint."

"Don't you turn your back on me, you little bitch."

It was shock as much as pain that had Keeley gasping when he grabbed her arm and dragged her around.

When she tried to jerk free, the sleeve of her shirt tore at the shoulder. Beside her, Finnegan whinnied nervously and shied.

"You look at me when I talk to you. You think you're better than me." He shoved her back against the gelding's side, then yanked her forward again. "You think you're special 'cause your daddy's rolling in money."

"I think," Keeley said with deceptive calm, "that you'd better take your hands off me." She reached in her pocket, closed her fingers, and they were rock steady, around a hoof pick.

It happened fast, a blur of motion and sound. Even as she tugged the makeshift defense free, Finnegan whipped his head and bit Tarmack's shoulder. For the second time Tarmack rapped her hard against the solid wall of the gelding's side, and as he drew back his fist she shouted, leaping to block it from connecting with Finnegan's head.

It skidded over her temple instead, sending a shocking ribbon of pain across her skull, and a haze of pale red over her vision. As she staggered, stumbling around to defend herself and her horse, Brian came through the doors like a vengeful god.

Instinctively Keeley grabbed Finnegan's bridle, to calm him, to balance herself. "It's all right. It's all right now."

But hearing the unmistakable sound of fists against flesh and bone, she ran out.

"Brian, don't!"

His face was blank, a mask without emotion. It seemed all sharp bones and cold eyes. He had Tarmack braced against the wall with a hand over the man's throat, an arm cocked back to deliver another blow. Tarmack's mouth and nose were already bleeding. Keeley grabbed Brian's arm, and hung on like a burr. It felt like gripping hot iron.

"That's enough. It's all right."

Without even a glance, so much as a flicker of acknowledgment, Brian shook her off, rammed a ready fist into Tarmack's gut. "He put his hands on you."

"Stop it." Panting, she grabbed his arm again, and wrapped both hers around it. "He didn't hurt me. Let him go, Brian." She could hear Tarmack struggling for air through the hand Brian had banded around his windpipe. "I'm not hurt."

Very slowly, Brian turned his head. When his eyes, flat and cold with violence met hers, she trembled. "He put his hands on you," he said again, carefully enunciating each word. "Now step back."

"No." She could hear the shouts behind her, see out of the corner of her eye the crowd already forming. And she could smell the blood. "It's enough. Just let him go."

"It's not enough." He started to shake her off again, and Keeley had an image of herself flying free as he flicked her off like a gnat.

She hadn't feared Tarmack, but she was afraid now. "What's the problem here?"

She could have wept with relief at the sound of her father's voice. The crowd parted for him. She'd never known one not to. He took one long look at her face, skimmed his gaze over the torn sleeve, and though the hand he laid on her shoulder was gentle, she'd seen the edge come into his eyes.

"Move back, Keeley," he said in a voice of quiet steel.

"Dad." She shook her head, twined around Brian's arm like a vine. "Tell Brian to let him go now. He won't listen to me."

Brian rapped the gasping Tarmack's head against the wall, a kind of absent violence as he once again spoke with rigid patience. "He put his hands on her."

The edge in Travis's eyes went keen, sharp as silver. "Did he touch you?"

"Dad, for God's sake." She lowered her voice. "He'll kill him in a minute."

"Let him go, Brian." Adelia hurried up, took in the situation in one glance. Gently she touched a hand to Brian's shoulder. "You've dealt with him. There's a lad. You're frightening Keeley now."

"Her shirt's torn. Do you see her shirt's torn?" He continued to speak slowly, as if in a foreign tongue. "Take her out of here."

"I will, I will. But let that pathetic man go now. He's not worth it."

Perhaps it was the voice, the lilt of his own country that broke quietly through the rage. Brian loosened his grip and Tarmack wheezed in air.

"He had her trapped in the stall. Trapped, you see, and his hands were on her."

Adelia nodded. Her gaze shifted briefly to her husband's. A lifetime ago he'd dealt with a drunk who'd had her trapped. She understood the barely reined violence in Brian's eyes. "She's all right now. You saw to that."

"I'm not finished." He said it so calmly, Adelia could only blink when his fist flashed out again and had Tarmack sagging to his knees.

"Stop it." Seeing no other way, Keeley stepped between the two men and shoved Brian with both hands. She didn't move him an inch, but the gesture made a point. "That's enough. It's just a torn shirt. He's drunk, and he was stupid. Now that's enough, Brian."

"You're wrong. It won't ever be enough. You've tender skin, Keeley, and he'll have marked it, so it won't ever be enough."

Tarmack was on his hands and knees, retching. In an almost absent move, Travis dragged him to his feet. "I suggest you apologize to my daughter and then be on your way, or I might let this boy loose on you again."

His stomach was jellied with pain, and he could taste his own blood in his mouth. Humiliation struck nearly as hard as he saw the blur of faces watching. "You can go to hell. You and all the rest. I'm bringing charges."

"Go ahead." Travis bared his teeth in a killing smile. "You're drunk and you're stupid, just as my daughter said. And you touched her."

"He was shouting at her, Mr. Grant." Larry elbowed his way through the crowd. "I heard him threatening her when I was coming in to see the horse."

Travis blocked Brian's move forward, felt Brian's muscle quiver under his hand. "Hold on," he said quietly, and turned his attention back to Tarmack. "You stay away from what's mine, Tarmack. If you ever lay hands on my girl again, what Brian can do to you will be nothing against what I will do."

Emboldened as he assumed Brian was now on a leash, Tarmack swiped blood from his face with the back of his fist. "So what if I touched her? Just getting her attention was all. She's not so particular who has his hands on her. She wasn't minding when this two-bit mick was pawing her."

Brian surged forward, but Travis was closer, and nearly as quick. His fist cracked, one short-armed hammer blow, against Tarmack's jaw. The man's eyes rolled back as he collapsed.

"Dee, take Keeley home, will you?" Travis glanced

at the crowd, one brow lifted as if he dared for comments. "Would someone call security?"

"We shouldn't have left." Keeley paced the kitchen, stopping at the windows on each pass. Why weren't they back?

"Darling, you're shaking. Come on now, sit and drink your tea."

"I can't. What's wrong with men? They'd have beaten that idiot to a pulp. I'm not that surprised at Brian, I suppose, but I expected more restraint from Dad."

Genuinely surprised, Adelia glanced over. "Why?"

As worry ate through her she raked her hands through her hair. "He's contained. Now you, I could see you taking a few swings…" She winced. "No offense," she said, then saw that her mother was grinning.

"None taken. My temper might be a bit, we'll say, more colorful than your father's. His tends to be cold and deliberate when it's called for. And it was. The man hurt and frightened his little girl."

"His little girl was about to attempt to gut the man with a hoof pick." Keeley blew out a breath. "I've never seen Dad hit anyone, or look like he wanted to keep right on with it."

"He doesn't use his fists overmuch because he doesn't have to. He'll be upset about this, Keeley."

Adelia hesitated, then gestured her daughter to a chair. "Sit a minute. Years ago," she began, "shortly after I came to work here, I was down at the stables at night. One of the grooms had been drinking. He had me down in one of the stalls. I couldn't fight him off."

"Oh, Mama."

"He was starting to tear at my clothes when your father came in. I thought he would beat the man to death. He didn't even raise a sweat about it, just laid in with his fists, systematic like, in a cold kind of rage that was more terrifying than the fire. That's what I saw in Brian's face today." Gently she touched the faint bruise on Keeley's temple. "And I can't blame him for it."

"I don't blame him." She gripped her mother's hands. "This today, this wasn't like that. Tarmack was mad over the horse, and wanted to bully me."

"Threats are threats. If I'd gotten there first, likely I'd have waded in myself. Don't fret so, darling."

"I'm trying not to." She picked up her tea, set it down again. "Ma, what Tarmack said about Brian. About him pawing me. It wasn't like that. It's not like that between us."

"I know that. You're in love with him."

"Yes." It was lovely to say it. "And he loves me. He just hasn't gotten around to saying so yet. Now I'm worried that Dad… Tempers are up, and if he takes what that bastard said the wrong way." She pushed away from the table again. "Why aren't they back?"

She paced another ten minutes, then finally took some aspirin for the headache that snarled in both temples. She drank a cup of tea and told herself she was calm again.

And was up like a shot the minute she heard wheels on gravel. She got to the door in time to see Brian's truck drive by, and her father's pull in behind the house.

"I missed all the excitement." Though his voice was light, Brendon's eyes carried that same glint of temper she'd seen in their father's. "You okay?"

"I'm fine." Though she patted his arm, her gaze was fixed on her father. She could read nothing in his face as he climbed out of the truck. "I'm absolutely fine," she said again, stepping toward him.

"I'd like you to come inside."

Contained, she thought again. It was impressive, and not a little scary, to see all that rage and fury so tightly contained. "I will. I have to see Brian." Her eyes pleaded with his for understanding. "I have to talk to him. I'll be back."

With one quick squeeze of her hand on his arm, she dashed off.

"Let her go, Travis," Adelia said from the doorway. "She needs to deal with this."

Eyes narrowed, he watched his daughter run to an-other man. "She's got five minutes."

Keeley caught up with Brian before he climbed the steps to his quarters. She called out, increased her pace. "Wait. I was so worried." She would have leaped straight into his arms, but he stepped back. And his face was glacier cold. "What happened?"

"Nothing. Your father dealt with it. The man won't be bothering you again."

"I'm not worried about that," she said shortly. "Are you all right? I started to think you might be in trou-ble. I should have stayed and given a statement. Ev-erything got so confused."

"There's no trouble, and nothing to be worried about."

"Good. Brian, I wanted to say that I… Oh, God! Your hands." She snatched them, the tears swimming up as she saw his torn knuckles. "Oh, I'm so sorry. Your poor hands. Let's go up. I'll take care of them."

"I can take care of myself."

"They need to be cleaned and—"

"I don't want you hovering."

He yanked his hands free, then cursed when he saw her cheeks go pale with shock, and the first tear slid down. "Damn it, swallow those back. I'm not in the mood to deal with tears on top of everything else."

"Why are you slapping at me this way?"

Guilt and misery rolled through him. "I've things

to do." He turned away, started up the stairs. And fury caught up with guilt and misery. "You didn't want me standing up for you." He spun back, his eyes brilliant with temper.

"What are you talking about?"

"I'm good enough for a roll on the sheets or to help with the horses. But not to stand up for you."

"That's absurd." The tears came fast now as reaction from the last few hours set in. "Was I just supposed to stand by and watch while you beat him half to death?"

"Yes." He snapped, gripped her shoulders, shook. "It was for me to see to. You took that from me, and in the end, handed it to your father. It was for me, two-bit mick or not."

"What's going on here?" For the second time that day, Travis walked in on tempers and shouts, Adelia by his side. And this time, he saw his daughter's tear-streaked face. His eyes shot hotly to Brian. "What the hell is going on here?"

"I'm not sure." Keeley blinked at tears as Brian released her. "This idiot here seems to think I share Tarmack's opinion of him because I didn't stand back and let him beat the man to pieces. Apparently by objecting I've tread on his pride." She looked wearily at her mother. "I'm tired."

"Go up to the house," Travis ordered. "I want to speak with Brian."

"I refuse to be sent away like a child again. This is my business. Mine, and—"

"You don't speak in that tone to your father." Brian's sharp order brought varying reactions. Keeley gaped, Travis frowned thoughtfully and Adelia fought back a grin.

"Excuse me, but I'm very tired of being interrupted and ordered around and spoken to like a recalcitrant eight-year-old."

"Then don't behave like one," Brian suggested. "My family might not be fancy, but we were taught respect."

"I don't see what—"

"Be quiet."

The command left her stunned and speechless.

"I apologize for causing yet another scene," he said to Travis. "I'm not altogether settled yet. I didn't thank you for smoothing out whatever trouble there might have been with security."

"There were enough people who saw most of what happened. There'd have been no trouble. Not for you."

"A minute ago you were angry because my father smoothed things out."

Brian spared her a glance. "I'm just angry altogether."

"Oh, that's right." Since violence seemed to be the mood of the day, she gave in to it and stabbed a finger into his shoulder. "You're just angry period. He's got some twisted idea that I don't think he's good enough to defend me against a drunk bully. Well, I have news for you, you hardheaded Irish horse's ass."

Now that her own temper was fired, she curled her hand into a fist and used it to thump his chest. "I was defending myself just fine."

"You half Irish, stiff-necked birdbrain, he's twice your size and then some."

"I was handling it, but I appreciate your help."

"The hell you do. It's just like with everything else. You've got to do it all yourself. No one's as smart as you, or as clever, or as capable. Oh it's fine to give me a whistle if you need a diversion."

"Is that what you think?" She was so livid her voice was barely a croak. "That I make love with you for a diversion? You vile, insulting, disgusting son of a bitch."

She raised her own fists, and might have used them, but Travis stepped in and gripped Brian by the shirt. His voice was quiet, almost matter-of-fact. "I ought to take you apart."

"Oh, Travis." Adelia merely pressed her fingers to her eyes.

"Dad, don't you dare." At wit's end, Keeley threw up her hands. "I've got an idea. Why don't we all just beat each other senseless today and be done with it?"

"You've a right." Brian kept his eyes on Travis's and kept hands at his sides.

"The hell he does. I'm a grown woman. A grown

woman," she repeated rapping a fist lightly on her
father's arm. "And I threw myself at him."

She gained some perverse satisfaction when her
father turned that frigid stare on her. "That's right. I
threw myself at him. I wanted him, I went to him, and
I seduced him. Now what? Am I grounded?"

"It doesn't matter how it happened. I was experienced, and she wasn't. I'd no right to touch her, and I
knew it. In your place I'd be doing some pounding of
my own."

"No one's doing any pounding." Adelia moved forward, laid a hand on Travis's arm. "Darling, are you
blind? Can't you see what's between them? Now let
the boy go. You know damn well he'll stand there
and let you pummel him, and you'd get no satisfaction from it."

No, Travis wasn't blind. Looking in Brian's eyes
he saw his life shift. His baby, his little girl, had
become someone else's woman. The someone else,
he noted, looked about as miserable and baffled by
the whole business as he felt himself. "What do you
intend to do?"

"I can be gone within the hour."

Amusement was bittersweet. "Can you?"

"Yes, sir." For the first time he knew he'd never
pack all he needed, all he wanted into his bag. "Reiv-
ers is capable enough to hold you until you find another
trainer."

Stubborn Irish pride, Travis thought. Well, he'd had a lifetime of experience on how to handle it. "I'll let you know when you're fired, Donnelly. Dee, we still have that shotgun up at the house, don't we?"

"Oh aye," she said without missing a beat. And wondered if she'd ever been more proud of the man she'd married, or had ever loved him more. "I believe I could lay my hands on it."

Yes, amusement was bittersweet, Travis thought as he watched every ounce of color drain from Brian's face. "Good to know. It's always pleased me that my children recognize and appreciate quality." He released Brian, turned to Keeley. "We'll talk later."

Tears were threatening again as she watched her parents walk off, saw her father reach for her mother's hand, forge that link that had always held strong.

"I've competed for a lot of things," she said quietly. "Worked for a lot of things, wanted a lot of things. But underneath it all, what they have has always been the goal." She turned as Brian walked unsteadily to the steps and sat down. "He won't shoot you, Brian, if you decide you still need to run."

It wasn't the shotgun that worried him, but the implication of it. "I think the lot of you are confused. It's been an emotional day."

"Yes, it has."

"I know who I am, Keeley. The second son of not-quite middle-class parents who are one generation out of poverty. My father liked the drink and the horses a bit too much, and my mother was dead-tired most of the time. We got by is all, then got on. I know what I am," he continued. "I'm a damn good trainer of racehorses. I've never stayed in one job, in one spot, more than three years. If you do, it might take hold of you. I never wanted to find myself fenced in."

"And I'm fencing you in."

He looked up then with eyes both weary and wary. "You could. Then where would you be?"

"Talk about birdbrains." She sighed then walked over to him. "I know who I am, Brian. I'm the oldest daughter of beautiful parents. I've been privileged, brought up in a home full of love. I've had advantages."

She lifted a hand when he said nothing, and brushed at the hair that tumbled over his forehead. "I know what I am. I'm a damn good riding teacher, and I'm rooted here. I can make a difference here, have been making one. But I realize I don't want to do it alone. I want to fence you in, Brian," she murmured, framing his face with her hands. "I've been hammering at that damn fence for weeks. Ever since I realized I was in love with you."

His hands came to her wrists, squeezed reflexively, before he got quickly to his feet. "You're mixing things up." Panic arrowed straight into his heart. "I told you sex complicates things."

"Yes, you did. And of course since you're the only

man I've been with, how would I know the difference between sex and love? Then again, that doesn't take into account that I'm a smart and self-aware woman, and I know the reason you're the only man I've been with is that you're the only man I've loved. Brian…"

She stepped toward him, humor flashing into her eyes when he stepped back. "I've made up my mind. You know how stubborn I am."

"I train your father's horses."

"So what? My mother groomed them."

"That's a different matter."

"Why? Oh, because she's a woman. How foolish of me not to realize we can't possibly love each other, build a life with each other. Now if you owned Royal Meadows and I worked here, then it would be all right."

"Stop making me sound ridiculous."

"I can't." She spread her hands. "You are ridiculous. I love you anyway. Really, I tried to approach it sensibly. I like doing things in a structured order that makes a beeline for the goal. But…" She shrugged, smiled. "It just doesn't want to work that way with you. I look at you and my heart, well, it just insists on taking over. I love you so much, Brian. Can't you tell me? Can't you look at me and tell me?"

He skimmed his fingertips over the bruise high on her temple. He wanted to tend to it, to her. "If I did there'd be no going back."

"Coward." She watched the heat flash into his eyes, and thought how lovely it was to know him so well.

"You won't push me into a corner."

Now she laughed. "Watch me," she invited and proceeded to back him up against the steps. "I've figured a lot of things out today, Brian. You're scared of me—of what you feel for me. You were the one always pulling back when we were in public, shifting aside when I'd reach for you. It hurt me."

The idea quite simply appalled him. "I never meant to hurt you."

"No, you couldn't. How could I help but fall for you? A hard head and a soft heart. It's irresistible. Still, it did hurt. But I thought it was just the snob in you. I didn't realize it was nerves."

"I'm not a snob, or a coward."

"Put your arms around me. Kiss me. Tell me."

"Damn it." He grabbed her shoulders, then simply held on, unable to push her back or draw her in. "It was the first time I saw you, the first instant. You walked in the room and my heart stopped. Like it had been struck by lightning. I was fine until you walked into the room."

Her knees wanted to buckle. Hard head, soft heart, and here, suddenly, a staggering sweep of romance. "Why didn't you tell me? Why did you make me wait?"

"I thought I'd get over it."

"Get over it?" Her brow arched up. "Like a head cold?"

"Maybe." He set her aside, paced away to stare out at the hills.

Keeley closed her eyes, let the breeze ruffle her hair, cool her cheeks. When the calm descended, she opened her eyes and smiled. "A good strong head cold's tough to shake off."

"You're telling me. I never wanted to own things," he began with his back still to her. "It was a matter of principle. But when a man decides to settle, things change."

Things change, he thought again. Maybe she had the right of it, and he'd been running for a long time. But in running, hadn't he ended up where he'd been meant to be in the end?

Destiny. He was too Irish not to embrace it when it kept slugging him between the eyes. "I've money put by. Considerable as I've never spent much. There's enough to build a house, or start one anyway. You'd want one close by—for your school, for your family."

She had to close her eyes again. Tears would only fluster him. "Those are the kind of details I usually appreciate, but they just aren't the priority right now. Will you just tell me, Brian. I need you to tell me you love me."

"I'm getting to it." He turned back. "I never thought

I wanted family. I want to make children with you, Keeley. I want ours. Please don't cry."

"I'm trying not to. Hurry up."

"I can't be rushed at such a time. Sniffle those back or I'll blunder it. That's the way." He moved to her. "I don't want to own horses, but I can make an exception for the gift you gave me today. As a kind of symbol of things. I didn't have faith in him, not pure faith, that he'd run to win. I didn't have faith in you, either. Give me your hand."

She held it out, clasping his. "Tell me."

"I've never said the words to another woman. You'll be my first, and you'll be my last. I loved you from the first instant, in a kind of blinding flash. Over time the love I have for you has strengthened, and deepened until it's like something alive inside me."

"That's everything I needed to hear." She brought his hand to her cheek. "Marry me, Brian."

"Bloody hell. Will you let me do the asking?"

She had to bite her lip to hold off the watery chuckle. "Sorry."

With a laugh, he plucked her off her feet. "Well, what the hell. Sure I'll marry you."

"Right away."

"Right away." He brushed his lips over her temple. "I love you, Keeley, and since you're birdbrain enough to want to marry a hardheaded Irish horse's ass, I believe it was, I'll go up now and ask your father."

"Ask my—Brian, really."

"I'll do this proper. But maybe I'll take you with me, in case he's found that shotgun."

She laughed, rubbed her cheek against his. "I'll protect you."

He set her on her feet. They began to walk together past the sharply colored fall flowers, the white fences and fields where horses raced their shadows.

When he reached to take her hand, Keeley gripped his firmly. And had everything.

* * * * *

SULLIVAN'S WOMAN

For Don,
the most Irish of my brothers.

Chapter 1

Cassidy waited. Mrs. Sommerson tossed a third rejected dress into her arms.

"Simply won't do," the woman muttered and scowled at a midnight-blue linen. After a moment's consideration this, too, was dumped into the pile over Cassidy's arms. Valiantly Cassidy held on to her patience.

After three months as a sales clerk in The Best Boutique, she felt she'd learned patience, but it hadn't been easy. Dutifully she followed the solid bulk of Mrs. Sommerson to another display of dresses. After twenty-seven minutes of standing around like a clothes rack, Cassidy thought, shifting the weight on her arms, her hard-earned patience was sorely strained.

"I'll try these," Mrs. Sommerson finally announced and marched back to the changing room. Mumbling only a little, Cassidy began to replace unsuitable dresses.

She jammed a loose hairpin into her scalp in irritation. Julia Wilson, The Best's owner, was a stickler for neatness. No hair was allowed to tumble over the shoulders of her clerks. Neat, orderly and unimaginative, Cassidy concluded, and wrinkled her nose at the midnight-blue linen. It was unfortunate that Cassidy was disorganized, imaginative, and not altogether neat. Her hair seemed to epitomize her personality. There were shades from delicate blond to rich brown melding into a tone like gold in an old painting. It was long and heavy and protested against the confines of pins by continuously slipping through them. Like Cassie herself, it was unruly and stubborn yet soft and fascinating.

It had been the appeal of Cassidy's slightly unconventional looks that had prompted her hiring. Experience had not been among her qualifications. Julia Wilson had recognized a potential advertisement for her merchandise and knew that Cassidy's long, supple body would set off the bold colors and styles of her more adventurous line. The face was undoubtedly a plus, too. Julia hadn't been certain it was a beautiful face, but she'd known it was striking. Cassidy's features were sharp and angular, undeniably aristocratic.

Her brows arched over long, lidded eyes that seemed oversized in her narrow face and were a surprising violet.

Julia had seen Cassidy's face, figure and her well-pitched voice as references but had insisted on having her pin up her hair. With it down around her shoulders, it lent a distressingly wanton quality to the aristocratic features. She was pleased with Cassidy's youth, with her intelligence and with her energy. Soon after hiring her, however, Julia had discovered she was not as pliable as her age had suggested. She had, Julia felt, an unfortunate tendency to forget her place and become overly friendly with the customers. More than once, she'd come upon Cassidy as she asked customers impertinent questions or gave unwarranted advice. From time to time her smile suggested she was enjoying some private joke. And often, far too often, she daydreamed. Julia had begun to have serious doubts about Cassidy St. John's suitability.

After returning Mrs. Sommerson's rejected choices to their proper place, Cassidy took up her post by the changing room. From inside she could hear the faint rustle of materials. Idle, her mind did what it invariably did when given the opportunity. It drifted back to the manuscript that lay spread over her desk in her apartment. Waiting.

As far back as memory took her, writing had been her dream. For four years of college she had studied

the craft seriously. At nineteen she'd been left without family and with little money. She had continued
to work her way through college in various odd jobs
while learning the discipline and art of her chosen
profession. Between her education and employment,
Cassidy had been left with meager snatches of free
time. Even these had been set aside for work on her
first novel.

To Cassidy writing was not a career but a voca-
tion. Her entire life had been guided toward it, leaving
her room for few other attachments. People fascinated
her, but there were few with whom she was deeply involved. She wrote of complex relationships, but her
knowledge of them came almost entirely secondhand.
What gave her work quality and depth were her sharp
talent for observation and her surprising depth of emotion. For the greater part of her life, her emotions had
found their release in her work.

Now, a full year after graduation, she continued
to take odd jobs to pay the rent. Her first manuscript
worked its way from publishing house to publishing
house while her second came slowly to life.

As Mrs. Sommerson opened the door of the changing room, Cassidy's mind was deep into the reworking
of a dramatic scene. Seeing her standing with proper
handmaidenly reserve, Mrs. Sommerson nodded ap-
provingly. She preened ever so slightly.

"This should do nicely. Don't you agree?"

Mrs. Sommerson's choice was a flaming-red silk. The color, Cassidy noted, accented her florid complexion but was an attractively sharp contrast to her fluffy black mane of hair. The dress might have been more appropriate if Mrs. Sommerson had been a few pounds lighter, but Cassidy saw possibilities.

"You'll draw eyes, Mrs. Sommerson," she announced after a moment's deliberation. With the proper accessories, she decided, Mrs. Sommerson might very likely look regal. The silk, however, strained over her ample hips. A sterner girdle, Cassidy diagnosed, or a larger dress. "I think we have this in the next size," she murmured, thinking aloud.

"I beg your pardon?"

Preoccupied, Cassidy failed to note the dangerous arch of Mrs. Sommerson's brows. "The next size," she repeated helpfully. "This one's a bit snug through the hips. The next size up should fit you perfectly."

"This is my size, young woman." Mrs. Sommerson's bosom lifted then fell. It was an awe-inspiring movement.

Deep into solving the accessory problem, Cassidy smiled and nodded. "A splashy gold necklace, I should think." She tapped her fingertip against her bottom lip. "Just let me find your size."

"This," Mrs. Sommerson stated in a tone that arrested Cassidy's full attention, "*is* my size." Indignation seethed in every syllable. Recognizing her mistake, Cassidy felt a sinking sensation in her stomach.

Whoops, she said silently then pulled her scattered wits together. Before she could begin soothing Mrs. Sommerson's ruffled ego, Julia stepped from behind her.

"A stunning choice, Mrs. Sommerson," she stated in her well-modulated contralto. With a noncommittal smile, she glanced from her customer to her clerk then back again. "Is there a problem?"

"This young woman…" Mrs. Sommerson heaved another deep breath. "Insists I've made a mistake in my size."

"Oh, no, ma'am," Cassidy protested, but subsided when Julia arched a penciled brow in her direction.

"I'm certain what Miss St. John meant to say was that this particular style is cut a bit oddly. The sizes simply do not run true."

I should've thought of that, Cassidy admitted to herself.

"Well." Mrs. Sommerson sniffed and eyed Cassidy with disapproval. "She might have said so, rather than suggesting that *I* was a larger size. Really, Julia." She turned back to the changing room. "You should train your staff better."

Cassidy's eyes kindled and grew dark at the tone. She watched the seams of the red silk protest against

Mrs. Sommerson's generous posterior. The quick glare from Julia had her swallowing retorts.

"I'll fetch the dress myself, Mrs. Sommerson," Julia soothed, slipping her personable smile back into place. "I'm certain it will be perfect for you. Wait for me in my office, Cassidy," she added in an undertone before gliding off.

With a sinking heart, Cassidy watched Julia's retreat. She recognized the tone all too well. Three months, she mused, then sighed. Oh, well. With one backward glance at Mrs. Sommerson, she moved down the narrow hallway and into Julia's small, smartly decorated office.

She surveyed the square, windowless room, then chose a tiny, straight-backed, bronze cushioned chair. It was here, she remembered, I was hired. And it's here I'll be fired. She jammed another rebellious pin into place and scowled. In a few minutes she'll walk in, lift her left brow and sit behind her perfectly beautiful rosewood desk. She'll look at me a moment, gently clear her throat and begin.

"Cassidy, you're a lovely girl, but your heart isn't in your work."

"Mrs. Wilson," Cassidy imagined herself saying, "Mrs. Sommerson can't wear a size fourteen. I was—"

"Of course not." Cassidy pictured Julia interrupting her with a patient smile. "I wouldn't dream of selling her one, but—" here Cassidy envisioned Julia lifting up one slender, rose-tipped finger for emphasis "—we must allow her illusions *and* her vanity. Tact and diplomacy are essential for a salesperson, Cassidy. I'm afraid you've yet to fully develop these qualities. In a shop such as this—" Julia would fold her hand on the desk's surface "—I must be able to depend, without reservation, on my staff. If this were the first incident, of course, I'd make allowances, but…" Here Cassidy imagined Julia would pause and give a small sigh. "Just last week you told Miss Teasdale the black crepe made her look like a mourner. This is not the way we sell our merchandise."

"No, Mrs. Wilson." Cassidy decided she would agree with an apologetic air. "But with Miss Teasdale's hair and her complexion—"

"Tact and diplomacy," Julia would reiterate with a lifted finger. "You might have suggested that a royal-blue would match her eyes or that a rose would set off her skin. The clientele must be pampered while the merchandise moves. Each woman who walks out the door should feel she has acquired something special."

"I understand that, Mrs. Wilson. I hate to see someone buy something unsuitable; that's why—"

"You have a good heart, Cassidy." Julia would smile maternally then drop the ax. "You simply have no talent for selling…at least, not the degree of talent I require. I shall, of course, pay you for the rest of the week and give you a good reference. You've been prompt and dependable. Perhaps you might try clerking in a department store."

Cassidy wrinkled her nose at this point in her scenario, then quickly smoothed her features as the door behind her opened. Julia closed it quietly then lifted her left brow and moved to sit behind her rosewood desk. She studied Cassidy a moment then gently cleared her throat.

"Cassidy, you're a lovely girl, but…"

Cassidy's shoulders lifted and fell with her sigh.

An hour later, unemployed, she wandered Fisherman's Wharf, enjoying its cheerful shabbiness, its traveling carnival atmosphere. She loved the cornucopia of scents and sound and color. Here there was always a crowd. Here there was life in ever-changing flavors. San Francisco was Cassidy's concept of a perfect city, but Fisherman's Wharf was the end of the rainbow. Make-believe and reality walked hand in hand.

She passed through the emporiums, poking idly through barrels of trinkets, fingering newly imported silk scarfs and soaking up the noise. But the bay drew her. She moved toward it at an easy, meandering pace as the afternoon gave way to evening. The scent of fish dominated the air. Beneath it were the aromas of onions and spice and humanity.

She listened to the vendors hawk their wares and watched as a crab was selected and boiled in a sidewalk cauldron. The wharf was rimmed with restaurants and crammed with stores. Without apology, its ambience was vaguely dilapidated and faintly tawdry. Cassidy adored it. It was old and friendly and content to be itself.

Nibbling on a hot pretzel, she moved through stalls of hanging Chinese turnips, fresh abalone and live crabs. Wisps of fog began to curl at her feet, and the sun sank lower. She was grateful for her plum-colored quilted jacket as the breeze swept in from the bay.

If nothing else, she thought ruefully, I acquired some nice clothes at a tidy discount. Cassidy frowned and took a generous bite of her pretzel. If it hadn't been for Mrs. Sommerson's hips, I'd still have a job. After all, I did have her best interests at heart. Annoyed, she pulled the pins from her hair then tossed them into a trash can as she passed. Her hair tumbled to her shoulders in long, loose curls. She breathed a sigh of relief.

Rats. She chewed her pretzel aggressively and headed for the watery front yard of Fisherman's Wharf. I needed that job. I really needed that stupid job. Depression threatened as she walked the dock between lines of moored boats. She began a mental accounting of her finances. The rent was due the following week, and she needed another ream of typing paper. According to her shaky calculations, both of these necessities could be met if she didn't put too much emphasis on food for the next few days.

I won't be the first writer to have to tighten her belt

in San Francisco, she decided. The four basic food groups are probably overrated anyway. With a shrug she finished off the pretzel. That could be my last full meal for some time. Grinning, she stuck her hands in her pockets and strolled to the rail at the edge of the dock.

Like a gray ghost, the fog rolled in over the bay. It crept closer to land, swallowing up the water along the way. It was thin tonight, full of patches, not the thick mass that often coated the bay and blinded the city. To the west the sun dipped into the sea and shot spears of flame over the rim of the water. Cassidy waited for the last flash of gold. Already her mood was lifting. She was a creature of hope and optimism, of faith and luck. She believed in destiny. It was, she felt, her destiny to write. The sale of articles and occasional short stories to magazines kept the dream alive. For four years of college her life had revolved around perfecting her craft. Jobs kept a roof over her head and meant nothing more. Dating had been permitted only when her schedule allowed and was kept casual. As yet, Cassidy had met no man who interested her seriously enough to make her veer from the straight path she had chosen. There were no curves in her scheme of things. No detours.

The loss of her current job distressed her only temporarily. Even as the evening sky darkened and the lights of the wharf fluttered on, her mood shifted. She was young and resilient.

Something would turn up, she decided as she leaned over the rail. Wavelets slapped gently against the hull of a fishing boat beside her. She had no need for a great deal of money; any job would do. Clerking in a department store might be just right. Perhaps something in home appliances. It would be difficult to step on anyone's vanity while selling a toaster. Pleased with the thought, Cassidy pushed worries out of her head and watched the fog tumble closer. Its fingers reached toward her.

There was a chill in the air now as the breeze picked up. She let it wash over her, tossing her hair and waking up her skin. The sounds and calls from the stands became remote, muffled by the mist. It was nearly dark. She heard a bird call out as it flew overhead and lifted her face to watch it. The first thin light of the moon fell over her. She smiled, dreaming a little. Abruptly she drew in her breath as a hand gripped her shoulder. Before she could make a sound, she'd been turned around and was staring up into a stranger's face.

He was tall, several inches taller than Cassidy, with a shock of black curls around a lean, raw-boned face. Her mind worked quickly to categorize the face, rejecting handsome in favor of dangerous. Perhaps it was her surprise and the creeping fog and darkening sky that caused the adjective to leap into her mind. But she thought, as she looked up at him, that his features were more in tune with the Barbary Coast than Fisherman's Wharf. His eyes were a deep, intense blue under black, winged brows, and his forehead was high under the falling black curls. His nose was long and straight, his mouth full, and his chin faintly cleft. It was a compelling, hard-hitting face with no softening features. He had a rangy build accentuated by snug jeans and a black pullover. After her initial shock passed, Cassidy gripped her purse tight and squared her shoulders.

"I've only got ten dollars," she told him, keeping her chin fearlessly lifted. "And I need it at least as badly as you."

"Be quiet," he ordered shortly and narrowed his eyes. They were oddly intent on her face, searching, probing in a manner that made her shiver. When he cupped her chin in his hand, Cassidy's courage slipped away again. Without speaking, he turned her head from one side to the other, all the while studying her with absolute concentration. His eyes were hypnotic. She watched him, speechless, as his brows lowered in a frown. There was speculation in the look. She tried to jerk away.

"Be still, will you?" he demanded. His deep voice sounded annoyed, and his fingers were very firm.

Cassidy swallowed. "Now listen," she said with apparent calm. "I've a black belt in karate and will cer-

tainly break both your arms if you try to molest me."
As she spoke she glanced past his shoulder and was
dismayed to see the lights of the restaurants behind
them had dimmed in the fog. They were alone. "I can
break a two-by-four in half with my bare hand," she
added when his expression failed to register terror and
respect. She noted that the fingers on her chin were
strong, and that despite his rangy build his shoulders
were broad. "And I can scream very loudly," she continued. "You'd better go away."

"Perfect," he murmured and ran his thumb along her
jawline. Cassidy's heart thudded with alarm. "Absolutely perfect. Yes, you'll do." All at once the intensity
cleared from his eyes, and he smiled. The transforma-
tion was so rapid, so startling, Cassidy simply stared.
"Why would you want to do that?"

"Do what?" Cassidy asked, astonished by his meta-
morphosis.

"Break a two-by-four in half with your bare hand."

"Do *what?*" Her own bogus claim was forgotten.
Confused, she frowned at him. "Oh, well, it's—it's for
practice, I suppose. You have to think right through the
board, I believe, so that—" She stopped, realizing she
was standing on a deserted dock in the fog holding an
absurd conversation with a maniac who still had her
chin in his hand. "You'd really better let me go and be
on your way before I have to do something drastic."

"You're exactly what I've been looking for," he told

her but made no attempt to act on her suggestion. She noted there was a slight cadence to his speech that suggested an ethnic background, but she did not pause to narrow the choices.

"Well, I'm sorry. I'm not interested. I have a husband who's a linebacker for the 49ers. He's six feet five, two hundred and sixty-three pounds and *very* jealous. He'll be along any minute. Now let me go and you can have the blasted ten dollars."

"What the devil are you babbling about?" His brows lowered again. With the fog swirling thinly at his back, he looked fierce. Abruptly, one black brow flew up to disappear beneath the careless curls. "Do you think I'm going to mug you?" A flash of irritation crossed his face. "My dear child, I've no designs on your ten dollars or on your honor. I'm going to paint you, not ravish you."

"Paint me?" Cassidy was intrigued. "Are you an artist? You don't look like one." She considered his dashing, buccaneer's features. "What sort of an artist are you?"

"An excellent one," he replied easily and tilted her face a tad higher. A splash of moonlight found it. "I'm famous, talented and temperamental." The charming smile was back in his face, and the cadence was Irish. Cassidy responded to both.

"I'm desperately impressed," she said. He was obviously a lunatic but an appealing one. She forgot to be afraid.

"Of course you are," he agreed and turned her head to left profile. "It's only to be expected." He freed her chin at last, but the tingle of his fingers remained on her skin. "I've a houseboat just outside the city. We'll go there and I can start sketching you tonight."

Cassidy's eyes lit with wary amusement. "Aren't you supposed to offer to show me sketches, or is this a variation on an old theme?" She no longer considered him dangerous, merely persistent.

He sighed, and she watched the quick annoyance flash over his face. "The woman has a one-track mind. Listen…what is your name?"

"Cassidy," she answered automatically. "Cassidy St. John."

"Oh, no, half Irish, half English. We'll have trouble there." He stuck his hands into his pockets. His eyes seemed determined to know every inch of her face. "Cassidy, I have no need for your ten dollars, and no plans to tamper with your virtue. What I want is your face. I've a sketch pad and so forth on my houseboat."

"I wouldn't go on Michelangelo's boat if he handed me that line." Cassidy relaxed the grip on her purse and pushed her hair from her shoulders. Though he made a swift sound of exasperation, she grinned.

"All right." She sensed the impatience in his stance as he glanced behind him. "We'll get a cup of coffee in a well-lit, crowded restaurant. Will that suit you? If I try anything improper, you can break the table in half with your famous bare hand and draw attention."

Cassidy's lips trembled into a fresh grin. "I think I could agree to that." Before she could say anything else, he had her hand in his and was pulling her toward the cluster of restaurants. She felt an odd intimacy in the gesture along with a sense of his absolute control and determination. He was a man, she decided, who wouldn't take no for an answer. He walked quickly. She wondered if he were perpetually in a hurry. His stride was smooth, loose-limbed.

He pulled her into a small, rather dingy café and found a booth. The moment they were seated he again fixed her with his intent stare. His eyes, she noted, were even more blue than they had seemed in the dim light. Their color was intensified by his thick black lashes and bronze-toned skin. Cassidy met him stare for stare as she wondered what sort of man lived behind that incredible shade of blue. It was the waitress who broke her attention.

"What'll ya have?"

"Oh…coffee," she said when her companion made no move to speak or cease his staring. "Two coffees." When the waitress clomped away, Cassidy turned back to him. "Why do you stare at me like that?" she demanded. It annoyed her that her nerves responded to the look. "It's very rude," she pointed out. "And very distracting."

"The light's dreadful in here, but it's some improvement over the fog. Don't frown," he ordered. "It gives you a line right here." Before she could move he had lifted a finger and traced it down between her brows. "You have a remarkable face. I can't decide whether the eyes are an advantage or a drawback. One tends to disbelieve violet."

As Cassidy attempted to digest this, the waitress returned with their coffee. Glancing up, he plucked the pencil from her pocket and gave her one of his lightning smiles. "I need this for a few minutes. Drink your coffee. Relax," he directed with a careless gesture of his hand. "This won't hurt a bit."

Cassidy obeyed as he began to sketch on the paper placemat in front of him. "Do you have a job we'll need to work around or does your fictitious husband support you with his football prowess?"

"How do you know he's fictitious?" Cassidy countered and forced her eyes away from the planes of his face.

"The same way I know you'd have a great deal of trouble with a two-by-four." He continued to sketch. "Do you have a job?"

"I was fired this afternoon," she muttered into her coffee.

"That simplifies matters. Don't frown, I'm not a

patient man. I'll pay you the standard sitting fee." He glanced up as Cassidy's brows lifted. "What I have in mind should take no more than two months, if all goes well. Don't look so shocked, Cassidy, my intentions were pure and honorable from the beginning. It was only your lurid imagination—"

"My imagination is not that lurid," she tossed back indignantly. She shifted in her seat as she felt her cheeks warm. "When people come looming up out of the fog and seizing other people—"

"Looming?" he interrupted and stopped sketching long enough to give her a dry look. "I don't believe I did any looming or seizing tonight."

"It seemed a great deal like looming and seizing from my perspective," she grumbled before she sipped her coffee. Her eyes dropped to the sketch he made. She set down the cup, her eyes widening with surprised admiration. "That's wonderful!"

In a few bold strokes he had captured her. She saw not just the shape of her own hair, but an expression she recognized as essentially her own. "It's really wonderful," she repeated as he began another sketch. "You really *are* talented. I thought you were bragging."

"I'm unflinchingly honest," he murmured as his borrowed pencil moved across the placemat.

Recognizing the quality of his work, Cassidy became more enthusiastic. Her mind raced ahead. Steady employment for two months would be a god-

send. By the end of that time she should have heard
from the publishing house that had her manuscript
under consideration. Two months without having to
sell toasters! She would have her evenings free to
work on her new plot. The benefits began to mount
and multiply. Destiny must have sent Mrs. Sommerson in search of a dress that afternoon.

"Do you really want me to sit for you?"

"You're precisely what I need." His manner suggested that the matter was already settled. The second
sketch was nearly completed. His coffee cooled, untouched. "I want you to start in the morning. Nine
should be early enough."

"Yes, but—"

"Keep your hair down, and don't pile on layers of
makeup, you'll just have to wash it off. You might
smudge up your eyes a bit, but little else."

"I haven't said I'd—"

"You'll need the address, I suppose," he continued,
ignoring her protests. "Do you know the city well?"

"I was born here," she told him with a superior
sniff. "But I—"

"Well then, you shouldn't have any trouble finding
my studio." He scrawled an address on the bottom of
the placemat. Abruptly he lifted his eyes and captured
hers again.

They stared at each other amid the clatter of cutlery
and chatter of voices. What Cassidy felt in that brief

moment she could not define, but she knew she had never experienced it before. Then, as quickly as it had occurred, it passed. He rose, and she was left feeling as if she had run a very long race in a very short time.

"Nine o'clock," he said simply; then as an afterthought he dropped a bill on the table for the coffee. He left without another word.

Reaching over, Cassidy picked up the placemat with the sketches and the address. For a moment she studied her face as he had seen it. Was her chin really shaped that way? she wondered and lifted her thumb and finger to trace it. She remembered his hand holding it in precisely the same fashion. With a shrug she dropped her hand then carefully folded the placemat. It wouldn't do any harm to go to his studio in the morning, she decided as she slipped the paper into her purse. She could get a look at things and then make up her mind if she wanted to sit for him or not. If she had any doubts, all she had to do was say no and walk out. Cassidy remembered his careless dominance and frowned. All I have to do, she repeated to herself sternly, is to say no and walk out. With this thought she rose and strolled out of the café.

Chapter 2

The morning was brilliantly clear, with a warmth promising more before afternoon. Cassidy dressed casually, not certain what was *de rigueur* for a prospective artist's model. Jeans and a full-sleeved white blouse seemed appropriate. As instructed she had left her hair loose, and her makeup was light enough to appear nonexistent. She had yet to decide if she would sit for the strange, intriguing man she had met in the fog, but she was curious enough to keep the appointment.

With the address safely copied onto her own notepad and tucked in her purse, Cassidy grabbed a cable car that would take her downtown. The scribbled address had surprised her, as she had recognized the exclusiveness of the area. Somehow she'd expected her artist to have his studio near her own apartment in North Beach. There the atmosphere was informal and enduringly bohemian. Traditionally, clutches of writers and artists and musicians inhabited that section of the city and maintained its flavor. She wondered if perhaps he had a patron who had set him up in an expensive studio. He hadn't fit her conception of an artist. At least, she corrected herself, until she had seen his hands. They were, Cassidy recalled, perhaps the most beautiful hands she had ever seen, long and narrow with lean, tapering fingers. The bones had been close to the surface. Sensitive hands. And strong, she added, remembering the feel of his fingers on her skin.

His face remained clear in her mind, and she brooded over its image for several moments. Something about it tugged at a vague memory, but she couldn't bring her recollection into focus. It was a distinctive face, unique in its raw appeal. She thought if she were an artist, it would be a face she would be compelled to paint. There were good bones there and shadows and secrets, dominated by the terrifying blue of his eyes.

The trolley's bells clanged and snapped Cassidy out of her reverie. Stupid, she thought and lifted her face to the breeze. I didn't even get his name, and I'm obsessed with his face. He's supposed to be obsessed with mine, not the other way around. She jumped from the trolley and stepped onto the sidewalk. She scanned the street numbers looking for the address. I was right, she mused, about the quality of the neighborhood.

Still, like all of the city, it was a fascinating mixture of the exotic and the cosmopolitan, the romantic and the practical. San Francisco's dual personality was as prevalent here as it was in Chinatown or on Telegraph Hill. There remained a blending of the antique and the revolutionary. Cassidy could hear the clang of the old-fashioned trolley as she looked up at a radically new steel-and-glass skyscraper.

The day was fine and warm, and her body enjoyed it while her mind drifted back to the plot that sat on her desk at home. She brought her attention back to the present when she reached the number corresponding to the address in her purse. She stood frowning.

The Gallery. Cassidy scanned the number on the door for confirmation, and her frown deepened. She'd browsed through The Gallery only a few months before, and she remembered quite well when it had opened five years ago. Since its opening it had gained an enviable reputation as a showcase for the finest art in the country. A showing at The Gallery could make a fledgling artist's career or enhance that of a veteran. Collectors and connoisseurs were known to gather there to buy or to admire, to criticize or simply to be seen. Like much of the city it was a combination of the elegant and the unconventional. The architecture of the building was simple and unpretentious, while inside was a treasure trove of paintings and sculpture. Cassidy was also aware that one of The Gallery's biggest draws was its owner, Colin Sullivan. She searched her memory for what she had read of him, then began to put the bits and pieces into order.

An Irish immigrant, he had lived in America for more than fifteen years; his career had taken off when he had been barely twenty. Oil was his usual medium, and a unique use of shading and light his trademark. He had a reputation for impatience and brilliance. He would be just past thirty now and unmarried, though there had been several women linked romantically with him. There had been a princess once, and a prima ballerina. His paintings sold for exorbitant sums, and he rarely took commissions. He painted to please himself and painted well. As she stood in the warmth of the morning sunlight piecing together her tidbits of gossip and information, Cassidy recalled why the face of her artist had jarred a memory. She'd seen his picture in the newspaper when The Gallery had opened five years before. Colin Sullivan.

She let out a long breath then lifted her hands to either side of her head to push at her hair. Colin Sullivan wanted to paint her. He had once flatly refused to do a portrait of one of Hollywood's reigning queens, but he wanted to paint Cassidy St. John, an unemployed writer whose greatest triumph to date was a short story printed in a woman's magazine. All at once she remembered that she'd thought he'd been a mugger, that she had said absurd things to him, that she had told him with innocent audacity that his sketches were good. In annoyance and humiliation she chewed on her lip.

He might have introduced himself, she thought with a frown, instead of sneaking up behind me and grabbing me. I behaved quite naturally under the circumstances. I've nothing to be embarrassed about. Besides, she reminded herself, he told me to come. He's the one who arranged the entire thing. I'm only here to see if I want to take the job. Cassidy shifted her purse on her shoulder, wished briefly she had worn something more dignified or more exotic and moved to the front door of The Gallery. It was locked.

She pushed against the door again then concluded with a sigh that it was too early for The Gallery to be open. Perhaps there was a back entrance. He had spoken of a studio; surely it would have its own outside door. With this in mind Cassidy strolled around the side of the building and tried a side door, which refused to budge. Undaunted, she continued around the square brick building to its rear. When another door proved uncooperative, she turned her attention to a set of wooden steps leading to a second level.

Craning her neck, she squinted against the sun and

scanned the ring of windows. The glass tossed back the light. If I were an artist with a studio, she reflected, it would definitely be up there. She began to climb the L-shaped staircase. The treads were open and steep. Faced with another door at the top, she started to test the knob, hesitated and opted to knock. Loudly. She glanced back over her shoulder and discovered the ground was surprisingly far below. A tiny sound of alarm escaped her when the door swung open.

"You're late," Colin stated with a frown of impatience and took her hand, pulling her inside before she could respond. Her senses were immediately assailed with the scents of turpentine and oils. He looked no less formidable in broad daylight than he had in the murky fog. In precisely the same manner he had employed the night before, he caught her chin in his hand.

"Mr. Sullivan…" Cassidy began, flustered.

"Ssh!" He tilted her head to the left, narrowed his eyes and stared. "Yes, it's even better in decent light. Come over here, I want some proper sketches."

"Mr. Sullivan," Cassidy tried again as he yanked her across a high, airy room lined with canvases and cluttered with equipment. "I'd like to know a little more about all this before I commit myself."

"Sit here," he commanded and pushed her down on a stool. "Don't slouch," he added as he turned away.

"Mr. Sullivan! Would you please listen to me?"

"Presently," he replied as he picked up a wide pad and a pencil. "For now be quiet."

Totally at a loss, Cassidy sighed gustily and folded her hands. It would be simpler, she decided, to let him get his sketches out of his system. She allowed her eyes to wander and search the room.

It was large, barnlike, with wide windows and a skylight that pleased her enormously. The expanses of glass let in all the available sunlight. The floor was wood and bare, except for splatters of paint, and the walls were a neutral cream. Unframed canvases were stacked helter-skelter, facing the walls. Easels were propped here and there, and a large table was scattered with paints and brushes and rags and bottles. There was a couch at the far end of the room, sitting there as if added in afterthought. Three wooden chairs were placed at odd intervals as if pushed aside by an impatient hand and left wherever they landed. There were two other stools, two inside doors and a large goose-necked high-intensity lamp.

"Look out the window," Colin ordered abruptly. "I want a profile."

She obeyed. The vague annoyance she felt slipped away as she spotted a sparrow building a nest in the crook of an oak. The bird moved busily, carrying wisps of this and that in her beak. Patient and tenacious, she swooped and searched and built, then swooped again. Her wings caught the sun. Enchanted,

Cassidy watched her. A quiet smile touched her lips and warmed her eyes.

"What do you see?" Colin moved to her, and her absorption was so deep she neither jolted nor turned.

"That bird there." She pointed as the sparrow made another quick dive. "Look how determined she is to finish that nest. The whole thing built from bits of string and grass and whatever other treasures sparrows find. We need bricks and concrete and prefabricated walls, but that little bird can build a perfectly adequate home out of next to nothing, without hands, without tools, without a union representative. Marvelous, don't you think?" Cassidy turned her head and smiled. He was closer than she had imagined, his face near hers in order for him to follow her line of vision. As she turned, he shifted his eyes from the window and caught hers. She felt a sudden jolt, as if she had stood too quickly and lost her inner balance.

"You might be even more perfect than I had originally thought," Colin said. He brushed her hair behind one shoulder.

She suddenly remembered her resolve to be businesslike. "Mr. Sullivan—"

"Colin," he interrupted. He continued to arrange her hair. "Or just Sullivan, if you like."

"Colin, then," she said patiently. "I had no idea who you were last night. It didn't occur to me until I was standing outside The Gallery." She shifted, faintly disturbed that he remained standing so close. "Of course, I'm flattered that you want to paint me, but I'd like to know what's expected of me, and—"

"You're expected to hold a pose for twenty minutes without fidgeting," he began while he pushed her hair forward again then back over her other shoulder. His fingers brushed Cassidy's neck and caused her to frown. He appeared not to notice. "You're expected to follow instructions and keep quiet unless I tell you otherwise. You're expected to be on time and not to babble about leaving early so you can meet your boyfriend."

"I was on time," Cassidy retorted and tossed her head so that his arrangement of her hair flew into confusion. "You didn't tell me to come to the back, and I wandered around until I found the right door."

"Bright, too," he said dryly. "Your eyes darken dramatically when your Irish is up. Who named you Cassidy?"

"It's my mother's family name," she said shortly. She opened her mouth to speak again.

"I knew some Cassidys in Ireland," he commented as he lifted her hands to examine them.

"I don't know any of my mother's family," Cassidy murmured, disconcerted by the feel of his hands on hers. "She died when I was born."

"I see." Colin turned her palms up. "Your hands are very narrow-boned. And your father?"

"His family was from Devon. He died four years ago. I don't see what this has to do with anything."

"It has to do with everything." He lifted his eyes from her hands but kept them in his. "You get your eyes and hair from your mother's family, and your skin and bone structure from your father's. It's a face of contradictions you have, Cassidy St. John, and precisely what I need. Your hair must have a dozen varying shades and it looks as though you've just taken your head from a pillow. You're wise not to attempt to discipline it. Your eyes go just past Celtic-blue into violet and add a touch of the exotic with the shape of them. They tend to dream. But your bones are all English aristocracy. Your mouth tips the balance again, promising a passion the cool British complexion denies. Pure skin, just a hint of rose under the ivory. You haven't walked through life without having to scale a few walls, yet there's a definite aura of the ingenue around you. The painting I want to do must have certain elements. I need very specific qualities in my model. You have them." He paused and inclined his head. "Does that satisfy your curiosity?"

She was staring at him, transfixed, trying to see herself as he described. Did her heritage so heavily influence her looks? "I'm not at all certain that it does," Cassidy murmured. She sighed, then her eyes found him again. "But I'm vain enough to want Colin Sullivan to paint me and destitute enough to need the job." She smiled. "Shall I be immortal when you've finished? I've always wanted to be."

Colin laughed, and the sound was warm and free in the big room. He squeezed her hands, then surprisingly brought them to his lips. "You'll do me, Cass."

Cassidy's fumbling reply was interrupted as the studio door swung open.

"Colin, I need to—" The woman who swirled into the room halted abruptly and fixed sharp eyes on Cassidy. "Sorry," she said as her gaze drifted to their joined hands. "I didn't know you were occupied."

"No matter, Gail," Colin returned easily. "You know I lock the door when I'm working seriously. This is Cassidy St. John, who'll be sitting for me. Cassidy, Gail Kingsley, a very talented artist who manages The Gallery."

Gail Kingsley was striking. She was tall and thin as a reed with a long, triangular face set off by a spiky cap of vivid red hair. Everything about her was vital and compelling. Her eyes were piercingly green and darkly accented, her mouth was wide and slashed in uncompromising scarlet. Gold hoops poked through the spikes of vibrant hair at her ears. Her dress was flowing, without a definite line, a chaotic mix of greens washed over silk. The effect was bold and breathtaking. She moved forward, and her entire body seemed charged with nervous energy. Even her movements were quick and sharp, her eyes probing as they rested on Cassidy's face. There was something in the look that made Cassidy instantly uncomfortable. It was a purposeful intrusion while it remained completely impersonal.

"Good bones," Gail commented in a dismissing tone. "But the coloring's rather dull, don't you think?"

Cassidy spoke with annoyed directness. "We can't all be redheads."

"True enough," Colin said and, lifting a brow at Cassidy, turned to Gail. "What was it you needed? I want to get back to work."

There is a certain aura around people who have been intimate, Cassidy thought. It shows in a look, a gesture, a tone of voice. In the moment Gail's eyes left Cassidy to meet Colin's, she knew they were, or had been, lovers. Cassidy felt a vague sense of disappointment. Uncomfortable, she tried vainly to pull her hands from Colin's. She received an absentminded frown.

"It's Higgin's *Portrait of a Girl.* We've been offered five thousand, but Higgin won't accept unless you approve. I'd like to have it firmed up today."

"Who made the offer?"

"Charles Dupres."

"Tell Higgin to take it. Dupres won't haggle and he's fair. Anything else?" There was a simple dismissal in the words. Cassidy watched Gail's eyes flare.

"Nothing that can't wait. I'll go give Higgin a call."

"Fine." Colin turned back to Cassidy before Gail was halfway across the room. He was frowning at her hair as he pushed it back from her face. Over his shoulder, Cassidy watched Gail's glance dart back when she reached the door. Gail shut it firmly behind her. Colin stepped away and scanned Cassidy from head to toe.

"It won't do," he announced and scowled. "It won't do at all."

Confused by his statement, shaken by what she had recognized in Gail's eyes, Cassidy stared at him then ran her fingers through her hair. "What won't?"

"That business you have on." He made a gesture with his hand, a quick flick of the wrist, which encompassed her blouse and jeans and sandals.

Cassidy looked down and ran her palms over her hips. "You didn't specify how I should dress, and in any case I hadn't decided to sit for you." She shrugged her shoulders, annoyed with herself for feeling compelled to justify her attire. "You might have given me some details instead of scrawling down the address and bounding off."

"I want something smooth and flowing—no waist, no interruptions." He ignored Cassidy's comments. "Ivory, not white. Something long and sleek." He took her waist in his hands, which threw her into speechless shock. "You haven't any hips to speak of, and the waist of a child. I want a high neck so we won't worry about the lack of cleavage."

Blushing furiously, Cassidy slipped down from the stool and pushed him away. "It's my body, you know. I don't care for your observations on it or your—your hands on it, either. My cleavage or the lack of it has nothing to do with you."

"Don't be a child," he said briskly and set her back on the stool. "At the moment, your body only interests me artistically. If that changes, you'll know quickly enough."

"Now just a minute, Sullivan." Cassidy slipped off the stool again, tossing back her head as she prepared to put him neatly in his place.

"Spectacular." He grabbed a handful of her hair to keep her face lifted to his. "Temper becomes you, Cass, but it's not the mood I'm looking for. Another time, perhaps." The corners of his mouth lifted as his fingers moved to massage her neck. His smile settled lazily over his face, and though Cassidy suspected the calculation, it was no less effective. She was conscious of his fingers on her skin. The essential physicality of the sensation was novel and intrigued her into silence. This was something new to be explored. His voice lowered into a caress no less potent than the hand on her skin. The faint lilt of Ireland intensified. "It's an illusion I'm looking for, and a reality. A wish. Can you be a wish for me, Cass?"

In that moment, with her face inches from his, their bodies just touching, the warmth of his fingers on her skin, Cassidy felt she could be anything he asked. Nothing was impossible. This was where his power over women lay, she realized: in the quick charm, the piratical features, the light hint of an old country in his speech. Added to this was an undiluted sexuality he turned on at will and an impatience in the set of his shoulders. She knew he was aware of his power and used it shamelessly. Even this was somehow attractive. She felt herself submitting to it, drawn toward it while her emotions overshadowed her intellect. She wondered what his mouth would feel like on hers, and if the kiss would be as exciting as she imagined. Would she lose or find herself? Would she simply experience? As a defense against her own thoughts, she placed her hands on his chest and pushed herself to safety.

"You're not an easy man, are you, Colin?" Cassidy took a deep breath to steady her limbs.

"Not a bit." There was careless agreement in his answer. She defined what flicked over his face as something between annoyance and curiosity. "How old are you, Cassidy?"

"Twenty-three," she answered, meeting his eyes levelly. "Why?"

He shrugged, stuck his hands in his pockets then paced the room. "I'll need to know all there is to know about you before I'm done. What you are will creep into the portrait, and I'll have to work with it. I've got to find the blasted dress quickly—I want to start.

The time's right." There was an urgency in his movements that contrasted sharply with the man who had seduced her with his voice only moments before. Who was Colin Sullivan? Cassidy wondered. Though she knew finding out would be dangerous, she felt compelled to learn.

"I think I know one that might do," she hazarded while his mood swirled around the room. "It's more oyster than ivory, actually, but it's simple and straight with a high neck. It's also horribly expensive. It's silk, you see—"

"Where is it?" Colin demanded and stopped his pacing directly in front of her. "Never mind," he continued even as she opened her mouth to tell him. "Let's go have a look."

He had her by the hand and had passed through the back door before she could say another word. Cassidy took care to go along peacefully down the stairs, not wishing to risk a broken neck. "Which way?" he demanded as he marched her to the front of the building.

"It's just a few blocks that way," she said and pointed to the left. "But, Colin—" Before she could finish her thought, she was being piloted at full speed down the sidewalk. "Colin, I think you should know… Good grief, I should've worn my track shoes. Would you slow down?"

"You've got long legs," he told her and continued without slackening his pace. Making a brief sound of disgust, Cassidy trotted to keep up. "I think you should know the dress is in the shop I was fired from yesterday."

"A dress shop?" This appeared to interest him enough to slow him down while he glanced at her. With a gesture of absent familiarity, he tucked her hair behind her ear. "What were you doing working in a dress shop?"

Cassidy sent him a withering stare. "I was earning a living, Sullivan. Some of us are required to do so in order to eat."

"Don't be nasty, Cass," he advised mildly. "You're not a professional dress clerk."

"Which is precisely why I was fired." Amused by her own ineptitude, she grinned. "I'm also not a professional waitress, which is why I was fired from Jim's Bar and Grill. I objected to having certain parts of my anatomy pinched and dumped a bowl of coleslaw on a paying customer. I won't go into my brief career as a switchboard operator. It's a sad, pitiful story, and it's such a lovely day." She tossed back her head to smile at Colin and found him watching her.

"If you're not a professional clerk or waitress or switchboard operator, what are you, Cass?"

"A struggling writer who seems singularly inept at holding a proper job since college."

"A writer." He nodded as he looked down at her. "What do you write?"

"Unpublished novels," she told him and smiled again. "And an occasional article on the effects of perfume on the modern man. I have to keep my hand in."

"And are you any good?" Colin skirted another pedestrian without taking his eyes from Cassidy.

"I'm positively brimming with fresh, undiscovered talent." She tossed her hair behind her shoulders then pointed. "There we are, The Best Boutique. I wonder what Julia will have to say about this. She'll probably think you're keeping me." She bit her lip to suppress a giggle then slid her glance back to his. "Have you any smoldering looks up your sleeve, Colin?" Mischief danced in her eyes as she paused outside the front door of the shop. "You could send me a few and give Julia something to talk about for weeks." She swung through the door, her lovely face flushed with laughter.

True to form, Julia greeted Colin with scrupulous politeness and only the faintest glimmer of curiosity. There was a speculative glance for her former clerk, then recognition of Colin widened her eyes. She lifted a brow at Cassidy's request for the oyster silk dress then proceeded to wait on them personally.

In the changing room Cassidy stripped off her jeans and marveled at the irony of life. Little more than twenty-four hours before, she had been standing outside that very room with discarded dresses heaped over her arms...without a thought of Colin Sullivan in her head. Now he seemed to dominate both her thoughts and her actions. The thin, cool silk was slipping over her head because he wished it. Her heart beat just a fraction quicker because he waited to see the results. Cassidy fastened the zipper, held her breath and turned. Her reflection stared back at her with undisguised awe.

The dress fell from a severely high neck in a straight line, softened by the fragility of the material. Her arms and shoulders gleamed under the thin transparency of its full sleeves. Her hair glowed with life against the delicacy of color. Cassidy let out her breath slowly. It was a wish of a dress, as romantic as the material, as practical as its line. In it she not only looked both elegant and vulnerable but felt it. With taut nerves she moistened her lips and stepped from the changing room.

Colin was charming Julia into blushes. The incongruity of flirtatious color in the cool, composed face turned Cassidy's nerves into amusement. There was the devil of a smile in Colin's eyes as he lifted Julia's hand and brushed his lips over her knuckles. Cassidy schooled her features to sobriety. A hint of a smile lurked on her lips.

"Colin."

He turned as she called his name. The smile that lit his face and brightened his eyes faded then died. Releasing Julia's hand, he took a few steps closer but kept half the room between them. Cassidy, who had been about to grin and spin a circle for inspection, stood still, hypnotized by his eyes.

Very slowly, his eyes left her face to travel down the length of her then back again. Cassidy's cheeks grew warm with the flurry of her emotions. How could he make her feel so vitalized then so enervated with just a look? She wanted to speak, to break her own trance, but the words were jumbled and uncooperative. She found she could only repeat his name.

"Colin?" There was the faintest hint of invitation in the word, a question even she did not understand.

Something flashed in his eyes and was gone. The intense concentration was inexplicably replaced by irritation. When he spoke it was brisk and dismissive.

"That will do very well. Have it packed up and bring it with you tomorrow. We'll start then."

Cassidy's mind raced with a hundred questions and a hundred demands. His tone stiffened her pride, however, and hers was cool when she spoke. "Is that all?"

"That's all." Temper hovered in his voice. "Nine o'clock tomorrow. Don't be late."

Cassidy took a deep breath and let it out carefully. In that moment she was certain she despised him. They watched each other for another minute while the air crackled with tension and something more volatile. Then she turned her back on him and glided into the changing room.

Chapter 3

Cassidy spent most of the night lecturing herself. By morning she felt she had herself firmly in hand. There had been absolutely no reason for her to be annoyed with Colin. His brisk, impersonal attitude over the dress was only to be expected. As she rode the trolley across town, she shifted the dress box into her other arm and determined to preserve a cool, professional distance from him.

He's simply my employer. He's an artist, obviously a temperamental one. She added the modifier with a sniff. Deftly she jumped from the cable car to finish the trip on foot. He's a man who sees something in my face he wants to paint. He has no personal feelings for me, nor I for him. How could I? I barely know Colin

Sullivan. What I felt yesterday was simply the over-
flow of his personality. It's very strong, very magnetic.
I only imagined that there was an immediate affinity
between us. Things don't happen that way, not that
fast. All there is between us is the bond between artist
and subject. I was writing scenes again.

Cassidy paused at the base of the stairs that led to
Colin's studio. Still, he might have thanked me for
finding the dress he was looking for, she thought.
Never mind. She made an involuntary gesture with her
hand as she climbed the steps. He's so self-absorbed he
probably forgot I suggested the shop in the first place.
With a quick toss of her head, Cassidy knocked, prepared to be brisk and professional in her new employ.
Her resolve wavered a bit when Gail Kingsley opened
the door.

"Hello," she said and smiled despite the cool assess-
ment in Gail's eyes. For an answer Gail made a sweeping arm gesture into the room that would have seemed
overdone on anyone else. Flamboyance suited her.

Gail was just as striking today in a shocking-pink
jumpsuit no other redhead would have had the courage to wear. Colin was nowhere in sight. Cassidy was
torn between admiration for the redhead's style and
disappointment that Colin hadn't answered the door.
She felt juvenile and ragged in jeans and a pullover.

"Am I too early?"

Gail placed her hands on her narrow hips and walked

around Cassidy slowly. "No, Colin's tied up. He'll be along. Is that curl in your hair natural or have you a perm?"

"It's natural," Cassidy replied evenly.

"And the color?"

"Mine, too." Gail's bold perfume dominated the scents of paint. When she came back to stand in front of her, Cassidy met her eyes levelly. "Why?"

"Just curious, dear heart. Just curious." Gail flashed a quick, dazzling smile that snapped on and off like a light. It was momentarily blinding, then all trace of it vanished. "Colin's quite taken with your face. He seems to be drifting into a romantic period. I've always avoided that sort of technique." She narrowed her eyes until she seemed to be examining the pores of Cassidy's skin.

"Want to count my teeth?" Cassidy invited.

"Don't be snide." Gail touched a scarlet-tipped finger to her lips. "Colin and I often share models. I want to see if I can use you for anything."

"I'm not a box lunch, Miss Kingsley," retorted Cassidy with feeling. "I don't care to be shared."

"A good model should be flexible," Gail reproved, stretching her slender arms to the ceiling in one long, luxurious movement. "I hope you don't make a fool of yourself the way the last one did."

"The last one?" Cassidy responded then immediately wanted to bite off her tongue.

"She fell desperately in love with Colin." Gail gave her quick light-switch smile again. Her sharp, rapid gestures skittered down Cassidy's nerves. She was a cat looking for something to stalk. "Worse, she imagined Colin was in love with her. It was really quite pathetic. A lovely little thing—milky skin, dark gypsy eyes. Naturally Colin was beastly to her in the end. He tends to be when someone tries to pin him down. There's nothing worse than having someone mooning and sighing over you, is there?"

"I wouldn't know," Cassidy returned in mild tones. "But you needn't worry that I'll be mooning and sighing over Colin. He needs my face, I need a job." She paused a moment. Perhaps, she thought, it's best to be clear from the start. "You won't have any trouble from me, Gail. I'm too busy to orchestrate a romance with Colin."

Gail stopped her pacing long enough to fix her with a speculative frown. The frown vanished, and she moved swiftly to the door. "That simplifies matters, doesn't it? You can change through there." She flung out an arm to her left and was gone.

Cassidy took time to inhale deeply. She shook her head. Artists, she decided, were all as mad as hatters. Shrugging off Gail's behavior, she moved to the door indicated and found a small dressing room. Closeting herself inside, Cassidy began to change. As before, the gown made her feel different. Perhaps, she thought as she pulled a brush through her hair, it's the sensation of real silk against my skin, or the elegant simplicity of the line and color. Or is it because it's the image of what Colin wants me to be?

Whatever the reason, Cassidy couldn't deny that she felt heightened when she wore the gown—more alive, more aware, more a woman. After giving herself one last quick glance in the mirror, she opened the door and stepped into the studio.

"Oh, you're here," she said foolishly when she saw Colin scowling at a blank canvas. She had only a side view of him, and he didn't turn at her entrance. His hands were stuffed in his pockets, and his weight was distributed evenly on both legs. There was an impression of sharp vitality held in check—waiting, straining a bit for release. He was dressed casually, as she was now accustomed to seeing him, and the clothes seemed to suit his rangy, loose-limbed build. His face was in a black study: brows lowered, eyes narrowed, mouth unsmiling. The thought crossed Cassidy's mind that he was unscrupulously attractive and would be a terrifying man to care for. She remained where she was, certain he had not even heard her speak.

"I'm going to start on canvas straight away," he said. Still he did not turn to acknowledge her. "There're violets on the table." With one shoulder he made a vague gesture. "They match your eyes."

Cassidy looked over and saw the small nosegay

tossed amid the artistic rubble. Her face lit with instant pleasure. "Oh, they're lovely!" Moving to the table, she took them then buried her face in their delicate petals. The fragrance was subtle and sweet. Touched and charmed, Cassidy lifted her smile to thank him.

"I want a spot of color against the dress," Colin murmured. His preoccupation was obvious and complete. He did not glance at her or change expression.

Pleasure shattered, Cassidy stared down at the tiny flowers and sighed. It's my fault, she thought ruefully. He bought them for the painting, not for me. It was ridiculous to think otherwise. Why in the world should he buy me flowers? With a shake of her head and a wry smile, she moved over to join him. "Do you see me there already?" she asked. "On the empty canvas?"

He turned then and looked at her, but the frown of his concentration remained. He lifted the hand that held the flowers. "Yes, they'll do. Stand over here, I want the light from this window."

As he propelled her across the room, Cassidy twisted her head to look up at him. "Good morning, Colin," she said in the bright, cheerful voice of a kindergarten instructor.

He lifted a brow as he stopped by the window. "Manners are the least of my concerns when I'm working."

"I'm awfully glad you cleared that up," Cassidy replied, smiling broadly.

"I've also been known to devour young, smart-tongued wenches for breakfast."

"Wenches!" Cassidy's smile became a delighted grin. "How wonderfully anachronistic. It sounds lovely when you say it, too. I do wish you'd said lusty young wenches, though. I've always loved that phrase."

"The description doesn't fit you." Colin lifted her chin with one finger and brushed her hair over her shoulder with his other hand.

"Oh." Cassidy felt vaguely insulted.

"Once I've set the pose, don't fidget. I just might throw an easel at you if you do." While he spoke, he moved her face and body with his hands. His touch was as impersonal as a physician's. I might as well be a still-life arrangement, Cassidy thought. By his eyes, she saw that his mind had gone beyond her and into his art. She recognized his expression of absolute concentration from her own work. She, too, had a tendency to block out her surroundings and step into her own mind.

At length he stood back and studied her in silence. It was a natural pose and simple. She stood straight, with the nosegay cupped in both hands and held just below her right hip. Her arms were relaxed, barely bent at the elbows. He had left her hair tumbled free, without design, over both shoulders. "Lift your chin a fraction higher." He held up a hand to stop the movement. "There. Be still and don't talk until I tell you."

Cassidy obeyed, moving only her eyes to watch him as he strode behind the easel again. He lifted a piece of charcoal. Minutes passed in utter silence as she watched the movements of his arms and shoulders and felt the probing power of his eyes. They returned again and again to her face. She knew he could look into her eyes and see directly into her soul, learning more perhaps than she knew herself. The sensation made her not nervous so much as curious. What would he see? How would he express it?

"All right," Colin said abruptly. "You can talk for the moment, but don't move the pose. Tell me about those unpublished novels of yours."

He continued to work with such obsessed concentration that Cassidy assumed he had invited her to talk only to keep her relaxed. She doubted seriously if her words made more than a surface impression. If he heard them at all, he would forget them moments later.

"There's only one actually, or one and a half. I'm working on a second novel while the first bounces from rejection slip to rejection slip." She started to shrug but caught herself in time. "It's about a woman's coming of age, the choices she makes, the mistakes. It's rather sentimental, I suppose. I like to think she makes the right choices in the end. Do you know it's very difficult to talk without your hands? I had no idea mine were so necessary to my vocabulary."

"It's your Gaelic blood." Colin frowned deeply at the canvas then lifted his eyes to hers. By the movement of his shoulders she knew he continued to work. "Will you let me read your manuscript?"

Surprised, Cassidy stared a moment before gathering her wits. "Well, yes, if you'd like. I—"

"Good," he interrupted and slashed another line on the canvas. "Bring it with you tomorrow. Be quiet now," he commanded before Cassidy could speak again. "I'm going to work the face."

Silence reigned until he put down the charcoal and shook his head. "It's not right." He scowled at Cassidy then paced. Unsure, she held the pose and her tongue. "You're not giving me the right mood. Do you know what I want?" he demanded. There was impatience and a hint of temper in his voice. She opened her mouth then closed it again, seeing the question had been rhetorical. "I want more than an illusion. I want passion. You've passion in you, Cassidy, more, by heaven, than I need for this painting." He turned to face her again, and she felt the room vibrate with his tension. Her heart began to quicken in response. "I want a promise. I want a woman who invites a lover. I want expectation and the freshness that springs from innocence. Untouched but not untouchable. It's that you have to give me. That's the essence of it." In his frustration, the cadence of his native land became more obvious. The fire of his talent flickered in his eyes. Fascinated, Cassidy watched him, not speaking even when he stopped directly in front of her. "There would be a softness in your eyes and just a trace of heat. There would be a giving in the set of your mouth that comes from having just been kissed, from waiting to be kissed again. Like this."

His mouth took hers quickly, stunningly. He framed her face with his hands, thumbs brushing her cheeks while he took the kiss into trembling intimacy with terrifying speed. His lips were warm and soft and experienced. His tongue plundered without warning. Somewhere deep within her came an answer. Passion, long overlooked, smoldered then kindled then licked tentatively into flame. She tasted the flavor of power. As quickly as his mouth had taken, it liberated.

Though she was unaware of it, her expression was exactly what he'd demanded of her—expectant, inviting, innocent. Fleetingly he dropped his gaze to her mouth; then, taking his time, he removed his hands from her face. Impatience flickered in his eyes before he turned and strode to his easel.

Cassidy tried to steady her spinning brain. Reason told her the kiss had meant nothing, a means to an end, but her heart thudded in contradiction. In a few brief seconds he had stirred up a hunger she hadn't been aware of having, had stirred up desires she hadn't been aware she had. It was more a revelation, she thought bemusedly, than a kiss. Forcing her breathing to slow, she tried to keep the quick encounter in perspective.

She was a grown woman. Kisses were more common than handshakes. It was her treacherous imagination that had turned it into something else. *Only my imagination,* she decided as she calmed, and his utter effrontery. He'd taken her totally by surprise. He'd kissed her when he'd had no right to do so, and in a way that had been both proprietary and intimate. No man had ever been permitted either of the privileges, and his seizure of them had left her shaken. Cassidy could justify her reaction to Colin by intellectually dissecting the scene, its cause and results. She turned her emotions over to her mind and plotted the scene. She examined motivations. Still, something lingered inside her that could not quite be rationalized or explained away. Disturbed, she tried to ignore it.

"We'll stop now," Colin stated abruptly and put aside the charcoal. He glanced up as he cleaned his hands on a paint rag. She thought perhaps he saw Cassidy St. John again for the first time since he had set the pose. "Relax."

When Cassidy obeyed, she was surprised to find her muscles stiff. "How long have I been standing there?" she demanded as she arched her back. "A good bit more than twenty minutes."

Colin shrugged, his eyes back on the canvas. "Perhaps. It's moving nicely. Do you want coffee?"

Cassidy scowled at his casual dismissal of the time. "Twenty minutes is quite long enough to stand in one position. I'll bring a kitchen timer with me from now on, and yes, I want coffee."

He ignored the first two-thirds of her statement and headed for the door. "I'll fix some."

"Am I allowed to look?" She gestured toward the canvas as he drew back the bolt.

"No."

She made a sound of disgust. "What about the others?" Her gesture took in the canvases against the wall. "Are they a secret, too?"

"Help yourself. Just stay away from the one I'm working on." Colin disappeared, presumably to fetch the promised coffee.

Making a face at the empty doorway, Cassidy set down the nosegay and wandered toward the neglected canvases. They were stacked here and tilted there, without order or design. Some were small while others were large enough to require some effort on her part to turn them around. Within moments, whatever minor irritation she'd felt was eclipsed by admiration for his talent. She saw why Colin Sullivan was considered a master of color and light. Moreover she saw the sensitivity she had detected in his hands and the strength she had felt there. There was insight and honesty in his portraits, vitality in his city scenes and landscapes. A play of shadows, a splatter of light, and the paintings breathed his mood. She wondered if he painted what he saw or what he felt, then understood it was a marriage of both. She decided that he saw more than the average mortal was entitled to see. His gift was as much in his perception as in his hands. The paintings moved her almost as deeply as the man had.

Carefully she turned another canvas. The subject was beautiful. The woman's undraped body lounged negligently on the couch that now sat empty at the far end of the studio. There was a lazy smile on her face and a careless confidence in the attitude of her naked limbs. From the milky skin and gypsy eyes, Cassidy recognized the model Gail had spoken of that morning.

"A lovely creature, isn't she?" Colin asked from behind. Cassidy started.

"Yes." She turned and accepted the proffered mug. "I've never seen a more beautiful woman."

Colin's brow arched as he moved his shoulders. "Of a type, she's nearly perfect, and her body is exquisite."

Cassidy frowned into her coffee and tried to pretend the stab of irritation didn't exist.

"She has a basic sexuality and is comfortable with it."

"Yes." Sipping her coffee, Cassidy spoke mildly. "You've captured it remarkably well."

Her tone betrayed her. Colin grinned. "Ah, Cass, it's an open book you are and surely the most delightful creature I've met in years." The thickened brogue rolled easily off his tongue. Better women than she, Cassidy was certain, had fallen for the Gaelic charm.

She tossed her head, but the glare she had intended to flash at him turned of its own volition into a smile. "I can't keep up with you, Sullivan." She studied him over the rim of her mug. Sunlight shot through her hair and shadowed the silk of the dress. "Why did you settle in San Francisco?" she asked.

Colin straddled one of the abandoned wooden chairs, keeping his eyes on her. She wondered if he saw her as a person now or still as a subject. "It's a cross section of the world. I like the contrasts and its sordid history."

"And that it trades on that sordid history rather than apologizing for it," Cassidy concluded with an agreeing nod. "But don't you miss Ireland?"

"I go back now and then." He lifted his coffee and drank deeply. "It feeds me, like a mother's breast. Here I find passion, there I find peace. The soul requires both." He glanced up at her again and searched her face. The violet of her eyes had darkened. Her expression revealed her thoughts. They were all on him. Colin turned away from the innocent candor of her eyes. "Finish your coffee. I want to perfect the preliminary outline today. I'll start in oil tomorrow."

The morning passed almost completely in silence while she took advantage of Colin's absorption to

study him. She had read of the dark devil looks and
fiery blue eyes of the volatile black Irish, and now she
found them even more compelling in the flesh. She
wondered at the strange quirk in her own personality
that caused her to find moodiness appealing.

With only the barest effort she could feel the swift
excitement of his lips on hers. Warmed, she drifted
with the sensation. For a moment she imagined what
it would be like to be held by him in earnest. Though
her experience with men had been limited, her instincts told her Colin Sullivan was dangerous. He interested her too much. His dominance challenged her,
his physicality attracted her, his moodiness intrigued
her.

Gail Kingsley's scathing comment about Cassidy's
predecessor came back to her. She had a quick mental
picture of the redhead's demanding beauty and the
model's sultry allure. Cassidy St. John, she mused,
is at neither end of the spectrum. She isn't strikingly
vivid nor steamily sexy. Feminine extremes apparently appeal to Colin both as an artist and as a man.
She caught herself, annoyed with the train of her own
thoughts. It would not do to get involved or form any
personal attachments with a man like Colin Sullivan.
Don't get too close, she cautioned herself. Don't open
any doors. *Don't get hurt.* The last warning came from
nowhere and surprised her.

"Relax."

Cassidy focused on Colin and found him staring down at the canvas. His attention was concentrated on what only he could see. "Go change," he directed without glancing up. Cassidy's thoughts darkened at his tone. Rude, she decided, was a mild sort of word for describing Sullivan the artist. Controlling her temper, Cassidy went back to the dressing room.

My worries are groundless, she told herself and closed the door smartly. No one could possibly get close enough to that man to be hurt.

A few moments later Cassidy emerged from the dressing room in her own clothes. Colin stood, facing the window, his hands jammed into his pockets, his eyes narrowed on some view of his own.

"I've left the dress hanging in the other room," Cassidy said coldly. "I'll just be off, since you seem to be done." She snatched up her purse from the chair. Even as she swung it over her shoulder and turned for the door, Colin took her hand in his.

"You've that line between your brows again, Cass." He lifted a finger to trace it. "Smooth it out and I'll buy you some lunch before you go."

The line deepened. "Don't use that patronizing tone on me, Sullivan. I'm not an empty-headed art groupie to be patted and babied into smiles."

His brow lifted a fraction. "Quite right. Then again, there's no need to go off in a tiff."

"I'm not in a tiff," Cassidy insisted as she tried to

jerk out of his hold. "I'm simply having a perfectly normal reaction to rudeness. Let go of my hand."

"When I'm through with it," he replied evenly. "You should mind your temper, Cass my love. It does alluring things to your face, and I'm not one for resisting what appeals to me."

"It's abundantly clear the only appeal I have for you is on that canvas over there." Cassidy wriggled her hand in an attempt to free it. With a quick flick of the wrist, Colin tumbled her into his chest. Mutinous and glowing, her face lifted to his. "Just what do you think you're doing?"

"You challenge me to prove you wrong." There was amusement in his eyes now and something else that made her heart beat erratically.

"I don't challenge you to anything," she corrected with a furious toss of her head. Her hair swung and lifted with the movement then settled into its own appealing disarray.

"Oh, but you do." His free hand tangled in her hair and found the base of her neck. "You threw down the gauntlet the night I found you in the fog. I think it's time I picked it up."

"You're being ridiculous." Cassidy spoke quickly. She realized her temper had carried her into territory she would have been wise to avoid. As she began to speak again, he caught her bottom lip between his teeth. The movement was sudden, the pressure light, the effect devastating.

Though she made a tiny sound of confused protest, her fingers clutched at his shirt instead of pushing him away. The tip of his tongue traced her lip as if experimenting with its flavor. When he released it, she stood still. Her eyes locked with his.

"This time when I kiss you, Cass, it's to pleasure myself," he said as his mouth lowered to take hers. Knowing he would meet no resistance, he circled her waist to mold her against him. Cassidy responded as if she'd been waiting for the moment all of her life. Her body seemed to know his already and fitted its soft, subtle curves to his firm, taut lines. Her hands traveled from his neck to tangle in his hair, while her mouth grew more mobile under his. For one brief instant, he crushed her to him with staggering force, ravishing her conquered mouth. Just as swiftly, her lips were freed. Her breath came out in a quick rush as she gripped him for balance. He held her close, keeping their bodies as one, his eyes boring into hers. Only the sound of their mixed breathing disturbed the silence.

The weakness Cassidy felt was a shock to her. Her knees trembled beneath her and she shook her head in a quick attempt to deny what he had awakened. Something deep and secret was struggling for release. The strength of it alarmed and fascinated her. Still, her fear outweighed her curiosity. Instinct warned her it was not yet time. Even as she found the will to draw away, Colin pulled her closer.

"No, Colin, I can't." She swallowed as her hands pushed against his chest. She watched his eyes darken as his lips lingered just over hers.

"I can," he murmured, then crushed her mouth. She swirled back into the storm.

Nothing in her experience had ever prepared her for the new demands of her own body. With innocent allure, she moaned against his mouth. She felt his lips move against hers as he murmured something. Then he plundered, pulling her down into a world of heat and darkness. A quickening fear rose with her passion. When he released her mouth, her breath came in short gasps. Her eyes clouded with desire and confusion.

"Please, Colin, let me go. I think I'm frightened."

He was capable of taking her, she knew, and of making her glad that he had. His eyes were blazing blue, and she kept hers locked on them. To let her eyes drift to his mouth would have been her downfall. The fingers at her neck tightened, then relaxed and dropped away. Seizing the moment, Cassidy stepped back. The narrowness of her escape shook her, and she dragged her hand through her hair.

Colin watched her, then folded his arms across his chest. "I wonder if you had more difficulty fighting yourself or me."

"So do I," Cassidy replied with impulsive candor.

He tilted his head at her response and studied her. "You're an honest one, Cassidy. Mind how honest you are with me——I'd have few qualms about taking advantage."

"No, I'm sure you wouldn't." After blowing out a long breath, Cassidy straightened her shoulders. "I don't suppose that could have been avoided forever," she began practically. "But now that it hasn't been, and it's done, it shouldn't happen again." Her brow furrowed as Colin tossed back his head and roared with laughter. "Did I say something funny?"

"Cass, you're unique." Before she could respond, he had moved to her and had taken her shoulders in his hands. He kneaded them quickly in a friendly manner. "That streak of British practicality will always war with the passionate Celt."

"You're romanticizing," she claimed and lifted her chin.

"The door's been opened, Cassidy." She frowned because his words reminded her of her earlier thoughts. "Better for you perhaps if we'd kept it locked." He shook her once, rapidly. "Yes, it's done. The door won't stay closed now. It'll happen again." He released her then stepped back, but their eyes remained joined. "Go on now, while I'm remembering you were frightened."

The strong temptation to step toward him alarmed her. In defense against it, she turned swiftly for the door. "Nine o'clock," he said, and she turned with her hand on the knob.

He stood in the room's center, his thumbs hooked in his front pockets. The sun fell through the skylight, silhouetting his dark attraction. It occurred to Cassidy that if she were wise, she would walk out and never come back.

"Not a coward, are you, Cass?" he taunted softly, as if stealing her thoughts from her brain.

Cassidy tossed her head and snapped her spine straight. "Nine o'clock," she stated coolly then slammed the door behind her.

Chapter 4

As the days passed Cassidy found herself more at
ease in the role of artist's model. As for Colin himself,
she felt it would be a rare thing for anyone to remain
relaxed with him. His temperament was mercurial,
with a wide range of degrees. Fury came easily to him,
but Cassidy learned humor did as well. As she began to
uncover different layers of the man, he became more
fascinating.

She justified her concentrated study of Colin Sullivan as a writer's privilege. It was a personality like
his—varied, unpredictable, bold—that she needed as
grist for her profession. There was nothing between
them, she told herself regularly, but an artistic exchange. She reminded herself that he hadn't touched

her again, except to set the pose, since the first day he had begun work on the canvas. The stormy kiss was a vivid memory, but only that...a memory.

Sitting at her typewriter in her apartment, Cassidy told herself she was fortunate—fortunate to have a job that kept the wolf from the door, and fortunate that Colin Sullivan was absorbed in his work. Cassidy was honest enough to admit she was more than mildly attracted to him. It was much better, she mused, that he was capable of pouring himself into his work to the extent that he barely noticed she was flesh and blood. *Unless I move the pose.* She frowned at the reflection of her desk lamp in the window.

Being attracted to him is perfectly natural, she decided. I'm not behaving like my predecessor with the milky skin and falling in love with him. I'm much too sensible. *Don't be so smug,* a voice whispered inside her head. Cassidy's frown became a scowl. I *am* sensible. I won't make a fool of myself over Colin Sullivan. He has his art and his Gail Kingsley. I have my work. Cassidy glanced down at the blank sheet of paper in her typewriter and sighed. But he keeps interfering with it. No more, she vowed then shifted in her seat until she was comfortably settled. I'm going to finish this chapter tonight without another thought of Sullivan.

At once the keys on her typewriter began to clatter with the movement of her thoughts. Once begun, she became totally involved, lost in the characters of her own devising. The love scene developed on her pages as she unconsciously called on her own feelings for her words. The scene moved with the same lightning speed as had the embrace with Colin. Now Cassidy was in control, urging her characters toward each other, propelling their destinies. It was as she wanted, as she planned, and she never noticed the influence of the man she had vowed to think no more about. The scene was nearly finished when a knock sounded on her door. She swore in annoyance.

"Who is it?" she called out and stopped typing in midsentence. She found it simpler to pick up her thoughts when returning to them that way.

"Hey, Cassidy." Jeff Mullans stuck his friendly, red-bearded face through her door. "Got a minute?"

Because he was her neighbor and she was fond of him, Cassidy pushed away the urge to sigh and smiled instead. "Sure."

He eased himself, a guitar and a six-pack of beer through the door. "Can I put some stuff in your fridge? Mine's busted again. It's like the Mojave Desert in there."

"Go ahead." Cassidy spun her chair until she faced him, then quirked her brow. "I see you brought all your valuables. I didn't know your six-string needed refrigeration."

"Just the six-pack," he countered with a grin as he marched back into her tiny kitchen. "And you're the only one in the building I'd trust with it. Wow, Cassidy, don't you believe in real food? All that's in here's a quart of juice, two carrots and half a stick of oleo."

"Is nothing sacred?"

"Come next door and I'll fix you up with a decent meal." Jeff came back into the room holding only his guitar. "I got tacos and stale doughnuts. Jelly-filled."

"It sounds marvelous, but I really have to finish this chapter."

Jeff's fingers pawed at his beard. "Don't know what you're missing. Heard anything from New York?" After glancing at the papers scattered over her desk, he settled Indian-fashion on the floor. He cradled his guitar in his lap.

"There seems to be a conspiracy of silence on the East Coast." Cassidy sighed, shrugged and tucked up her feet. "It's early days yet, I know, but patience isn't my strong suit."

"You'll make it, Cassidy, you've got something." He began to strum idly as he spoke. His music was simple and soothing. "Something that makes the people you write about important. If your novel is as good as that magazine story, you're on your way."

Cassidy smiled, touched by the easy sincerity of the compliment. "You wouldn't like to apply for a job as an editor in a New York publishing house, would you?"

"You don't need me, babe." He grinned and shook back his red hair. "Besides, I'm an up-and-coming songwriter and star performer."

"I've heard that." Cassidy leaned back in her chair. It occurred to her suddenly that Colin might like to paint Jeff Mullans. He'd be the perfect subject for him—the blinding red hair and beard, the soft contrast of gray eyes, the loving way the long hands caressed the guitar as he sat on her wicker rug. Yes, Colin would paint him precisely like this, she decided, in faded, frayed jeans with a polished guitar on his lap.

"Cassidy?"

"Sorry, I took a side trip. Have you got any gigs lined up?"

"Two next week. What about your gig with the artist?" Jeff tightened his bass string fractionally, tested it then continued to play. "I've seen his stuff... some of it, anyway. It's incredible." He tilted his head when he smiled at her. "How does it feel to be put on canvas by one of the new masters?"

"It's an odd feeling, Jeff. I've tried to pin it down, but..." She trailed off and brought her knees up, resting her heels on the edge of the chair. "I'm never certain it's me he's seeing when he's working. I'm not certain I'll see myself in the finished portrait." She frowned then shrugged it away. "Maybe he's only using part of me, the way I use parts of people I've met in characterizations."

"What's he like?" Jeff asked, watching her eyes drift with her thought. The glow of her desk lamp threw an aura around her head.

"He's fascinating," she murmured, all but forgetting she was speaking aloud. "He looks like a pirate, all dashing and dangerous with the most incredible blue eyes I've ever seen. And his hands are beautiful. There's no other word for them; they're perfectly beautiful."

Her voice softened, and her eyes began to dream. "He exudes a thoughtless sort of sensuality. It seems more obvious when he's working. I suppose it's because he's being driven by his own power then, and is somehow separate from the rest of us. He tells me to talk, and I talk about whatever comes into my head." She moved her shoulders then rested her chin on her knees. "But I don't know if he hears me. He has a dreadful temper, and when he rages his speech slips back to Ireland. It's almost worth the storm to hear it. He's outrageously selfish and unbearably arrogant and utterly charming. Each time I'm with him I find a bit more, uncover another layer, and yet I doubt I'd really know him if I had years to learn."

There was silence for a moment, with only Jeff's music. "You're really hung up on him," he observed.

Cassidy snapped back with a jolt. Her violet eyes widened in surprise as she straightened in the chair. "Why, no, of course not. I'm simply...simply..." *Simply what, Cassidy?* she demanded of herself. "Simply interested in what makes him the way he is," she answered and hugged her knees. "That's all."

"Okay, babe, you know best." Jeff stood in an easy fluid motion, the guitar merely an extension of his arm. "Just watch out." He smiled, leaned over and cupped her chin. "He might be a great artist, but if the gossip columns are to be believed, he's very much a man, too. You're a fine-looking lady, and you might as well be fresh from the farm."

"I'd hardly call four years at Berkeley fresh from the farm," Cassidy countered.

"Only someone utterly naive could evade every pass I make and still make me like her." Jeff closed the distance and gave her a gentle invitation of a kiss. It was as pleasant and as soothing as his music. Cassidy's heartbeat stayed steady. "No dice, huh?" he asked when he lifted his head. "Think of the rent we could save if we moved in together."

Cassidy tugged on his beard. "You're only lusting after my refrigerator."

"A lot you know," he scoffed and headed for the door. "I'm going home to write something painfully sad and poignant."

"Good grief, I'm always inspiring someone these days."

"Don't get cocky," Jeff advised then closed the door behind him.

Cassidy's smile faded as she stared off into space. Hung up on, she repeated mentally. What a silly phrase. In any case, I'm not hung up on Colin. Can't a woman express an interest in a man without someone reading more into it? Thoughtfully she ran her fingertip over her bottom lip and brought back the

feel of Jeff's kiss. Easy, undisturbing, painless. What
sort of chemistry made one man's kiss pleasant and
another's exhilarating? The smart woman would go
for the pleasant, Cassidy decided, knowing Jeff would
be basically kind and gentle. Only an idiot would want
a man who was bound to bring hurt and heartache.

With a quick shake of her head she swung back to
her typewriter and began to work. Her fingers had
barely begun to transfer her thoughts when a knock
sounded again. Cassidy rolled her eyes to the ceiling.

"You can't possibly be finished writing a painfully
sad and poignant song," she called out and continued
to type. "And the beer certainly isn't cold yet."

"I can't argue with either of those statements."

Cassidy spun her chair quickly and stared at Colin.
He stood in her opened doorway, negligently leaning
against the jamb and watching her. There was light
amusement on his face and male appreciation in his
eyes as they roamed over her skin. It was scantily covered in brief shorts and a T-shirt that had shrunk in
the basement laundry. His lazy survey brought out a
blush before she found her tongue.

"What are you doing here?"

"Enjoying the view," he answered and stepped
inside. He closed the door at his back then lifted a
brow. "Don't you know better than to keep your door
unlatched?"

"I'm always losing my key and locking myself out,

so I..." Cassidy stopped because she realized how ridiculous she sounded. One day, she promised herself, I'll learn to think before I speak. "There isn't anything in here worth stealing," she said.

Colin shook his head. "How wrong you are. Wear your key around your neck, Cass, but keep your door locked." Her brain formed an indignant retort, but before she could vocalize it he spoke again. "Who did you think I was when I knocked?"

"A songwriter with a faulty refrigerator. How did you know where I lived?"

"Your address is on your manuscript." He gestured with the thick envelope before setting it down.

Cassidy glanced at the familiar bundle with some surprise. She had assumed Colin had forgotten her manuscript as soon as she'd given it to him. Suddenly it occurred to her why she hadn't asked him before if he had read it, or what he'd thought of it. His criticism would be infinitely harder to bear than an impersonal rejection slip from a faceless editor. Abruptly nervous, she looked up at him. Any critique she was expecting wasn't forthcoming.

Colin wandered the room, toying with an arrangement of dried flowers, examining a snapshot in a silver frame, peering out of the window at her view of the city.

"Can I get you something?" she asked automatically then remembered Jeff's inventory of her refrigerator.

She bit her lip. "Coffee," she added quickly, knowing she could provide it as long as he took it black.

Colin turned from the window and began to wander again. "You have a proper eye for color, Cass," he told her. "And an enviable way of making a home from an apartment. I've always found them soulless devices, lacking in privacy and character." He lifted a small mirror framed with sea shells. "Fisherman's Wharf," he concluded and glanced at her. "It must be a particular haunt of yours."

"Yes, I suppose. I love the city in general and that part of it in particular." She smiled as she thought of it. "There's so much life there. The boats are all crammed in beside each other, and I like to imagine where they've been or where they're going." As soon as the words were spoken Cassidy felt foolish. They sounded romantic when she had been taking great pains to prove to Colin she was not. He smiled at her, and her embarrassment became something more dangerous. "I'll make coffee," she said quickly and started to rise.

"No, don't bother." Colin laid a hand on her shoulder to keep her seated then glanced at her desk. It was cluttered with papers and notes and reference books. "I'm interrupting your work. Intolerable."

"It seems to be the popular thing to do tonight." Cassidy shook off her discomfort and smiled as he continued to pace the room. "It's all right because I was nearly done, otherwise I suppose I'd behave as rudely as you do when you're interrupted." She enjoyed the look he gave her, the ironical lift of his brow, the light tilt of a smile on his mouth.

"And how rudely is that?"

"Abominably. Please sit, Colin. These floors are thin, you'll wear them through." She gestured to a chair, but he perched on the edge of her desk.

"I finished your book tonight."

"Yes, I thought perhaps that's why you brought the manuscript back." She spoke calmly enough, but when he made no response she moaned in frustration. "Please, Colin, I'm no good with torture. I'd confess everything I knew before they stuck the first bamboo shoot under my fingernail. I'm a marshmallow. No, wait!" She held up both hands as he started to speak. She rose and then took a quick turn around the room. "If you hated it, I'll only be devastated for a short time. I'm certain I'll learn to function again...well, nearly certain. I want you to be frank. I don't want any platitudes or cushioned letdowns." She pushed her mane of hair back with both hands, letting her fingers linger on her temples a moment. "And for heaven's sake, don't tell me it was interesting. That's the worst. The absolute worst!"

"Are you finished?" he asked mildly.

Cassidy blew out a long breath, tugged her hand through her hair and nodded. "Yes, I think so."

"Come here, Cass." She obeyed instantly because his voice was quiet and gentle. Their eyes were level, and he took her hands in his. "I haven't mentioned the book until now because I wanted to read it when I wouldn't be interrupted. I thought it best not to talk about it until I finished." His thumbs ran absently over the back of her hands. "You have something rare, Cass, something elusive. Talent. It's not something they taught you at Berkeley, it's something you were born with. Your college years polished it, perhaps, disciplined it, but you provided the raw material."

Cassidy released her breath. Astonishing, she thought, that the opinion of a man known barely a week should have such weight. Jeff's opinion had pleased her; Colin's had left her speechless.

"I don't know what to say." She shook her head helplessly. "That sounds trite, I know, but it's true." Her eyes drifted past him to the disorder of papers on her desk. "Sometimes you just want to chuck it all. It just isn't worth the pain, the struggle."

"And you would choose to be a writer," Colin said.

"No, I never had any choice." She brought her eyes back to his. The violet glowed almost black in the shadowed light. "If anything, it picked me. Did you choose to be an artist, Colin?"

He studied her a moment, then shook his head. "No." He turned her hands, palms up, and looked at them with lowered brows. "There are things that come to us whether we ask for them or not. Do you believe in destiny, Cass?"

She moistened her lips, finding them suddenly dry, then swallowed. "Yes." The single syllable was little more than a breath.

"Of course, I was certain you did." He lifted his eyes and locked them on hers. Cassidy's heartbeat jumped skittishly. "Do you think it's our destiny to be lovers, Cassidy?" Her mouth opened but no words came out. She shook her head in mute denial. "You're a poor liar," he observed; then, cupping her chin in his palm, he moved his lips to hers. In direct contrast to the ease and pleasantness of Jeff's kiss, this brought a pain that seemed to vibrate in every cell of her body. Defensively Cassidy jerked her head back.

"Don't!"

"Why?" he countered, and his voice was soft. "A kiss is a simple thing, a meeting of lips."

"No, it's not simple," Cassidy protested, feeling herself being pulled to him by his eyes only. "You take more."

He kissed one cheek, then the other, barely touching her skin. Cassidy's eyelids fluttered down. "Only as much as you'll give me, Cass. That much and no more." His lips moved over hers, teasing, persuading, until her blood thundered in her brain. His fingers were gentle on her face. "You taste of things I'd forgotten," he murmured. "Fresh, young things. Kiss me, Cass, I've a need for you."

With a moan, half despair, half wonder, she answered his need.

The flames that leapt between them were intense and wild. Her brain sent out quick, desperate protests and was ignored. A hunger for him drove her; her mouth became urgent and searching as his hands began to explore her soft curves. The fear she felt only added to her excitement, the exquisite terror of losing control. She was overwhelmed by a primitive need, an ageless necessity. When their lips parted and met again, hers ached for the joining.

Abruptly he tore his mouth from hers and buried it against her neck. Cassidy shuddered from the onslaught even as she tilted back her head to offer him more. With his teeth he brought her skin alive with delicious pain. His hands found their way under her shirt, running up her rib cage. With his thumbs he stroked the sides of her breast while she strained against him.

Her joints went fluid, leaving her helpless but for his support. For a moment, when their lips met again, there was nothing she had that was not his. The offer was complete and unconditional. Slowly, with his hands on her shoulders, Colin drew her away. Her lashes fluttered up then down, before she found the strength to open her eyes. His expression was dark and forbidding. Briefly his hands tightened.

"It seems you were right," he began in a voice thick with desire. "A kiss isn't a simple thing. I want you, Cass, and you'd best know nothing in heaven or hell will keep me from taking you when I've a mind to." His hands relaxed, the grip becoming a caress. "When the painting's finished, we'll have no choice but to meet our destinies."

"No." Frightened, disturbed by feelings that were too intense, Cassidy pulled out of his arms. She dragged a trembling hand through her hair, and her breath came quickly. "No, Colin, I won't be the latest in your string of lovers. I won't! I think more of myself than that. That's something you'd best understand." She stepped away from him, her shoulders straightening with inherent pride.

Colin's eyes narrowed. She could see his temper rising. "It should be an interesting contest." He took a step forward and grabbed a handful of her hair. With a quick jerk he brought her face to his, then gave her a hard, brief kiss. Cassidy's breath trembled out, but she kept her eyes steady. "Time will tell, Cass my love. Now it's late, nearly midnight, and I'd best be on my way." Lifting her hand, he brushed her fingers with his lips. "Sinning is much more appealing after midnight." With another careless smile, he turned for the door. Reaching it, he pushed the latch so that it would engage when he shut it. "Find your keys," he ordered and was gone.

Chapter 5

Another week passed without any clash between Colin and Cassidy. She had returned to his studio the day after his visit to her apartment determined to resist him. She'd spoken the truth when she'd told him she wouldn't be one of his lovers.

All her life she had waited for a relationship with depth and permanence. Her own ideals and her dedication to her studies had kept her aloof from men, and her aloofness had prolonged her naiveté. She'd grown up with only a father and had never closely witnessed the commitment of a man and a woman to each other. She had watched her father enjoy several light relationships as she'd grown up, but none of the women in his life had become important to him. Watching him drift through life with only his work, Cassidy had vowed she would find someone one day to share hers.

She didn't consider her vow romantic, but as necessary to her soul as food was to her body. Until she found what she searched for, she would wait. Before Colin there had never been any temptation to do otherwise. Still, when she returned to his studio, she was prepared to stand firm against him. Her preparation proved unnecessary.

Colin spoke to her only briefly, and when he set the pose his touch was impersonal. But there seemed to be some surge of emotion just under the surface of his face, something that just stirred the air. Whether it was temper or passion or excitement, Cassidy had no way of knowing. She knew only she was vitally aware of it…and of him.

They passed the days with only what needed to be said, and long gaps of silence filled the sessions. By the end of the week Cassidy's nerves were stretched taut. She wondered if Colin felt the tension, or if it was simply within her. He seemed intent only on the painting.

The sun fell over Cassidy warmly, but her muscles were growing stiff from holding the pose. Colin stood behind his easel, and she watched his brush move from palette to canvas. He could work for hours without a moment's rest. Cassidy tried to imagine how he had painted her.

Will I hang in The Gallery or face the wall in a corner up here until he decides what to do with me? she thought. Will I be sold for some astronomical price and hang in a manor house in England? What will he title me? *Woman in White. Woman with Violets.* She tried to imagine being discussed and pondered over by an art class in a university. A century from now, will someone see me in some dusty gallery and wonder who I was or what I was thinking when he painted me?

The idea gave Cassidy an odd feeling, one she was not certain wholly pleased her. How much of her soul could Colin see, and how much would be revealed with oil and canvas? Would she, in essence, be as naked as the model who'd lounged on the couch?

Colin swore roundly, snapping her attention back to him. Her eyes widened as he slammed down his palette.

"You've moved the pose." He stalked toward her as her mouth opened to form an apology. "Hold still, blast you," he ordered curtly, adjusting her shoulders with impatient hands. His brows were lowered in annoyance. "I won't tolerate fidgeting."

Cassidy's mouth snapped shut on her apology. Swift and heated, her temper rose. With one quick jerk she pulled out of his hands. "Don't you speak to me that way, Sullivan." She threw her nosegay on the windowsill and glared at him. "I was not fidgeting, and if I were, it would be because I'm human, not a—a robot or a dime-store dummy." She tossed her head, effectively destroying his arrangement of her hair. "I'm sure it's difficult to understand a mere mortal when one is so lofty and godlike, but we can't all be perfect."

"Your opinions are neither requested nor desired." Colin's voice was as cold as his eyes were heated. "The only thing I require from a model is that she hold still." He took her shoulders again, firmly. "Keep your temper to yourself when I'm working."

"Go paint a tree, then," she invited furiously. "It won't give you any back talk." Cassidy turned to stalk to the dressing room, but Colin grabbed her arm and spun her around. His face was alive with temper.

"No one walks away from me."

"Is that so?" Cassidy lifted her chin, infuriated with his arrogance. "Watch this." She turned her back on him only to be whirled around again before she had taken two steps. "Let go of me," she ordered as blood surged angrily under her skin. Nerves that had been stretched for a week strained to the breaking point. "I've nothing more to say, and I'm through holding your blasted pose for the day."

His grip on her arm tightened. "Very well, but there's more between us than painting and talking, isn't there?" He bit off the words as he dragged her against him.

Cassidy's heart jumped to her throat when she felt the violence of his fingers against her skin. She saw that temper ruled him now, a temper sharp enough to cut through any protest she could make. He was a man of passion, and she was aware that his darker side could carry them both past the turning point. In a desperate attempt to hold him off, Cassidy arched away from him. Even as she made the move, his mouth crushed hers. She tasted his fury.

Her sounds of protest were muffled, her arms pinioned by his. In her throat, her heart thudded with the knowledge that she was totally at his mercy. His lips were bruising, unyielding, as his tongue penetrated her mouth. The kiss became as intimate as it was savage. When she tried to turn her face from his, he gripped her hair tightly and held her still. His mouth was hard and hot and ruthless. Behind her closed lids, a dull red mist swirled. For the first time in her life, Cassidy feared she would faint. Her protests became slighter. Colin took more.

He was pulling her too deep too quickly, down dark corridors, beyond the border of thought and into sensation. There was no gentleness on the journey, only hard, uncompromising demand. Unable to fight him any longer, Cassidy went limp. She made no struggle when his hand moved to unfasten the dress. Her body was consumed by fire, instinctively responding to his touch. The knock on the studio door vibrated like a cannon through the room. Ignoring it, Colin continued to ravish her mouth.

"Colin." Dimly Cassidy heard Gail Kingsley's voice and the sound of another knock. "There's someone here to see you."

With a savage oath, Colin tore his mouth from Cassidy's. He released her abruptly, and freed of support she staggered and fell against him. Cursing again, he took her arms and held her away, but his words halted as he studied her wide, frightened eyes.

Her mouth was trembling, swollen by his demands. Her breath sobbed in and out of her lungs as she clung to him for balance.

"Colin, don't be nasty." Gail's voice sounded with practiced patience through the door. "You must be pretty well finished by now."

"All right, blast it!" he called out brusquely to Gail but kept his eyes on Cassidy. Leading her by the arm, he walked to the dressing room. Inside he turned her again to face him. In silence she looked up, struggling to balance her system and discipline her breathing. The need to weep was tearing at her.

An expression came and went in Colin's eyes. "Change," he said in a quiet voice. He seemed to hesitate, as if to say more, then he turned away. When he shut the door, Cassidy turned to face the wall.

She let the trembling run its course. Several minutes passed before the voices in the studio penetrated.

There was Gail's quick, nervous tone and Colin's, calm now, without any trace of the temper of passion that had dominated it before. An unfamiliar voice mixed with theirs. It was light and male with an Italian accent. Cassidy concentrated on the voices rather than the words. Turning, she stared at her own reflection. What she saw left her stunned.

Color had not yet returned to her cheeks, leaving them nearly as white as the dress she wore. Her eyes were haunted. It was the look of utter vulnerability that disturbed her the most; the look of a woman accepting defeat.

No. No, I won't. She pressed her palm over the face in the glass. He'll win nothing that way, and we both know it. Quickly she stripped out of the dress and began to pull on her clothes. The straight, uncompromising lines of her khakis and button-down shirt made her appear less frail, and she began a careful repair of her face. The conversation in the outer room started to penetrate her thoughts. The first moments of eavesdropping were unconscious.

"An interesting use of color, Colin. You seem to be working toward a rather dreamlike effect." Hearing Gail's comment, Cassidy realized they were discussing the painting. She frowned as she applied blusher to her cheeks. He lets her look at it, she thought resentfully. Why not me? "It seems almost sentimental. That should be a surprise to the art world."

"Sentimental, yes." The Italian voice cut in while Cassidy now eavesdropped shamelessly. "But there is passion in this play of color here, and a rather cool practicality in the line of the dress. I'm intrigued, Colin—I can't figure out your intention."

"I have more than one," Cassidy heard him answer in his dry, ironic tone.

"How well I know." The Italian chuckled then made a sound of curiosity. "You have not begun the face."

"No." Cassidy recognized the dismissal in the word, but the Italian ignored it.

"She interests me…and you, too, it appears. She would be beautiful, of course, and young enough to suit the dress and the violets. Still, she must have something more." Cassidy waited for Colin's reply, but none came. The Italian continued, undaunted. "Will you keep her hidden, my friend?"

"Yes, Colin, where is Cassidy?" Gail's question held an undertone of amusement that made Cassidy's eyes narrow. "You know she'd adore meeting Vince." She gave a light laugh. "She is rather a sweet-looking thing. Don't tell me we ran her off?"

Thoroughly annoyed with the condescending description, Cassidy turned and opened the door. "Not at all," she said and gave the trio by the easel a brilliant smile. "And of course I'd adore meeting Vince." She saw Gail's eyes glitter with a quick fury then shifted her gaze to Colin. His face told her nothing, and again her gaze shifted.

The man beside Colin was nearly a head shorter, but his lean build and proud carriage gave the illusion of height. His hair was as dark as Colin's, but straight, and his eyes were darkly brown against the olive of his skin. He had smooth, handsome features, and when he smiled he was all but irresistible.

"Ah, *bella*." The compliment was a sigh before he crossed the room to take both of Cassidy's hands in his. "*Bellisima.* But of course, she is perfection. Where did you find her, Colin?" he demanded as his eyes caressed her face. "I will go and set up camp there until I find a prize of my own."

Cassidy laughed, amused by his undisguised flirtation. "In the fog," she told him when Colin remained silent. "I thought he was a mugger."

"Ah, my angel, he is much worse than that." Vince turned to Colin with a grin but retained Cassidy's hand. "He is a black Irish dog whose paintings I buy because I have nothing better to do with my money."

Colin lifted a brow as he moved to join them. "Vince, Cassidy St. John. Cass, Vincente Clemenza, the duke of Maracanti."

At the introduction Cassidy's eyes grew wide. "Ah, now you have impressed her with my title." Vince's teeth flashed into a grin. "How accommodating of you." With perfect charm he lifted both of Cassidy's hands to his lips. "My pleasure, *signorina.* Will you marry me?"

"I've always thought I'd make a spectacular duchess. Do I curtsy?" she asked, smiling at him over their joined hands. "I'm not certain I know how."

"Vince normally requires that one kneel and kiss his ring." At the comment, Cassidy let her eyes drift to Colin. His gaze was dark and brooding on her face. Fractionally, she lifted her chin. Though he said nothing, she sensed his acknowledgment of the gesture.

"You exaggerate, my friend." Vince released Cassidy's hands then laid his own on Colin's shoulder. "As never before, I envy you your gift. You will give me first claim on the portrait."

Colin's eyes remained fixed on Cassidy's face. "There's been a prior claim."

"Indeed." Vince shrugged. The movement was at once elegant and foreign. "I shall have to outbid my competition." There was an inflection in his tone of a man used to having his own way. Hearing it Cassidy wondered how he and Colin dealt together with such apparent amiability.

"Vince wanted to see *Janeen,*" Gail cut in and moved across the room to a stack of canvases.

"If you'll excuse me, then," Cassidy began, but Vince scooped up her hand again.

"No, *madonna,* stay. Come peruse the master's work

with me." Without waiting for her assent he urged her across the room.

Gail took a canvas then propped it on an easel. It was the portrait of the nude with the milky skin. Cassidy glanced up to see Gail smiling.

"Cassidy's predecessor," she announced then stepped back to stand with Colin. Cassidy recognized the proprietary nature of the gesture. She turned her attention back to the portrait without looking at Colin.

"An exquisite animal," Vince murmured. "One would say a woman without boundaries. There is quite an attractive wickedness about her." He turned his head to smile at Cassidy. "What do you think?"

"It's magnificent," she replied immediately. "She makes me uncomfortable, and yet I envy her confidence in her own sexuality. I think she would intimidate most men...and enjoy it."

"Your model appears to be an astute judge of character." Vince rubbed his thumb absently over Cassidy's knuckles. "Yes, I want it. And the Faylor Gail showed me downstairs. He shows promise. Now, madonna..." He turned to face Cassidy again. His eyes were dark and appreciative. "You will have dinner with me tonight? The city is a lonely place without a beautiful woman."

Cassidy smiled, but before she could speak Colin laid a hand on her shoulder. "The paintings are yours, Vince. My model isn't."

"Ah." Vince's one syllable was ripe with meaning. Cassidy's eyes narrowed with fury. Smoothly Colin turned to take the painting from the easel.

"Have someone package this and the Faylor for Vince," he told Gail as he handed her the canvas. "I'll be down shortly and we'll discuss terms."

Without a word Gail crossed the studio and swung through the door. Vince watched her with a thoughtful eye then turned back to Cassidy.

"*Arrivederci,* Cassidy St. John." He kissed her hand then sighed with regret. "It seems I must find my own dream in the fog. I will expect a bargain price to soothe my crushing disappointment, my friend." He shot a look at Colin as he moved to the door. "If you are ever in Italy, madonna…" With a final smile he left them.

Trembling with rage, Cassidy turned on Colin the moment the door closed. "How *dare* you?" Now she had no need of blusher to bring color to her cheeks. "How dare you imply such a thing?"

"I merely told Vince he could have the paintings but not my current model," Colin countered. Carelessly he moved across the room and covered Cassidy's portrait. "Any implication was purely coincidental."

"Oh, no!" Cassidy followed him, propelled by fury. "That was no coincidence. You knew precisely what you were doing. I won't tolerate that sort of interference from you, Sullivan." She took a finger and poked him in the chest. "I'm perfectly free to see whomever

I choose, whenever I choose, and I won't have you implying otherwise."

Colin hooked his hands in his pockets. For a moment he studied her face in silence. When he spoke it was with perfect calm. "You're very young and remarkably naive. Vince is an old friend and a good one. He's also a charming rake, if you'll forgive the archaic term. He has no scruples with women."

"And you do?" Cassidy retorted in an instant of blind heat. She saw Colin stiffen, saw his eyes flare and the muscles in his face tense. For the first time she witnessed his calculated control of his temper.

"Your point, Cass," he said softly. "Well taken." His hands stayed in his pockets as he watched her. "Don't come back until Thursday," he told her and turned to walk to the door. "I need a day or two."

Cassidy stood alone in the empty studio. I may have scored a point, she thought wretchedly, but this victory isn't sweet. She was drained, physically as well as emotionally. She returned to the dressing room for her purse. Colin wasn't the only one who needed a day or two.

"Oh, what luck, I've caught you." Gail swept into the studio just as Cassidy emerged from the dressing room. "I thought we might have a little chat." Gail shot her a quick, flashing smile and leaned back against the closed door. "Just us two," she added.

Cassidy sighed with undisguised weariness. "Not

now," she said and shifted her purse to her shoulder. "I've had enough temperament for one day."

"I'll make it brief, then, and you can be on your way." Gail spoke pleasantly enough, but Cassidy felt the antagonism just below the surface.

It's best not to argue, Cassidy decided. It's best to hear her out, agree with everything she says and go quietly. That's the sensible thing to do.

She gave her what she hoped was an inoffensive smile. "All right, go ahead, then."

Gail took a quick, sweeping survey. "I'm afraid perhaps I haven't made myself clear…about myself and Colin." Her voice was patient—teacher to student. Cassidy ignored a surge of annoyance and nodded.

"Colin and I have been together for quite some time. We meet a certain need in each other. Over the years he's had his share of flirtations, which I'm quite capable of overlooking. In many cases these relationships were intensified for the press." She shrugged a gauze-covered shoulder. "Colin's romantic image helps maintain the mystique of the artist. I'll sanction anything when it helps his career. I understand him."

As if unable to remain still for more than short spurts, Gail began to roam the room.

"I'm afraid I don't see why you're telling me this," Cassidy began. The last thing she needed to hear at the moment was how experienced Colin Sullivan was with women.

"Let's you and I understand each other, too." Gail stopped pacing and faced Cassidy again. Her eyes were hard and cold. "As long as Colin's doing this painting, I have to tolerate you. I know better than to interfere with his work. But if you get in my way…" She wrapped her fingers around the strap of Cassidy's purse. "I can find ways of removing people who get in my way."

"I'm sure you can," Cassidy returned evenly. "I'm afraid you'll find I don't remove easily." She pried Gail's fingers from her strap. "Your relationship with Colin is your own affair. I've no intention of interfering with it. Not," she added as a satisfied smile tilted the corner of Gail's mouth, "because you threaten me. You don't intimidate me, Gail. Actually, I feel rather sorry for you."

Cassidy ignored Gail's harsh intake of breath and continued. "Your lack of confidence where Colin is concerned is pathetic. I'm no threat to you. A blind man could see he's only interested in what he puts on that canvas over there." She flung out a hand and pointed to the covered portrait. "I interest him as a *thing,* not as a person." She felt a quick slash of pain as her own statement came home to her. She continued to speak, though the words rushed out in desperation. "I won't interfere with you because I'm not in love with Colin, and I have no intention of ever being in love with him."

Whirling, she darted through the back door of

the studio, slamming it at her back. Only after she had gulped in enough air to steady her nerves did Cassidy realize she had lied.

Chapter 6

For the next two days Cassidy buried herself in her work. She was determined to give herself a time of peace, a time of rest for her emotions. She knew she needed to cut herself off from Colin to accomplish it. The disruption of their day-to-day contact wasn't enough. She knew she needed to block him from her mind. In addition, Cassidy forced herself not to consider the knowledge that had come to her after the scene with Gail. She wouldn't think of being in love with Colin or of the circumstances that made her love impossible. For two days she would pretend she'd never met him.

Cassidy wrote frantically. All her fears and pain and passion were expressed in her words. She worked late the studio, slamming it at her back. Only after she had gulped in enough air to steady her nerves did Cassidy realize she had lied.

Chapter 6

For the next two days Cassidy buried herself in her work. She was determined to give herself a time of peace, a time of rest for her emotions. She knew she needed to cut herself off from Colin to accomplish it. The disruption of their day-to-day contact wasn't enough. She knew she needed to block him from her mind. In addition, Cassidy forced herself not to consider the knowledge that had come to her after the scene with Gail. She wouldn't think of being in love with Colin or of the circumstances that made her love impossible. For two days she would pretend she'd never met him.

Cassidy wrote frantically. All her fears and pain and passion were expressed in her words. She worked late into the night, until she could be certain there would be no dreams to haunt her. When she slept, she slept deeply, exhausted by her own drive. More than once she forgot to eat.

On the second day it began to rain. There was a solid gray wall outside Cassidy's window of which she remained totally unaware. Below, pedestrians scrambled about under umbrellas.

Cassidy's concentration was so complete that when a hand touched her shoulder, she screamed.

"Wow, Cassidy, I'm sorry." Jeff tried to look apologetic but grinned instead. "I knocked and called you twice. You were totally absorbed."

Cassidy held a hand against her heart as if to keep it in place. She took two deep breaths. "It's all right. We all need to be terrified now and again. It keeps the blood moving. Is it your refrigerator?"

Jeff grimaced as he ran a finger down her nose. "Is that where you think my heart is? In your refrigerator? Cassidy, I'm a sensitive guy, my mother'll tell you." Cassidy smiled, leaning back in her chair.

"I've got that gig in the coffeehouse down the street tonight. Come with me."

"Oh, Jeff, I'd love to, but—" She began to make her excuses with a gesture at the papers on her desk. Jeff cut her off.

"Listen, you've been chained to this machine for two days. When are you coming up for air?"

She shrugged and poked a finger at her dictionary. "I've got to go back to the studio tomorrow, and—"

"All the more reason for a break tonight. You're pushing yourself, babe. Take a rest." Jeff watched her face carefully and pressed his advantage. "I could use a friendly face in the audience, you know. We rising stars are very insecure." He grinned through his beard.

Cassidy sighed then smiled. "All right, but I can't stay late."

"I play from eight to eleven," he told her then ruffled her hair. "You can be home and tucked into bed before midnight."

"Okay, I'll be there at eight." Cassidy glanced down at her watch, frowned then tapped its face with her fingertips. "What time is it? My watch stopped at two-fifteen."

"A.M. or P.M.?" Jeff asked dryly. He shook his head. "It's after seven. Hey." He gave her a shrewd look. "Have you eaten?"

Cassidy cast her mind back and recalled an apple at noon. "No, not really."

With a snort of disgust Jeff hauled her to her feet. "Come on with me now, and I'll spring for a quick hamburger."

Cassidy pushed her hair back out of her face. "Golly, I haven't had such a generous offer for a long time."

"Just get a coat," Jeff retorted, stalking to her door. "In case you haven't noticed, it's pouring outside."

Cassidy glanced out her window. "So it is," she agreed. She pulled a yellow slicker out of the closet and dragged it on. "Can I have a cheeseburger?" she asked Jeff as she breezed past him.

"Women. Never satisfied." He closed the door behind them.

The rain didn't bother Cassidy. It was refreshing after her hibernation. The hurried cheeseburger and soft drink were a banquet after the scant meals of the past two days. The smoky, crowded coffeehouse gave her a taste of humanity that she relished after her solitude.

Seated near the back, she drank thick café au lait and listened to Jeff's soothing, introspective music. The evening had grown late when she realized she had relaxed her guard. Colin had slipped over her barrier without her being aware. He stood clearly in her mind's eye. Once he had breached her defenses, Cassidy knew it was useless to attempt to force him out again. She closed her eyes a moment, then opened them, accepting the inevitable. She could not avoid thinking of him forever.

Colin Sullivan was a brilliant artist. He was a confident man who twisted life to suit himself. He had wit and charm and sensitivity. He was selfish and arrogant and totally dedicated to his work. He was thoughtless and domineering and capable of violence.

And I love him completely.

Cassidy trembled with a sigh, then stared into her coffee. I'm an idiot, a romantic fool who knew the pitfalls then fell into one anyway. I see he has a lover, I understand he sees me as important only as a subject for his painting. I'm aware he would make love to me without his heart ever being touched. I know there've been dozens of women in his life, and none of them have lasted.

No, not even Gail, she mused, for all her claims. She's just another woman who's touched the corners of his life. Colin's never made a commitment to a woman. Knowing all this, and wanting a healthy, one-to-one relationship with a man, I fall in love with him. Brilliant.

It's insane. He'll trample me. So what do I do? Slowly Cassidy lifted her coffee and sipped. She drifted away from her surroundings.

I have to finish the portrait; I gave my word. It would be impossible to be in the studio together day after day and not speak. I'm not capable of feuding in any case. Her elbows were propped on the table, the cup held between her hands, but her eyes were staring over the rim and into the distance.

Fighting with him is too dangerous because it brings the emotions to the surface. I don't know how deeply inside me he's capable of seeing. I won't humiliate myself or embarrass him with the fact that I've been stupid enough to fall in love with him. The only thing to do is to behave naturally. Hold the pose for him, talk when he asks me to talk and be friendly. The painting seems to be moving well; it should be finished in a few more weeks. Surely I can behave properly for that amount of time. And when it's finished...

Her thoughts trailed off into darkness. And when the painting's finished, what? I pick up the pieces, she answered. For a moment her eyes were lost and sad. When the painting's finished and Colin drops out of my life, the universe will still function. What a small thing one person's happiness is, she reflected. What a tiny, finite slice of the whole.

With a sigh Cassidy shook off her thoughts and finished the coffee. Setting down the cup she let herself be stroked by Jeff's quiet music.

Cassidy pulled her jacket closer as she stood outside the studio door and searched her bag for the key Colin had given her.

Blasted key, she grumbled silently as she groped for it. She blew her hair from her eyes then pulled out a notepad, three pencils and a linty sourball.

"How did that get in there?" she mumbled. Her eyes flew up when Colin opened the door. "Oh. Hello."

He inclined his head at the greeting then dropped his eyes to her laden hands. "Looking for something?"

Cassidy followed his gaze. Embarrassed, she dumped everything back into her bag and fumbled for poise. "No, I...nothing. I didn't think you'd be here so early." She shifted her purse back to her shoulder.

"It appears it's fortunate I am. Have you lost your key, Cass?" There was a smile on his face that made her feel foolish and scatter-brained.

"No, I haven't lost it," she muttered. "I just can't find it." She walked past him into the studio. Her shoulder barely brushed his chest and she felt a jolt of heat. It wasn't going to be as easy as she'd thought. "I'll change," she said briefly then went directly to the dressing room.

When she emerged, Colin was setting his palette and gave her not so much as a glance. His ignoring of her brought a wave of relief. There, you see, she told herself, there's nothing to worry about.

"I'm going to do some work on the face today," Colin stated, still mixing paints. His use of the impersonal pronoun was further proof his thoughts were not on Cassidy St. John. She denied the existence of the ache in her chest. Keeping silent, she waited until he was finished then stood obligingly while he set the pose. She would, she determined, give him absolutely no trouble. But when he cupped her chin in his hand, she stiffened and jerked away.

Colin's eyes heated. "I need to see the shape of your face through my hands." He set the pose again with meticulous care, barely making contact. "It's not enough to see it with my eyes. Do you understand?"

She nodded, feeling foolish. Colin waited a moment then took her chin again, but lightly, with just his fingertips. Cassidy forced herself to remain still. "Relax, Cassidy, I need you relaxed." The patient tone of the order surprised her into obeying. He murmured his approval as his fingers trailed over her skin.

To Cassidy it was an agony of delight. His touch was gentle, though he frowned in concentration. She wondered if he could feel the heat rising to her skin. Colin traced her jawline and ran his fingers over her cheekbones. Cassidy focused on bringing air in and out of her lungs at an even pace. She tried to tell herself that his touch was as impersonal as a doctor's, but when his hand lingered on her cheek she brought her eyes warily to his.

"Hold steady," he commanded briskly, then turned to go to his easel. "Look at me," he ordered as he picked up his palette and brush.

Cassidy obeyed, trying to put her mind on anything but the man who painted her. Even as her eyes met his, she realized it was hopeless. She could not look at him and not see him. She could not be with him and not be aware of him. She could not block him out of her mind with any more success than she could block him out of her heart.

Would it be wrong, she wondered, to let myself dream a little? Would it be wrong to look for some pieces of happiness in the time I have left with him?

Unhappiness will come soon enough. Can't I just enjoy being near him and pay the price after he's gone? It seemed a small thing.

Cassidy watched him work, memorizing every part of him. There would come a time, she knew, when she would want the memories. She studied the dark fullness of the hair falling on his forehead and curling over his collar. She studied the black arched brows which were capable of expressing so many moods. The planes of his face fascinated her. His eyes lifted again and again to her face as he painted. There was a fierce concentration in them, an urgency that intensified an already impossible blue.

She couldn't see his hands, but she envisioned them, long and narrow and beautiful. She could feel them learning her face, seeing what perhaps she herself would never see, understanding what she might never understand. If one has to fall foolishly in love, she decided, there couldn't be a more perfect man.

They worked for hours, taking short breaks for Cassidy to stretch her muscles. Colin was always impatient to begin again. She sensed his mood, his excitement, and knew something exceptional was being created. The studio was alive with it. Eagerness, anticipation, tingled in the air.

"The eyes," he muttered and set down his palette. Quickly he stalked over to her. "Come, I need to see you closer." He pulled her to just behind the easel. "The eyes can be the soul of a portrait."

Colin took her by the shoulders, and his face was barely an inch from hers. The smell of paint and turpentine was sharp in her nostrils. Cassidy knew she would never smell them again without thinking of him.

"Look at me, Cass. Straight on."

She obeyed, though the look of his eyes nearly undid her. It was deep, intruding, reaching past what was offered and seeking the whole. Reflected in his eyes, she saw herself.

I'm a prisoner there, she thought. His. Their breaths mingled, and her lips parted, inviting his to close the minute distance. Something flickered and nearly caught flame. Abruptly he stepped back to his canvas.

Cassidy spoke without thinking. "What did you see?"

"Secrets," Colin murmured as he painted. "Dreams. No, don't look away, Cass, it's your dreams I need."

Helplessly Cassidy brought her eyes back. It was far too late for resistance. Setting down his palette and brush, Colin frowned at the canvas for several long moments, then he stepped toward Cassidy and smiled.

"It's perfect. You gave me what I needed."

Cassidy felt a tiny thrill of alarm. "Is it finished?"

"No, but nearly." He lifted her hands and kissed them one at a time. "Soon."

"Soon," she repeated and thought it an ugly word.

Quickly she shoved back depression. "Then it must be going well."

"Yes, it's going well."

"But you're not going to let me see it yet."

"I'm superstitious." He gave her hands a gentle squeeze. "Humor me."

"You let Gail see it." Unable to prevent herself, Cassidy let resentment slip into her tone.

"Gail's an artist," Colin pointed out. He released her hands then patted her cheek. "Not the model."

With a sigh of defeat Cassidy turned to wander the room. "You must have painted her...at one time or other," she commented. "She's so striking, so vital."

"She can't hold a pose for five minutes," Colin said. He began to clean his brushes at the worktable.

Smiling, Cassidy leaned on the windowsill. "Do you have a hard time with your seascapes?" she asked him. "Or do you simply command the water and clouds to stop fidgeting? I believe you could do it." She stretched then lifted the weight of her hair from her neck. With an expansive sigh, she let it fall again to tumble as it chose. The sun shimmered through its shades.

When she turned her head to smile at Colin again, she found him watching her, the brush he was cleaning held idly in one hand. Something pulled at her, urging her to go to him. Instead, she walked to the other end of the room.

"The first painting of yours I ever saw was an Irish

landscape." Cassidy kept her back to him and tried to speak naturally. "It was a small, exquisite work bathed in evening light. I liked it because it helped me imagine my mother. Isn't that odd?" She turned back to him as the thought eclipsed her nerves. "I have several pictures of her, but that painting made her seem real. She rarely seems real to me." Her voice softened with the words; then, suddenly, she smiled at him. "Are your parents alive, Colin?"

His eyes held hers for a moment. "Yes." He went back to cleaning his brushes. "Back in Ireland."

"They must miss you."

"Perhaps. They've six other children. I don't imagine they find much time to be lonely."

"Six!" Cassidy exclaimed. Her lips curved at the thought. "Your mother must be remarkable."

Colin looked over again, flashing a grin. "She had a razor strap that could catch three of us at one time."

"No doubt you deserved it."

"No doubt." He scrutinized the sable of his brush. "But I recall wishing a time or two her aim hadn't been so keen."

"My father lectured," Cassidy remembered, taking a long breath in and out. "I'd often wish he'd whack me a time or two and be done with it. Lectures are a great deal more painful, I think, than a razor strap."

"Like Professor Easterman's at Berkeley?" Colin asked with a grin. Cassidy blinked at him.

"How did you know about him?"

"You told me yourself, Cass my love. Last week, I think it was. Or perhaps the week before."

"I never thought you were listening," she murmured. Cassidy tried to remember all she had rambled about since the sittings had begun. Her teeth began to worry her bottom lip. "I can't think of half the things I talked about."

"That's all right, I do…well enough." After wiping his hands on a rag, Colin turned back to her. She was frowning, displeased. "You've got those lines between your brows again, Cass," he said lightly and smiled when she smoothed them out. "Well now, I've made you miss lunch, and that's a crime when you're already thin enough to slip under the door. Shall I poison you with whatever's in the kitchen, or will you settle for coffee?"

"I think I'll pass on both those gracious invitations." She swung around and glided toward the dressing room. "I'll take my chances at home. I have a neighbor who hoards stale doughnuts."

Cassidy closed the door behind her and smiled. That wasn't so bad, she told her reflection. The ground was only shaky a couple of times. Now that the worst of it's over, the rest of the sittings should be easy.

Humming lightly, she began to strip out of the gown. Everything's going to be all right. After all, I'm a grown woman. I can handle myself.

After she had slipped out of the dress, Cassidy held it aloft to shake out the folds. When the door opened, her humming turned to a shriek. In a quick jerk she pressed the dress against her naked skin and held on with both hands.

"What about dinner?" Colin asked and leaned against the open door.

"Colin!"

"Yes?" he asked in a pleasant tone.

"Colin, go away. I'm not dressed." She hugged the dress close and hoped she was somewhat covered.

"Yes, so I see, but you haven't answered my question."

Cassidy made an anxious sound and swallowed. "What question?"

"What about dinner?" he repeated. His eyes skimmed over her bare shoulders.

"What about dinner?" she demanded.

"You can't eat stale doughnuts for dinner, Cass. It's not healthy." He smiled at the incredulity on her face. She shifted the dress a bit higher.

"He keeps tacos as well," she said primly. "Now, would you mind shutting the door on your way out?"

"Tacos? Oh, no, that won't do." Colin shook his head and ignored her request. "I'll have to feed you myself."

Cassidy began to demand her privacy again then

stopped. For a moment she studied him thoughtfully. "Colin, are you asking me for a date?"

"A date?" he repeated. For a moment he said nothing as he appeared to consider the matter. One brow arched as he studied her. "It certainly seems that way."

"To dinner?" Cassidy asked cautiously.

"To dinner."

"What time?"

"Seven."

"Seven," she repeated with a nod as she shut her ears on her practical side. "Now, close the door so I can get dressed."

"Certainly." A wicked gleam shot into his eyes, making her clutch the dress with both hands. She took one wary step in retreat. "By the way, Cass, you'd never've been a successful general."

"What?"

"You forgot to cover your flank," he told her as he shut the door behind him.

Twisting her head, Cassidy caught the full rear length of herself in the mirror.

Chapter 7

As Cassidy dressed that evening she blessed her short skip into the boutique business. The wisteria crepe de chine was worth all the hours she had practiced patience. It was a thin, dreamlike dress with floating lines. Her shoulders were left bare as the bodice was caught with elastic just above her breasts. The material nipped in at the waist then fell fully to the knees. She slipped on the cap-sleeved matching jacket and tied it loosely at the waist. The color was good for her eyes, she decided, bringing out the uniqueness of their shade. This was a night she didn't want to feel ordinary.

You shouldn't even be going. Cassidy brought the brush through her hair violently in response to the nag-

ging voice. I don't care. I am going. *You'll get hurt.*
I'll be hurt in any case. Moving quickly, she fastened
small gold lover's knots to her ears. Doesn't everyone
deserve one special moment? Aren't I entitled to a
glimpse of real happiness? I'll have my one evening
with him without that blasted painting between us.
I'll have my moment when he's looking at me, seeing
me, and not whatever it is he sees when we're in the
studio.

She lifted her scent and sprayed a cloud as delicate
as the wisteria. I won't think about tomorrow, only tonight. The painting's almost finished and then it'll be
over. I have to have something. One evening isn't too
much to ask. I'll pay the price later, but I'm going to
have it. After tossing her hair behind her shoulders,
Cassidy glanced at her watch.

"Oh, good grief, it's already seven!" Frantically she
began to search for her key. She was on her hands and
knees, peering under the convertible sofa that doubled
as her bed, when the knock came. "Yes, yes, yes, just
a minute," she called out crossly and stretched out for
something shiny in the dark beneath the sofa.

She pulled it out with an "Aha!" of triumph, then
sighed when she saw a quarter and not a key in her fingers.

"I said I'd buy," Colin told her, and Cassidy's head
shot up. He stood inside her door, looking curiously at

the woman on her hands and knees. Cassidy straightened up, blew her hair from her eyes and studied him.

He wore a slimly tailored black suit. Its perfect cut accentuated the width of his shoulders and leanness of his build. His shirt was a splash of white in contrast and opened at the throat. Cassidy concluded Colin Sullivan would never restrict himself with a tie. She leaned back on her heels.

"I've never seen you in a suit before," she commented. The lamplight fell softly on her upturned face. "But you don't look too conventional. I'm glad."

"You're an amazing creature, Cassidy." He held out a hand to help her up, touching the other to her hair as she rose.

Standing, she tilted her head back and smiled at him. "Do you think so?"

A smile was his answer as he stepped back, keeping her hand in his. "You look lovely." The survey he made was quick and thorough. "Perfectly lovely." Taking her other hand, he turned it palm up and revealed the quarter. "Cab fare?" he asked. "It won't take you far."

Cassidy frowned down at her own hand. "I thought it was my key."

"Of course." Colin took the quarter and examined it critically. "It looks remarkably like one."

"It did in the dark under the sofa," Cassidy retorted then resumed her search. "It has to be here somewhere," she muttered as she shuffled through papers on her desk. "I've looked everywhere, positively everywhere."

"Where's the bedroom?" Colin asked, watching her shake out the pages of a dictionary.

"This *is* the bedroom," Cassidy informed him and poked through the leaves of a fern. "And the living room, and the study and the parlor. I like things all in one place, it saves steps." She found an eraser under a pile of notebooks and scowled at it. "I looked all over for this yesterday." With a long sigh she set it down.

"All right, just a minute," she said to the room in general as she leaned back on the desk. "I'll get it." Her eyes closed as she rubbed the tip of her finger over the bridge of her nose. "Last time I had it, I'd been to the market. I came in," she said, pointing to the door, "and I took the bag into the kitchen. I put a can of juice into the freezer, and…" Her eyes widened before she scrambled into the next room.

When she came back, she bounced the key from palm to palm. "It's cold," she explained and flushed under Colin's amused glance. "I must have been thinking of something else when I left it in there." Picking up a small gold bag, Cassidy dropped the frozen key inside. "That should do it." She moved to the door and engaged the lock. Gravely, Colin walked to her then cupped her face in his hands.

"Cass."

"Yes?"

"You don't have any shoes on."

"Oh." She lifted her shoulders then let them fall. "I suppose I'll need them."

He kissed her forehead and let her go. "It's best to be prepared for anything." A grin accompanied the gesture of his arm. "They seem to be by your desk."

In silence, Cassidy walked to the desk and slipped into her shoes. Her eyes were smiling as she returned to Colin. "Well, have I forgotten anything else?"

He took her hand, interlocking their fingers. "No."

"Do you like organized people particularly, Colin?" She tilted her head with the question.

"Not particularly."

"Good. Shall we go?"

Cassidy's first surprise of the evening was the Ferrari that sat by the curb. It was red and sleek and flashy. "That must be yours," she murmured, taking her eyes from bumper to bumper then back again. "Or my neighbor has suddenly inherited a fortune."

"One of Vince's bribes." Colin opened the door on the passenger side. "For this I did a portrait of his niece. A remarkably plain creature with an overbite. Shall I put the top up?"

"No, don't." Cassidy settled into the seat as she watched him round the hood. Cinderella never had a pumpkin like this, she thought and smiled. "I thought you didn't paint anyone unless you were particularly interested in the subject."

"Vince is one of the few people I have difficulty refusing." The Ferrari roared into life. Excitement vibrated under Cassidy's feet.

"Did you know you can buy a three-bedroom brick rambler in New Jersey for what this car costs? With a carport and five spreading junipers."

Colin grinned and swung away from the curb. "I'd make a lousy neighbor."

Colin drove expertly through the city. They skirted Golden Gate Park, and avoided the labyrinthine stretches of freeway. They took side roads, narrow roads, and he maneuvered through traffic with smooth skill.

Cassidy could smell the varied scents from the sidewalk flower vendors and hear the brassy clang of the trolley bell. Tilting her head back, she could see the peak of a slender skyscraper. "Where're we going?" she asked but cared little as the breeze fluttered over her cheeks. It was enough to be with him.

"To eat," Colin returned. "I'm starving."

Cassidy turned to face him. "For an Irishman, you're not exactly talkative. Look." She sat up and pointed. "The fog's coming in."

It loomed over the bay, swallowing the bridge with surprising speed. As Cassidy watched, only the pinnacles of the Golden Gate speared the tumbling cloud.

"There'll be foghorns tonight," she murmured then looked at Colin again. "They make such a lonely sound. It always makes me sad, though I never know why."

"What sound makes you happy?" He glanced over to her, and she brushed wisps of flying hair from her face.

"Popping corn," she answered instantly then laughed at herself.

Leaning her head back, Cassidy looked up at the sky. It was piercingly blue. How many cities could have tumbling fog and blue skies? she wondered. When Colin pulled to the curb, her gaze traveled down until it encountered the huge expanse of the hotel. Her lips parted in surprise as she recognized the area. Nob Hill. She had paid no attention to their direction.

Her door was opened by a uniformed doorman who offered his hand to help her alight. She waited while Colin passed him a bill then joined her.

"Do you like seafood?" He took her hand and moved toward the entrance.

"Why, yes, I—"

"Good. They have rather exceptional seafood here."

"So I've heard," Cassidy murmured.

In a few steps she walked from a world she knew into one she had only read of.

The restaurant was huge and sumptuous. High, iridescent glass ceilings crowned a room dripping with chandeliers. The carpet was rich, the tables many and elegantly white clothed. The maître d' was immediately attentive, and as Colin called him by name Cassidy realized the artist was no stranger there.

The secluded corner table set them apart from the vastness of the restaurant yet left Cassidy with a full view of the splendor. Jeff's cheeseburger seemed light-years away. Having gawked as much as she deemed proper, Cassidy turned to Colin.

"It seems I'm going to do better than tacos after all."

"I'm a man of my word," he informed her. "That's why I give it as seldom as possible. Wine?" he asked and smiled at her in his masterfully charming fashion. "You don't look the cocktail type."

"Oh?" Her head tilted. "Why not?"

"Too much innocence in those big violet eyes." He brushed her hair behind her shoulder. "It almost makes me consider doing something bourgeois like cutting the wine with water."

A black-coated waiter stood respectfully at Colin's elbow. "A bottle of Château Haut-Brion blanc," he ordered, keeping his eyes on Cassidy. With a slight bow the waiter drifted backward and away. She watched him then took another long look around the room, trying to absorb every detail. "I noticed by your desk that you've been working. Is it going well?"

Cassidy studied Colin with some surprise. Perhaps

he saw more than she assumed he did. "Yes, actually, I think it is. I'm having one of those periods when everything falls into place. They don't last long, but they're productive. Does it work like that with painting?"

"Yes. Times when everything seems to flow without effort, and times when you scrape the canvas down again and again." He smiled at her, and his long fingers traced her wrist. "Somewhat like you tearing up pages, I imagine."

The waiter returned with their wine, and the ritual of opening and tasting began. Gratefully, Cassidy remained silent. The pulse in her wrist had leapt at Colin's casual touch, and she used the time to quiet its skittish rhythm. When her glass was filled, she was able to lift it with complete composure. The wine was lightly chilled and exquisite.

"To your taste?" Colin asked as he watched her sip.

Cassidy's eyes smiled into his. "It could become a habit."

"Tell me what you're writing about." He, too, lifted his glass, but his free hand covered hers.

"It's about two people and their life together and apart from each other."

"A love story?"

"Yes, a complex one." She frowned a moment at their joined hands then brought her eyes to Colin's again. The flame of the candle threw gold among the violet. She reminded herself to enjoy the moment, not to think of tomorrow. A smile lifted her lips as she touched the glass to them. "They both seem to be volatile characters and get away from me sometimes. There's a fierce determination in them both to stand separate, yet they're drawn together. I'd like to think love allows them to remain separate in some aspects."

"Love makes its own rules, depending on who's playing." His finger trailed over her knuckles then down to her nails before they traveled back. The simple gesture quickened her heartbeat. "Will they have a happy ending?"

Cassidy allowed herself to absorb the pure blue of his eyes. "Perhaps they will," she murmured. "Their destinies are in my hands."

Watching her, Colin brought her hand to his lips. "And for tonight, Cass," he said softly, "is yours in mine?"

Her eyes were dark and steady on his. "For tonight."

He smiled then, with the flash of the pirate. Lifting his glass, he toasted her. "To the long evening ahead."

It was a luxuriously lengthy meal. Wine sparkled in crystal. Even after endless courses, they lingered long over coffee. Cassidy savored each moment. If she was to have only one evening with the man she loved, she would relish each morsel of time. Perhaps by the force of her own will, she could slow the hands of the clock.

The candle flickered low when they rose from the table. Her hand slipped into his. Just as they reached the lobby Cassidy heard Colin's name called. Looking up, she saw a round, balding man in an impeccably cut suit coming toward them. He had a full smile and an extended hand. On reaching Colin, he pumped it enthusiastically while his other thumped on Colin's shoulder. Cassidy saw a large diamond flash from the ring on his hand.

"Sullivan, you rascal, it's good to see you."

"Jack." An easy grin spread over Colin's face. "How've you been?"

"Getting by, getting by. Have a little job in town." His eyes drifted to Cassidy and lingered.

"Cass, this is Jack Swanson, a perfect reprobate. Jack, Cassidy St. John, a perfect treasure."

Cassidy was torn between pleasure at Colin's description and astonishment as she put Swanson's face and name together. Over the past twenty-five years he had produced some of the finest motion pictures in the industry. As he took her hand and squeezed it, she struggled to conceal her feelings.

"Reprobate?" Swanson snorted and kept possession of Cassidy's hand. "You can't believe half the things this Irishman says. I'm a pillar of the community."

"There's a plaque in his den that says so," Colin added.

"Never did have an ounce of respect. Still…" Swanson's eyes roamed over Cassidy's face. There was appreciation in the look. "His taste is flawless. Not an actress, are you?"

"Not unless you count being a mushroom in the fourth-grade pageant." Cassidy smiled.

Swanson chuckled and nodded. "I've dealt with actresses who had lesser credits."

"Cassidy's a writer," Colin put in. He draped an arm around her shoulders, running his hand lightly down her arm. "You warned me to stay away from actresses."

"Since when have you listened to my sage advice?" Swanson scoffed. He pursed his lips as he studied Cassidy. Appreciation became speculation. "A writer. What sort of writer are you?"

"Why, a brilliant one, of course," she told him. "Without a scrap of ego or temperament."

Swanson patted her hand. "I've a late meeting or I'd steal you away from this young scamp now. We'll have dinner before I leave town." He cast an eye at Colin. "You can bring him along if you like." With another slap for Colin's shoulder, he lumbered away.

"Quite a character, isn't he?" Colin asked as he steered Cassidy toward the door again.

"Marvelous." It occurred to her that since meeting Colin, she had held hands with an Italian duke and one of Hollywood's reigning monarchs.

They stepped outside into the soft light of evening.

The sun was gone, but some of its light still lingered. Cassidy slipped into the Ferrari with a contented sigh. She watched the first star flicker into life. With surprise she noted that Colin was headed away from the direction of her apartment.

"Where are we going?"

"There's this little place I know." He turned a corner and eased into traffic. "I thought you'd enjoy it." He shot her a glance and a smile. "Not tired, are you?"

Cassidy's lips curved. "No, I'm not tired."

The nightclub was dimly lit and smoky. Tables were small and crowded together. Jeans sat next to elegant evening dresses and splashy designer outfits. Brassy music blared from a band near a postage-stamp dance floor. Couples swayed together as they moved to the beat.

Colin escorted Cassidy to a dark table at the side of the room. His name was called now and again, but he only made a gesture of acknowledgment and continued until they were seated.

"This is wonderful! I'm certain it's a front for gun running or jewel smuggling," Cassidy exclaimed.

Colin laughed, taking both her hands. "You'd like that, would you?"

"Of course." She grinned, and her eyes lit with mischief.

A waitress had pushed her way over to them and

stood, impatient, with her weight on one hip. "The lady needs champagne," Colin told her.

"Who doesn't," she mumbled and shoved her way back through the tables.

Cassidy laughed with unbridled delight. "No deferential bows for Mr. Sullivan in here," she commented.

"It's all a matter of atmosphere. I'm rather fond of sassy waitresses in the right setting. And," he added softly, turning her hand over and kissing the inside of her wrist, "crowded tables that require very close contact. Poor lighting," he continued, pressing his lips to her palm. "Where I can enjoy the taste of your skin in relative privacy." With a slight movement of his head, he kissed the sensitive skin behind her ear.

"Colin," she said breathlessly and lifted her hand to his lips in defense. He merely took it in his and kissed her fingers.

The bottle of champagne came down on the table with a bang. Colin pulled out a bill and handed it to the waitress. Shoving it in her pocket, she stalked away.

"Annoyingly speedy service tonight," he murmured as he opened the bottle. The pop was drowned out by the loud horns of the band. Cassidy accepted the wine and took a long, slow sip in the hope of stabilizing her pulse.

They drank champagne in quiet companionship, watching the raucous nightlife revolve around them. Cassidy's mood grew mellow and dreamy. Reality and make-believe became too difficult to separate. When Colin stood and took her hand, she rose to go with him to the dance floor.

The music had turned low and bluesy. He slipped both arms around her waist, and in response she lifted hers to circle his neck. Their bodies came together. The air was thick with smoke and clashing perfumes. Other couples were little more than shadows in the dim light. Their movement was only a slow swaying with their bodies pressed close.

Cassidy tilted back her head to look at him. Their eyes joined, their lips tarried less than a whisper apart. She felt a quick surge of desire. If they had been on an island without a trace of humanity, she could not have felt more alone with him. The music ended on a haunted bass note.

Silently Colin took her hand and led her from the crowd.

The moon was a white slice. Cooler air blew some of the heat from Cassidy's blood and some of the clouds from her brain. The Ferrari climbed a hill then descended. Cassidy smiled to herself. There was nothing in the evening she would have changed. No regrets.

Fog curled in twisting fingers on the road ahead. As she glanced to the side Cassidy saw the solid mass of clouds over the bay below them. Again she turned to Colin.

"To my houseboat," he told her before she could form the question. "I have something for you."

Warning lights flashed on and off in her brain. The bittersweet taste of danger was in her mouth. Cassidy looked out on the fog-choked bay and told herself she should ask Colin to take her home. But the night isn't over, she reminded herself. I promised myself tonight.

Fog swirled more thickly as they drove toward sea level. Now and again, from somewhere deep in the mist, came the low warning horns. She'd lost all sense of time when Colin stopped the car. Once again she was in a make-believe world. This one had drifting mists and the sigh of lapping water. Colin led her toward a shrouded shape. The high, maniacal call of a loon speared the silence. A narrow rope bridge swayed lightly under her feet as they crossed it. A breeze blew aside a curtain of fog, and the houseboat jumped into the opening.

"Oh, Colin." She stopped to stare at it with delight and surprise. "It's wonderful."

She saw a wide structure of aged wood in two levels with a high deck on the bow. Fog misted over again as they approached.

Inside Cassidy shook the dampness from her hair as Colin switched on a light. They walked down two steps and into the living room. It was a large square room with a low, inviting couch and tables scattered for convenience. To the right another short set of stairs led to the galley.

"How marvelous to live on the water." Cassidy spun to Colin and smiled.

"On a clear night the city's all prisms and crystals. In the fog it's brooding and wrapped in mystery." He came to her and, with a habitual gesture, brushed her hair behind her shoulder. His fingers lingered. "Your hair's damp," he murmured. "Do you know how many shades of gold and brown I used to paint your hair? It changes in every light, daring someone to define its color." Colin frowned suddenly and dropped his hand. "You should have a brandy to ward off the chill."

He turned away and walked to a cabinet. Cassidy watched him pour brandy into snifters while she dealt with the effect the intimate tone of his voice and the touch of his hand had had on her.

After accepting the brandy she turned to wander around the room. On a far wall was a painting of the bay at sunrise. The sky was molten with color, reds and golds at their most intense. There was a feeling of frenzied motion and brilliance. Even before she looked for the signature, Cassidy knew it was a Kingsley.

"She's immensely talented," Colin commented from behind.

"Yes," Cassidy agreed with sincerity. The painting gripped her. "It makes the start of a day demand your attention. A sunrise like this would be exciting, but I don't think I could begin each morning with such violence, however beautiful."

"Are you speaking of the painting or of the artist?"

Realizing his question had followed her thoughts, Cassidy shrugged and stepped away. "Strange," she began again. "One would think an artist would cover his walls with paintings. You have relatively few." She began to examine his collection, moving slowly from one to the next. Abruptly she stopped, staring at a small canvas. It was the Irish landscape she had told him of that morning.

"I wondered if you'd remember it." He stood behind her again, but this time his hands came to her shoulders. There was something casually possessive in the gesture.

"Yes, of course I do."

"I was twenty when I painted that. On my first trip back to Ireland."

"How odd that I should have spoken of it just this morning," Cassidy murmured.

"Destiny, Cass," Colin claimed and kissed the top of her head. Stepping around her, he took the canvas from the wall. "I want you to have it."

Cassidy's eyes flew to his. "No, Colin, I couldn't." Distress and amazement mingled in her voice.

"No?" His brow arched under his fall of hair. "You appeared to like it."

"Oh, Colin, you know I do. It's beautiful, it's wonderful." Her distress deepened, reflecting clearly on her face. "I can't just take one of your paintings."

"You're not taking it, I'm giving it to you," he countered. "That's one of the privileges of the artist."

"Colin." Her eyes went back to the painting then lifted to his. "You wouldn't have kept it all this time if it hadn't meant something special to you. You'd have sold it."

"Some things you don't sell. Some things you give." He held the small canvas out to her. "Please."

Tears thickened in her throat. "I've never heard you say 'please' before."

"I save it for special occasions."

Cassidy looked back at him. He had given her more than the painting; it was a bond—between herself and a woman she had never known. Her smile came slowly. "Thank you."

Colin traced her lips with a fingertip. "This is one of the loveliest things about you," he murmured. "Come," he said abruptly. "Sit down and drink your brandy." He took the canvas and set it aside, then led Cassidy to the sofa.

"Do you paint here, too?" she asked as she sipped her brandy.

"Sometimes."

"I remember the night I met you, your wanting me to come back here for sketches."

"And you threatened me with a husband in a football helmet."

"It was the best I could think up on the spur of the moment." She turned her head to grin at him and found his face dangerously close. His fingers tangled in her hair before she could ease away. Slowly he leaned closer until his lips brushed her cheek. Feather light, the kiss moved to her other cheek, lingering over her lips without touching. Still, she could taste the kiss on them.

"Colin," Cassidy whispered. She put a hand to his chest as his lips moved to her temple. She knew the warmth she felt was not from the brandy.

"Cassidy." He trailed his mouth down to her jawline then drew away. His eyes were grave as he looked down at her, his hand light on her shoulder. "The last time I kissed you, I hurt you. I regret that."

"Please, Colin." Cassidy shook her head to halt his words. "We were both angry."

"You've already forgiven me, because it's your nature to do so. But I remember the look on your face." He ran his hand down her arm until it linked with hers. "I want to kiss you again, Cass, the way you should be kissed." He took his hand and gently circled her neck. "But I need you to tell me it's what you want."

It would be so easy to refuse. She had only to form the word "no," and she knew he'd let her go. But she was as truly his prisoner now as if she were chained to him. "Yes," she said and closed her eyes. "Yes."

His mouth touched hers lightly, and her lips parted. His kisses were soft and gentle, lingering before one ended and another began. She felt him slip the light jacket from her shoulders and enjoyed the warmth of his hands on her skin. Slowly the kisses grew deeper. Her arms found their way around him. The languor that spread through her went far beyond the effects of the wine. Her limbs were pliant, her mind clouded as her senses grew sharper.

When their lips parted, Colin loosened his hold. "Cass."

With a sigh she snuggled against him, brushing his neck with a kiss. She ran a hand experimentally up the silk of his shirt. "Yes?" she murmured, lifting her face to his. Her eyes were slumberous, her lips a temptation. Colin swore under his breath before he crushed his mouth to hers.

Cassidy's response was instantaneous. Her passion went from languid to flaming in the space of a heartbeat. Blood pounded thickly in her brain as she found herself falling backward onto the cushions of the sofa. Colin's body was taut. His hands caressed the bare skin of her shoulders as the kiss deepened. At the base of her throat he found more pleasure, and his mouth lingered there as her pulse beat wildly beneath it.

The elastic of her bodice slid down at his insistence,

freeing her breasts to his searching hands. Unbridled, her passion raced through her, bringing a moan that spoke of longing and delight. His mouth trailed down through the valley between her breasts, devouring her heated skin. His fingers brushed over the peak of her breasts, exploring, learning, until his mouth replaced them. Cassidy gave a shuddering moan as he brought his lips back to hers, accepting the fierce, final urgency that flared before he ended the kiss. Her eyes opened to meet the dark fire of his.

Seeing the tumble of his hair over his brow, she lifted a hand to push it back. She murmured his name. Colin caught her hand in his as she took it to his cheek. Carefully he drew the bodice of her dress into place then pulled her with him to a sitting position.

"I make few noble gestures, Cassidy." His voice was husky, and under her palm she could feel the rapid beat of his heart. "This is one of them." Rising, he drew her to her feet then draped her jacket over her shoulders. "I'll take you home."

"Colin," she began, knowing only that she wanted to be his.

"No, don't say anything." He dropped his hands from her shoulders and put them in his pockets. "You put your destiny in my hands for tonight. I'll take you home. Next time the decision will be in your hands."

Chapter 8

The sun was high and bright. Cassidy watched it spear through her window as she lay in bed. It fell in a patch on the floor and shimmered. Her eyes drifted to the painting that hung to her left. It had hung there for only two days, but she knew every minute detail of the canvas. She knew the very texture of the brush strokes. Sighing, she stared up at the ceiling.

She remembered every moment of her evening with Colin, from the instant she had looked up from her hands and knees by her couch to the brief good-bye at the door.

When she had returned to the studio the morning after their date, Colin had fallen into his work pattern with apparent ease. Whatever had been between them,

Cassidy decided, had been for that night. For him, it was over. For me, she thought, studying the painting again, it's forever.

I should be grateful to him for taking me home when he did. If I had stayed... If I had stayed, she repeated after a long breath, I would have become one of his lovers. And then he would have picked up his life exactly where he left off, and I would be even more alone than I am now. As it is, I have one exceptional evening to remember. Wine and candlelight and music.

"Romantic fool," she muttered abruptly then rolled over and punched her pillow.

"Cassidy." The knock sounded as a brief concession before Jeff burst through the door. "Hey, Cassidy." He stopped and gave her a look of disgust. "Still in bed? It's eleven o'clock."

Cassidy pulled the sheet up to her chin and scrambled to sit up. "Yes, I'm still in bed. I worked till three-thirty." She frowned past him. "I thought I'd remembered to lock that door."

"Uh-uh." Jeff hurried over and plopped on the bed while she flushed with embarrassed amusement.

"Make yourself at home," she said with a grand gesture of her free arm. "Don't mind me."

"Take a look at this! You got yourself in the paper."

"What?" Cassidy glanced down at the newspaper Jeff had clutched in his hand. "What are you talking about?"

"I splurged on a Sunday paper," he began then his lips spread in a grin. He touched her nose with a fingertip. "And who do I see when I take a look at the society section, but my friend and neighbor, Cassidy St. John."

"You're making that up," Cassidy accused and tossed back her sleep-tumbled hair. "What would I be doing on the society page?"

"Dancing with Colin Sullivan," Jeff informed her as he waved the paper under her nose.

Cassidy grabbed his wrist to stop the movement, then her mouth fell open in astonishment. She stared, unbelievingly, at the picture. In two quick moves she had dropped the sheet and grabbed the paper from Jeff's hand. "Let me see that."

"Help yourself," he said amiably. He settled back on one elbow to watch myriad expressions cross her face. The flush sleep had put into her cheeks grew deeper. "Seems you were seen together in some hot spot. A picture gets snapped, and they add a bit of interesting speculation of who Sullivan's latest flame is." He pulled on his beard and chuckled. "Little do they know she's sitting right here in a number fifty-three football jersey that looks a lot better on her than it would on a right tackle." He chuckled again then peered down at the newspaper. "You look real good in there, too."

"This is all—all drivel!" Cassidy slammed down the paper then scrambled to her knees. Pushing Jeff aside she stepped over him to the floor. "Did you read that story?" she demanded and kicked a stray tennis shoe into a corner. "How dare they imply such things?"

Jeff sat back up, watching her spin around the room. "Hey, Cassidy, it's just a story, nothing to get all worked up about. Besides…" He picked up the discarded paper and smoothed it out. "They're really pretty complimentary where you're concerned. Listen, they call you a…" He paused while he searched down the phrase. "Oh, yeah, here it is. A 'nubile young beauty.' Sounds pretty good."

Cassidy made a low sound in her throat then kicked the mate to the tennis shoe into an opposing corner. "That's just like a man," she stormed back at him. Turning away, she pulled open a drawer and yanked out a pair of cutoffs; then, spinning around, she waved them at him. "Toss out a few compliments and it makes everything all right." Cassidy dove back into the drawer and came up with a crimson scoop-necked T-shirt. "Well, it's not, it's absolutely not." She pushed her hair out of her face and drew in a deep breath. "Can I keep that?" she asked in more controlled tones.

"Sure." Warily, Jeff rose and handed her the paper. He cleared his throat. "Well, I guess I'll just go read the rest of the paper," he told her, but she was already scowling down at the picture again. Taking advantage of her preoccupation, he slipped out the door.

* * *

Less than an hour later Cassidy was stalking down the pier toward Colin's houseboat. Gripped in her hand was the folded page of the Sunday paper. Filled with righteous indignation, she crossed the narrow swaying bridge then pounded on the door. There was silence and the lapping of waves. She glanced around then scowled at the Ferrari.

"Oh, you're home all right, Sullivan," she muttered darkly then pounded again.

"What the devil are you banging about?" Colin's voice boomed over her head. Cassidy backed away from the door, looked up and was blinded by the sun. Furious, she flung up a hand to shade her eyes.

She saw him leaning over the rail of the top deck. He was bare-chested, his cutoffs a slight concession to modesty. He held a paint brush tipped in blue in his hand.

"I've got to talk to you!" Cassidy shouted and waved the paper at him.

"All right then, come up, but stop that idiotic banging." He disappeared from the rail before she could speak again. Cassidy walked toward the bow until she spotted a steep set of stairs. After climbing them, she stood on the upper deck with her hands on her hips. She scowled at his back.

He was on a three-legged stool in front of a canvas, painting with sure, rapid strokes. Glancing over, she saw the sailboats he was recreating. They skimmed over the bay with spinnakers billowing in a riot of color.

"Well, what brings you rapping at my door, Cass?" His voice was muffled as he held the stem of a brush between his teeth like a pirate's saber. Another glided over the canvas. Cassidy stomped over and fearlessly waved the paper in front of his face.

"This!"

With surprising calm, Colin put down both of his brushes, cast her a raised-brow look, then took the paper from her. "It's a good likeness," he said after a moment.

"Colin!"

"Ssh. I'm reading." He lapsed into silence, eyes on the paper, while Cassidy ground her teeth and stalked around the deck. Once he laughed outright but held up a hand when she started to speak. She shut her mouth on something like a growl and turned her back on him. "Well," he said at length. "That was highly entertaining."

Cassidy whirled around. "Entertaining? *Entertaining?!* Is that all you have to say about this—this trash?"

Colin shrugged. "It could be better written, I suppose. Do you want coffee?"

"Did you *read* that?" she demanded and stormed forward until she stood in front of him. The wind tugged at her hair, and she pushed it back, annoyed.

"Did you read the things it said, the things…" Cassidy sputtered to a halt, stomped her foot in frustration then gave him a firm rap on the chest with her fist. "I am not your latest flame, Sullivan."

"Ah."

Her eyes kindled. "Don't you use that significant 'ah' on me. I am *not* your latest flame, or your flame of any sort, and I resent the term. I resent all the little insinuations and innuendos in that article. I resent the unstated fact that you and I are lovers." She tossed back her head. "What sort of logic is it that because we dance together, we have to be lovers?"

"You have to admit the idea is appealing." He chuckled at her smoldering glare. The breeze rolling in from the bay continued to blow her hair around her face. Absently Colin brushed it back then laid a hand on her shoulder. "Would you like to sue the paper?"

She heard the soft amusement in his voice and stuck her hands in her pockets. "I want a retraction," she said stubbornly.

"For what?" he countered. "For snapping a picture? For writing a bit of gossip? My dear child, the picture's enough all by itself." He held it out, drawing her eyes to it. "These two people appear to be totally absorbed in each other."

Cassidy turned away and walked to the rail. She knew it had been the picture that had set her off. Their bodies were close, her arms around his neck, their eyes locked. The dark, smoky nightclub was a backdrop. No words were needed to complete the picture. She remembered the moment, the feeling that had rushed through her, the utter intimacy they had shared.

The picture was an invasion of her private self, and she hated it. She detested the chatty little column beside it that linked her so casually with Colin. Without even having learned her name, they had titled her his woman, his woman of the moment…until the next one. Cassidy frowned out at the water, watching the gulls swoop.

"I don't like it," she muttered. "I don't like being splashed in print for speculation over cornflakes and coffee. I don't like being made into something I'm not by someone's lively imagination. And I don't like being described as a…"

"'Nubile young beauty'?" Colin provided.

"I see nothing funny in that grand little phrase. It makes me feel absurd." She folded her arms over her chest. "It's not a compliment, whatever you and Jeff might think."

"Who the devil is Jeff?"

"He thought the article was just peachy," she continued, working up to a high temper again. "He sat on my bed this morning, telling me I should be flattered, that I should—"

"Perhaps," Colin interrupted and walked to her,

"you'd tell me who Jeff is and why he was in your bed this morning?"

"Not in, *on*," Cassidy corrected impatiently. "And stick to the point, Sullivan."

"I'd like this matter cleared up first." He took a final step toward her then captured her chin. His fingers were surprisingly firm. "In fact, I insist."

"Will you stop it?" she demanded and jerked away. "How can I get anywhere when you're constantly badgering and belittling me."

"Badgering and belittling?" Colin repeated then tossed back his head and roared with laughter. "Now *that's* a grand little phrase. Now, about Jeff."

"Oh, leave him out of it, would you?" Cassidy blew out a frustrated breath, making a wide sweep with her arms. Her eyes began to glitter again. "He brought me the article this morning, that's all. I'm telling you, Colin, I won't be lumped in with all your former and future flames. And I won't be used to sustain the romantic mystique of the artist."

His brows drew together. "Now what precisely is the meaning of that last sentence, for those of us who missed the first installment?"

"I think it's clear, a simple declarative sentence in the first person. I mean it, Colin."

"Yes." He studied her curiously. "I can see you do."

They watched each other in silence. She was painfully aware of the lean attraction of his build, of the bronzed skin left bare but for low-slung cut-offs. Thrown off balance by her own thoughts, Cassidy turned away again and leaned over the rail. For a moment she listened to the gentle slap of water against the wood of the boat. Her shoulders moved with her sigh.

"I'm basically a simple person, Colin. I've never been out of the state and scarcely been more than a hundred miles from the city. I don't have a fascinating background. I'm not a woman of mystery." Composed again, she turned back to him. The breeze picked up her hair and tossed it behind her. "I don't like being misrepresented." She lifted her hands a moment then dropped them to her sides. "I'm not the sort of woman they made me seem in that paper."

Colin folded the paper then tucked it in his back pocket before he crossed to her. "You are infinitely more fascinating than the sort of woman they made you seem in that paper."

Cassidy shook her head. "I wasn't fishing for a compliment."

"A simple statement of fact." He kissed her before she could decide whether to accept or evade him. "Feel better now?"

Cassidy frowned at him. "I'm not a child having a temper tantrum."

His brow lifted. "A nubile young beauty, then."

Cassidy narrowed her eyes at him then glanced down at herself. "I'm nubile enough, I should think."

"And certainly young."

Bringing her eyes back up, she gave him a provocative look. "Don't you think I'm beautiful?"

"No."

"Oh."

Colin laughed then captured her face with his hands. "That face," he said as his eyes roamed over her, "has superb bones, exquisite skin. There's strength and frailty and vivacity, and you're totally unaware of it. A unique, expressive face. *Beautiful* is far too ordinary a word."

Color warmed Cassidy's cheeks. She wondered why, after so many close examinations, her blood still churned when he studied her face. "A charming way to make up for an insult," she said lightly. "It must be the Irish in you."

"I've a much better way."

The kiss was so quickly insistent, Cassidy had no time for thought, only response. A sound of pleasure escaped her as she moved her hands up the taut, bare skin of his chest. She felt the heat of the sun and her own instant need. Her mouth became avid. Desire swirled through her blood, causing her to demand rather than surrender. The passion he released in her ruled her, changing submission to aggression. She felt Colin's arms tighten around her and heard his low moan of approval.

"Cassidy," he murmured as his lips roamed over her face. "You bewitch me."

With a curiosity of their own, her hands explored the long line of his torso, the wiry muscles of his arms and back. His heart hammered against hers as she touched him. Here was a whole new world, and her mouth searched his ravenously as she tested it.

"Oh, dear, I seem to be interrupting."

Startled, Cassidy pulled her mouth from Colin's but was unable to break his hold. Twisting her head, she stared at Gail Kingsley. She stood just at the top of the stairs, one hand poised on the railing. An emerald silk scarf rippled at her throat and trailed in the breeze.

"That seems obvious enough," Colin returned evenly. Flushing to the roots of her hair, Cassidy wriggled for freedom.

"I do apologize, Colin darling. I had no idea you had company. So rare for you on a Sunday, after all." She gave him a smile that established her knowledge of his habits. "I needed to pick up those Rothchild canvases, you remember? And we do have one or two things to discuss. I'll just wait downstairs." She crossed the deck as she spoke and opened a door that led inside. "Shall I make coffee for three?" she added then disappeared without waiting for an answer.

Cassidy twisted her head back to Colin, pressing her

hands against his chest. "Let me go," she demanded between her teeth. "Let me go this minute."

"Why? You seemed happy enough to be held a moment ago."

She threw back her head as she shoved against him. The muscles she had just tested made her movements useless. "A moment ago I was blinded by animal lust. I see perfectly now."

"Animal lust?" Colin repeated. He grinned widely in appreciation. "How interesting. Does it come over you often?"

"Don't you grin at me, Sullivan. Don't you dare!"

Colin released her without sobering his features. "At times it's difficult not to."

"I won't have you holding me while Gail stands there with her superior little smile." With a sniff, she brushed at her T-shirt and shorts.

"Why, Cass, are you jealous?" His grin grew yet wider. "How flattering."

Her head snapped up, her breathing grew rapid. "Why you smug, insufferable—"

"You were perfectly willing to suffer me when you were blinded by animal lust."

A sound of temper came low in her throat. Tested past her limit, Cassidy took an enthusiastic swing at him that carried her in a complete circle. He dodged it, catching her neatly by the waist.

"Women are supposed to slap," he instructed. "Not punch."

"I never read the rules," she snapped then jerked away. Cassidy turned, intending to leave in the same manner she had arrived. Colin caught her hand and spun her back until she collided with his chest. He smiled then kissed the tip of her nose.

"What's your hurry?"

"There's an old Irish saying," she told him as she pushed away again. "Three's a crowd."

He chuckled, patting her cheek. "Cass, don't be a fool."

She rolled her eyes to the sky and prayed for will-power. Screaming wouldn't solve anything. She took several deep breaths. "Oh, go...go paint your spinnakers," she suggested and stalked down the steps to the lower deck.

"Sure and it's a fine-looking woman you are, Cassidy St. John," Colin called after her in an exaggerated brogue. She glanced back over her shoulder with eyes blazing. He leaned companionably over the rail. "And it's the truth it's no more hardship watching your temper walking away than it is watching it coming ahead. Next time I'll be wanting to paint you in a pose that shows your more charming end."

"When pigs fly," she called back and doubled her pace. His laughter raced after her.

Chapter 9

Cassidy knew the painting was nearly finished. She had the frantic, hollow sensation of one living on borrowed time. Though she sensed the end would be almost a relief, a release from the tension of waiting, she tried to hold it off by sheer force of will. As she held the pose, she sensed Colin was perfecting, polishing, rather than creating fresh. His quick impatience had relaxed.

He made no mention of her Sunday visit, and she was grateful. In retrospect, with her temper at a reasoning degree, she knew she had overreacted. She was also forced to admit that she had made a fool of herself. A complete fool.

It's not the first time, she mused. And perhaps, in

a way, excusable. All I could see was a very public picture revealing my very private feelings. Then that silly little article… Then remembering Gail's spouting off about romantic press and Colin's image. Cassidy caught herself before she scowled. *Well, I won't have to listen to her much longer. I'd better start picking up the pieces. It's time to start thinking about tomorrow. A new job,* she concluded dismally. *A new start,* she corrected. *New experiences, new people. Empty nights.*

"Fortunately, I finished the face yesterday," Colin commented. "Your expression's altered a dozen times in the last ten minutes. Amazing what a range you have."

"I'm sorry. I was…" She searched for a word and settled on an inanity. "Thinking."

"Yes, I could see." His eyes caught hers. "Unhappy thoughts."

"No, I was working out a scene."

"Mmm," Colin commented noncommittally then stepped back from the easel. "Not a particularly joyful one."

"No. They can't all be." She swallowed. "It's finished, isn't it?"

"Yes. Quite finished." Cassidy let out a quiet sigh as she watched his critical study. "Come, have a look," he invited. He held out his hand, but his eyes remained on the canvas.

It surprised her that she was afraid. Colin glanced up at her and lifted a brow.

"Come on, then."

Her fingers tightened around the nosegay, but she walked toward him. Obediently she slipped her hand into his extended one. She turned and looked.

Cassidy had tried to imagine it a hundred times, but it was nothing like what she'd thought. The background was dark and shadowy, playing on shading and depth. In its midst, she stood highlighted in the oyster-white dress. Her nosegay was a surprising splash of color calling attention to the frailty of her hands. Pride was in the stance, in the tilt of her head. Her hair was thick and gloriously tumbled, offsetting the quiet innocence of the dress. It was hair that invited passion. There was a delicacy in the bones of her face she had been unaware of, a fragility competing with the strength of the features. She had been right in thinking he would see her as she had never seen herself.

Her lips were parted, unsmiling but waiting to smile. The smile would be to welcome a lover. The knowledge was in her expression, along with the anticipation of something yet to come. The eyes told everything. They were the eyes of a woman consumed by love…the eyes of innocence waiting to be surrendered. No one could look at it and remain unaware that the woman in the painting had loved the man who painted it.

"So silent, Cass?" Colin murmured and slipped an arm around her shoulders.

"I can't find the word," she whispered then drew a trembling breath. "Nothing's adequate, and anything less would sound platitudinous." She leaned against him a moment. "Colin." Cassidy tried to forget for a moment that the eyes in the painting were naked with love. She tried to see the whole and not the revelation of her emotions. Secrets, he had said. Dreams.

Colin kissed her neck above the silk of the dress then released her. "Rarely, an artist steps back from his work and is astonished that his hands have created something extraordinary." She could hear the excitement in his voice, a wonder she had not expected him to be capable of feeling. "This is the finest thing I've ever done." He turned to her then. "I'm grateful to you, Cassidy. You're the soul of it."

Unable to bear his words, Cassidy turned away. She had to cling to some rags of pride. Desperately she kept her voice calm. "I've always felt the artist is the soul of a painting." Cassidy dropped the nosegay on the work-table then continued to wander around the room. The silk whispered over her legs. "It's your—your imagination, your talent. How much of me is really in that painting?"

There was silence for a long moment, but Cassidy didn't turn back to him. "Don't you know?" Cassidy moistened her lips and struggled to keep her tone light as she turned around.

"My face," she agreed; then, gesturing down the dress, she added, "My body. The rest is yours, Colin, I can't take credit for it. You set the mood, you drew out of me what you already saw. You had the vision. It was a wish you asked me to be, and that's what you've made. It's your illusion." Saying the words caused her more pain than she had believed possible. Still, she felt they had to be said.

"Is that how you see it?" Colin's look was speculative, but she sensed the anger just beneath the surface. "You stood, and I pulled the strings."

"You're the artist, Colin." She shrugged and answered lightly. "I'm just an unemployed writer."

After a long, silent study, he crossed to her. There was a steady calculation about the way his hands took her shoulders. She had felt that seeking, probing look before and stiffened her defenses against it. His fingers tightened on her skin. "Has the woman in that portrait anything to do with you?" He asked the question slowly.

Cassidy swallowed the knot in her throat. "Why, of course, Colin, I've just told you—"

He shook her so quickly, the words slid back down her throat. She saw the fury on his face, the vivid temper she knew could turn violent. "Do you think it was only your face I wanted? Just the shell? Is there nothing that's inside you in that painting?"

"Must you have everything?" she demanded in despair and anger. "Must you have it all?" Her voice thickened with emotion. "You've drained me, Colin. That's drained me." She flung a hand toward the canvas. "I've given you everything, how much more do you want?"

She pushed him away as a tidal wave of anguish engulfed her. "You never looked at me, thought of me, unless it was because of that painting." She pushed her hair back with both hands, pressing her fingers against her temples. "I won't give you anymore. I can't, there isn't any. It's all there!" She gestured again, and her voice shook. "Thank God it's over."

With a quick jerk, she was out of his hold and running from the studio.

Cassidy spent the next two weeks in the apartment of vacationing friends. Leaving a brief note for Jeff, she packed up her typewriter and buried herself in work. She unplugged the phone, bolted the door and shut herself in. For two weeks she tried to forget there was a world outside the people and places of her imagination. She lost herself in her characters in an attempt to forget Cassidy St. John. If she didn't exist, she couldn't feel pain. At the end of the interlude, she'd shed five pounds, produced a hundred pages of fresh copy and nearly balanced her nerves.

As she returned, hauling her typewriter back up the steps to her apartment, she heard Jeff's guitar playing through his door. For a moment she hesitated, thinking to stop and tell him she was back, but she passed into her own apartment. She wasn't ready to answer questions. She considered calling Colin at The Gallery to apologize, then decided against that as well. It was best that their break had been complete. If they parted on good terms, he might be tempted to get in touch with her from time to time. Cassidy knew she could never bear the casual friendliness.

She packed up the dress she had worn on her flight from the studio. Her fingers lingered on the material as she placed it back in the dress box. So much had happened since she had first put it on. Quickly she smoothed the tissue over it and closed the lid. That part of her life was over. Turning, she went to the phone to call The Gallery. The clerk who answered referred her immediately to Gail.

"Why, hello, Cassidy. Where did you run off to?"

"I have the dress from the portrait and the key to the studio," Cassidy told her. "I'd like someone to come pick them up."

"I see." There was a brief hesitation before Gail continued. "I'm afraid we're just terribly busy right now, dear. I know Colin particularly wanted that dress. Be sweet and drop it by? You can just let yourself into the studio and leave everything there. Colin's away, and we're just swamped."

"I'd rather not—"

"Thank you, darling. I must run." The phone clicked. With a quick oath of annoyance, Cassidy hung up.

Colin's away, she thought as she picked up the dress box. Now's the time to finish it completely.

A short time later Cassidy pushed open the back door of Colin's studio. The familiar scents reached out and brought him vividly to her mind. Resolutely she pushed him away. Now is not the time, she told herself and walked briskly to his worktable to set down the dress and key.

For a moment she stood in the room's center and looked about her. She had spent hours there, days. Every detail was already etched with clarity on her memory. Yet she wanted to see it all again. A part of her was afraid she would forget something, something small and insignificant and vital. It surprised her that the portrait still stood on the easel. Forgetting her promise to leave quickly, Cassidy walked over to study it one last time.

How could he look at that, she wondered as she gazed into her own eyes, and believe the things I said? I can only be grateful that he did. I can only be grateful he believed what I said rather than what he saw. Reaching out a hand, she touched the painted violets.

When the door of the studio opened, Cassidy jerked her hand from the painting and whirled. Her heart flew to her throat.

"Cassidy?" Vince strolled into the room with a wide smile. "What a surprise." In seconds, her hands were enveloped by his.

"Hello." Her voice was a trifle unsteady, but she managed to smile at him.

He heard the breathlessness in her voice and saw there was little color in her face. "Did you know Colin has been looking for you?"

"No." She felt a moment's panic and glanced at the door. "No, I didn't. I've been away, I've been working. I just…" She drew her hands away and clasped them together as she heard herself ramble. "I just brought back the dress I wore for the portrait."

Vince's dark eyes became shrewd. "Were you hiding, madonna?"

"No." Cassidy turned and walked to a window. "No, of course not, I was working." She saw the sparrow, busily feeding three babies with gaping mouths. "I didn't realize you were going to be in America this long." Say anything, she told herself, but don't think until you're out of here.

"I have stayed a bit longer in order to convince

Colin to sell me a painting he was reluctant to part with."

Cassidy gripped the windowsill tightly. *You knew he would sell it.* You knew from the beginning all that would be left would be dollars and cents. Did you expect him to keep it and think of you? Shaking her head, she made a quiet sound of despair.

"Cassidy." Vince's hand pressed lightly on her shoulder.

"I shouldn't have come here," she whispered, shaking her head again. "I should've known better." She started to flee, but he tightened his grip and turned her to face him. As he studied her, he lifted a hand to brush her cheek. "Please…" She closed her eyes. "Please don't be kind to me. I'm not as strong as I thought I was."

"And you love him very much."

Cassidy's eyes flew open. "No, it's only that I—"

"Madonna." Vince stopped her with a finger to her lips. There was a wealth of understanding in his eyes. "I've seen the portrait. It speaks louder than your words."

Lowering her head, Cassidy pressed the heel of her hand between her brows. "I don't want to… I'm trying so very hard not to. I have to go," she said quickly.

"Cassidy." Vince held her shoulders. His voice was gentle. "You must see him…speak to him."

"I can't." She placed her hands on his chest, shaking

her head in desperation. "Please, don't tell him. Please, just take the portrait and let it be over." Her voice broke, and when she found herself cradled against Vince's chest she made no protest. "I always knew it was going to be over." She closed her eyes on the tears, but allowed herself to be held until the need to release them faded. He stroked her hair and kept silent until he felt her breathing steady. Gently he kissed the top of her head then tilted her face to his.

"Cassidy, Colin is my friend—"

"Interesting." Cassidy's eyes darted to the doorway...and to Colin. "I'd thought so myself." His voice was quiet. "It appears I've been mistaken about more than one person recently." Even before he crossed the room, Cassidy felt the danger. "Gail told me I'd find you up here," he said when he stood directly in front of them. "With my *friend.*"

"Colin..." Vince began, only to be cut off with a fierce look.

"Take your hands off her, and keep out of this. When I've finished, you can pick up where you left off."

Hearing the fury in his words, Cassidy nudged out of Vince's hold. "Please," she murmured, not wanting to cause any trouble between them. "Leave us alone for a moment." When Vince's hand stayed on her arm, she turned her eyes to him. "Please," she repeated.

Reluctantly Vince dropped his hand. "Very well,

cara." He turned briefly to Colin. "I've never known you to be mistaken about anyone, my friend." He walked across the room then closed the door quietly behind him. Cassidy waited an extra moment before she spoke.

"I came to return the dress and the key." She moistened her lips when he only stared down at her. "Gail told me you were away."

"How convenient the studio was available for you and Vince."

"Colin, don't."

"Setting yourself up as a duchess?" he asked coldly. "I should warn you, Vince is known for his generosity, but not his constancy." His eyes raked her face. "Still, a woman like you should do very well for herself in a week or two."

"That's beneath you, Colin." She turned and took a step away, but he grabbed a handful of her hair. With a small sound of surprise and pain, she stared up at him.

His eyes were shadowed and dark, as was his chin with at least a day's growth of beard. It occurred to her suddenly that he looked exhausted. Thinking back, she knew he had never shown fatigue after hours of painting. His fingers tightened in her hair.

"Colin." In defense, she lifted a hand to his.

"Such innocence," he said softly. "Such innocence. You're a clever woman, Cassidy." His hands came to her shoulders, quickly, ruthlessly. She stared up at him in silence, tasting fear. "It's one thing to lie with words, but another to lie with a look, to lie with the eyes day after day. That takes a special kind of cheat."

"No." She shook her head as his words brought back the tears she had stemmed. "No, Colin, please." She wanted to tell him she had never lied to him, but she couldn't. She had lied the very last time they had been together. She could only shake her head and helplessly let the tears come.

"What is it you want from me?" he demanded. His voice became more infuriated as tears slipped down her cheeks. The sun fell through the skylight and set them glinting. "Do you want me to forget that I looked at you day after day and saw something that was never there?"

"I gave you what you wanted." Tears became sobs and she struggled against him. "Please, let me go now. I gave you what you wanted. It's finished."

"You gave me a shell, a mask. Isn't that what you told me?" He pulled her closer, forcing her head back until she looked at him. "The rest was my imagination. Finished, Cass? How can something be finished when it never was?" His hand went back to her hair as she tried to lower her head. "You said that I'd drained you. Have you any idea what these past weeks have done to me?" He shook her, and her sobs grew wilder.

"You were right when you told me that painting

was nothing more than your face and body. There's no warmth in you. I created the woman in that painting."

"Please, Colin. Enough." She pressed her hands over her ears to shut out his words.

"Do you cringe from the truth, Cassidy?" He tore her hands away, forcing her face back to his again. "Only you and I will know the painting's a lie, that the woman there doesn't exist. We served each other's needs after all, didn't we?" He pushed her aside with a whispered oath. "Get out."

Freed, Cassidy ran blindly for escape.

Chapter 10

It was late afternoon when Cassidy approached her apartment building. She had walked for a long time after her tears had dried. The city had been jammed with people, and she had sought the crowd while remaining separate. The pain had become numbed with fatigue. She was two blocks from home when the rain started, but she didn't increase her pace. It was cool and soft.

Inside her building she began an automatic search for her mailbox key. Her movements were mechanical, but she forced herself to perform the routine task. She would not crawl into a hole of despair. She would function. She would survive. These things she had promised herself during the long afternoon walk.

With the key at last in the lock, Cassidy lifted the cover on the narrow slot and pulled out her mail. She riffled through the advertisements and bills automatically as she started for the stairs. Her feet came to an abrupt halt as she spotted the return address on one of the envelopes. *New York.*

For several minutes she merely studied it, turning it over then back again. Walking back to her mailbox, she pushed the rest of her mail back inside then leaned against the wall. A rejection slip? she reflected, nibbling her bottom lip. Then where was the manuscript? She turned the envelope over again and swallowed.

"Oh, the devil with it," she muttered and ripped it open. She read the letter twice in absolute silence. "Oh, why now?" she asked and hated herself for weeping again. "I'm not ready for it now." She forced back the tears and shook her head. "No, it's the perfect time," she corrected then made herself read the letter again. There couldn't be a better time.

She stuffed the letter into her pocket and ran back into the rain. In ten minutes she was banging on Jeff's door.

Guitar in hand, he pulled open the door. "Cassidy, you're back! Where've you been? We were ready to call out the marines." Stopping, he took his eyes from the top of her head to her feet. "Hey...you're drenched."

"I am not drenched," Cassidy corrected as she dripped on the hall floor. She hoisted up a bottle of champagne. "I'm much too extraordinary to be drenched. I've been accepted into the annals of literature. I shall be copywritten and printed and posted in your public library."

"You sold your book!" Jeff let out a whoop and hugged her. His guitar pressed into her back.

Laughing, Cassidy pulled away. "Is that any way to express such a momentous occurrence? Peasant." She pushed back her sopping hair with her free hand. "However, I'm a superior person, and will share my bottle of champagne with you in my parlor. No dinner jacket required." Turning, she walked to her own door, pushed it open then gestured. Grinning, Jeff set down his guitar and followed her.

"Here," he said after he had closed the door and taken the bottle from her. "I'll open it, you go get a towel and dry off or else you'll die of pneumonia before the first copy hits the stands."

When she came back from the bathroom wrapped in a terry-cloth robe and rubbing a towel over her hair, Jeff was just releasing the cork. Champagne squirted out in a jet.

"It's good for the carpet," he claimed and poured. "I could only find jelly glasses."

"My crystal's been smashed," Cassidy told him as she picked up her glass. "To a very wise man," she said solemnly.

"Who?" Jeff raised his glass.

"My publisher," she announced, then grinned and drank. "An excellent year," she mused, gazing critically into the glass. The wine fizzed gently.

"What year is it?" Jeff lifted the bottle curiously.

"This one." Cassidy laughed and drank again. "I only buy new champagne."

They drank again then Jeff leaned over and kissed her. "Congratulations, babe." He pulled the damp towel from her shoulders. "How does it feel?"

"I don't know." She threw her head back and closed her eyes. "I feel like someone else." Quickly she filled her glass again. She knew she had to keep moving, had to keep talking. She couldn't think seriously about what she had won that day or she would remember what she had lost. "I should've bought two bottles," she said, spinning a circle. "This is definitely a two-bottle occasion." She drank, feeling the wine rise to her head. "The last time I had champagne..." Cassidy stopped, remembering, then shook her head. Jeff eyed her in puzzlement. "No, no." She gestured with her hand as if to wipe the thought away. "I had champagne at Barbara Seabright's wedding in Sausalito. One of the ushers propositioned me in the cloakroom."

Jeff laughed and took another sip. A knock sounded. Cassidy called out, "Come in, there's enough for—" Her words were cut off as Colin opened the door.

Cassidy's color drained slowly. Her eyes darkened.

Jeff looked quickly from one to the other, then set down his glass.

"Well, I gotta be going. Thanks for the champagne, babe. We'll talk later."

"No, Jeff," Cassidy began. "You don't have to—"

"I've got a gig," he announced, lifting her restraining hand from his arm. She saw him exchange one long look with Colin before he slipped through the door.

"Cass." Colin stepped forward.

"Colin, please go." Shutting her eyes, she pressed her fingers between her brows. There was a pressure in her chest and behind her lids. Don't cry. Don't cry, she ordered herself.

"I know I haven't any right to be here." There was a low harshness in his tone. "I know I haven't the right to ask you to listen to me. I'm asking anyway."

"There isn't anything to say." Cassidy forced herself to stand straight and face him. "I don't want you here," she said flatly.

He flinched. "I understand, Cassidy, but I feel you have a right to an apology…an explanation."

Her hands were clenched, and slowly she spread her fingers and stared down at them. "I appreciate the offer, Colin, but it isn't necessary. Now—" she lifted her eyes to his "—if that's all…"

"Oh, Cass, for pity's sake, show more mercy than I did. At least let me apologize before you shut me out of your life."

Unable to respond, Cassidy merely stared at him. He stooped to pick up the bottle of champagne. "I seem to have interrupted a celebration." He set the bottle back and looked at her. "Yours?"

"Yes." Cassidy swallowed and tried to speak lightly. "Yes, mine. My manuscript was accepted for publication. I had a letter today."

"Cass." He moved toward her, lifting a hand to touch her cheek.

Cassidy stiffened and took a quick step back. Catching the look that crossed his face, she knew she had hurt him. Colin slowly dropped his hand.

"I'm sorry," Cassidy began.

"Don't be." His voice had a quiet, final quality. "I can hardly expect you to welcome my touch. I hurt you." He paused, looking down at his hand a moment before bringing his gaze back to her face. His eyes searched hers. "Because I know you as well as I know myself, I'm aware of how badly I hurt you. I have to live with that. I haven't the right to ask you to forgive me, but I'll ask you to hear me out."

"All right, Colin, I'm listening," Cassidy said wearily. She drew a deep breath and tried to speak calmly. "Why don't you sit down."

He shook his head and, turning, moved back to the window and looked out, resting his hands in the sill. "The rain's stopped and there's fog. I still remember how you looked that night, standing in the fog looking up at the sky. I thought you were a mirage." He murmured the last sentence, as if to himself. "I had an image in my mind of a woman. My own idea of perfection, a balance of qualities. When I saw you, I knew I had found her. I had to paint you."

For a moment he lapsed into silence, brooding out at the gloom. "After we'd started, I found everything in you I'd ever looked for—goodness, spirit, intelligence, strength, passion. The longer I painted you, the more you fascinated me. I told you once you bewitched me; I almost believe it. I've never known a woman I've wanted more than I've wanted you."

He turned then and faced her. The play of the light threw his features into shadows. "Each time I touched you, I wanted more. I didn't make love to you that night on the houseboat because I wouldn't have you think of yourself as just one of my lovers. I couldn't take advantage of your being in love with me."

At his words, Cassidy's eyes closed. She made a soft sound of despair.

"Please, don't turn away. Let me finish. The day the painting was finished, you denied everything. You said the things I'd seen had been in my own imagination. You were so cool and dispassionate. You very nearly destroyed me…. I had no idea anyone had such power over me," he continued softly. "It was a revelation, and it hurt a great deal. I wanted more from you, I needed more, but you told me you had nothing left. I was angry when you ran away, and I let you go. When I came here later, you were gone.

"I've been out of my mind for over two weeks, not knowing where you were or when—worse, *if*—you were coming back. Your friend next door had your cryptic little note and nothing else."

"You saw Jeff?" she asked.

"Cassidy, don't you understand? You disappeared. The last time I saw you, you were running away from me, and then you were gone. I didn't know where you were, or how to find you, if something had happened to you. I've been going slowly mad."

She took a step toward him. "Colin, I'm sorry. I had no idea you'd be concerned…."

"Concerned?" he repeated. "I was frantic! Two weeks, Cassidy. Two weeks without a word. Do you know what a helpless feeling it is to simply have to wait? Not to know. I've haunted Fisherman's Wharf, been everywhere in the city. Where in heaven's name were you?" he demanded furiously then held up a hand before she could answer. She watched him take a deep breath before turning away from her. "I'm sorry. I haven't had much sleep lately, and I'm not completely in control."

His movements became restless again. He stopped and lifted Cassidy's discarded glass of champagne. Thoughtfully, he studied the etchings on the side. "An interesting concept in a wineglass," he murmured.

Turning back, he toasted her. "To you, Cass. To only you." He drank then set down the empty glass.

Cassidy dropped her eyes. "Colin, I am sorry you were worried. I was working, and—"

"Don't." The word stopped her, and her eyes shot back to his. "Don't explain to me," he said in more controlled tones. "Just listen. When I walked into the studio today and saw you with Vince, something snapped. I can give you excuses—pressure, exhaustion, madness, take your pick. None of them make up for the things I said to you." His eyes were eloquent on hers. "I despise myself for making you cry. I hated the things I said to you even as I said them. Finding you there, with Vince, after looking for you everywhere for days…" He stopped, shaking his head, then moved back to the window.

"Gail arranged the timing very well," he said. "She knew what I'd been through the past two weeks and knows me well enough to predict how I'd react finding you alone with Vince. She sent him up to the studio on a fictitious errand before I got back to The Gallery. She told me the two of you were meeting up there. She made the suggestion, but I grabbed on to it with both hands." He rubbed his fingers over the back of his neck as if to release some tension.

"We'd been occasional lovers up until about a year ago when things got a bit complicated. I should have remembered whom I was dealing with, but I wasn't thinking too clearly. Gail's decided to take a long—perhaps permanent—sabbatical on the East Coast." He paused a moment then turned to study her. "I'd like to think you could understand why I behaved so abominably."

In the silence Cassidy could just hear Jeff's guitar through the thin walls of the apartment. "Colin." Her eyes searched his face then softened. "You look so tired."

His expression altered, and for a moment she thought he would cross to her. He stood still, however, keeping the distance between them. "I don't know when I fell in love with you. Perhaps it was that first night in the fog. Perhaps it was when you first wore that dress. Perhaps it was years before I met you. I suppose it doesn't matter when."

Cassidy stared at him, robbed of speech. "I'm not an easy man, Cassidy, you told me that once."

"Yes," she managed. "I remember."

"I'm selfish and given to temper and black moods. I have little patience except with my work. I can promise to hurt you, to infuriate you, to be unreasonable and impatient, but no one will love you more. No one." He paused, but still she could only stare at him, transfixed. "I'm asking you to forget what makes sense and be my wife and my lover and mother my children. I'm asking that you share your life with me, taking me as I am." He paused again, and his voice softened. "I love you, Cass. This time, my destiny's in your hands."

She watched him as he spoke, heard the cadence of his native land grow stronger in his speech. Still he made no move toward her, but stood across the room with shadows playing over his face. Cassidy remembered how he had looked when she had flinched away from his touch.

Slowly she walked to him. Reaching up, she circled his neck with her arms then buried her face against his shoulder. "Hold me." His arms came gently around her as his cheek lowered to the top of her head. "Hold me, Sullivan," she ordered again, pressing hard against him. She turned her head until her mouth found his.

His arms drew tight around her, and she murmured in pleasure at their strength. "I love you," she whispered as their lips parted then clung again. "I've needed to tell you for so long."

"You told me every time you looked at me." Colin buried his face in her hair. "I refused to believe I'd fallen in love with you, that it could have happened so quickly, so effortlessly. The painting was nearly finished when I admitted to myself I'd never be able to live without you."

His voice lowered, and he drew her closer. "I've been crazy these last two weeks, staring at your portrait and not knowing where you were or if I'd ever see you again."

"Now you have me," she murmured, making no objection when his hands slipped under the terry cloth to roam her skin. "And Vince will have the portrait."

"No, I told you once some things can't be sold. The portrait has too much of both of us in it." He shook his head, breathing in the rain-fresh fragrance of her hair. "Not even for Vince."

"But I thought…" She realized that she had only assumed Vince had been speaking of her portrait. There was a new wealth of happiness in the knowledge that Colin had not intended to sell what was to her a revelation of their love.

"What did you think?"

"No, it's nothing." She pressed her lips against his neck. "I love you." Her mouth roamed slowly up his jawline, savoring what she knew now was hers.

"Cass." She felt his heart thud desperately against hers as his fingers tightened in her hair. "Do you know what you do to me?"

"Show me," she whispered against his ear.

With a groan, Colin kissed her again. She could taste his need for her and wondered at the strength of it. Her answer was to offer everything.

"We'll get married quickly," Colin murmured then took her lips again, urgently. Inside her robe, his hands ran in one long stroke down her sides, then roamed to her back to bring her closer. "Very quickly."

"Yes." Cassidy closed her eyes in contentment as his cheek rested against hers. "I already have the perfect dress." She sighed and nestled against him. "What will you title the painting, Colin?"

"I've already titled it." He smiled into her eyes. *"Sullivan's Woman."*

* * * * *